Gabriel Chevallier (1895–1969) is widely known as the author of *Clochemerle*, which was published in 1934, translated into twenty-six languages and which sold several million copies. Chevallier was called up at the start of WWI and wounded a year later, but returned to the front. *Fear* draws on his experience.

'What Chevallier wanted to write with *Fear* is a straightforward, honest book, from which all artifice is absent; a work that gives the reader the exact measure of war. Chevallier has had the courage to strip war of all its prestige by admitting: I was frightened' *Liberté*

'Gabriel Chevallier, best known for his magnificent novel *Clochemerle*, has used his experiences during World War I to produce a work of great intensity, comparable to such great literary masterpieces of the period as Henri Barbusse's *Under Fire*' Kathy Stevenson, *Daily Mail*

'There are enough flashes of intense colour and incident to make this translation a worthwhile exercise' Toby Clements, *Sunday Telegraph*

'Chevallier's pen is as sharp as a bayonet in exposing the arrogance and stupidity of commanding officers… The power of the novel is inc_____ of pace… There are eloquer___ so_____liberty, and impassioned arguments on the nature of war and its effects on those who wage it, by the only men truly qualified to speak of them... *Fear* is being billed as a French *All Quiet on the Western Front*, and in this fine translation by Malcolm Imrie it is a fair claim' Gavin Bell, *Herald*

'One of the most affective indictments of war ever written' Tobias Grey, *Bookshelf*

'Elegant and compelling... should be required reading' *Scotsman*

'The most beautiful book ever written on the tragic events that blood-stained Europe for nearly five years... a classic' *Le Libertaire*

'All the horrors of war are there, but atrocity alone would not be enough to explain the grandeur of this text. It is the healthy defiance and controlled anger which earned the book its stripes' *Le Figaro*

'It is the fear of the condemned man that is described here: fear that sometimes paralyses and sometimes excites by separating strength from courage. These pages, which would have had the author shot during the war, we read with amazement brought on by their complete honesty' *Le Soir*

FEAR

Gabriel Chevallier

TRANSLATED BY MALCOLM IMRIE

Introduced by John Berger

Ouvrage publié avec le soutien du Centre national du livre
Published with the support of the Centre national du livre

A complete catalogue record for this book can be obtained from the
British Library on request

First published as *La Peur* in 1930 by Editions Stock, Paris

First published in this paperback edition in 2012 by Serpent's Tail
First published in English in 2011 by Serpent's Tail,
an imprint of Profile Books Ltd
3A Exmouth House
Pine Street
London EC1R 0JH
website: www.serpentstail.com

ISBN: 978 1 84668 727 3
eISBN: 978 1 84765 643 8

Designed and typeset by sue@lambledesign.demon.co.uk

Printed by CPI Group (UK) Ltd, Croydon, CR0 4YY

10 9 8 7 6 5 4 3 2 1

THE IMPERATIVE NEED
Introduction by John Berger

'THE YELLOW LIGHT OF A DAY that seemed to falter as if it too was struck by horror, illuminated a lifeless, soundless battle-field. It was as if everything around us and off into infinity was dead, and we did not dare raise our voices. It felt as if we had come to some place in the world which was part of a dream, that had gone beyond all the limits of reality and hope.'

The 'we' refers to French soldiers (*poilus*, not officers) serving in the trenches. The 'place' is near Douai in Flanders. The horrific experiences related in this book were lived almost a century ago. 1914–1918. The book itself was first published in 1930. My guess is that it took several years to write because indignation – more often than not, and contrary to what one might expect – slows writing down.

What this written book achieves, however, is of the utmost urgency and relevance today. As a graphic day-to-day account of survival, pain and death in the trenches, dugouts and saps, it is unique and almost insupportable, and, at the same time, it is about something more: about the endless outrages which separate official bulletins (and then History books) from the millions of maimed and lost lives on the killing fields.

Its fury is directed against the deliberate and manufac-tured ignorance existing between speeches and bloodshed. The ignorance not of those on the ground and under fire, but of the war leaders and decision-making commanders.

Most rulers lie, yet lies are less shocking, less corrosive than the chosen, cultivated ignorance Chevallier addresses here. This ignorance denies the reality of anything which provokes pity. It is an error to think of such war leaders (or, today, economic strategists) as pitiless; they are abject. And this is what we have to learn and act upon. They are abject.

At the literary checkpoints this book probably claimed to be a novel. It isn't. A memoir, then, for Chevallier himself served in the trenches. It isn't a memoir. A passionate plea, then, plea for pacifism. Again it won't pass. It's a book without papers. Consisting of what? A chorus of voices. It's a choral work. The voices have come together to break a silence, the silence of deliberate ignorance, and to fill it with stories and descriptions and remarks and confessions until now unheard. This book, wonderfully translated, is like a choral avalanche of anger, pity and hopes deferred. I can think of three other books which are comparable avalanches: Tolstoy's *Resurrection*, Victor Serge's *Years Without Pity* and Andrei Platanov's *Chevengur*. Such great books wait a long while before being finally admitted for what they are.

When I write that, I think of my father reading this book, which he never did. He endured four years in the trenches with the British infantry. I was born eight years after the end of the war. But the war was part of the map with which I tried to find my way about, during my early childhood, my adolescence, and later too. The war marked an area on that map which covered one of the extreme limits of human experience, close to the tragic, unanswerable, but, unlike the tragic, silent and perhaps futile.

My father talked about the experience of those four years to nobody. Or anyway that was my impression. In my presence he would sometimes finger and look at his mementos: a field compass, a revolver, some trench maps, a few letters and lists, some machine-gun rounds, the ring of a hand grenade. Sometimes he named them but said no more. The rest was indescribable, and the fact that I was a child, to whom so much was still indescribable, made this sharing natural and possible.

When I was nearly fifty, I wrote a poem about the battlefields of Ypres, which are about sixty miles to the north of Douai. I gave it to my father. He read it – he did not read many poems – he looked at me, he lowered his eyelids, then he nodded, folded the paper in four and slipped it into his pocket.

Base: fields whose mud is waterlogged

Perpendicular: thin larches
                        planted in rows
                                with broken
                                        branches

Horizontal: brick walls the colour of
                        dead horses

Sinking: lower
                        and lower
                                houses with dark windows

Sometimes a wall is white-washed
a rectangle of dead lime
                        under the indifferent clouds

Here all poultry should have webbed feet
At dusk drowned soldiers cross the field to steal chickens

Through base
                perpendicular
                and horizontal
                        there is order:
                        the order of split wood
                        broken branches
                        walls the colour of dead horses
                        and roofs fallen in

There is no way out except across
Nothing reaches any heaven from here

Between earth and sky there is
        a transparent canopy
        plaited from cock crows
        and the cries of soldiers

This book consists of the chorus of the cries of those soldiers. And I believe that if my father had read it and heard the silence filled, he would have been confirmed by the declared pain and anger, by the raised voices and by the imperative need for us today to learn from them.

John Berger's poem appeared in his *Pages of the Wound: Poems, Drawings, Photographs, 1956–96*, Bloomsbury, 1996.

'Can anything be more ridiculous than that a man should
have the right to kill me because he lives on the other side of
the sea, and because his ruler has a quarrel with mine,
though I have none with him.'

Pascal, *Pensées*

EXTRACT FROM THE PREFACE
TO THE 1951 EDITION

FIRST PUBLISHED IN 1930, this anti-war book had the misfortune to run into a new one.[1] In 1939, its author and publisher freely agreed to suspend sales. Once war has come, the time has passed for warning that it is a disastrous venture with unforeseeable consequences. That is something that must be understood earlier, and acted on accordingly.

When I was young we were taught – when we were at the front – that war was edifying, purifying and redemptive. We have all seen the repercussions of such twaddle: profiteers, arms dealers, the black market, denunciations, betrayals, firing squads, torture; not to mention famine, tuberculosis, typhus, terror, sadism. And heroism, I agree. But the small, exceptional amount of heroism does not make up for the immensity of evil. Besides, few people are cut out for true heroism. Let those of us who came back have the honesty to admit it.[2]

The great novelty of this book, whose title was intended as a challenge, is that its narrator declared: I am afraid. In all the 'war books' I had read, fear was indeed sometimes mentioned, but it was other people's fear. The authors themselves were always phlegmatic characters who were so busy jotting down their impressions that they calmly greeted incoming shells with a happy smile.

The author of the present book believed that it would be dishonest to speak of his comrades' fear without mentioning his. That is why he decided to admit, indeed to proclaim, his own fear. To have written about the war without writing about fear, without emphasising it, would have been a farce. You do not spend time in places where at any moment you may be blown to pieces without experiencing a degree of apprehension.

Responses to the book varied widely and its author was sometimes taken to task. But two points are worth noting. Some of those who had attacked him would later come to grief, their valour having chosen the wrong camp. And since then some proud pens have avowed that shameful little word, fear.

As for those who fought as infantrymen, they wrote: 'True! This is what we experienced but could not express.' Their opinion is worth a great deal. […]

I should add two other points. I have not looked at these pages for fifteen years and have just reread them. It is always a surprise for an author to confront a text to which he once put his name. A surprise and a test. For men like to think they learn something as they grow older, That, at least, is how they console themselves.

The tone of *Fear* is extremely scornful and arrogant in places. It is the arrogance of youth and nothing in it could be changed without eliminating youth itself. The young Dartemont thinks what cannot be thought officially. He is still naïve enough to believe that everything is susceptible to reason. He fiercely asserts weighty and unpalatable truths. It is a matter of choosing whether to speak these truths or keep quiet about them. But he is too angry to be cautious. And acquiescence is often a mark of decrepitude.

A second point. Today I would not write this book in exactly the same way. But should I alter it, and to what extent? I am aware that former readers would take me to task if I changed the original text, that they would see it as a concession or capitulation. So, apart from some rare replacements of words or epithets, the text remains that of the first edition. I have even resisted the temptation to add more artistry, reminding myself that literary embellishments to a finished book only weaken it and there is no going back on the risk I took at the start.

One last thing. How will this book be 'used', for what propaganda? My answer is simply that it stood apart from all propaganda, and was not written to serve any.

G.C.

THE WOUND

'I am not a sheep, which means I am nothing'
Stendhal

1

THE PROCLAMATION

'The danger in these strong communities, founded on similar, steadfast individual members, is an increasing, inherited stupidity, which follows all stability like its shadow.'

Nietzsche, *Human, All Too Human*, I, 224 (trans. Helen Zimmern)

THE FIRE WAS ALREADY SMOULDERING somewhere down in the depths of Europe, but carefree France donned its summer costumes, straw hats and flannel trousers, and packed its bags for the holidays. There wasn't a cloud in the sky – such an optimistic, bright blue sky. It was terribly hot and drought was the only possible worry. It would be so lovely out in the countryside, or down by the sea. The scent of iced absinthe hung over the café terraces and gypsy orchestras played popular tunes from the *The Merry Widow*, which was then all the rage. The newspapers were full of details from a big murder trial that everyone was talking about; would the woman who some were calling the 'blood clot' be condemned or acquitted, would the thundering Labori, her lawyer, and the crimson-faced, raging little Borgia in a tail-coat, who had once led us (saved us, some said) carry the day?[3] We could see no further than that. Trains were packed and the booking offices did a roaring trade in round-trip tickets: the well-to-do were looking forward to a two-month holiday.

Then, all of a sudden, bolts of lightning pierce the perfect sky, one after another: ultimatum... ultimatum... ultimatum... But France, gazing at the clouds gathering in the east, says: 'That's where the storm will be, over there.'

A clap of thunder in the clear sky above the Île-de-France. Lightning strikes the Ministry of Foreign Affairs.

Priority! The telegraph is working flat out, for reasons of state. Post offices send out telegrams in cipher, marked 'Urgent'.

The proclamation is posted up on every town hall in the country.

The shouting starts: 'It's official!'

Crowds of people swarm on to the streets, pushing and shoving, running in all directions.

Cafés empty. Shops empty. Cinemas, museums, banks, churches, bachelor flats and police stations empty.

The whole of France now stands gazing at the poster and reads: 'Liberty, Equality, Fraternity – General Mobilisation.'

The whole of France stands on tiptoe to see the poster, all squeezed together in a fraternal huddle, dripping with sweat beneath a burning sun, and repeats the word 'mobilisation' without understanding it.

A voice goes off in the crowd like a firecracker: IT'S WAR!

And then France goes into a spin, rushing along the streets and boulevards that are too narrow for such crowds, through the villages, and out across the countryside: war, war, war...

Hey! Over there! War!

The country policemen bang their little drums and all the churches ring all the bells in their ancient Romanesque towers and tall, fine Gothic steeples. All together now! War!

The sentries in their tricolour sentry-boxes present arms. The mayors put on their sashes. The prefects put on their old uniforms. The generals assemble their staff. The ministers, in a tizzy, consult each other. War! Whatever next?

No one can keep still. Not the bank clerks, not the drapers' assistants or the factory workers or the dressmakers or the typists or even the concierges. We're closing! We're closing! The ticket offices are closed, the strong-rooms are closed, the factories and the offices are closed. The steel shutters are down. We are all off to see what's happening!

Military men take on a great importance and smile at the public acclaim. Career officers tell themselves: 'Our hour has come. No more grovelling around in the lower ranks for us.'

In the teeming streets, men and women, arm in arm, launch themselves into a great dizzy, senseless farandole, because it's war, a farandole which lasts through part of the night that follows this extraordinary day on which the posters went up on the town hall walls.

It starts just like a festival.

Only the cafés stay open.

And you can still smell the scent of iced absinthe, the scent of peacetime.

Women are crying. Why? A foreboding? Or just nerves?

War!

Everyone is getting ready. Everyone is going.

What is war?

No one has the foggiest idea…

It's more than forty years since the last one. The few surviving witnesses, identifiable by their medals, are old men who talk a lot of drivel, whose youth has deserted them and are well on their way to a place in Les Invalides.[4] It was not because we lacked valour that we lost the war of 1870 but because we were betrayed by Bazaine,[5] think the French. Ah, if it hadn't been for Bazaine…

In recent years we have learned of other, more distant wars. The one between the English and the Boers, for example. We know about that one mainly through the caricatures of Caran d'Ache[6] and the engravings in illustrated magazines. The courageous president Kruger led the Boers in their resolute resistance;

we admired him for it, and hoped he would triumph, so as to upset the English who burned Joan of Arc and made a martyr of Napoleon on Saint Helena. Then there was the Russo-Japanese war, Port Arthur and all that. Those Japanese must be formidable soldiers; they beat the famous Cossacks, our allies, who, it must be said, lacked railways. The colonial wars do not seem to us to be very alarming. They evoke expeditions to the heart of the desert, pillaging Arab encampments, the Spahis with their red burnous, Arabs firing Damascene muskets into the air and galloping off on their little horses kicking up the golden sand. As for the Balkan wars, the province of journalists, they didn't bother us. Living in the centre of Europe as we do, and convinced of the superiority of our civilisation, we consider that these regions are inhabited by coarse, inferior people. To us their wars resemble brawls between hooligans on suburban wastelands.

War was far from our thoughts. To imagine it, we had to refer back to History, to what little we knew of it. This was reassuring. For History offered us a past packed with glorious wars, great victories and ringing declarations, with a cast of remarkable and celebrated figures: Charles Martel,[7] Charlemagne, Saint Louis[8] sitting under an oak tree on his return from Palestine, Joan of Arc who kicked the English out of France, the hypocrite Louis XI who put people in cages while kissing his devotional medals, the gallant Francois I ('All is lost save honour'), Henri IV, good-natured and cynical ('A kingdom is well worth a Mass'[9]), the majestic Louis XIV, prolific producer of bastards, indeed all our skirt-lifting, jingoist kings, our eloquent revolutionaries, and Bayard, Jean Bart, Condé, Turenne, Moreau, Hoche, Masséna... And towering over them all, the mirage of Napoleon, in which the brilliant Corsican looms through the cannon smoke in his simple military uniform surrounded by his marshals, his dukes, his princes, his scarlet kings, in all their plumes and finery.

It must be said that after bothering all of Europe with our turbulence over so many centuries we have calmed down with age. But if anyone should dare to challenge us, we are ready for them... And now the die is cast, we must go to war! We are not afraid, to war we will go. We are still French, are we not?

Men are stupid and ignorant. That is why they suffer. Instead of thinking, they believe all that they are told, all that they are taught. They choose their lords and masters without judging them, with a fatal taste for slavery.

Men are sheep. This fact makes armies and wars possible. They die the victims of their own stupid docility.

When you have seen war as I have just seen it, you ask yourself: 'How can we put up with such a thing? What frontier traced on a map, what national honour could possibly justify it? How can what is nothing but banditry be dressed up as an ideal, and allowed to happen?'

They told the Germans: 'Forward to a bright and joyous war! On to Paris! God is with us, for a greater Germany!' And the good, peaceful Germans, who take everything seriously, set forth to conquer, transforming themselves into savage beasts.

They told the French: 'The nation is under attack. We will fight for Justice and Retribution. On to Berlin!' And the pacifist French, the French who take nothing at all seriously, interrupted their modest little *rentier* reveries to go and fight.

So it was with the Austrians, the Belgians, the English, the Russians, the Turks, and then the Italians. In a single week, twenty million men, busy with their lives and loves, with making money and planning a future, received the order to stop everything to go and kill other men. And those twenty million individuals obeyed the order because they had been convinced that this was *their duty*.

Twenty million, all in good faith, following God and their prince... twenty million idiots... like me!

Or rather, no, I did not believe this was my duty. Nineteen

years old and I had not yet come to believe that there was anything great or noble in sticking a bayonet into a man's stomach, in rejoicing in his death.

But I went all the same.

Because it would have been hard for me to do anything else? No, that is not the real reason and I should not make myself out to be better than I am. I went against all my convictions, but still of my own free will – not to fight but out of curiosity: to see.

Through my own behaviour I can explain that of a great many others, especially in France.

In just a few hours, war turned everything upside down, spread the semblance of disorder everywhere – something the French always enjoy. They set off without any hatred at all, drawn by an adventure from which everything could be expected. The weather was lovely. This war was breaking out right at the beginning of August. Ordinary workers were the most eager: instead of their fortnight's annual holiday, they were going to get several months, visiting new places, and all at the expense of the Germans.

A great medley of clothes, customs and classes, a great clamour, a great cocktail of drinks, a new force given to individual initiatives, a need to smash things up, to leap over fences, to break laws – all this, at the start, made the war acceptable. It was confused with freedom, and discipline was then accepted in the belief that it was lacking.

Everywhere had the atmosphere of a funfair, a riot, a disaster and a triumph; a vast, intoxicating upheaval. The daily round had come to a halt. Men stopped being factory workers or civil servants, clerks or common labourers, in order to become explorers and conquerors. Or so at least they believed. They dreamed of the North as if it were America, or the pampas, or a virgin forest, of Germany as if it were a banquet; they dreamed of laying waste to the countryside, breaking open wine barrels, burning towns, the white stomachs of the blonde women of Germania, of pillage and plunder, of all that life normally denied them. Each individual believed in his destiny, no one thought of death, except the death of others.

In short, the war got off to a pretty good start, with the help of chaos.

In Berlin those who wanted all this make an appearance on the palace balconies, in their finest uniforms, in postures suitable for the immortalising of famous conquerors.

Those who are unleashing on us two million fanatics, armed with rapid-fire artillery, machine guns, repeater rifles, hand grenades, aeroplanes, chemicals and electricity, shine with pride. Those who gave the signal for the massacre are smiling at their coming glory.

This is the moment when the first – and last – machine gun should have done its work, emptied its belt of bullets on to that emperor and his advisors, men who believe themselves to be strong, superhuman, arbiters of our destinies, and who are nothing but miserable imbeciles. Their cretinous vanity is destroying the world.

Meanwhile in Paris those who did not know how to prevent all this, who are surprised and overwhelmed by it, run around consulting each other, advising each other, rushing out reassuring communiqués, and mobilising the police against the spectre of revolution. The police, zealous as ever, strike down anyone who is not displaying sufficient enthusiasm.

In Brussels, in London, in Rome, those who feel threatened assess the balance of forces, weigh up their chances, and choose their camp.

And millions of men, because they believed what they were taught by emperors, legislators and bishops in their legal codes, their manuals of instruction and their catechisms, by historians in their history books, by ministers on their platforms, teachers in their colleges, and decent, ordinary people in their living rooms, these millions of men form countless flocks that shepherds with officers' braids lead to the slaughterhouses, to the sound of music.

In a few short days, civilisation was wiped out. In a few short days, all our leaders became abject failures. For their role, their only role that mattered, was precisely to prevent all this.

If we did not know where we were going, they, at the very least, should have known where they were leading their nations. A man has the right to be stupid on his own account, but not on behalf of others.

On the afternoon of 3 August, I take a walk through the city with Fontan, a friend the same age as me.

Outside a café in the centre, an orchestra is blasting out the *Marseillaise*. Everyone removes their hats and stands up to listen. Everyone, that is, except for one frail, humbly dressed little man with a sad face crowned by a straw hat, who sits alone in a corner. One of the bystanders spots him, rushes up and, with a flick of his hand, knocks his hat flying. The man goes pale, shrugs his shoulders and says 'Bravo! Brave citizen!' The other man orders him to stand up. He refuses. Other people come over, surrounding him. The aggressor continues: 'You are insulting the nation, I will not put up with it!' The little man, by now very pale but stubborn, replies: 'And you, in my opinion, are insulting reason but I'll say nothing. I am a free man and I won't celebrate war.' Someone shouts: 'Give the coward a damn good hiding!' People run up from behind him, walking sticks are raised, tables overturned, glasses broken. In no time at all, a mob has formed. Those at the back, who haven't seen anything, tell newcomers what is happening. 'He's a spy. He shouted "Long live Germany!"' Indignation grips the mob, drives them on. There is the sound of blows striking home, cries of hatred and of pain. Eventually the café manager scurries over, a napkin still draped over his arm, and pulls them off. The little man, knocked off his chair, lies on the floor among the spit and cigarette ends. His badly bruised face is unrecognisable, with one eye closed and blackened; blood trickles from his forehead and his open, swollen mouth; he is breathing with difficulty and cannot get up. The manager calls two waiters: 'Get him out of here!' They drag him on to the pavement and leave him there. But then one of the waiters goes back, leans over and shakes him threateningly: 'And what about your bill?' As the unfortunate man doesn't answer, the waiter rifles through his pockets and pulls a fistful of coins from his waistcoat, taking what he considers the right amount with the mob as his witness. 'The bastard would have gone off without paying!' General approval – 'These people are capable of anything! Lucky he was disarmed! He had a gun? He threatened people with a revolver. We're always too nice in France! The socialists are playing Germany's game, no mercy for those wretches. We're not having a repeat of 1870 this time round.'

To mark this great victory, people demand an encore of the *Marseillaise*. They stand and listen, looking down at the little man who is bleeding and whimpering quietly. Beside me I notice a beautiful, pale woman who murmurs to her companion: 'What a dreadful sight. That poor man had the courage...' '...of an idiot,' he interrupts. 'It is folly to go against public opinion.'

'There we see the war's first casualty,' I say to Fontan.

'Indeed,' he says, absently, 'there's a great deal of enthusiasm.'

I am the silent witness of this great frenzy.

From one day to the next, civilians dwindle away, transforming themselves into hastily dressed soldiers who run around town to make the most of their last hours and get themselves admired, and no longer button up their army tunics because this is war. In the evenings, those who have drunk too much insult passers-by, whom they take for Germans. The passers-by see this as a good sign and applaud them.

Wherever you go you hear martial music. Old gentlemen wish they were young, children bitterly wish they were not, and women bemoan the fact that they are only women.

I lose myself in the crowds which fill the approaches to the barracks, these sordid barracks that have become the storage batteries of national energy. I watch the regiments leave for the front. The crowd surrounds them, hugs them, showers them with flowers, and gets them drunk. Every line of soldiers is accompanied by clusters of delirious, dishevelled women, who are crying and laughing, offering their waists and their breasts to these heroes as if to the nation; who kiss the sweating faces of the rough, honest warriors and scream their hatred for the enemy, which makes them look ugly.

I watch the cavalry trot by, the army's aristocracy. The heavy cuirassiers, their breastplates blinding in the sunshine, an unstoppable force in a headlong charge. The dragoons, like medieval jousters preparing for a tournament with their plumed helmets, lances and pennants. The mounted chasseurs of the light cavalry, capering and prancing in their pale blue uniforms, chasseurs of the forward posts, who surge out of a fold in the landscape to cut down an enemy detachment with their sabres, or capture a village in a surprise attack. The artillery makes the houses shake; they say that the 75s fire twenty-five rounds a minute and always hit the target by the third shell. People gaze with respect at the silent muzzles of these little monsters that in a few days' time will be tearing whole divisions to shreds.

The Zouaves and the colonials are especially popular: bronzed, tattooed and fierce, straight-backed despite their huge packs, with wide, godless grins. People think they are bandits who will give no quarter; this is reassuring. And here come the blacks, whom we can spot from a distance by the white teeth shining in their dark faces, these childlike and cruel blacks who decapitate their enemies and cut off their ears to make amulets. A charming little detail. Good old blacks! People offer them alcohol and affection, relish the strong scent, that exotic scent they associate with the Colonial Exhibition, that lingers in the air as they pass. The blacks are happy, happy suddenly to merit the friendship of white men, and because they think the war will be like one of those wild dances they have in their own countries.

Railway stations are now closed to the public. Their surroundings look like military encampments, with stacks of rifles everywhere, and crowds of troops waiting their turn to be swallowed up by the trains alongside the platforms. The stations are the hearts through which the nation's blood is flowing, pumped out along the arteries, the tracks, to the North and the East, where men in their madder-dyed breeches multiply like red corpuscles. 'Destination Berlin' is chalked on the carriages. The trains set off for adventure, filling the countryside with a clamour that is more joyful than bellicose. At every level-crossing, people shout back to them, handkerchiefs waving. With all these overexcited, empty-headed passengers, you would think these were holiday trains.

All across Europe, right up to the borders of Asia, armies are on the move, impatient to take on the enemy, certain of the justice of their cause and confident of victory.

Who is afraid? No one! No one yet…

Twenty million men, whom fifty million women have covered in flowers and kisses, hasten towards glory, bellowing out their national anthems.

The people are fired up and raring to go. The war is coming along very nicely. The statesmen of Europe can be proud!

2

TRAINING

IT WAS RAINING on the morning I set off for the army medical board which had been set up in the town hall of my *arrondissement*. Guessing that the cloakroom would be inadequate, I had put on my oldest clothes, the dirtiest ones I had left. I anticipated the examination with some irritation; I was annoyed at the idea of having a fully clothed man assess me at his leisure when I was completely naked, and pass judgement on my anatomy, taking advantage of the subordinate position in which I was placed. How unfair it seemed that in such circumstances someone could demand so much from my body, a body that society usually insisted I keep hidden, and that no intellectual guile on my part would be of any help in the affair. Making judgements on such a basis was already quite enough to condemn the military system, in my opinion. And, though I most certainly have no deformity, I was not quite sure that my body was perfectly proportioned (having never had it judged before except, rarely, by women, who usually don't know much about such things), and I would have been offended if anyone had looked askance at it.

I had always hoped that I could avoid military service and its insulting rules and regulations by some last-minute ruse, but on this December day, on the contrary, my only worry was that I might be turned down. The war was already a few months old and I was beginning to fear that it might end before I got there. I saw war neither as a career nor an ideal, but as a show – in the same category as a motor race, an air display or a sports match. I was full of natural curiosity and, since this war would be the most remarkable spectacle of the age – I would not want to miss it.

The ceremony was quickly concluded, and the medical officers handled it with inattentive discretion. Their patriotism consisted of accepting every kind of body, puny or not, to feed the front. The only way to get a proper examination would be to announce your physical defects without embarrassment, and that would arouse suspicion.

We had to undress in a cramped antechamber, bumping into each other's naked bodies, and it soon resembled a steam bath. Then, rather awkwardly, we entered the gloomy room, its walls lined with shelves packed with box files, where the medical officers waited, surrounded by their assistants, the town hall clerks. My only wish was to get this cursory examination over with as fast as possible. When my name was called I went under the height gauge and then quickly got on the scales.

An army doctor read my form:

'Dartemont, Jean, one metre seventy-two, sixty-seven kilos. Is that you?'

'Yes, sir.'

'Fit for service. Next...'

I had to rummage through a heap of shoes and socks and shirts to find my clothes. Once dressed, I hurried out into the city, happy and if truth be told rather proud to be suitable material for a soldier, not to belong to that category of despised citizens in the prime of life who have stayed at home. Unwittingly, I was rather a victim of the general mood. Moreover, physical health had always seemed to me to be greatly desirable, and my own had just been confirmed by the medical officer's decision.

I told my family the news, which they immediately and proudly circulated, thus gaining public esteem. I also told a young woman with whom I was sharing vain dreams of a future, but I discouraged her a little too tenderly.

* * * * *

On a cold evening in December 1914, the conscript train deposited its cargo of young men at the garrison. We set off in a crowd for the barracks. But the sentry would not let us in and summoned the NCOs. A sergeant, and then an adjutant, alarmed by our numbers, ran off to alert a commandant,[10] who soon appeared, not happy at the disturbance.

'What's going on here?' he inquired.

'Class 15 has disembarked, sir.'

'What on earth am I supposed to do about it at six in the evening?' he said, cursing.

'We can always go away again...' suggested a voice at the back.

'Silence!' barked the sergeant.

Hastily summoned, the barracks chief and the quartermaster declared that nothing was ready since they had not been told of our arrival. There was no food, no mattresses, and no blankets. The major paused for thought, then resolved the situation without further ado.

'I don't give a damn!' he told the quartermasters. 'I want these men fed and bedded down within two hours. Jump to it!'

And off he went. We exchanged comments.

'Seems an awfully charming bloke, that commandant!'

'Efficiently run here, don't you think?'

Most of us decided to remain civilians for one more night and come back the next day. We set off to explore the town.

The chaos that reigned in barracks at this time made our lives tolerable. We naturally exploited the disorder and soon picked up the tricks of the trade of soldiering: how to fake passes, fake sickness, and fake being present at roll-call. There were not enough NCOs to supervise us, and, faced with war in the very near future, we had decided to enjoy ourselves in base camp and not let anyone treat us as ordinary conscripts. In the absence of veterans, the usual barracks traditions had been forgotten, and this also encouraged our insubordination since we did not have to endure the cruel initiation rituals of peacetime.

The first month of military service was like a fancy dress ball. Since the stores lacked uniforms all we were given were army trousers and collarless army shirts, which stuck out below our civilian jackets. Forage caps and képis were also missing, so many people had kept their own headwear. Soldiers could be seen walking around in bowler hats; one joker gained fame by bowing and doffing his hat with an exaggerated sweep of the arm as officers passed by. It was in these outfits that we were taught the external marks of respect and the basic rudiments of the discipline which is the main strength of armies, a discipline which we cheerfully resisted. For our strange disguises stopped us taking anything very seriously and, as a reminder of the exceptional circumstances, tempered any anger from our superiors. Most of our instructors, in any case, were corporals from the previous class, with only three months' training, who were not entirely convinced of the military effectiveness of the exercises we were carrying out.

To us this training seemed a pointless sham, which could not have anything in common with the adventures in store for us – adventures whose prospect didn't bother us but which we used as an excuse for our disobedience.

At this time I was faced with a challenge that could have affected my life and completely changed my military career.

We had been soldiers for about a fortnight when the unit leaders were asked to select men whom they considered suitable candidates for the entry exam to officer school. It was up to us to make ourselves known to them.

So I needed to know if I was going to participate in this war as an officer or a soldier. Getting myself promoted would mean making some sort of commitment to the army, an institution that I instinctively loathed, like anything else that restricted the individual and made him part of a crowd, and it would put me in conflict with myself. But I already felt that, whatever my position, my freedom was slipping away, and that by remaining an ordinary soldier I would have to endure tougher discipline, an intolerable encroachment on my own ideas and opinions which I considered to be my rights. I did not see why, out of some questionable loyalty, I should be expected to subordinate myself to inferior and ignorant authority figures whom reason taught me to loathe, and I also wanted to avoid fatigues, and other manual tasks that I naturally found repugnant. Finally, I told myself that the role of officer, by giving me a degree of initiative and responsibility, would make my job more useful and interesting. I did not have a very clear idea of what it would be like to be an officer under fire, but I believed I had enough dignity, decency or pride to shoulder the obligations it would entail. It seemed to me that the individual qualities which I vaguely felt I possessed would stand in for military qualities, and might even be superior to them. For I had nothing but contempt for purely military values. Having had this debate with myself, I put my name forward.

For the written exam, we were given a prophetic theme: 'Show the historical origins of the present war and predict its development, its conclusion and its consequences.' To exhaust this vast subject, we were shut away for three hours. I made up for my scant knowledge of history with a lyricism borrowed from our most eloquent patriots: I derided the Central Powers, exalted our own courage and that of our allies, and concluded with a swift victory that would astonish the whole world and save it from barbarism. This brilliant piece of work put me in fourth place out of five hundred candidates, just beside a former companion from school, a very talented pupil who already had a place at the Ecole Centrale Paris. I thought I was through.

But there was still the oral. On an icy day, in the peculiar outfits already described, we were assembled on the training ground. After a long wait, a car drew up with flags on its bonnet. From it stepped a colonel who strode forward with that masculine assurance that comes from the certainty of never being contradicted. With his stiff moustache, bushy eyebrows, and the tanned complexion of a man who has spent a lot of time outdoors doing very little, this superior officer exuded energy. He sought it, too, and clearly felt it could be distinguished by how fiercely orders were barked on a parade square.

With an eye accustomed to judging men by the shine on their boots and buttons, the length of their hair, and their ability to stand in line, he surveyed our ranks, and decided:

'We are going to find out who has military aptitude!'

The test began straight away. We were instructed to put a section through various manoeuvres. Not having the faintest idea how to do this, we were extremely awkward. However, since this test had begun with those who were top so far, after two hours of demonstration the men who had almost failed the written exams finally managed to imitate the false tone that lends power to a command. When it was over, an officer held out a package of scripts to the colonel.

'Here are the essays, sir.'

'Never mind the paperwork, the decision is made!' replied the perspicacious leader.

And the next day twenty candidates were named, all carefully chosen from the bottom.

The decision of this colonel who was such a great connoisseur of men put an end to my ambitions and relegated me to the rank of private, a rank which I resolved – as my own revenge against stupidity – never to change. It was then that I was automatically selected to join the squad of men training to be corporals, a squad where I was forced to remain despite my protests. Luckily I found many of my former fellow students there and we enjoyed our time together when we were not on exercises. This camaraderie was the only benefit I derived from it, for we were never made corporals.

That is why, after a year of army life, I am still a private. Many people are in the same position, men who would have been able to do better if they had been better employed. I regret nothing, but it should be recorded that it was the army, in the person of one obdurate colonel, which refused my well-meaning offer.

Searching through my memories I find something that I had forgotten and which, at the time, annoyed me. Today I see it in a different light and regret my anger.

I had been with the regiment for three weeks when I was summoned to the company office. There I found our old captain, a rather paternal figure, who had a question to ask me.

'What's the matter, my friend, is something wrong?'

'Not at all, sir,' I replied in astonishment.

'Really? Quite sure?'

'Absolutely sure!'

'So tell me then, what is the meaning of this letter?'

I read it:

'*Monsieur le Commandant*, I am taking the liberty of writing to you about my grandson, Private Jean Dartemont. I have looked after this boy for a long time and he has always been delicate. I am certain that he could not bear the strain of a campaign. It is very unfortunate that no one is thinking of the health of our children during these sad times, and instead people take advantage of their enthusiasm and their lack of experience. Only people who are strong should be sent to war, and not young people who are too frail and are prey to violent emotions, who will not be of any use at all over there. Everyone should serve the nation according to his abilities and I am sure my grandson, who has been well educated, will be much more help working in an office. I know that the child will not dare to complain, and that is why, given my age and the misfortunes that I have witnessed over the years, I am writing to you, sir, so that in the light of his feeble constitution you may take the necessary steps…'

I shrugged my shoulders, with a grin.

'So?' demanded the captain.

'A grandmother's exaggerations. I am really not that weak!'

'And you have no complaints? There is nothing you need?'

'Nothing at all, sir.'

'Very good. Off you go then!'

Smiling, he watched me leave. I was furious at this clumsy meddling in my life, and at the thought that anyone could think I had encouraged my grandmother to intervene on my behalf. 'She's always been the same, always scared of everything!' I muttered. I remembered all the warnings she used to give me when I stayed with her in the holidays, how anxious she was when I fired my little pistol at the bottom of the garden, or when I went across the river in a boat. I had to hide in order to go swimming, and also to avoid going to Mass. 'When will they leave me alone?' I asked myself, thus confusing her with the rest of the family, something I did not usually do, for I was grateful for her gentle, heartfelt affection, however anxious it may have been.

Today I am ashamed of my anger. Writing as she did, my grandmother was certainly far from being a true Spartan, and no doubt her confessor could have chided her for a lack of Christian resignation. But now I can appreciate that her nervousness in the face of what was going on was more human, closer to the truth, than all the fine poses of people for whom courage cost precious little, since they exercised it at others' expense. Her faltering heart allowed her to imagine what war would be like for me, while I had no idea, and she dreaded to think of those she loved suffering or being in danger. She put my safety above all vanity, my life above all conventions. And her letter, which my ignorance had made appear ridiculous, now seems to me to be the best reason that this dear old woman has given me to cherish her.

*****

I am always either happy or bored: there is nothing in between. The only things I can do well are those that I enjoy and I can only enjoy things where I use my brain. Army life makes fewer demands on the brain than any other activity. Necessarily so, because it allows the army to swell its ranks with more and more soldiers, and because it can easily reconstitute itself once they've been decimated. 'Atten-shun!' – the army's entire strength rests on that command, on silent obedience which destroys the capacity for rational thought. You can see why it is vital. What would become of the army if soldiers had the idea of asking generals where they were leading them and then started arguing? It would be an embarrassing question for a general, for no leader should ever have to answer an inferior with 'I don't know any more than you do'.

After a year of army life, I have come to the conclusion that I'm a bad soldier and I regret it, just as I once regretted being a bad pupil. I am simply unable to submit to any rule. Should I blame myself? Is the fact that I have never accepted the principles that I've been taught a serious failing? I usually think that it is something good, and that it is the principles that are terribly wrong. But when I see so many people lined up against me, certain of their convictions, I sometimes have my doubts: I have my weaknesses just like everyone else and I give way to public opinion… I am afraid of being unfit for a war which asks for nothing save passivity and endurance. Would I not feel easier if I was a wholehearted combatant, like all the others (but have I ever actually met any?), fighting fiercely for his nation and certain that his god will reward him with indulgences for the death of each enemy he kills? Unfortunately I am quite unable to do something if it does not make sense to me, and the rules that various guardians have tried to impose on me never make sense. My former schoolmasters took me to task for my independence;

later I understood that they feared my judgement and that my adolescent logic was raising questions that they had chosen to avoid. But today the guardians are more powerful, and the people in that role may have me killed.

Back at the base our initial training was complete and we had been made privates first class (the selection of corporals would only be made at the front) and each given a squad. In my case this meant commanding twenty-five men. I never managed to get interested in this command, in checking the shine on rifle sights or whether buttons were correctly fastened or packs kept neat and tidy, in other words in harassing other men to demonstrate their dependency and my superiority, imposing on them what in their place I would have hated myself. It requires a certain level of mediocrity to develop a taste for such things and those above me, who had that taste, quickly saw that I was not one of them. They took their revenge by putting me down for the first train to the front. I could perceive a threat in their attitude which I did not understand until later. At the time I just laughed at this ominous choice and saw in it a contradiction (which should have enlightened me) with army doctrine: if honour is to be found in perilous situations then why send me off before more merito- rious candidates? But I had already decided to go to the front. The sooner the better, and I was getting tired of being stuck at the rear, where conditions were gradually reverting to the usual rigours of barracks life.

Our departure was very jolly. We had been issued with fresh kit and horizon-blue uniforms in a new design in which we pranced around like dandies. We had forty-eight hours to strut through town and read in the eyes of passing women the tender interest that our youth and daring merited. We were rather proud of ourselves.

I took my leave of someone who had shown me all the kindness and indulgence of an older sister, based on experience of men's ingratitude and the fact that one should not expect too much from them. Knowing that she was only a staging-post in my life, I had not questioned her about her past (which I suspected was quite murky) and, in two months, had known nothing about her beyond her first name, which was indispensable for conversation. In other words, my strength was unimpeded, destined for other goals, and I was not enfeebled by all those silly emotions that can weaken a virile heart. I separated from this convenient woman resolutely, with no regrets or wish to return. I believe I would have refused to devote a week to her, that I would have even have sacrificed the vanity of feeling myself loved to my desire to visit a battlefield, to finally know what was going on there. I still imagined the war in terms of sightseeing.

Ten months after the first to go, we set off for the front in good cheer, and the local people, who were getting rather used to all this by now, still gave us an honourable send-off because, after all, we were scarcely nineteen years old.

3

WAR ZONE

THE ENCHANTED CIRCLE, when at last we reached it, was a disappointment. When the train set us down in the middle of the countryside, we had to begin a long march in the rain, during which our beautiful new kit, our full packs, our bandoliers and our tools all weighed heavily. At nightfall we reached a rather grand country house, its terrace crowded with strutting officers. But we had to erect our tents on the spongy lawns under trees dripping with rainwater. This exercise, which we carried out clumsily, took a great deal of time and it was dark by the time we finished. Then, already soaked, we had to sleep in this swamp.

The next day we were ordered to join a march battalion. Battalions like this provided reserves of men which were moved up parallel to the front line so that they could be brought in to places that were under attack and provide immediate reinforcements. These battalions also acted as front-line depots into which were poured those who passed through the first-aid posts: the sick, the walking wounded. These wounded men, veterans, could be recognised by their washed-out uniforms, their faked submissiveness and their anxious demeanour. The NCOs treated them better.

I managed to get myself into the same squad as my friend Bertrand, with whom I had been through initial training and who was, like me, a private first class. But we very soon realised that this single stripe had no value here, that it only attracted ridicule, and we decided to get rid of it, with a quick slash of the knife. Not quickly enough, though, to stop our corporal noticing and taking umbrage. No doubt he saw in this stripe the start of an ambition that threatened his power. We had been marked out, and these two unfortunate privates first class, even self-demoted, became the unhappy objects of his ill-temper and abuse. I should say that I was his main target. Betrand had a rather gentle character and a mild face to match his mild emotions. My own face, on the contrary, by the disgust which it clearly revealed, was a constant challenge to our superior. One can only describe this NCO, whose name I have forgotten, as a thug. His repulsive appearance made it all too clear: a big red face, square head, thick neck, powerful but ugly chest, thin legs with knock knees, club feet, huge fists, something base in his expression, and the voice of a drunken navvy. He ordered us around with revolting coarseness and constantly boasted of his courage. Later we had proof that this was an empty boast.

In the army it is always easy to find fault with people and persecute them. Especially easy in my case, since, out of training as I was, fatigue overwhelmed me to the point where I failed to look after my weapons or the fine details of my uniform. I was, in particular, very bad at marching. Our torturer was aware of this, and never failed to force me to carry an extra load whenever we were on the move. He made me add to my pack a dixie containing food for the whole squad. These few, awkwardly balanced, kilos were pure torture for me. I soon decided to head for the latrines after the second break in the march. Lying flat on my back I let the column set off without me and then waited for one of the convoys that rumbled along the roads. Hopping from one vehicle to another I made it to my destination quite comfortably. But at one point my pack, falling from an artillery truck on which I was hanging, slipped beneath the wheels. The dixie was flattened and that evening the squad had nothing to eat. That was the last time I was ordered to carry food.

Digging latrines, sweeping out the camp, stuffing straw mattresses – these tasks left us no time to rest. To them we brought a cheerful nonchalance and unfailing incompetence. Our good humour was sustained by the thought that there was nothing else to do here in the countryside and so we might as well pass the time together, straining to botch a job or make it last forever, and pretend we enjoyed it. In the end it stopped us being bored. When we were ordered out on fatigues, we got in the habit of declaiming a line from Cicero: 'Quid abutere, Catilina, patienta nostra?'[11] 'What was that you said?' shouted our little boss, the first time he heard these words, suspecting rebellion. 'It is not my duty to teach you Latin, corporal,' I replied very sweetly.

In the end, my patience ran out. I can still picture the exact spot. On a bare plateau beneath a fierce June sun, our squad was exercising under the orders of Catiline (the name had stuck). With no other motive than hatred, he let my comrades take a break, leaving me alone to repeat the exhausting movements of bayonet drill; point! thrust!… A man's strength has its limits, of which he took no account, and this test was a kind of duel which I would necessarily lose. I knew that when I could no longer move my arms he was quite capable of provoking me into disobeying an order. More than anything, the sight of his hideous face was driving me mad. I suddenly strode up to him, with my fixed bayonet, only stopping when the point was touching his chest. 'I'm going to k…!' I snarled. I don't know if I would have killed him. But, seeing the look on my face, he didn't doubt it. He went very pale and didn't say another word. The whole, trembling squad knew he was beaten.

With that moment of madness I was risking prison. But honour where honour's due! This senseless act, which could have been the end for me, put a stop to our persecution. Afterwards the corporal tried to make friends with us. We made it clear that this would be even more repugnant than his hatred, and that in any case we were not afraid of him any more. But this thug had spoilt

our first month at the front and poisoned in advance the new life
we were hoping for.

For several weeks, we had to march all over the place. We did
our cooking in the open air and slept under canvas. I remember
two marches in particular. One was on a scorching hot day when
we all succumbed to the heat. Our battalion fell apart completely
leaving groups of men staggering about like sunstroke victims by
the roadside. Some tried to drag themselves along, others flopped
down in the fields, or attempted to force their way on to passing
convoys. True to my principles, I had dropped out of the ranks at
the start. I knew I couldn't make it to the end and told myself it
was better not to wait till I was exhausted. By the end of the day,
the march looked like a rout.

The second march took twelve hours and lasted right through
the night. We were ordered to set off without any warning. The
whole battalion was half-asleep and we marched with our eyes
shut, bumping into each other. At every halt we nodded off by the
roadside. Night marches are dreadful, because there is nothing to
look at, nothing to catch your attention and to take your mind off
your worn-out body. We were constantly forced into the ditches
by ammunition wagons galloping past, by columns of lorries and
heavy supply buses which paid no heed to the staggering columns
of infantry. The traffic raised up thick clouds of white dust, which
stuck to our sweating faces like a brittle glaze. We were a troop of
ghosts and old men, and all we could do was keep crying out for
a breather. But always the whistles would summon us back up on
our feet, set in motion our onerous role as beasts of burden, until
it no longer felt like a march with a destination but a journey to
the end of a night that spread across the earth into infinity.

We were shaken out of this torpor by a world in flames. We had
just marched over the crest of a hill, and suddenly there before us
lay the front line, roaring with all its mouths of fire, blazing like

some infernal factory where monstrous crucibles melted human flesh into a bloody lava. We shuddered at the thought that we were nothing but more coal to be shovelled into this furnace, that there were soldiers down there fighting against the storm of steel, the red hurricane that burned the sky and shook the earth to its foundations. There were so many explosions that they merged into a constant roar and glare. It was as if someone had set a match to the petrol-soaked horizon, or an evil spirit was stoking up the flames in some devil's punch-bowl, dancing naked and sneering at our destruction. And so that nothing was missing from this macabre carnival, so that there was something to highlight the tragedy by its contrast, we saw rockets rising gracefully, like flowers of light, fading at the summit of this inferno and dropping down, dying, trailing stars. We were mesmerised by this spectacle, whose poignant meaning only the old hands knew. This was my first sight of the front line, my first sight of hell unleashed.

It was on the following day that I felt an itch and slipped my hand into my trousers to find something soft which stuck under my fingernail. I pulled out my first louse, pallid and fat, the sight of which made me shudder with disgust. As I was concealed by a hedge, I checked through all my clothes. The creature already had a few companions, and in the seams and hems I found the little white dots of their eggs. I was contaminated, but I still had to keep these repulsive clothes, endure the tickling and the biting of the vermin, to which my imagination lent an incessant activity. The foul family must now prosper upon my body, month after month, and contaminate my intimate life with its multiplication. This discovery demoralised me and made me hate my solitude, now haunted by a swarm of parasites. Lice marked the fall into ignominy and a man could only escape this squalor of war by spilling his blood. Heroes now lived as sordidly as the denizens of night shelters, and their quarters, filthier than those shelters, were also deadlier.

The whole area behind the front line was swarming with

troops of all kinds. Since the few villages could not provide shelter for so many soldiers, primitive encampments had sprung up everywhere, with tents, huts and barracks, spreading their smoke across the countryside. Every clump of trees, every gulley hid a tribe of combatants, busy preparing food or doing their washing. The landscape had been devastated: the ground churned up by tramping feet, military transport and general depredations, covered in debris and rubbish. It bore the mark of that desolation which armies always bring to the regions they traverse. Only wine was in plentiful supply. The lukewarm barrels in the canteens dispensed oblivion to those who had the money to fill their flasks.

In the morning, we heard a buzzing in the air, and up in the blinding blue sky where the sun breaking through the last patches of mist promised a scorching day, we could see an aeroplane climbing up, dipping and turning like a lark. We watched it for a long time until it dissolved into the atmosphere way off in the distance so that there was nothing left but a glittering shard of mica fluttering in the wind. How we envied that man up there who made war in the purity of the heavens, an angel with a machine gun.

Before us, the line of observation balloons, known as 'sausages', marked the front line, the thundering front of the attack sector, whose rage reached us in waves of dull thuds. Sometimes we would pass frantic columns of lorries on the road, full of haggard infantrymen, some of them venting their joy at having survived in frenzied cries that sounded like curses, others just stretched out, still as corpses, and all of them stained with blood and dirt. These were the troops who had just distinguished themselves at Notre-Dame-de-Lorette, Le Labyrinthe, Souchez, and La Targette, and we knew from the number of empty lorries the price these regiments had paid for clawing from the enemy a few ruined houses or a few bits of trench.

* * * * *

The battalion finally moved to quarters a few kilometres behind the front, in a village where we could reorganise ourselves. The road passing through this village was the main thoroughfare for the whole Neuville-Saint-Vaast sector. So we were posted at a crossroads and could get a picture of life at the front through the movement of relief troops, supply columns and ambulances. The permanent traffic jams on the access roads forced units to wait under our gaze for a long time. We were thus able to observe at close quarters men who had already fought, terrifying, hardened men who were returning to attack again. They uttered nothing but curses, as if to spit in the face of death, but we could see the anxiety beneath the bravado, at the edge of despair. They were shepherded by officers with tense faces, in plain uniforms, officers who would mix in with them, rarely seemed to stand on ceremony and kept orders to a minimum. The soldiers hung around in pre-occupied groups by the rifle stacks, argued bitterly with the NCOs whom they threatened with terrible retributions, and whenever no one was looking would rush off to the few places in the village where they could get a drink. Many were drunk, and not only the ordinary soldiers. In the evening they would slowly take the road that led back up there. The uproar they made would slowly fade, soon lost in the noise of the bombardment into which they were marching.

We slept on straw in huts of wood and tarpaulin that were swelteringly hot in the daytime. We were used as navvies, repairing old trenches in readiness for a new offensive. We set off at dusk, marched for a long time through former positions. Once we got to the right spot we were assigned our tasks in groups of two: one pick, one shovel. After a certain hour, the nights were calm. We could only hear the crackle of grenades far away, and brief fusillades, and see rockets going up: stray bullets buzzed like mosquitoes. A few artillery shells exploded ahead of us, also far off, and an invisible battery, somewhere down in the shadows, barked its response. We returned to camp at daybreak and had the morning to rest.

Our huts were so infested with lice that I would often go and sleep in a field, rolled up in my blanket and tent canvas. The trouble with that was the damp morning dew. That was surely the cause of the stomach upsets that wore me out and for a long time gave me no peace at all. In a situation where everything depends on your body, a discomfort like this became something very serious.

Along with Bertrand and some other soldiers, I was attached to the company office as a runner or, if they needed one, a secretary. This did not spare us from work, but it brought a few advantages. We got out of afternoon drill and other petty annoyances, and we were given food separately which we could cook in kitchens in the village, paying the people who lived there a bit of extra money to improve on our rations. This cooking was also an occasion for frequent quarrels, because of the work it entailed, to which we brought very little good will. I often noticed at the front how men's boredom and misery changed to anger at the slightest pretext; they did not know who to blame and so turned violently against each other. Too much suffering made them lose control. And since material concerns were all they thought about (all intellectual life being suspended, having nothing there to nourish it), the pettiest issues were the cause of their arguments. In war all instincts are given free rein, with nothing to impede or stop them, except for death's arbitrary intervention. And even that limit did not exist for those whose jobs usually kept them out of danger. Among the many senior officers staying in the village I saw two examples.

The first was the colonel of an infantry regiment, idling away the time in a camp that had been set up on the outskirts of the village. A former colonial, red-faced and robust, he derived great pleasure from beating up soldiers. His way of doing this, as I witnessed, showed clearly that he was deranged. He would hail someone, call him over, and then, with a warm smile, ask him a few friendly questions to put him at ease – but his eyes shone in a strange way, and his veins swelled up. And then suddenly he would strike the subordinate a blow full in the face, accompanied by a torrent of insults, which made him even more excited: 'Take that, you swine! You son of a bitch!' He would carry on hitting the man until, having got over his surprise, his victim would flee. Then the colonel would resume his stroll, moving in a jerky, unco-ordinated fashion like someone suffering from ataxia, smacking his jaws, with a contented air. It would often happen that a soldier walking along with nothing much to do would be stopped and get a fierce kick in the arse: the colonel had passed. Very soon, people learned to get well out of the way when they saw him coming, and he could no longer approach anyone. Such a cruel deprivation changed him; he became sad and withdrawn. He only brightened up when a man from another unit or regiment fell into his hands, someone who did not know about his mania. But these windfalls were rare. He experienced a few happy days when four hundred reinforcements were sent up from the rear to join his regiment. For one week, he kept himself busy punching and insulting and his good humour was restored. Old hands, hiding in corners, watched this massacre of newcomers astonished to learn that war consisted of having your face knocked in by a superior officer. Soldiers actually said that – this fault excepted – their colonel was not a bad man. On several occasions he had even overruled severe punishments imposed by court martials. It was true that the culprits still left with bloody faces and broken teeth.

'I'm amazed that no one has hit him back,' Bertrand said to me.

'It would be too dangerous. A man who defended himself would no doubt carry the day. But there would be nothing to stop his colonel then ordering him on a mission where he'd get himself killed.'

Once a week we were sent to the showers. The sanitation service had dreamt up the idea of eradicating parasites by soaking us in cresol. Medical orderlies washed us down with a sponge. This treatment made our skin burn for an hour but had no effect at all on the lice we rediscovered afterwards in our clothes – which had not been disinfected – in fine form and with healthy appetites. But still the weekly showers became an attraction, thanks to 'Old Father Rosebud'. This was the name we had given to a divisional general, a thin, dirty, hunched man with bloodshot eyes, who was always there. This sadistic officer only liked to see soldiers when they were naked. He would inspect each new batch, lined up under the showers, moving along the line with the little mincing steps of an old man, keeping his eyes fixed somewhere not far below their waist. If one of the objects of his gaze struck him by its dimensions he would congratulate the possessor: 'You've got a fine one there!' His face would wrinkle up in pleasure, and he dribbled. The only other place one encountered him was the latrines. There, he would lose himself in contemplation of the ditches, plunge his cane in, and welcome the men, who were surprised to see him. 'Go on, lads, don't be shy, let it go. Healthy bowels make healthy soldiers. I'm just here to check on your morale.' This behaviour, which would have been unacceptable anywhere except in a war, entertained the troops, who were not fussy about their distractions.

'It is terrifying to think that the lives of ten thousand men may depend on a general like this,' said Bertrand. 'How are we expected to win the war with people like him at the top?'

'We don't see what is going on in the other camp,' I replied. 'They've got their own mad brutes who make just as many mistakes. The best proof is that they set off to conquer with everything they needed for a swift victory, and they failed.'

'How do you think this is going to end?'

'No one knows. The men who are running the war have been overwhelmed by events. The forces on both sides are still so huge that they balance each other out. It's like when you play draughts: you have to remove a lot of pieces before you can get a true picture of the game. A lot more people must be killed before things will take shape.'

'We keep *nibbling* at them, as...'[12]

'The nibbling is mutual. The generals of both sides fight the war with the same military principles and cancel each other out. It takes a great idea to win a war: the wooden horse of Troy, Hannibal's elephants, Napoleon crossing the Alps through the Saint Bernard Pass... those were real ideas.'

'And the Paris taxis?'[13]

'An idea too – which didn't really come from the military. And still...'

'And what about valour?'

'Valour is a virtue for ordinary soldiers; leaders need the virtue of intelligence. What we lack are leaders with outstanding intelligence. Genius shakes up the old rules and principles, genius *invents*.'

'Do you think that Napoleon...?'

'Napoleon would have done what he always did. He'd make something new from whatever was available to him in 1914 just like he did in 1800. Alexander, Caesar, Napoleon, they were *thinkers*. Today all we've got are *specialists*, blinded by dogma, who can't think beyond the narrow boundaries of their military training.'

'But they know how to do their job.'

'No, they don't even know that. Who was there to teach them? This war followed forty years of peace. The only training they could have got was through war games, manoeuvres, empty shams whose results couldn't be measured. Our generals are like students fresh from college: all theory and no practice. They came to war with modern equipment and a military system that's a century out of date. But now they're learning, they are *experimenting with us*. The people of Europe are in the hands of arrogant, all-powerful, ignoramuses.'

'So what do you think it takes to make a great military leader?'

'Maybe the first requirement would be that they came from outside the army, so they could bring a fresh approach to understanding war. It isn't so much a military leader we need as a real leader, which would be something much greater.'

'Perhaps they'll still find one...'

'Perhaps...'

The heat, the dirt, and the boredom had worn us out.

My most vivid memory from this time was of a dead body, not one I saw but one I smelt. It was a night when we were trying to deepen a communication trench, hardly able to see where we were digging. As one of us struck his pick into the earth there was a squelch, the sound of something bursting. The pick had hit a damp, rotten stomach, which released its miasma right into our faces, in a sudden blast of foul vapour. The stench filled the air, covered our mouths like a foetid flannel so we could not breathe, pricked our eyelids with poisonous needles which brought tears to our eyes. This pestilential geyser caused a panic and the diggers fled the accursed spot. The decomposing body's disgusting gasses spread out, filled the darkness and our lungs, reigned over the silence. The NCOs had to force us back to this angry corpse, and then we shovelled furiously, desperate to cover it up and calm it down. But our bodies had caught the awful, fecund smell of putrefaction, which is life and death, and for a long time that smell irritated our mucous membranes, stimulated the secretions of our glands, aroused in us some secret organic attraction of matter for matter, even when it is corrupt and almost extinguished. Our own promised, perhaps imminent, putrefaction found communion with this other, powerful extreme of putrefaction, which holds dominion over our pale souls and hunts them down remorselessly.

That night I reflected on the destiny of the unknown soldier whose grave we had disturbed, and upon which many others would trample. I imagined a man like me, someone young, full of plans and ambitions, of loves still uncertain, scarcely out of childhood and about to launch himself into life. To me life is like a game you begin at twenty where victory is called success: money for most people, reputation for some, esteem for a very few. To live, to endure, that is nothing; to achieve is everything. I compare someone who dies young to a player who has just been dealt his cards and then forbidden to play. Maybe this particular player was taking his revenge... Twenty years of learning, of subordination, of hopes and desires, the sum of feelings that a human being carries within himself and which gives him his value, had all found their conclusion in a corner of a communication trench. If I must die now, I will not say it is awful or terrible, but it is unjust and absurd, because I have not yet attempted anything, I have done nothing but wait for my chance and my moment, built up my resources and waited. The life of my will and my tastes is only just starting – or will start, because the war has deferred it. If I disappear now, I will have been nothing but subordinate and anonymous. I will have been defeated.

I got my first proper view of a wide section of the front on 15 August 1915. A few kilometres outside our village was a hill called Mont-Saint-Éloi, somewhere near the famous Berthonval farm, I think, from where our spring offensive was launched and which must now therefore be nothing but a pile of rubble. There was a monument on this hill, a church, damaged by shellfire and out of bounds because it was dangerous. But, being curious to see, I managed to slip away with Bertrand and we climbed one of the towers, up a stone stairway that was shaky in places, and partially blocked by debris from the walls, cracked by the bombardment.

From up there you could see right across the plains of Artois, but it was impossible to make out any real signs of a battle. A few white puffs of smoke, followed by explosions, told us that this was indeed where the war was, but we could not see any trace of the armies on the ground observing and destroying each other slowly in this arid, silent landscape. Such a calm expanse, baking in the sunshine, confounded our expectations. We could see the trenches quite clearly but they looked like tiny embankments, or narrow, winding streams, and it seemed incredible that this fragile network could offer serious resistance to attacks, that people did not simply step across it to move forward. I later thought that some generals, who had never done sentry duty at a lookout post nor charged at barbed wire under machine-gun fire, must have seen the trenches as we saw them then, with our novice eyes, and had the same illusions. Such illusions seem to have determined the murderous and pointless offensive in which I took part.

Soon after, we joined a fighting unit.

4

BAPTISM OF FIRE

WE MOVED UP TO THE LINE at the beginning of September, on a quiet, cool evening. The trench system spread out over eight to ten kilometres, but we wandered around all night, packs on our backs, as the guides who led our column kept getting lost at the various junctions. We often had to retrace our steps and wait while scouts explored the desolate, silent labyrinth in which they, in their turn, got lost. Behind us, some small groups had vanished altogether, through the fault of men who had dropped back a few metres, lost sight of those in front of them, and then set off in the wrong direction. So we all had to take responsibility for those behind us. The march was forever being stopped by shouts of 'Halt!' and 'Turn here!' which made it very tiring.

I was sustained by the notion that this night was my baptism of fire, and my equipment seemed less of a burden than usual. Little by little we advanced into the active zone, the danger zone. It felt warmer and stuffier, like a place that was lived in; there was a powerful smell of human bodies, a mixture of fermentation and excrement, and food that had gone bad. Men were snoring behind the embankments we brushed past, and glimmers of light marked the openings of the dugouts where they lay. We had to keep ducking to avoid the tangle of wires, traverses, and plank bridges. The first stray bullets began to plough through the air, but the rifle shots themselves were scarcely audible. Shells passed over us like great birds of passage, way up high, then came to earth somewhere off in the depths of the battlefield where they burst with dull thuds. Now rockets were illuminating a flickering landscape, briefly bathing the tattered natural world in baleful moonlight. After these bursts of false day, the night was even blacker and we groped our way forward like blind men. The more we advanced, the more tortuous the passageways became, and the more densely populated too, so it seemed. We finally emerged into ruins and I had the impression that I was entering some town that had been exhumed from the dead. But now the night was nearly over. We saw our pale faces, tinged with green by the dawn and exhaustion. Our squad slipped down into the nearest cellar, settled in by the light of a candle, and slept.

When I woke a few hours later I remembered that I was in Neuville-Saint-Vaast, just a few hundred metres from the front lines. At last, I told myself, I was at the heart of the adventure, with my luck, my strength, and my curiosity intact. I hurried out like an eager tourist, leaving my weapons behind. I was greeted by a beautiful, clear sky, which seemed to me to bode well, and I set off to see the sights, drifting aimlessly along the main street, a real boulevard of war. It was crowded with soldiers bustling about who took no notice of me. The confusion was a delight. I had been transported to an unknown country, like none I had ever seen, and this chaos, which I intended to explore, enchanted me, for I saw it as the symbol of the freedom that surely awaited me here. Nothing remained of the houses except some walls and piles of rubble above the cellars where soldiers sheltered; a few kept parts of their broken timber frames, which stretched out their burned beams in anguish. Mutilated trees were frozen in the postures of supplicants. One, which still had leaves, made me think of the poignant good humour of an invalid. It was pleasant to lose myself in the infinite maze of streets, to feel alone and adrift, and then to find my path again, with the special sense of a true warrior.

The shelters, of all shapes and sizes, dug out of mounds of

earth, offered a curious sight. What was particularly striking about these makeshift constructions was that the materials used were themselves just bits of scrap and rubbish: old pieces of wood, old weapons, old pots and pans. With no resources except their wits, the combatants had come up with this primitive solution. A few metal implements sufficed for all their needs and life thus returned to the most basic conditions, as if to the dawn of time.

I went back to our cellar, then set off once more. Continuing my explorations away from the main thoroughfares, I came upon the bodies of two long-dead Germans in the basement of a house. These men must have been hit by grenades and then walled up, in the haste of battle. In this airless space they had not decomposed but shrivelled and then a more recent shell had blown apart their tomb and scattered their remains. I spent some time in their company, turning them over with a stick, not out of hatred or disrespect but motivated rather by a kind of fraternal pity, as if asking them to deliver up the secret of their death. The flattened uniforms seemed empty. Of the scattered remains nothing really survived except for half a head, a mask, but a mask of magnificent horror. The skin on it had dried and turned green, taking on the dark tones of an antique bronze with its patina of age. A pitted eye socket was empty and around it had streamed like tears a paste, now hardened, which must have been brains. It was the only blemish that spoilt the whole thing, but perhaps it really added to it, like the marks of wear add something to the worn stone of ancient statues. It was as if a pious hand had closed the eye, and, beneath the eyelid you could imagine the smooth contour and the shape of the eyeball. The mouth was fixed in the last screams of a terrible death agony, with a rictus of the lips baring the teeth, a mouth wide open, spitting out the soul like a clot of blood. I wished I could have kept this mask that death had fashioned, on which its fatal genius had achieved a synthesis of war, so that a cast could be made and given to women and zealots. I did at least make a sketch which I've kept in my notebook, but it does not express the holy horror with which I was filled by its model. The skull lent the chiaroscuro of the ruins a grandeur that I found hard to leave behind, and I only went outside again when the fading daylight cast formless shadows over the forehead, cheek bones and teeth, turning it into a grinning Asian.

I went back slowly through a dusk pierced by the noise of gunfire and exploding shells, which heralded the night's uneasy quarrel, when men shoot more to comfort themselves than to destroy.

Inside our shelter an old hand said to me:

'You shouldn't stay outside, young lad. You'll come to harm!'

But I was proud of my afternoon discovery and at the thought that in one day at the front I had already found something that people at the rear could not imagine: this pathetic mask, this death mask of some Beethoven who had been savagely executed.

The next morning we were taken to the front lines and put to work.

Our job was to dig out 'Russian saps', in preparation for the next offensive, now imminent. These were low, narrow underground trenches, dug straight out from the front line for some twenty metres towards the enemy lines, so that our troops could advance and only appear at the last moment. Some unknown engineer had come up with this idea which was supposed to allow our assault units to move forward stealthily under cover, and to charge out close to the German positions, and at the same time to eliminate the need for taking down our own barbed wire so as not to warn the enemy of an impending attack. But the Germans had other sure ways of knowing, and the eventual surprise was not the one hoped for.

It was long and tiring job. One man, bent double, moved forward with his pick, and those behind passed back sacks full of earth, which those at the rear would empty in the second, reserve lines so that the digging wasn't visible. One sap was allotted to each squad, with gaps between them, all the way along the front of the offensive as far as I knew. Completing the task took us a fortnight, interrupted by other bits of repair work, day and night, all over our sector. Our military function was limited to the role of navvies working under fire, exposed and passive, terms which in fact defined the general situation of soldiers in this war. But I did not know that yet and was disappointed that our initiation began with fatigues.

The sector was fairly quiet, as often happens in the periods before a big battle, and only disturbed by the bombardments of our own artillery, either for range-finding or to cause general damage. The German batteries, no doubt trying to save ammunition, only answered with short, concentrated fire on targeted objectives.

The only people we encountered at the front line were mud-encrusted men, who trudged about like peasants, wary and arrogant. When they ate they did it with intense concentration, as if it were the most important task in the world and their greasy mess-tins and battered dixies contained very possible pleasure. They would spend long hours just standing behind an observation slit, not talking, smoking their pipes, and cursing loudly whenever there was an explosion in the vicinity.

I had been astonished to find myself in the middle of the war yet not be able to find it, unable to accept that in fact the war consisted precisely of this stasis. But I had to see it, and so I clambered up on a fire-step and stuck my head above the parapet. Through the tangle of barbed wire an embankment very like ours could be seen less than a hundred metres away, silent as if abandoned, yet full of eyes and gunsights focused on us. The other army was there, under cover, holding its breath to surprise us, and menacing us with its own guns and gadgets and the conviction of its strength. Between the two embankments, ours and theirs, lay this strip of shattered land, no man's land, where anyone who stands up is a target immediately struck down, where rotting corpses serve as bait, where patrols venture only at night, suffocated by their pounding hearts and dizzied by the blood roaring in their temples, so loud it seems to hide all other sounds, when they creep out into this macabre land defended by dread and death.

But I didn't have time for a good look. Someone had grabbed my feet and was pulling me down. I heard a low, angry voice:

'If you really want to be a corpse there's no rush, you'll have plenty of chances. But don't show the Boche where your pals are!'

I wanted to reply. But the shrugs and sneers of the other soldiers made me think better of it:

'Berlin's straight ahead, lad, you can't miss it!'

'Looks like the new boys are dead keen to win the war for us!'

'Yeah, just look at this one! But they won't be cocky for long, these bloody conscripts!'

I realised that they had taken my curiosity for some pointless display of bravado and that I should watch what I said to men who were old hands at this game. I must not allow myself to look ridiculous by appearing reckless, and the wisest counsel was to imitate their prudence and passivity. From then on I only looked out through the narrow slit of a loophole, hidden by sparse clumps of grey grass which also cut off the view at a few metres. Instead of the enemy army all I glimpsed were ants and the occasional grasshopper, the only visitors to a landscape forbidden to men.

In any case, bullets kept smashing into the parapet.

And our sergeant gave us wise advice:

'Fritz will make sure he puts some lead in your brain. Leave it to him!'

We came under shellfire for the first time.

Since the days were still warm, we made ourselves comfortable in the afternoon among the ruins outside our cellar. Stripped to the waist, we inspected our underwear so we could kill the lice that were devouring us and which thrived in the rotten straw mixed with rubbish that we slept on. Lice-hunting was one of our most pressing tasks. We devoted an hour of our rest period to it, as well as a great deal of care. Our sleep depended on it.

One day, while we were thus occupied, a time-shell burst just over our squad, enveloping us in its hot breath and a chorus of shrill whistles. Shrapnel fell all around but, miraculously, no one was hit. It felt like I had been struck a blow on the neck and my head resounded with a painful, metallic vibration, as if someone had drilled into my skull. Instinctively, and too late, we had jumped down into the cellar. Then we gathered the shards of shell casing, still burning hot, and the way they were driven into the ground gave me an idea of their velocity.

One night while we were working behind the front line, repairing a trench that had been smashed by artillery fire, we were caught in an enfilade by two artillery batteries, to left and right. The Germans, having spotted the damage to our position, correctly assumed we were repairing it. Their gunfire alternated with perfect regularity. But they were 'shooting long' in both directions, so that we kept running to escape explosions first at one end then at the other. When we heard their guns fire, we hit the ground in a shameful heap of panting bodies, waiting for the explosion so we could breathe again, unclench our stomachs, and run further off. The artillery played with us in this way for an hour and forced us to roll in the mud. I was furious at being compelled to adopt such a posture and several times refused to 'bow' to the shells. Once they had stopped firing, a rocket revealed a sergeant on the planks over a latrine beside the trench, slowly pulling up his trousers.

'Here's another one they missed!' he called to us cheerfully.

His calm composure brought back our smiles.

But when we all reassembled I saw that all the old hands had vanished, and the corporal wasn't surprised. We found them further on, in the cellar, where some were already asleep.

On yet another occasion we endured a very fierce bombardment. All afternoon we had worked recklessly on a support trench, throwing the earth we dug over the parapet. The sun had just gone down, a perfect calm had descended over the battlefield, and we were rolling cigarettes while waiting for the relief section. Shells shattered the silence in an instant. They came in rapid succession, targeted right on us, landing within fifty metres. Sometimes they were so close that we were showered with earth and breathed in the smoke. Men who had been laughing were now nothing more than hunted prey, undignified animals whose bodies only moved instinctively. I saw my ashen-faced comrades jostling and huddling together so that they weren't struck alone, jerking about like puppets in spasms of fear, hugging the ground, pushing their faces into the mud. The explosions were so continuous that their hot, acrid breath raised the temperature of the trench and we poured with sweat which froze on us yet still did not know whether this cold was not in fact heat. Our nerves contracted with every little scratch and bruise and more than one person believed he'd been hit and truly felt the terrible laceration of his flesh that fear made him imagine.

In this torment I was sustained by my reason, however wrong it was. I do not know where I had got the notion that field guns have a very straight trajectory. Which would mean that shells fired at us from in front could not land in the trench and it was only a matter of enduring the dreadful noise they made. This idiotic theory calmed me down and I suffered less than the others.

At last the relief arrived. But the shellfire pursued us. We ran and I found myself the last in the line. Shells came over very low, above my head, and exploded just a little further on. At the first turning, I came upon two men lying in their own blood, appealing with the expressions of beaten, imploring children that you see on people whom misfortune has suddenly struck, and I stepped over them shuddering at their awful cries. Since I could do nothing for them, I ran even faster to get away. Outside the shelters, their names were called out: Michard and Rigot, two young men we knew from the same class as us. The war had stopped being a game...

At night we were often woken up by runners shouting at the entrance to our cellar:

'Alert! Everybody out!'

We lit our candle, took our packs and rifles and grudgingly climbed up the stairs behind our corporal. Outside, we were caught in a tornado of explosions. We came out into the main thoroughfare, now swarming with armed shadows, trying not to get mixed up, calling each other and heading to the support positions. The cold air woke us up, as did the clattering of bullets, thousands of which were smashing into the walls, deafening us with their sharp slaps. All the stray bullets from the German fusillade were converging on the ruins, and, if we had emerged from the trenches, nothing would have remained of this subterranean army that had suddenly filled the night. Ahead of us, on the front lines, grenades crackled like sparks on some piece of electrical equipment. Heavy shells, with no warning this time, burst at random, with a red flash, shaking us with their foetid breath, surrounding us with torrents of metal and stones, which sometimes reached our ranks. Long human screams would suddenly cut through the rest of the din, echoing in us in waves of horror and reminding us, enough to make us tremble, of the lamentable frailty of our flesh, amidst this eruption of steel and fire. Then the staccato frenzy of machine guns tore through the voices of the dying, riddled the night, pierced it with a stipple of bullets and sounds. Impossible to make oneself heard without shouting, to be seen except in the boreal light of rockets, to move forward except by squeezing into these trenches choked with men, all gripped with the same anxiety: was it an attack? Were we going to fight? For in the months before this sector had been fought over day and night with grenade and bayonet from one barricade to another, one house to another, one room to another in the same house. There was not a single metre of conquered ground that wasn't paved with a corpse, not a hectare than had not cost a battalion.

Was the butchery beginning again?

At last we reached a trench in front of the village, outside the range of shells, peaceful as a suburb. With our loaded rifles on the parapet, awaiting the order to aim and fire, we watched the line of attack light up with bursts of flame, like embers in a hearth stoked back to life. We wondered what would become of us in this darkness, how we would distinguish attackers from our own soldiers falling back, and we tried to remember how to defend ourselves if, by chance, it soon became necessary. The bullets wove their whistling web, like the mesh of an aerial net that had been stretched over us and we kept our heads down. Little by little, we felt the cold and we yawned. Imperceptibly, shadows filled the corners of the horizon, the sky darkened, and the explosions became rare. We went back.

Once our corporal asked me: 'You weren't too scared?'

'Oh,' replied an old hand, 'I was behind him and he never stopped whistling.'

This was true. I do not enjoy being suddenly woken up. So I brought to these alerts the ill humour of a man whose routine has been upset and who absolutely refuses to get interested in a spectacle that he blames for the disturbance. My whistling, which had so astonished the veteran, expressed my contempt for a war which prevented people from sleeping and made such a lot of racket for such small results. The conviction that my destiny was not to find its end on a battlefield had still not been shaken. I had not yet taken the war (I thought: *their war*) seriously, judging it absurd in all its manifestations which I had assumed would be quite different. There was too much squalor, too many lice, too much drudgery and too much excrement; too much destruction for what purpose? Finding the whole business so badly organised, I sulked. Sulking gave me strength and a kind of courage.

The morning after the night when we were relieved, lorries took us to an unknown village where we were put in barns to get some sleep. We believed we were going to have a rest. In fact we were being taken to the rear to regroup and take our place in the formations of assault troops.

After two days, we marched to a point near the front, which thundered without pause. In another village, the captain read us a proclamation from High Command, the gist of which was that the French army was attacking the Germans at two points, in Artois and Champagne, with every available division, every piece of artillery and ordnance, and with the certainty of carrying all before it. The commander didn't hesitate to give us the numbers, whether true or false, of the troops engaged, so sure was he that the Germans would be incapable of stopping them.

While old hands were muttering, the captain concluded by stating that the first day's objective was Douai, twenty-five kilometres behind the German lines, and our division would be there to support the artillery and occupy captured ground.

The perspective of getting out of the trenches and advancing in open country and through towns, returning at last to traditional, imperial war, the kind we had been taught, with its surprise attacks, plunder, unforeseen events, happy encounters with beautiful women, all this enchanted class 15. But the stony-faced, sarcastic veterans dampened our enthusiasm.

'We all know about their stupid offensives and the objectives they've dreamt up in the officer's mess at HQ!'

'You'll see what a nice little job it is, an attack!'

'It all comes down to the fact that we're going to get smashed up one more time!'

Back in our billet, an old hand was carefully testing the

strength of his belts and braces. Seeing I was watching him, he explained:

'Surprised are you, young conscript, to see me taking a good dekko at my straps? But remember this: your future old age depends on whatever helps you run. Agility is the best weapon of any clear-thinking, well-organised infantryman, when things don't quite turn out the way the general imagined – which isn't unusual, with all due respect to the general who does what he can, which isn't very much. You think the Boche are more stupid than we are? Well, there's a bit of truth in that. But we are no more stupid than them. One day you fool them, the next day you're one who's fooled! War is all a matter of chance, a complete shambles, which no one's ever understood. There are times you'd do better to whistle a tune than waste your spit on patriotic speeches. Just imagine you happen to run slap into three or four Fritz of a soldierly type… (just because you look like a decent young chap it doesn't mean it won't happen to you!) While you are affecting your strategic withdrawal, at the double, if your flies let you down and your trousers drop round your ankles, then you're well and truly collared by the comrades from Berlin. I'm not saying that some of them aren't good sorts in their way but it still ain't healthy to hang around with them. Since you don't speak the same lingo you might not be understood if you're in a rush… Like I was saying: shoelaces, braces, flies, belts, everything that holds your clobber together, they are tools of the trade and you'd better look after them!'

We were all issued helmets. We didn't like this rigid headgear, because, unlike the képi, you could not break off the visor, and adapt it to your own taste, *Bat d'Af*[14] style, with a braided chinstrap, which was the height of rakish elegance in the army. Under a helmet, you could not tell at first glance if someone was one of the lads. But orders were strict, and our képis were withdrawn. Many people kept theirs in a haversack, in the hope of better days back at the rear, when you could put it on and charm the women, skivvies in local bars – a mere glimpse of one could arouse a whole battalion.

Then the corporal chose the bombers or trench-clearers. I was one of them. He gave each of us a large kitchen knife with a white wood handle, apparently intended for slicing German guts. I took mine with revulsion. I found the bombs, the grenades, equally revolting. Considering these objects with my customary, gloomy reasoning, I told myself that a worker assembling the things was sooner or later bound to misjudge the length of the fuse to the detonator and that I was equally bound to pay the price of his distraction. And I was a bad thrower. The only proper weapon in my opinion was the revolver, with which a skilled shooter had a chance, and which avoided the need for repugnant hand-to-hand combat with an enemy whose smell could be disagreeable and who usually had the advantage of weight (those Germans are fatter than us), and of their supposed barbarity. I knew that the French were supposed to be wiry and fierce. But that is just hearsay and I did not want to test out its accuracy by grappling with the first enemy I encountered. Such, more or less, were my ideas on close combat. They did not square at all with the methods used. One more reason I had to blame this war.

While I was considering my knife, Poirier tugged at my sleeve.

'Will you give me your place as a trench-clearer?'

This Poirier was short, red-faced, stocky and boastful, and I had held him in low esteem ever since I had surprised him with his hand in my food pack, which had become a great deal lighter. 'There are a lot of rats in this sector,' he had said, nonchalantly. What is more he had for some days been wearing a fine pair of new canvas and leather 'rest' shoes, bearing an uncanny resemblance to mine, which had vanished. But his proposition suited me. I was just handing over my knife when the corporal turned up. I explained to him what we were doing.

'Poirier would like to take my place as a bomber, and it must be said that I don't know how to use grenades.'

'No!'

'But Poirier wants to do it, and it disgusts me!'

'Listen, Poirier won't do it and you will! I have my orders.'

'That's all right then,' I said with a smile, 'that's military reasoning.'

In fact our corporal, a very young, blond, cheerful Parisian, was a charming lad. But he had a lot of trouble leading our squad of twelve men, undisciplined, excitable newcomers or quarrelsome Norman malcontents. To get us to march he always put himself at the front, but en route he would sometimes lose part of his team. Their alacrity in escaping danger was a characteristic of the old hands, a result of their experience of the realities of war. I think that NCOs had been advised to pick men who had been tried and tested as bombers. Our young leader confused the curiosity I had displayed on our first time in the trenches with military merit, and he judged that I was more reliable than Poirier whom he knew well. It is true that the latter was to leave us, three days into the attack, on the pretext of getting some supplies, and never reappeared. It was later rumoured that he had been shot.

That same evening, 24 September, we moved off again for the front. It was raining.

5

THE PARAPET

'Savary is an excellent man for secondary operations, but lacks the experience and calculation to be at the head of such a great machine. He understands nothing of this war.

You were ten leagues from your advance guard; General Lasalle, who commanded it, was five leagues from Burgos, as a result of which it was all ended by a colonel who did not know what was wanted of him. Is that, Marshal, how you have seen me make war?'

Napoléon

THE NEXT MORNING I had a strange awakening. A metal monster was brushing up against me, threatening to crush me: I saw huge pistons and got a blast of steam. I was lying on the edge of a railway track, and an armoured train was passing right next to my head.

Then I remembered I had dropped out of the column during the night and completed the march on a wagon. Arriving after everyone else and not knowing where to shelter, I lay down by the track, under a bridge which protected me from the rain, not imagining a train could come this far.

Having survived this latest peril, I looked around me. My battalion was in shelters on the slopes and I found my squad without any difficulty.

The bombardment had become tremendously intense. Invisible

guns were firing on all sides, and on top of that we were soon deafened by the armoured train. Aeroplanes flew very low overhead, under the grey clouds. Observation balloons, 'sausages', which had moved forwards by a few kilometres, loomed above us. Everywhere there was feverish activity. The attack had been underway for several hours. In some of the villages, on camou-flaged roads, the cavalry was hidden, ready to move forward. Crossing the slope, I reached the neighbouring woods. They were full of men, all waiting their turn to march forward. We were certainly there in force. But we had to leave others, down below, the time to launch the first blows, to open the breeches where the army could go into action. Our own future depended on the success of our brothers-in-arms.

All day we waited anxiously, but no news came. Just rumours: the attack was advancing, the artillery was ready to follow. The sun broke through for a few hours then hid its face sadly. We despaired at knowing nothing and our immobility seemed a bad sign. It was already quite obvious that we would not get to Douai so easily.

We were supplied with a new kind of grenade, known as a racket bomb: a tin box attached to a wooden paddle, with a percussion detonator which you released by pulling a string with a kind of curtain ring at the end. This ring tended to slip off the nail which held it in place and dangle freely: I found the things terrifying and refused to touch the two I was given by our corporal. Instead of arguing, he simply took them himself and secured them beneath the flap on the top of my pack.

As evening fell, it started raining again. By now we had little faith left in the success of the offensive. At last we moved forward. Beyond Mont-Saint-Éloi, the battlefield, shrouded in smoke and fog, spread out before us on a gentle slope. We could make out red flames in the distance, and hear the terrible roaring, punctuated by diabolic machine guns. Silent and fearful, we all knew that was our destination. The sight of the wounded deepened our misery.

Cadaverous and caked in mud, they had lost most of their kit and looked like fugitives; there was a glint of madness in their eyes, the madness that comes from proximity to death. They staggered away in groaning groups, holding each other up. We could not take our eyes off the white patches of field dressings, with blood seeping through. Blood still dripped from them, marking their trail. Next came the silent stretchers, from which hung white, contorted hands. Four medical orderlies transported on their shoulders one unfortunate whose arm had been torn apart, exposing the frayed muscles. His screams were terrible, rising up to the impassive heavens, enough to shame God.

The captain passed along the column:

'Courage, lads! It seems the new helmets really do protect the head and they've already saved a lot of lives.'

That was the best he could find to say to us! We knew for sure then the attack was faltering and that our task down there in the fog would be a very hard one.

Shortly after, a shell burst just ahead of the column. We were ordered to take to the trenches. As we jumped down, one soldier cried out in pain. 'I've sprained my ankle!' 'What perfect timing!' muttered someone beside me.

It became very hard to advance at all. Trampled by thousands of men, the ground had turned into slippery dough, in which we kept getting stuck. We had to pull our feet out with every step forward. We also had to pass units going back to the rear. These encounters were a real torture, in trenches too narrow for two men to stand side by side, and where everyone was laden with packs which made them even bulkier. The two columns became entangled and we had to pull ourselves out of the ensuing crush. Suffering enough already, men lost their patience, cursed, even struck out at each other. Then, with horror, I remembered my grenades. I was carrying two potential explosions right beside my neck, which would be set off by a tug on a piece of string. In this melée, all it would need would be for a rifle barrel to bang into one of those wretched curtain rings to finish things off. So I was forced to march sideways, thus reducing the chances of an accident, and watch every move of anyone who bumped into me. And even so some uncontrollable, sneering voice in my brain kept repeating: 'Look where your head's going to be rolling!'

Night came. When it did, we got lost, as usual. The front had become a bit quieter. The two armies were tallying up the results of their first day and preparing for the morrow. After marching for two or three hours, we halted. We took over old dugouts, groping our way in the dark. Mine was waterlogged. Before settling down, I opened my pack and dumped my two grenades on the trench parapet, telling myself that I would surely find plenty of similar devices at the front line.

We were starting to fall asleep when the order came to set off again. It was a very dark night, streaked with rockets in the distance, too far off for us to see their flash, but which left mournful haloes in the sky. We came out on to a road cluttered with military transport. We encountered strange vehicles, like rubbish carts, full of stiffened debris, standing out against the sky, which we recognised with a shudder: 'Corpses!' So they were withdrawing our predecessors from the morning, the first waves of the unstoppable offensive that had come to a standstill ahead of us. They were cleaning the battlefield. 'A fine turn-out by the hearse section,' said one wag. Each cart carried grief to a score of families.

We came into a ruined village. My section took shelter in a cellar. There was very little room so we sat upright, squeezed between all our kit, leaning on our packs. A sergeant had stuck a candle on the point of a bayonet. The feeble light lent a tragic expression to our faces. One man expressed what we were all feeling:

'It doesn't look like this attack is working.'

'Seems to me it's the same old shit as always.'

'Brothers, our duty is to die!' sneered a pale corporal.

'Shut your mouth!' growled everyone.

Men were snoring, twitching and whimpering, struggling with nightmares less terrible than reality. Outside high explosive shells started coming in. We heard them fall near us, relentless in their attack on this wounded village, pounding it, shattering it all over again, tearing apart the very last walls, the very last wooden beams, showering brick and rubble over the paths. Sometimes their hot breath roared down into our cellar, extinguishing the candle, and the explosion shook everything. Then silence and darkness. 'Anyone hit?' asked a sergeant. 'No – no – no one!' came the response from the men on the steps, in turn, as they recovered from the shock. And so the candle was lit again, its yellow flame sealing us off, dulling the noise from outside.

'A pity that the only time these fools give us a rest is in the middle of a bombardment!'

'It's never any different!'

A man ran up and shouted down the steps: 'Get ready!'

'Where are we going?'

But the runner was already gone, shouting into other cellars.

'What's the time?' asked one of the sergeants.

'Three o'clock…'

'There'll be no sleep for us tonight.'

We were all ready, waiting for a lull, and for orders. We waited a long time. We had taken off our packs and sat down again. Shells still rained down. Then suddenly, blasting apart our drowsiness like a shell, came the short, imperative shout from outside:

'Forward!'

'Forward! Forward!' repeated the sergeants. 'Clear the entrance.'

The candle went out. Men moved up the steps – and then rapidly moved back.

'Watch out!' shouted the soldier standing on the top steps.

A burst of gunfire very close. The entrance was a red square, blinding us. The cellar shook. Our breath came in gasps.

'Forward! On the double! Hurry!'

We threw ourselves out, tumbling over, clutching each other, shouting. We threw ourselves into the cold night, the whistling, burning night, the night full of obstacles and snares and shards of metal and clamour, the night which hid the unknown and death, that silent prowler with explosions for eyes, seeking its terrified prey. Abandoned creatures, wounded, lying out there somewhere, perhaps from our regiment, howled like injured dogs. Ammunition wagons, the thunder's supply-train, passed by at full speed, wobbling and rattling, crushing everything in their mad rush to escape. We ran with all our might, on inadequate legs, overburdened, too small, too weak to get out of the way of the sudden trajectories. Our packs and bags squeezed our lungs, pulled us back, cast us out into the zone of sparks, and roaring and crashing, where it was suddenly too hot. And we always had our rifles which kept slipping off our shoulders, such useless, ridiculous weapons, never staying put, always a hindrance. And the bayonets that get in our way! We ran, following the back of the person in front, eyes wide but ready to shut so as not to see the fire, to shut on our shrivelled brains, which refused to work, which didn't want to know, didn't want to understand, which were dead weights on our racing bodies, driven on by the sharp lash of steel, fleeing the leaded knout howling at our ears. We ran, leaning forwards, ready to fall to the ground, faster than the shell. We ran, like beasts, no longer soldiers but deserters, yet towards the enemy, with this one word resounding in us: enough!, through the shaking houses, lifted up and falling back in clouds of dust on to their foundations.

A salvo, so direct that it caught us still standing, roared up out of the earth like a volcano, roasted our faces, burned our eyes, cut into our column as if cutting into the flesh of each one of us.

Panic booted us in the arse. Like tigers we leaped over the shells' smoking craters, rimmed with the wounded, and we leaped over the cries of our brothers, cries that come from the guts and

strike at the guts, we leaped over pity, honour, shame, we elimi-
nated all feeling, all that makes us human, according to moralists
– imposters who are not enduring an artillery bombardment and
yet exalt courage! We were cowards and we knew it and we could
be nothing else. The body was in charge and fear gave the orders.

We ran faster than ever, hearts pummelled by the panic of our
bodies, with such a rush of blood that it made purple sparks dance
in front of our eyes, that it gave us hallucinations of yet more
explosions. 'Trenches?' we asked. 'Where are the trenches?'

We were still bracketed by the artillery fire, suffocating with
anxiety. Then we moved away from it, away from the village.

We managed to reach a wide trench, half-collapsed, a calm
spot in the night, which hid us from the enemy's deadly vigilance.
We slid down to the ground, utterly exhausted, trying to deepen
the darkness above us, like children hiding. We heard houses
blowing up five hundred metres away, not understanding how we
had been able to save ourselves, overwhelmed with horror at such
bombardments against which there is no defence. We hesitated
between futile revolt and the resignation of beasts in a slaughterhouse. We clung on to this calm for dear life, refusing to imagine
the next stage of this adventure, which was only beginning. Other
men in their turn ran up. We could hear their gasping breath. We
waited for our hearts and lungs to return to their normal rhythms
before asking questions, finding out who was missing. We put
off the moment when we would know. We let the darkness fill
the gaps in our ranks. Every fallen comrade increased the chances
of our own deaths. But the cold, which penetrated our soaking
garments, gradually calmed us down. This new discomfort brought
us back to life. Men once more, we sadly considered our destiny.

Questions went round:

'Tell the captain: ten wounded in the 3rd section, six in the
2nd, and a machine gun out of action.'

Then came the orders, the same as ever:

'Forward!'

We slung on our packs and set off, hunched over, wearier than ever and less confident. Shells were hunting their targets in the darkness and we were heading in their direction. We came into the range of this new bombardment. Heavy-calibre time-shells, methodical and precise, were bursting twenty metres above the trench every minute and showering us with their raging shrapnel. With every one, we dived down into the mud and waited, frozen with terror, for the explosion to seal our fate. And then we'd get up and push ourselves forward. Once again, some men were hit. The battalion advanced past them and witnessed their suffering. But the episode came to an end. Further on, the night was calm and endless, concealing from us unknown, deadly objectives. Fatigue, the struggle that every infantryman has to endure with the load he is carrying, which constricts and exhausts him, prevented us from thinking.

Our last reserves of strength were concentrated in the muscles of our necks and shoulders. Would these trenches never end? Yet we feared that they would indeed end. We were approaching a goal that we were in no hurry to reach. Every metre we covered, every effort that we could claw out of our exhaustion, took us ever deeper into danger, brought a great many lives closer to their end. Who would be struck down?

I had a trivial accident during this march to which the circumstances lent great importance and which caused me considerable suffering. As we were leaping through the harassing fire, gasping for breath, the puttee on my right leg came undone, unravelled, dragged in the mud, was stepped on by the person behind me, tripping me up. There was no question of stopping, resisting the pressure of hundreds of men blindly fleeing the shells. I had to keep going forward, holding my puttee, shackled like a beast. Whenever I heard the whistle of a shell I dropped down on one knee and profited from the explosion to wind round the strip of cloth as fast as I could. But the pause was too short, and I learned the hard way that a man who cannot move freely feels more vulnerable. This uncomfortable situation lasted for some time, until we made a proper halt.

We had lost all notion of the time, of duration, of distance. We kept on marching along identical trenches, in the endless night, numbed by the growing cold. We could no longer feel our flayed shoulders. We did not even have enough lucidity left to imagine, or fear, anything…

At last dawn broke through the grey rainclouds. A pale, silent dawn, revealing a foggy, lifeless desert. A strange scent hung in the air, at first rather sweet and sickly but then giving off the richer notes of a still-contained putrefaction – in the way that a thick sauce slowly reveals the strength of its seasoning.

I kept going, bent down, blank, all my faculties absorbed by my pack, my rifle and my cartridge pouches. I stepped over pools of water and shaky duckboards which added to the difficulty of our progress. We skirted round the blast-proof traverses, changed direction without trying to keep our bearings, all in silence, a metre apart, and banged into each other whenever the pace slackened. The trenches widened out, and there were more and more signs of damage and destruction.

All of a sudden the soldier in front of me crouched down on his knees in order to get under an overhanging pile of material. I crouched down behind him. When he got back on his feet, he revealed a man of wax, stretched out on his back, his unbreathing mouth wide open, his eyes expressionless, a cold, stiff man who must have slipped beneath this illusory shelter of old planks to die. I suddenly found myself face to face with the first fresh corpse that I had seen in my life. My face passed within a few centimetres of his, my gaze met his terrifying glassy stare, my hand touched his frozen one, darkened by the blood that had frozen in his veins. It felt as if this dead man, in the brief tête-à-tête he had forced on me, was blaming me for his death and threatening me with revenge. It was one of the most horrible impressions that I took away from the front.

But this dead man was like the watchman for a whole kingdom of the dead. This first French corpse preceded hundreds of other French corpses. The trench was full of them. (We had come out into our former front line, from where our attack had been launched the day before.) Corpses contorted into every possible position, corpses which had suffered every possible mutilation, every gaping wound, every agony. There were complete corpses, serene and perfectly composed like stone saints in a chapel; undamaged corpses without any evident injuries; foul, blood-soaked corpses like the prey of unclean beasts; calm, resigned, insignificant corpses; the terrifying corpses of men who had refused to die, raging, upright, bulging, haggard, cursing and crying out for justice. All with their twisted mouths, their glassy eyes, and their skin like that of drowned men. And then there were the pieces of corpses, the shreds of bodies and clothes, organs, severed members, red and purple human flesh, like rotten meat in a butcher's, limp, flabby, yellow fat, bones extruding marrow, unravelled entrails, like vile worms that we crushed with a shudder. The body of a dead man is an object of utter disgust for those who are alive, and this disgust is itself the mark of utter prostration.

To escape such horror, I looked out at the plain. A new and greater horror: the plain was blue.[15]

The plain was covered with our comrades, cut down by machine guns, their faces in the mud, arses in the air, indecent, grotesque like puppets, but pitiable like men, alas! Fields of heroes, cargo for the nocturnal carts...

A voice, from somewhere in our ranks, found words for the thought we suppressed: 'Jesus, they copped it!' which immediately echoed in all our minds as: Jesus, we're going to cop it!

No life, no light, no colour caught the eye or distracted the mind. We had to follow the trench, look out for corpses, if only to avoid them. I had noticed that we no longer distinguished the living from the dead. We had encountered a few soldiers leaning on the parapet, not moving, and I had assumed they had fallen asleep. I saw that they were also dead and the slight slope had kept them upright against the side of the trench.

From a distance I saw the profile of a little bald man with a beard, sitting on the fire-step, who seemed to be laughing. It was the first relaxed, cheerful face we had seen, and I approached him thankfully, asking myself what he had to laugh about. He was laughing at being dead! His head was cleanly sliced down the middle. As I passed, I saw with a start that he had lost half this jovial head, the other profile.[16] The head was completely empty. His brains, which had dropped out in one piece, were placed neatly beside him – like an item in a tripe butcher's – next to his hand which pointed to them. This corpse was playing a macabre joke on us. Hence, perhaps, his posthumous laughter. The joke reached the nadir of horror when someone uttered a strangled cry and shoved us aside to run.

'What's got into you?'

'I think that it's… my brother!'

'Good God, look more closely!'

'I don't dare…' he said, as he fled the scene.

Before us in every direction spread a flat, dreary, silent expanse, as far as the rainy horizon, sunk beneath low clouds. The landscape was nothing but a pulverised mire, uniformly grey, overwhelmingly desolate. Though we knew that the bleeding armies paralysed with fear were somewhere down in that valley of devastation, there was no sign of their presence or their respective positions. It looked like a barren land, recently stripped bare by some terrible flood, which had retreated leaving in its wake shipwrecks and bodies buried under a coat of dark slime. The heavy sky weighed down on us like a tombstone. It all served to remind us of the inexorable fate for which we were destined.

We finally emerged into a kind of rallying point, with wide tracks running through it. The place must have been blown apart and then re-established using a vast number of sandbags. Marching in single file, we hadn't seen each other since the previous day, and were surprised to recognise ourselves, so much had we changed. We were as pallid as the corpses that surrounded us, filthy and tired. Hunger gnawed at our bellies and the chill of morning made us shudder. I met Bertrand, who was with another unit. On his face that was worn and aged by the night's anxieties, I recognised the signs of my own anguish. Seeing him made me aware of how I looked myself. He found a few words to express the fear and the astonishment of all the new recruits:

'Is this what war is?'

'What are we doing here?' asked the men.

No one knew. We had no orders. We had been abandoned in this wasteland full of corpses, some of them sneering, holding us in the menacing gaze of their glaucous eyes, others turned away, indifferent, as if they were saying: 'We've finished with all this. Get yourself ready to die. It's your turn next.'

The yellow light of a day that seemed to falter as if it too was struck by horror, illuminated a lifeless, soundless battlefield. It felt as if everything around us and off into infinity was dead, and we did not dare raise our voices. It felt as if we had come to some place in the world which was part of a dream, that had gone beyond all the limits of reality and hope. Ahead and behind merged into limitless desolation, all covered with the same churned up grey mud. We were stranded on some ice-floe out in space, surrounded by clouds of sulphur, ravaged by sudden bursts of thunder. We prowled in these accursed limbos which at any moment now would turn into hell.

Our bugles sounded the charge and unleashed all the instruments of war.

Rifles and grenades, guardians of space, threw up their deadly barriers, at the level of French soldiers' stomachs.

Shells of every calibre were crashing down on us, barrage after barrage, a mixture of shrapnel and high explosive. The burning sky fell on our backs, squeezing our necks, buffeting us from side to side, twisting our guts with waves of dry, painful colic. Our pounding hearts tore at our bodies, tried to burst out of our chests. Terror suffocated us, like an attack of angina. And our souls were on our tongues, like bitter communion wafers, and we kept gulping them down, kept swallowing, because we did not want to spit out our souls.

The bugles sounded again, a death knell. We knew that just a few hundred metres ahead our ashen-faced brothers were about to offer themselves up to the eager machine guns. We knew that once they had fallen, and then others had fallen too, men just like us, just as obsessed with staying alive, with running away, with putting an end to their torment, it would be our turn, that we were worth no more than them in the mass of sacrificed manpower. We knew that the massacre was well underway, that new corpses were piling up on the earth, their arms frozen in the last, despairing gestures of drowning men.

The shellfire had caught us at a crossroads pinpointed by the German artillery. We ducked down into a Russian sap to shelter from the explosions.

The attack quickly subsided. The roar of the guns died away. Now we could hear the screams, those terrible screams that we had heard before…

We stayed in that sap for three days and two nights.

Once we realised that we were being left there, we organised ourselves. There were twenty of us in a tunnel some twenty metres long; we had to crouch down, chins on knees, only going out to answer calls of nature.

Several times a day we heard the ominous bugle calls and the artillery barrage began again. The smallest shell would have shattered the thin layer of soil that protected us but we had piled up our packs by the entrance to cover ourselves on that side. The entrance was guarded by a dead body, buried right there. As if he had been buried standing up, his head still stuck out of the ground, along with one hand, a finger pointing in our direction, seeming to indicate: there they are! Whenever we crawled out we nearly bumped into the cold head. It reminded us what awaited us in this chaos.

We did not receive any new provisions. We ate our emergency rations, and some men who had gone out in the dark to rummage in the packs of the dead brought back biscuits and chocolate. But we were desperately thirsty. I had a little flask of peppermint liqueur in my haversack. We passed it round but no one was allowed to drink. Twenty mouths sucked at the rim to moisten their lips. That was our only drink throughout those three days. But a few men took water from the puddles where corpses bathed.

We also sorted ourselves out so that we could sleep and avoid cramp. We arranged ourselves like oarsmen, each making space between his legs for his neighbour. At night the whole row of us leaned back so that stomachs served as pillows.

The sap became a rather cosy little place that we did not dare leave. We cherished the illusion that we had been forgotten and no order would ever find us there. But the orders came on the third day. We set off at night.

In the morning, after various halts and hesitations, we found ourselves in recently taken German positions. We walked past big dugouts that echoed with the cries of the wounded who had been brought there to wait until they could be transported to the rear. There were so many of them that it held up their evacuation; there were not enough stretcher-bearers.

Finally we were left in a trench where we could just about stand upright. It began to drizzle and we were soon wet. Our feet sank into the mud, which held them so firmly that in order to extricate them we had to pull at our knees with both hands. We warmed up each leg in turn. Still no new provisions. Fortunately shells rarely fell in this spot.

In the evening we had the idea to dig out small niches in the trench wall, just deep enough to hold our backs and stop us from slipping. Over the front of these little niches we spread out our tent canvases, held in place by cartridges stuck in the ground. Sitting behind the dripping canvas, squeezed together in pairs, with our feet in the water and shivering with cold, we managed to get a few hours' sleep.

In the middle of the night we were woken. The call came that I had dreaded: 'Bombers to the front!' The Germans must have launched a counter-attack. But the firing died down before we reached the front line.

The next day we were moved forward again.

We took up positions in a trench perpendicular to the enemy lines, closed off by a barricade of sandbags, at the furthest point of our advance.

We were dirtier, more exhausted, paler and more silent than ever. We knew that our hour was approaching.

After all that we had seen, we could have no more illusions. As soon as one battalion was out of action, the next battalion was pushed forward to attack, over the same ground covered in our dead and wounded, after an inadequate artillery barrage, which did more to alert the enemy than to harm them. The useless victory which consisted of capturing a bit of the enemy trenches was paid for by the massacre of our soldiers. We could see the dead men in blue spread out between the lines. We knew that their sacrifice had been in vain and ours, which was about to

GABRIEL CHEVALLIER

follow, would be too. We knew that it was absurd and criminal
to throw men against unbroken barbed wire protecting weapons
that spat out hundreds of bullets per minute. We knew that
invisible machine-gunners were waiting for the targets that we
would be as soon as we went over the top, and would pick us off
like game birds. Only the assailants were exposed to view, while
the men we were attacking, dug in behind their earthen ramparts,
would stop us getting to them as long as they kept a cool head for
a couple of minutes.

As for a deep advance, all hope was lost. This offensive, which
was supposed to take us twenty-five kilometres forward in one go,
destroying every obstacle in its path, had just about managed to
gain a few hundred metres in a week. A handful of senior officers
had to justify their role to the nation by a few lines of communiqué that bore the scent of victory. We were there for no other
reason than to purchase those few lines with our blood. It was
now a matter of politics, not strategy.

One thing still gave us pause for thought. Among all the dead
that surrounded us, we saw very few Germans. There was no
equivalence of losses; our feeble territorial gains were lies, because
we were the only ones to die. Victorious troops are those who kill
more, and here we were the victims. This put the finishing touch
to our demoralisation. The soldiers had lost conviction long
ago. Now they lost confidence. Our attacking troops, supposed
conquerors, muttered to themselves: 'These fools are just killing
us all.'

As a witness to this chaos and carnage, it seemed to me that
'fools' was an inadequate word. In the Revolution they sent
incompetent generals to the guillotine. An excellent measure.
Why should men who had set up courts martial, advocated
summary justice, escape the sanctions they imposed on others?
Such a threat would cure these wielders of thunderbolts of their
Olympian arrogance, force them to reflect on what they were
doing. No dictatorship could compare with theirs. They prohibit

any scrutiny of what they are doing by the nations, the families, who have blindly put their trust in them. And if those of us who can see that their glory is an imposture, their power a menace, if we tell the truth, they will have us shot.

These were the thoughts that haunted us on the eve of the attack. Bowed down beneath the rain and the shells, the pale soldiers sneered:

'Morale is high! The troops are raring to go!'

Now begins our final agony.

The attack is certain. But, since frontal assaults that get nowhere must be abandoned, we are to move forward through the trenches. My battalion will attack the German defences with grenades. As a bomber, I will march in the front ranks.

We still don't know the hour of the attack. Around midday they tell us: 'It will be this evening or tonight.'

From the latrines which were above the trenches we can see the enemy line. The gently rising plain is crowned in the distance by a wood that has been blasted to pieces, 'Folly Wood', and our command apparently proposes to occupy it. A rumour goes round that we are facing the German Imperial Guard and they will greet us with exploding bullets.

What can we do until evening? I have little faith in my grenades, which I do not know how to use. I strip down my rifle, clean it carefully, oil it and wrap it in a cloth. I also check my bayonet. I have no idea how one fights in a trench, in Indian file. But a rifle is a weapon after all, the only one I understand, and I have to get ready to protect my life. I have no faith in my knife either.

Above all, I must not think... What could I expect? To die? *I must not* expect that. To kill? That is the unknown and I have no wish to kill. Glory? This isn't the place where you get glory; that happens much further back. To advance one, two, three hundred metres into the German positions? I have seen only too well that this will make no difference to events. I have no hatred, no ambition, and no motivation. Yet I must attack...

I have a single idea: get through the bullets, the grenades, the shells, get through them all, whether victorious or defeated. And moreover, *to be alive is to be victorious*. This was also the sole idea of everyone around me.

The old hands are anxious and grumble to calm themselves down. They refuse to do guard duty, but all eagerly volunteer to go to the rear in search of provisions.

Bursts of artillery and machine-gun fire sweep the plain. There's a bit of sunshine. Far off we can still hear bugles, gunfire, bombardments.

We would like to halt the march of time. Yet dusk descends on the battlefield, separates us from each other, makes us shiver with cold... the cold of death...

We wait.

Nothing gets any clearer.

I crouch down in a hole to get some sleep. Better not to know in advance!

I remember that I am twenty years old. The age of which the poets sing.

Daylight again. I stretch my stiff legs in the deserted trench and then go to our corporal's dugout.

'We're not attacking?'

'It's postponed to this evening.'

Here we go again! One more grim day!

It's early, and all is quiet on the front. Mist covers the plain and through it come long, heart-rending groans, punctuated by hoarse death-rattles. Our wounded lie between the lines, crying for help. 'Comrades, brothers, friends, come and get me... don't leave me, I can still live...' You can make out women's names, and the screams of those who are in unbearable pain: 'Finish me off!'

And those who curse us: 'Cowards, cowards!' There is nothing we can do but pity them, and shudder. In their cries we can hear the cries that are inside us, and which will come out, perhaps this evening... It is as if the two armies have kept quiet to hear them and must be red with shame in their trenches.

I withdraw to my hole, cover my head so as not to hear, and try to sleep.

I am awoken a few hours later. Food has finally come: a stew congealed in the dixies, wine, cold coffee, brandy. Our squad gathers round the corporal and he distributes it. I have no appetite, force it down, and finish first. The corporal gives me an armful of newspapers:

'Read us the news.'

'Yeah, let's hear the latest claptrap!' agree the men, clustering round so as not to miss anything.

First there was the rather confused official statement on the progress of the war. They shake their heads.

'Meaning, we're stuck in this shit for the winter!'

Then I scan the columns signed by great names: academicians, retired generals, even men of the Church, and pluck out these rare and precious flowers of prose:

'That war has an educational value can never be doubted by anyone with the slightest powers of observation...'

'It was time war came to France to revive the true meaning of the Ideal and the Divine.'

'One of the surprises of this war, and one of the wonders, is the brilliant role played by poetry.'

Someone interrupted:

'How much do these blokes get paid to write this fucking rubbish?'

Continuing, I indulged my audience:

'O dead, would that you were alive!'

'Merriment reigns in the trenches!'

'Now I can follow you into the attack; I can feel the joy that overwhelms you at the moment of supreme effort, the ecstasy, the transmigration of the soul, the unfettered flight of the spirit.'

They reflect for a moment. And then Bougnou, self-effacing, obedient little Bougnou, who never says a word, passes judgement on these famous writers in his little-girl voice:

'Oh, what scum!'

In the afternoon the corporal takes me aside: 'I want you to join a fatigue party this evening. We're going to go and collect some wicker hurdles.'[17]

'Oh no, not that. I am already a bomber. I don't want to go on fatigues as well.'

'Shut up. This way we'll miss the attack...'

His assurance calms me down. I pass quite a pleasant evening.

It has already been dark for some time when we set off. There are five of us. I've left my rifle and my pack in a little corner of the trench where I can get them later and just kept a haversack and the rest of my kit. We walk fast along the dark trenches that have been battered by shells, in a hurry to get to the rear where we can shelter.

Unfortunately the wet weather in the last few days and the damp biscuits I've eaten have brought back my upset stomach. I have to make frequent stops and force the others to wait, complaining, afraid that a shot will catch us at any moment. It isn't easy for me to find a suitable spot in the dark. At one point a man suddenly jumps up and tries to chase me off.

'Get out of here! These are the commandant's latrines.'

I tell this dutiful servant in no uncertain terms that no commandant in the world could make my guts stand to attention. His nose and the noises from my bowels convince him that I am telling the truth. He makes himself scarce.

We find the hurdles in a depot and assemble our load. Then

we sit in a covered shelter, huddled close together to keep warm, and light up our cigarettes.

Heavy shells start landing not far off and make a terrible racket in this deserted spot. We squeeze down into the depth of the shadows, telling ourselves that our shelter is solid. Above all, we are thinking of what's about to happen to the battalion up ahead. Better to be where we are.

And then the shelling stops and silence returns. We stop talking. We listen to the confused sounds from the front, off in the distance. We doze, we let the time pass. We feel like deserters.

'I suppose we'd better go back,' says the corporal.

Off we go again. It is quite a struggle moving forward with the wicker hurdles that are wider than the trenches so that we have to carry them at an angle. In normal times we would never have wanted such a task. But now we feel privileged.

We reach our positions.

The whole battalion is in the trench, bayonets fixed, in total silence.

'What are you doing?'

'We're about to attack.'

So the attack hasn't happened!

'Tell the captain that the hurdles have arrived,' says the corporal.

The message passes from man to man. I think of my rifle, and of going to get it... then an order comes:

'The men from the fatigue party to the front. Leave the hurdles.'

This is the limit! What is that supposed to mean? But there's no room for argument. We make our way through the battalion. Men move aside to let us pass, with unusual courtesy.

Beneath the parapet stands our captain, chinstrap in place, revolver in hand. He points to some boxes:

'Take your grenades.'

'I don't know how they work, sir.'

This is the truth. These are cylindrical tin grenades of a type I've never seen before. 'Just do it!' he snaps.

Yes sir! I dutifully take five or six grenades and slip them into my haversack. He points to the parapet.

'Over you go!'

I see a short ladder. I climb up. I straddle the sandbags and find myself on a level with the plain, above the trenches. I am blinded by flashes. Rockets, shells. Bullets whistling, whipping past me. I let myself drop down.

On the other side of the parapet...

A man is running in front of me. I am running behind him.

Thoughts flash through my mind: 'OK, here I am, I'm going into the attack at the front of a battalion. My only weapons are five grenades of an unknown type and I am running towards the German Imperial Guard...' That's as far as I can think. I wish I had not left my well-oiled rifle behind.

Other men are running behind me. I mustn't think of stopping, I don't think of stopping. One flare after another bathes us in light. I spot a rifle on the edge of a trench and grab it. An old French rifle: bolt jammed, bayonet bent and rusty. Better than nothing.

I cannot imagine combat at all, I just can't think like a soldier. I tell myself:

'This is all stupid, utterly stupid!' And I run, run like I'm in a hurry.

Am I afraid? My mind is afraid. But I'm not asking its advice. Stupid, stupid!

Behind the second parapet, four maniacs are lobbing grenades, bellowing to work themselves up into a frenzy.

So here we are, five chaps attacking the German army with tin cans. Unbelievable!

'Give me some grenades!' one of these lunatics shouts at me.

'With pleasure!' I think. I hand him the contents of my bag.

'More!'

The man behind hands me his. I pass them on. Others follow, passed along from hand to hand.

The four of them keep going like a machine: shout, ignite, throw... Can this go on forever?

I am lifted up, deaf, blinded by a cloud of smoke, pierced by a sharp smell. Something is clawing at me, tearing me. I must be shouting without hearing myself.

A sudden shaft of clarity. 'Your legs are blown off!' For a start...

My body leaps and runs. The explosion has set it off like some machine. Behind me, someone is shouting, 'faster!' in a voice of pain and madness. Only then do I actually realise I am running.

Some part of my reason returns, amazed, and starts to check: 'What are you running on?' I think I must be running on the stumps of my legs... My reason tells me to look. I come to a halt in the trench while invisible men run past. Fearful of finding something horrible, my hand goes slowly down the length of my limbs: thighs, calves, shoes. I still have my two shoes!... So my legs must be intact! Joy, but such incomprehensible joy. Yet something has happened to me, I've been hit...

My reason continues. 'You're running away... Have you the right to run away?' A new anxiety. I no longer know if I am hurt, or where. I examine my body, feeling it in the darkness. I discover that my right hand no longer works, the fingers don't close. A warm liquid is running out of my wrist. 'OK, good, I'm wounded, I can go now!'

This discovery calms me down and also makes me aware of pain. I groan quietly. I am dazed and dumbfounded.

I make it back to the first parapet where a gap has been opened to speed the advance. The captain is still there. No one stops me. Soldiers from my battalion, with their gleaming bayonets, turn their pale, frightened faces to see this, the first of the wounded. I recognise men from class 15. 'Lucky bastard!' they call out.

One comes forward. It's Bernard. He relieves me of my kit.

'Is it serious?' he asks.

'I have no idea.'

'Is it going OK out there?'

'I didn't have the time to find out.'

'Good luck!'

'You too, mate!'

'I only wish I was in your place.'

Their anxiety, their words, make me aware of my luck.

Now all I have to do is get to the rear, not get lost in the trenches, or hit by a shell… 'Lucky bastard!' I keep telling myself.

I'm starting to feel cold. My legs are stiffening and I'm limping on my right foot, which hurts. I move forward with difficulty through the network of dark, deserted trenches. We only passed through this sector at night and I don't know it. And now night covers it once more, and stretches to infinity. All I can do is to follow the most heavily trodden paths, the ones where more troops have passed. So I concentrate on the state of the ground and make sure I keep my back to the flares which must mark the front. I am alone and running out of strength.

My watch tells me it's three in the morning. I find a broken rifle to use as a stick to keep myself up. I feel more and more tired but if I stop to rest I don't think I'll get up again. I had the good fortune to be the first to get out of the attack, without the aid of stretcher-bearers. I must profit from this and avoid being caught in artillery fire. In fact the bombardments seem quite a way off, on the front lines.

Four o'clock. I still don't know where I am or where I am heading and I still haven't met anyone. Some shells fall nearby. I find myself on a sunken path. I hear footsteps, voices, and then bump into a supply party. The men give me something to drink, some coffee and brandy, point me in the direction of the village and the first-aid post beside it. They tell me it'll take an hour to get there.

An hour for them but a lot longer for me. In the village I leave the trenches and take the road, to save time. It's one of those typical Pas-de-Calais villages, stretching out in a long line, a mournful spot. And now there are shells coming down on my right, high explosives that go off above ground level, and shrapnel shells that throw rocks everywhere. If they get to me I cannot run or shelter; I am hobbling like a cripple. Now I am truly afraid, afraid I'll be finished off…

A red cross. I go down into a cellar. A medical officer gives me some first aid, is amazed at the number of shrapnel wounds I have, but is reassuring. The bottom of my coat is shredded and my leggings ripped apart. I haven't the strength left to move again. An orderly takes me on his back to the nearby clearing station. Daylight comes. It's now after six o'clock.

Outside the clearing station there are two stretchers, one of them occupied. I lie down on the other. I immediately feel a sense of well-being and safety; the worst is over, now I only have to let myself go, people will look after me.

A young priest with a pleasant face comes over and asks us kindly if we want anything. I ask for a cigarette. Once it's lit I give him a smile of gratitude. He spreads his arms in a somewhat liturgical gesture, and says:

'Such a spirit of self-sacrifice in our soldiers. Even in pain they have the courage to laugh!'

While he's off looking for something for us to drink, my wounded neighbour says:

'The old padre hasn't got a clue! Only reason we're laughing is that we're getting the hell out!'

We're taken down into a cellar that is still empty, with supports in place to take three rows of stretchers, one on top of the other. I am amazed that I have got here, at my incredible adventure... But I'm tired out and soon fall into a heavy sleep.

When I wake up some hours later the cellar is full of wounded men, screaming. All the places are full. Their occupants cover the whole range of expression of pain and despair. Some feel death approaching and struggle with it fiercely with imprecations and wild gestures. Others on the contrary let their lives slip away in a thin stream of liquid, with muffled sighs. Others try to soothe their suffering with measured, hoarse groans. Others plead for someone to stop their pain; others still beg to be finished off. Some call for help from beings we do not know. Some in their delirium are still fighting, uttering inhuman battle cries. Others confront us with their suffering and blame us for doing nothing for them. Some call upon God; some curse him, insult him, tell him to intervene if he is all-powerful.

To my left I recognise the young sub-lieutenant who led our section. From his flaccid mouth comes the monotonous, feeble cry of a little child. He is dying. He was a decent lad, and everyone liked him.

There isn't enough room. The most unfortunate are laid out on the ground, muddy lumps crowned with haggard faces, bearing that terrible expression of resignation that pain brings with it. They look like beaten dogs. Holding their shattered limbs, they intone a mournful chant that rises up from the depths of their flesh. One has a broken jaw hanging down that he dares not touch. The hideous hole of his mouth, blocked by an enormous tongue, is a well of thick blood. A man who has been blinded, walled up behind the bandage around his face, raises his head to heaven in the hope of catching some faint glimmer of light through the loophole of his eye sockets then slumps back down sadly into the darkness of his cell. He gropes around in the emptiness like someone scrabbling at the damp, slippery walls of a dungeon. A third has lost both his hands, the hands of a farmer or a worker, his tools, his means of earning a living; once he would have said, proclaiming his independence: 'When a man has two good, strong hands he'll always find work.' And now they are not even there to help him in his pain, to meet that most basic, habitual need of bringing them to the place that hurts, which they should hold, which they should calm. No hands to wring, no hands to clench, no hands to pray. Never again will he be able to *touch*. It occurs to me then that this is perhaps the most precious of all the senses.

They had also brought in a piece of human scrap so monstrous that everyone recoiled at the sight, that it shocked men who were no longer shockable. I shut my eyes; I had already seen far too much and I wanted to be able to forget eventually. This thing, this being, screamed in a corner like a maniac. The revulsion that turned our stomachs told us that it would an act of generosity, a fraternal act, to finish him off.

The German artillery has cut the road; we can hear the dull thud of the shells. We cannot be evacuated. Outside, more and more new batches of wounded men wait in the rain for us to die so they can come in. The nurses are overwhelmed. They go from one berth to another, checking the death-rattles. Once these subside into faint murmurs, indicating that the moribund is on the threshold of oblivion, the man is taken outside, where he can die just as well, and his place is filled by another wounded man who still has a chance of life. No doubt the choices are not always right, but the nurses are doing their best, and in war everything is a lottery. This is how our sub-lieutenant makes his exit.

All those who are removed are destined to become corpses, battlefield debris that no longer evokes pity in anyone. The dead get in the way of the living, wear them out. They are forgotten completely during periods of high activity, until their smell becomes insistent. The gravediggers really find them too much, and moan about all the extra work that is costing them sleep. Anything dead is irrelevant. To feel sympathy would weaken us.

An overworked, preoccupied doctor, with no medicine to offer, moves through the rows. With rough words, he brings whatever comfort he can, displaying his badges of rank to the more credulous to convince them they'll survive. His weariness is obvious, and you can smell the alcohol he uses to keep himself going. His face is streaked by so many splashes of blood that his smile, which he wants to be strong and kind, looks as cruel as an executioner's.

Most of the wounded bear the number of my regiment but I haven't been in it long enough to recognise them, and many of them are unrecognisable. From snatches of conversation I gather that the assault from the parapet had been murderous. It had cost the lives of more than a hundred and fifty men. After an initial advance we had been forced to retire to the positions we had started from. The Germans, less exhausted than we were, and well dug in to positions on the ridge, had then launched a vigorous counter-attack, profiting from the fact that our flanks were unprotected. I was curious to know the result of this action in which I had taken part in such an odd way. I also wanted to know what had become of my friends from class 15 and the men from my squad. We were such a disparate bunch in that squad, had so little in common, and quarrelled so often, but we were nonetheless a little family and I would have been distressed if harm had come to any one of them, especially to our young corporal. But I'm in a bad position, down at ground level, and can only see the wounded lying by the wall. They are too far away, too absorbed in their own suffering, for me to question them. And my wish to know more is less strong than my desire to avoid any effort.

And how am I?

I am ashamed. I am ashamed because I am suffering less than some of those around me and I have a whole berth to myself. I am ashamed but at the same time, while neither proud nor happy, I am satisfied with my fate. Despite everything egoism overwhelms the pity that I feel because I am not completely distracted by pain like all these unfortunates with terrible wounds. I am caught between two emotions: the discomfort of parading my good fortune in front of those who are suffering, and the somewhat insolent superiority of those whom destiny has favoured. My own body, turned towards hope, towards life, turns away from these other, smashed bodies; the animal in me, which wants to stay whole, tells me: 'Rejoice, you are saved!' But my mind keeps its solidarity with the poor men of the trenches, of whom I was one; it loves and pities them. We are united by the risks we have run together, the fear that has shaken us all. I am not yet detached from them and their cries find their echo in me. Is it just the sight of all these mutilations that could have been mine that moves me? Isn't our pity really a contemplation of ourselves, via others? I do not know. What should excuse me in their eyes is that we were all exposed to the same shells and bullets, and that what hit them could have hit me. Yet, lying still beneath my blanket, eyes closed, I hide the injustice of my good fortune.

I also have my own reasons for concern. If I lie flat on my back the wound in my chest suffocates me. If I try to turn over it feels as if daggers are being thrust into me. It may be that the hand which weighs so heavily at the end of my arm will never regain its flexibility... If I wasn't thinking of my comrades who are still out there in some ditch, up to their ankles in water, surrounded by corpses, their lives on the line at every moment, then no doubt I would be thinking that I have suffered a terrible misfortune. If something like this had happened to me outside of war I would surely have fainted away in shock. Whereas here I marched for three hours to find a first-aid post. The fact is that my fate has not been decided and I will only be reassured when the threat of amputation is lifted.

* * * * *

As evening falls, the cries and moans redouble, and delirium grips us. It is swelteringly hot, and the air is stifling, heavy with the sickly sweet smell of blood, of filthy dressings, and excrement. I am getting weaker, my head is spinning, and the cellar seems to be suffocating me, crushing down on my chest…

Fever claims me, makes me shudder, brings hallucinations. A parapet rises up before me, illuminated with flashes of light, a funeral pyre of flaming blue and grey men with the faces of grimacing corpses, with gumless jaws, like the death mask from Neuville-Saint-Vaast. They throw grenades at each other's heads which crown them with explosions. The smoke clears and they fight on desperately, half-decapitated and dripping with blood. One has an eye hanging out. So as not to waste time he sticks his tongue out and swallows it down. Another, a big German, has the top of his head open; a flap of skin like a hinge holds his scalp which swings like a lid. When he runs out of ammunition he sticks his hand into his head and pulls out his brains which he throws into the face of a Frenchman, covering it with a foul porridge. The Frenchman wipes this off in fury and then opens his coat. From inside he unrolls his intestines and makes them into a noose. This he throws, like a lasso, round the German's neck and then, pushing his foot against his enemy's chest, leaning back with his whole weight, he strangles him with his guts. The German's tongue comes out. The Frenchman cuts it off with his knife and then attaches it to his coat with a safety pin, like a medal. Then comes a woman suckling her baby. She removes the infant from her breast and places him on the top of the parapet where he starts to fry. The woman moves off sadly, moaning to herself: 'Oh, dear God, how has it come to this?' Then some officers' batmen arrive. On to a tin plate they place the baby, now grilled *à point* like a suckling pig, and fill buckets up with blood, then take all this to the field marshal, who is drinking an aperitif off in the distance while observing the battlefield through binoculars and yawning, because he's hungry. The parapet crumbles away and there are no victims or victors, because there's nothing left but corpses.

Now here I am at the front line, in a little machine-gun post. All of a sudden a black butterfly, streaked with red, flutters up above the barbed wire. I have been ordered to kill this butterfly. Finger on the trigger, I look for it through the machine-gun sight. Then I realise something terrible: the butterfly is my heart. Panic-stricken I call the sergeant and explain. 'It's an order! Shoot it or you'll be shot!' So I shut my eyes and fire off belt after belt to kill my heart... and the butterfly is still fluttering... The general arrives, in a fury: 'Where do you find these bloody useless conscripts? I'll get it myself with the first shot!' From a holster made of human skin he pulls out a golden revolver. He takes aim and kills my heart... I am crying... I will crawl out tonight and go and look for the poor little black butterfly...

And now I am alone, lying on a stretcher, between the trenches. Night is falling. The armies are leaving and abandoning me. I hear a bugle call, orders being shouted and down on the road I can see troops presenting arms. A colonel climbs out of a car with a flag on the bonnet. Despite the distance, I recognise him: he's the one who made me go through the test on the parade ground at training camp... He squats down, strikes a match and lights something close to the ground. Then he gets back in his car and drives off quickly. Once again soldiers present arms, once again there are bugle calls. The troops form up in lines of four and march off without looking back. I want to call out but something is blocking my throat. I'm alone again and cold. I think of all the rats swarming over the plain that might attack me. How could I protect myself? I've no strength and I'm strapped to the stretcher. I look for help in this bleak, freezing expanse... I can see a little speck of light that at first I take for a glow worm. But it is coming in my direction, wiggling along the ground. I thought it was miles away but it is only the fact that it is tiny that gives the impression of distance. Actually it is close and still advancing. What can it be? Suddenly, all is clear! My hair stands on end, I break into a terrified sweat. Yes, that colonel became my enemy after I had saluted him with my left hand by mistake. The light is the flame at the end of a fuse that he has lit, a fuse which runs from the road to me, which runs round my throat and stops me shouting. And my chest, my stomach, are stuffed with explosives, I am sure of it…

The hospital train has been travelling for an hour, taking us away from the front. In the cattle truck fitted with bunks there are a dozen of us, wounded and feverish, exhausted from having already had to wait for some days on stretchers, moving from one first-aid post to another. Some have serious injuries and are in great pain.

Struck by a sudden revelation, a man with a shrapnel wound in his hip forgot his pain for a moment, and announced the dawning of a new era:

'Hey, you lot, listen! We can't hear the guns any more!'

'For us,' someone answered, 'the war is over!'

That was a good month ago. I believed it too. Now I'm not nearly so sure.

6

THE HOSPITAL

*'He [Jesus Christ] has revealed to the world this truth, that
one's country is not everything, and that the man is before,
and higher than, the citizen.'*

Ernest Renan, *La Vie de Jésus*

I AM LYING IN A HOSPITAL BED and covered in dressings. A
sheet is attached to the head of the bed on which is sketched a
human body, front and back. A dozen marks in red ink indicate
the wounds on this body: my body. On the left wrist, the throat,
the legs, the right foot. 'Nothing in the chest or guts, jolly good!'
the little doctor had told me down in the cellar at La Targette
where I'd had to wait after the assault from the parapet. Next to
the sketch is a temperature chart, at the foot of which can be read:
'Admitted: 7 October 1915. Operated: 20 October. Discharged...'
I am hoping that this bit stays blank for as long as possible.

On my bedside table there are books, cigarettes, lozenges,
writing materials; in the drawer, my wallet, some letters, my
knife, my pen, my identity tag which is now useless, and my little
aluminium mug which I found in a haversack that had stayed
with me. Jolly good, indeed! I'm all right. I've escaped the winter
offensive, and the war will surely finish. I'm happy. I've saved my
skin...

* * * * *

The grenade had peppered me with shrapnel. Fortunately it was a tin grenade, blasted into such tiny pieces by the explosion that the shrapnel didn't hit me with much force. Almost all the wounds were skin deep and even now, after a few weeks, if I press hard on the spots that appear in the middle of my body, I squeeze out very sharp bits of metal. There must be quite a few left since when I change position I can feel sudden pricks like you get if you sit on a drawing-pin. For some time I was afraid that these little bits of shrapnel might cause abscesses. But the embarrassment of showing my buttocks to the nurses always stopped me mentioning it. (For me, buttocks are linked to the image of women and seem contrary to virility. And also, perhaps, there is some remnant of military prejudice, absurd today: a soldier should not be wounded in the back.) I carry out my own examination, groping under the bedclothes. When I've found a little hard spot, I twist myself around to investigate it with my mirror. Then I try to clean it out with the aid of my nail or a pin. This keeps me busy during moments when I'm tired of reading or smoking, and my neighbours find it entirely natural, as they busy themselves with similar activities. In any case, we have nothing to hide about our bodies, or their functions, and we look away from those who have to uncover themselves so as not to embarrass them. The only way we discomfort each other is with smell, however hard we try to be discreet.

I have pulled a lot of shrapnel out of my legs, along the tibias, using the point of my knife. I reckon I've found about forty pieces. However my body only has eleven serious wounds, none of them grave. The annoying thing is that the injuries are spread all over the place so that I have had to be almost entirely swathed in bandages. As the pus sticks to the gauze the bandages adhere to the wounds so that with the least movement I feel them tearing away. And because there is a little delay in transmission from one to the other my wincing is multiplied by a series of painful twinges. So I keep as still as I can. But because of lying permanently on my back, I get bed sores and so every day I have to spend a few hours on my side. Occasionally I manage to sit up. This is a movement that I prepare carefully so as to avoid any pain sharp enough to make me fall back down rapidly. Anyway, I have plenty of time. I even manage to get up briefly, while they are making my bed.

I 'went under the knife' and it wasn't so bad. The doctor in an ambulance at the front had probed my wounds and without any anaesthetic – or my consent – had pulled out the biggest pieces of shrapnel. One remained in my right foot and one in my left wrist which had lodged – without penetrating them – between the tendons which controlled the two middle fingers of my hand. To extract them they decided to put me to sleep. I was only afraid of being awake, of getting the same treatment as I had received at the front. After a day without food I was taken to the operating theatre around six o'clock, a stark, white room harshly lit by an arc lamp which gave a sharp blue shine to all the steel. I was laid out, naked, in the centre of this white space, offering myself up soft and shivering to all the instruments, as if in a torture chamber, and the nurses in their smocks seemed like the executioners of some grim inquisition. As they bent over me with the wad of cotton wool, the doctor said: 'Don't be afraid. Open your mouth wide and breathe deeply.' Which I did willingly, having no wish to witness the tortures they were going to inflict on my body.

The anaesthetic gave me the distinct impression of dying and since then I've thought that death, the crossing over, cannot be such a difficult moment as people believe, so long as it is not accompanied by the agonies that come with illness. One must overcome anxiety, resolve to vanish into nothingness. Under chloroform you quickly lose all sensation of your body; it stops existing. All life flows back into the humming brain. Mine, up to the moment when it vanished in its turn, did not lose its lucidity. Freed of the burden of the flesh, I was nothing more than a mind, and I had the fleeting idea of being pure spirit, an angel, a little dancing flame of joy. I told myself: 'You are dying!' and 'You are not really dying', and yet: 'All the same...' I offered no resistance to this advancing extinction. And then my thoughts, like a distant beacon, threw nothing but a dim light within me flickering over the chiaroscuro of my being and I slipped down into the darkness, into death, without being aware of it.

My mind came back first. Accompanied by a burning pain in my arm. And I could hear voices, make out what they were saying but as if they were in an antechamber of my self, for I was still wrapped in a thick web of sleep. The voices were saying: 'He's still out. Couldn't wake him down there.' I only had to open my eyelids, like shutters in the morning, to show them that my living soul was still inside. It was such a huge effort that I took some time deciding. At last I was gazing at faces leaning over me, I saw them light up, and closed my eyes again. All that remained of the chloroform was a nauseating taste that I exhaled through my lips in sickly bubbles. And fever wrapped me in its burning arms, shook me with its icy shivers and struck my temples with its hammer-blows.

After a fortnight, my temperature is back to normal, and there are no more reasons for concern about the consequences of my wounds. Only a few scars will remain, proof that I have indeed been through the great adventure of war, so that later, sated with pleasure, grateful and half-dreaming, women will feel pity and say 'Oh, how you must have suffered, my darling!' and their soft hands will gently caress those places once pierced by metal. Or so I imagine...

Sergeant Nègre from Limoges lies on my right. He must be about thirty-five. Small head, almost bald, a mischievous glint in his eyes and a little goatee beard. A typical French reserve NCO: quick to blame but slow to punish, taking charge of his little world but taking care of it too, even against orders if necessary, an obliging man with a wicked tongue. Like me he appreciates his good fortune and indeed has been even luckier than me. He has a hole in his calf; the wound isn't at all serious but a tendon has been damaged. He will need treatment so he can walk normally again. When he gets out of bed, he hops along on his good leg, down our row of beds by the windows, holding on to the frames. He stops at each one to inquire: 'So, my old pal, how's it going? We've made it to the hospital. And that's a bloody sight better than getting a medal, believe you me!' To those in pain, he points his finger to the north, cocks his ear as if listening to the gunfire: 'But they didn't get us! Think of all those fine bloated corpses, my lad, and give thanks to the god of armies!' To distract them from their pain he shouts: 'On your feet, the lot of you! Volunteers for patrol, get in line! Who can't wait to go and make a nice hole in the wire with a good pair of cutters?… One at a time, now, don't all rush!'

One day when we were all laughing at his antics as he hopped about, he explained: 'This war's given me bloody cramp. It comes from chasing after Glory. I've been chasing her ever since this war began, and then the bitch went to find General Baron de Poculotte who was at that precise moment planning his seventy-third Final Offensive with coloured pencils and tracing paper and rapid-writing rifles in his forward command post forty kilometres behind the lines. And you know what he replied when they told him that Glory had come at last? "God damn it, I don't like to be kept waiting, you old bat!" Oh yes, my lad, that's exactly what he said. You don't know the de Poculottes? A great family, from the old military aristocracy, so they say. A whole family of generals. These are the people who really know how to make decisions and counter-orders and manage the cavalry and the transport and supplies and the artillery and the engineers and sappers and mortars and the aeroplanes and the whole lot and how to really slaughter the infantry at zero hour, in industrial quantities. I mean, of course, the German infantry! Because your French infantryman is indestructible, as is well known in Perpignan…

First military principle: one French soldier is worth two German soldiers. Second military principle: obstacles don't bloody exist! Third military principle: one dead French soldier equals ten dead German soldiers, at least. Because the Germans attack in tight formations so as not to get lost in places they've never been before and to stop themselves being afraid. You only have to fire at them and you can knock down as many as you want. Any journalist will tell you. Don't you know yet that those chaps can see a lot further than you, you little earthworms, you cannon fodder, you stupid war cripples, and you better believe them.

'And now, you poor little moron, I'm going to teach you a whole load of good things. I got them from de Poculotte himself who was standing right next to me and explaining matters to a gentleman from parliament so that he in turn could explain them to the whole nation, which needs to see things clearly.

'So, first of all, we've got the bayonet. You stick it on the end of a Lebel and you get yourself an infantryman driven by French *furia*. Opposite, you've got your Boche. Now, what cannot fail to happen? They either run for it or throw in the towel. Why do you think they stuck barbed wire in the front of their lines? Because of the bayonet, says de Poculotte.

'Second, we've got our good French bread. The French hero stands up above the trench and shouts out in a scornful tone: "Hey, Fritz, want some nosh?" What cannot fail to happen? Fritz puts down his gun, says goodbye to his pals, and heads for the bread as fast as legs can carry him. Why do you think they stuck barbed wire in front of their lines? Because of our bread, with the sole purpose of stopping the whole lot of them running across at our dinner time leaving their crown-prince all on his own like an arsehole. We'd be in a right mess if this army of gluttons came over to stuff their faces with us! "They are pigs," says Poculotte, sipping his Burgundy. "They lack moral fibre. We can take them whenever we want!"

'And last but not least we've got the 75,[18] which flattens everything in a couple of shakes. Nothing's more accurate and nothing's faster. Why do you think they made Big Berthas? To hit back at our 75s, of course. Except that with our 75s, we always smash them. I can still hear Poculotte: "Races can be distinguished by their weapons. They have heavy artillery because they have heavy spirits, and we have light artillery because our spirits are light. Spirit over matter, my dear Minister. And war is the triumph of the spirit!" Don't ever forget it, old chum, war is the triumph of the spirit!'

When he's narrating the heroic deeds of General Baron de Poculotte, Nègre is unstoppable. That dashing superior officer has become a celebrity, a symbol, and we can all feel his presence among us. His resolute character rules over the ward; whenever we are surprised and confused by some new measure, we can turn to him for the correct military response. So, for example, someone who had just been reading the latest communiqué asks him:

'*Mon général*, how should we interpret "All quiet on the entire front"?'

'The true military mind does not permit interpretation,' replies the general through the mouth of Nègre. 'Good patriots should understand that "All quiet" means exactly what it says, and this plain description is easy enough to understand.'

'So should we understand that there were no dead or wounded?'

'No dead or wounded!' shouts the indignant general. 'Who is this miserable wretch who dares to question the abilities of our leaders? What would a war be like without dead and wounded?'

'Yes, *mon général*, but what about saving human lives?'

'Be quiet, you horrible underling, war is not about saving human lives but destroying them and don't you ever forget it. It is a noble mission and its goal is to deliver us from barbarism. Dismiss!'

It should be noted that the general normally makes his

appearance after the departure of the nurses. Then we are all soldiers together and Baron de Poculotte can express himself without inhibition, knowing that his words of wisdom will not be heard by stupid civilians, people for whom he feels the deepest contempt.

On my left is Diuré, a freckled redhead with milky skin who bears his suffering without complaint apart from rare and muffled groans. Suppurating phlegmon in the thigh from an infected wound. They've made a long gash, opening up the wound down to the bone and criss-crossing it with drainage tubes. He has so many pipes coming out that he looks like a piece of machinery. When his sheets are pulled back, the smell is very unpleasant, like a meat market in summer. Still he has the courage to bend down over this fissure in his decomposed flesh, soiled with green pus. He watches closely when his wound is being dressed, and seems very interested in the disgusting scraps of flesh that are pulled off him. He says little; we know nothing about him.

Next to him lies Peignard, the loudest screamer in the ward. They have removed the bones from part of his foot and this floppy foot, lacking its armature, pulls at his leg and his hips, causing his groin to swell and spreading its painful consequences across his stomach all the way to his heart. Sometimes he goes very pale and gasps for breath. The mere weight of a sheet on his foot can make him scream horribly. Fever takes him every evening at about six o'clock. Mouth open, lips trembling, he groans feebly and dribbles a stream of saliva on to his blanket. An hour later the real screaming starts: oh, ooh, ooh, ah, ah… aah, aah, the screams you'd hear at night in battle, the screams of abandoned men. At first we would shudder and pity him. Then, one night, when the lights were dimmed, someone turned over noisily with a sigh: 'Sure, but it's still a fucking pain in the arse for the rest of us!' Our silence indicated our approval. We are all suffering to one degree or another and it makes us selfish. When Peignard is hit by these attacks of pain he doesn't think to spare our nerves, he forces us to share in his suffering and makes us unhappy. Eventually they give him morphine which knocks him out, and we insist that this should be done promptly, as soon as he starts screaming.

Then comes Mouchetier, with what remains of his right forearm wrapped in a linen bandage. He can still feel his missing hand, thrown out with the rubbish a month ago. The networks of his nervous system stretch out into empty space and carry back pain that is constant and distracting. Often Mouchetier looks like he is rubbing his absent hand; his other hand seems to hold and squeeze it to stop the shooting pain. And yet he is slowly getting accustomed to his new condition. He's a wounded man like all the rest of us, and his infirmity won't make itself felt until he's a civilian again. Still, he must think about it. He sometimes stares at other people's right hands as if he's hypnotised – rough hands but so agile, so convenient, so useful in life. He was an accounts clerk before the war. This profession – which he might now have to give up – makes him obsessed with writing. He collects any envelopes or bits of paper with writing on that are scattered around in the ward, spreads them out on the corner of a table, and gazes dreamily at the neat copperplate, the elegant flourishes. Furtively, he tries to copy them in pencil with his untrained left hand. His pockets are full of sheets covered in clumsy letters, like a schoolboy's exercise book.

We often discuss the war. Those who were not seriously wounded claim that it will not last much longer. We are hoping less for a triumphal conclusion than for an end, which will remove us from further danger. *Going back* is a prospect that makes us freeze in horror and we refuse to contemplate it. The future offers us a break, varying in length according to our condition, which includes: recovery in hospital, convalescence, leave, and a spell at base. Four to six months in most cases. In our opinion, the war cannot last longer than that and the formidable alliance of France-

Great Britain-Russia-Italy-Belgium-Japan will inevitably prevail over the Central Powers, despite whatever merits we, as soldiers, may have seen in the Germans. Our spring offensive will carry all before it. Failing a great victory, then the exhaustion of one tribe or another should finish it off, that or general weariness.

Some, and Mouchetier first and foremost, argue that, on the contrary, 'it will go on for years the way things are going and there are still lots of surprises to come', with remarkable persistence. Listening to the debate the other day I suddenly understood: all the pessimists are cripples. It is too cruel for them to believe that they have lost a limb at the last moment, that with a little bit more luck they would have survived intact. Better for them to think that mutilation had not only saved their lives but spared them years of suffering. I shared my observation with Nègre and those with less serious injuries. From then on, we were less positive when the question came up.

To settle the dispute, we sought the advice of General de Poculotte, and he gave his answer:

'The great struggle exalts the lifeblood of the nation, it carries our country to the highest rank of humanity, and we must not wish for it to end too quickly. The France of the twentieth century is on the road to glory. Let us rejoice and place that glory higher than petty considerations about the life or death of a few hundred thousand soldiers. It is with their blood that we are writing these unforgettable pages, and their fate can never be a sad one!'

'He's a fine speaker, the old bugger!'

'So Mouchetier got it right, it isn't nearly over!'

Turning to the cripples, who always grouped together, we declared, with an air of jealousy: 'You're the lucky ones!' They smiled, and forgot some of their regrets. And Bardot, holding himself up on his crutches, spoke kindly to us:

'We wish you the same when you go back to the line.'

'Absolutely,' chipped in another, 'better to come back damaged than not come back at all!'

Only a few days ago, there were three in our ward whose condition gave cause for concern, out of thirty in all. Now there are only two, and that will not last long.

The first had a perforated intestine. He could only be fed through tubes, and his open stomach, into which these pipes fitted very loosely, gave off an odour of latrines. He struggled on, and went under the knife several times. From a distance all I could see was a bloodless face the colour of old ivory, and little by little this face seemed to acquire a dull, grey coating, as if someone had forgotten to dust it, and the beard, drawing strength from the compost of unhealthy flesh, spread rapidly, seeming to drive out life like ivy takes light from the front of a house. At last they took him down to a room on the first floor reserved for those needing constant care. Two days later, we learned that he had died.

The second is an adjutant – so we were told – who is suffering from acute toxaemia. Tests have shown fatally high levels of albumin. For the past two days the man has been completely blind, struggling feebly in the dark. Some spark of life still flickers, like a gas flame turned right down, but his mind has gone. No one stops by his bed any more; medicine has done all it can and must leave it to the organism to perform a miracle. He, too, will be taken downstairs. It seems most likely that nothing will interrupt his passage from the darkness of this death struggle to the darkness of the coffin. As he has never spoken we have not been able to form a bond with him, and his death will affect us less than that of a comrade whose voice is familiar. This is an unknown man whose name must be recorded somewhere on a list, and he is as much a stranger to us as a corpse would be that we encountered at a bend in the trench. And finally, he is dying of an illness, and illness doesn't inspire much pity in us.

The last is a small Breton lad, very young, with gangrenous wounds all along one side of his body. The doctors keep chipping away at two of his limbs: one arm and one leg, battling with the gangrene over his flesh, bit by bit, fifteen to twenty centimetres at a time. He has had five operations in eighteen days. Half the time he is knocked out by chloroform. They use this state of torpor to bind up his wounds, hiding from him the progressive shortening of his limbs. When he is lucid he won't let anyone come near, knowing that people only touch him to cause him pain. He is completely illiterate and speaks an incomprehensible patois, in which we can only understand the swear words he uses on the nurses. He is another one who emits the most horrible screams at certain times. But no one mutters complaints at these screams, for we know his situation is terrifying and will remain so even if he survives. On the contrary we are amazed at how rarely he screams and at how much resistance he has.

One evening four days ago, they brought a new patient into the ward and put him in a bed in a secluded corner. He seemed to be in very low spirits and kept his face turned resolutely to the wall. On his first day in the ward I thought I noticed the nurses displaying a certain degree of surprise when they questioned him. And over the next days they spoke to him in an odd tone in which, knowing them as well as I did, I could discern some cautious pity, along with an indefinable nuance of superiority. He became an object of curiosity and furtive glances for all of us. However, he didn't complain and ate normally.

A little while ago (I was beginning to take my first steps out of bed) I approached him rather stealthily. He didn't see me coming and our eyes met when I was right beside him.

'Nothing too serious, old man?'

He hesitated, then snapped:

'Me, I'm not a man any more.'

As I didn't grasp what he was saying he pulled back his blanket:

'See for yourself!'

Below his stomach I saw the shameful mutilation.

'Anything would have been better than that!'

'Are you married?'

'Two months before the war. A great little kid...'

He gave me a photo he took from under his pillow: a pretty brunette with bright eyes and firm bust.

'Anything would have been better.'

'So don't worry,' I said. 'You can still give pleasure to your wife.'

'You think?'

'For sure.'

I told him what I knew about eunuchs, about the pleasure they could give to women in the harems, explained that there were plenty of cases of having such surgery voluntarily. He seized my sleeve and, as if he wanted me to swear to the truth of what I was saying, demanded:

'You're sure of this?'

'Quite sure. I can find you a book which goes into these questions.'

He looked at the photograph.

'As for myself, well, perhaps, if I must... But you understand, it's because of her...'

He remained silent for a long time, then summed up his thoughts:

'Women, you know, you need *that* to keep them!'

I have told no one what I learned, not wanting to make it worse for him. There's no doubt everyone would feel pity for him, but it was precisely pity that would be so dreadful and he will have plenty of time to endure it. For now, the little edge in the nurses' voices (now I understood what it was) was quite enough. The tone they use with him astonishes me. Among their numbers are several very proper young women, from good families, some of them pious and probably virgins. Yet they are still sensitive to this. Faced with a man who is incomplete, they lose that very discreet air of submission and fear that women have with men. Their lack of respect means 'there's no danger in this one', the worst insult a woman can direct at us. He was right, the poor devil: *that* is essential with them, with all of them. The prudish ones, who are afraid of it, think about it just as much as the sensual ones, who need it.

As soon as she arrives at eight in the morning, the matron comes straight to my bed:

'Good morning, Dartemont. Sleep well?' she asks with a warm, sociable smile.

She is just being polite. I'm not in danger and always sleep well.

To Nègre, on my right, she says, cordially:

'Good morning, Nègre!' with a weaker smile, just what is left of the one she's given me.

To Diuré, on my left, now in a much more matronly tone: 'All right, Diuré?'

Then she hurriedly makes her rounds, addressing people as groups now, not as individuals – 'Everyone OK over here?'— while distributing haughty little nods of greeting.

The nuances are significant. They show that I have been granted the favour of the matron, who, to us wounded, was the equivalent of the colonel to the soldier. I have done nothing to merit this favour except to be myself, without concessions, accepting all the dangers of such frankness which must sometimes shock these women. It worked; they liked me. It must be said that the nurses find me more charming than many of my comrades. I come from the world of ideas and as I'm not in much pain, and stay lucid, and am not interested in drinking and card games, I can have long conversations with them which allow me to make sense of things – in my own fashion. I proceed to revise their values, which are not the same as mine. Their heads are stuffed with good intentions, which have been garnished with the bric-à-brac of noble sentiments tied up in a pretty bow, of honeyed breasts and make-believe men, as if their mothers had raised them to spend their whole lives sailing on some limpid blue lake with their heads on the shoulder of a faithful companion ... I make a mess of some of the drawers where they keep their ideas and break a few tasteless vases. But I get the feeling that they don't really detest what they would call cynicism, paradox or blasphemy. Being women, they like their ideas and opinions to be treated roughly, as, in some cases, their bodies. They experience a certain chaste thrill in listening to me, not so very different from the other kind of thrill, though they do not suspect it. They tell me a little anxiously of the things they admire. When they are at home they prepare questions for me at their leisure, which they note and then spring on me the next day. From my point of view, as long as they look after me, keep in their place and attend to my dressings every morning after washing me and applying iodine, then in the evenings, free from the tyranny of my wounded flesh, I can enjoy regaining my advantage over them, as a man, and one with a powerful intellect. It's funny to see how a little infantryman – little more than a servant, no doubt, in the eyes of some of their fathers – can give lessons to the daughters of superior officers, as indeed they admit I do, and pleasantly too. What adds piquancy to this little victory is the memory of the utter misery in which I found myself a few weeks ago, of my insignificance at the front, in a squad, behind a parapet, among the endless foothills of the Artois where a man with his personality and his ideas, with his past achievements if he's old and his future potential if he's young, is merely an anonymous unit in the vast hordes of serving soldiers, who will be decimated every day then replaced by other men who mean just as little to the leaders... A soldier, just another grain of the inexhaustible raw materials of the battlefield, little more than a corpse since he is destined to become one by chance in the great, anonymous massacre... And here, in mixed hospital no. 97, is the blessed Dartemont, to whom the matron remarked the other day, in the presence of some of these young ladies: 'Here we have the intellectual centre of the ward.'

Yesterday the lowliest herdsman, the lowliest navvy, with his thick skin and superior physical endurance, was better at war than me. His hard muscles and broad chest gave the country a safer frontier, in the ten metres of territory under his care. Yesterday, the meanest hoodlum with his stiletto and his hyena's taste for corpses, was a better assailant, a more dangerous enemy for the blond giant facing him than the unknown soldier Dartemont, taking his turn at drudgery ('just like one of the lads', and it was only fair), no good at marching, no good down in the trenches, untrained, scorned by the tough guys for all his useless student intellectual baggage, impressing them only when he gave away his brandy ration and didn't haggle over food. And here he is today chatting to ten young women who are smiling at him and listening to him, and who, when they discuss their wounded charges among themselves, must – I imagine – be saying: 'He's got an interesting mind, that boy!'

The hospital train that took us away from the front came into the station around nine in the morning, after an arduous, bumpy, and feverish three-day journey.

While we were being carried across the tracks and platforms, civilians looked at us with pity, and murmured: 'Poor children!' Their pity made me suddenly feel that my wound had a meaning, one revived from antiquity: 'Your blood has flowed for the country, and you are a hero!' But I knew just how hesitant and unwilling a hero I was, and that in fact I was a mere victim, or beneficiary, of a blow that had struck home, that I had not raised my arm to avenge it, that no enemy was dead because of anything I had done. I had no exploits to recount to all the zealous mothers and old men gathered on the ramparts to greet the returning warriors after their victorious battles. I was a hero without enemy scalps, taking advantage of the heroism of homicidal heroes. It could be that I felt just a little ashamed…

It was when we were brought into a great hall full of nurses in white, some of them young, smiling and fresh-faced, others grey and maternal, that we learned how special we were. Women! To be surrounded by the faces and voices and smiles of women! So we were not going to end up in some sinister military hospital...

We were assigned our beds. I was in ward 11, on the third floor, under the supervision of the matron, Miss Nancey. Each ward had its staff and head nurse; the hospital had twelve wards and must have held two or three hundred patients.

It was six days since I was wounded and this was the first time I had left the hard stretcher on which I couldn't turn round. My new bed felt infinitely soft, and to find myself in a bright, clean place, in white sheets, made me strangely astonished. Now I was certain of my salvation, I could at last let go, relinquish all the strength I'd summoned up to keep myself safe and sound while I was being transported by indifferent stretcher-bearers who had grown deaf to our screams having heard too many screams already, and who could only get the rest and calm which they also needed by abandoning us to our pain, forgetting us, sometimes letting us die. I gave in to the weakness that came so easily and closed my eyes, as a young nurse took charge of me.

I had not washed since we were in the trenches before the attacks of 25 September. Underneath its coating of bandages, my body was covered in filth and dried blood from top to toe, and there were still pallid lice crawling around beneath the gauze, lice which you could burst like fat pimples in one vile squelch with your fingernail. The young woman propped me up on my pillows, put a basin on my bed and wiped my face. I was transformed. From the haggard mask scarred by horror and exhaustion that I had acquired through three weeks of combat emerged my real face, my old one, the face of man destined to live. She considered this new face that she had just cleaned, now pink but still dazed, and asked me:

'What class are you in?'

'Class 15.'

'What were you doing before the war?'

'Student.'

'Ah! Two of my brothers were students.'

She washed my right hand (the left was still swathed in dressings), holding it in hers like you do with little children. The water in the basin was black and mucky. It was thick with the mud of Artois, the clay into which we were driven by the whistle of shells and which had plastered us with hard scales.

I thought she had finished with me but she came back, accompanied by a small, brusque woman who told me:

'We will move you near the windows.'

'I'm fine here,' I answered weakly, wanting nothing but sleep.

'No, you'll be better there, take my word for it.'

And without further ado she summoned the porters. I glared at her, I found her unpleasant. However, this turned out to be the first of Mademoiselle Nancey's kind deeds. From then on this was to be my bed, second in the row by the windows looking on to the hospital's main quadrangle, near the door, which I was soon convinced was a very good position. And I owed it to my social status, of which the young woman had immediately informed the head nurse.

I could sleep.

The next morning.

'It's not bad here,' says Nègre.

'It's not bad at all!'

Now that we were rested we could begin to take stock of our surroundings and companions. Before the war, mixed hospital no. 97 had been a religious boarding school called Saint-Gilbert, and ward 11 was in a former dormitory. It was very long room, lit by ten windows on either side, the darkest corner sectioned off, with beds lined up at two-metre intervals. In the middle of the room were dining tables; in the corner, the store cupboards, dispensary, and wash-hand basins. The ward was painted pale yellow, and was spotlessly clean; there were even vases of flowers.

'All in all,' continues Nègre, 'a pleasant place to be in pain.'

'I'm not in pain. You?'

'Not a lot.'

We watch the nurses scurrying around busily. ('The brunette's not bad.' 'The tall one's OK, too.'). They are getting the measure of this new batch of patients, choosing their favourites. They stop at the foot of each bed and call out to each other, a little too casually:

'Mademoiselle Jeanne, come and take a look at this one. Doesn't he look young?'

Unshaven and feverish, the wounded man who has lost the habit of talking to women, if he had ever acquired it, shrinks down under the blankets, blushes, and gives stupid answers to young ladies whose confidence intimidates him.

'You'd think these lasses were playing with their dollies!'

They are very polite and display considerable willingness to help. But you can still feel a certain distance in their tone, which shows that we are not from their milieu. Caring for us is a patriotic task, a humane gesture which they deign to make but which does not overcome the distance born of different upbringing. They keep the prejudices of their caste and address officers in a different tone. Nègre grumbles:

'We're going to look bloody stupid if this carries on! We didn't put up with shells and bullets in order to get pushed around by a bunch of hoity-toity brats!'

'You're right. It's high time we restored a bit of order.'

A nurse is just passing. I wave her over and, once she is at my bedside, I say:

'Mademoiselle, I need some notepaper, some cigarettes, and a newspaper. Can you sort that out?'

'Certainly, monsieur. We get the *Écho de Paris* here.'

'No doubt you do. But I want *L'Œuvre*, mademoiselle. Shall I give you the money?'

'And I need some pipe tobacco,' chips in Nègre, 'and a ballpoint pen.'

She notes all this down and assures us that we'll have it all in a couple of hours, then returns to her friends, looking a little astonished.

Nègre rubs his hands together.

'Excellent, excellent! As the general always said: "Attack, attack, attack! Always go on the offensive! Get the upper hand over your adversary and demoralise him! Attack and attack again!" Any staff officer from military college who knows what he's about would say the same.'

This is how I first hear of the famous General Baron de Poculotte, such an intimate friend of sergeant Nègre that he chose to make him his confidant. This leads me to question my neighbour on his past. I don't get anything very precise out of him. 'Ah well, you know, I've done this and that!' Later, in the course of various conversations, I learned that he had travelled abroad, had been a man of business, sold different products, some kind of trader. I think I also understood that he'd collected bets in cafés, and he seemed impressively well informed on drug-trafficking and the ways of the demi-monde… In short, he was a charming companion, his head full of stories and unexpected knowledge.

Our little initiative had been pointed out to the other nurses, who observed us at a distance, and, for the first few days, didn't come near us except to perform their medical duties.

We first made real contact when I asked for some books. When people like to read, they can readily find common ground. Preferences lead to debate, and give a rapid measure of each other's opinions. On my bedside table I soon had Rabelais, Montesquieu,

Voltaire, Diderot, Jules Vallès, Stendhal naturally; some Maeter-linck, Octave Mirbeau, and Anatole France, etc., all suspect authors for the young daughters of the bourgeoisie. And I rejected, as conventional and insipid, the writers whom they'd been fed.

Once I'd won over one nurse she'd bring along another one, and so it went. The conversations began and I was surrounded and bombarded with questions. They asked me about the war:

'What did you do at the front?'

'Nothing worth reporting if you're hoping for feats of prowess.'

'You fought well?'

'I really have no idea. What do you mean by "fought"?'

'But you were in the trenches... Did you kill any Germans?'

'Not that I know of.'

'But you saw them right in front of you?'

'Never.'

'How can that be? At the front line?'

'Yes, at the front line I never saw a living, armed German before me. I only saw dead Germans: the job had been done. I think I preferred it that way... Anyway, I can't tell you what I'd have done faced with some big, fierce Prussian, and how it would have turned out as regards national honour... There are actions you don't plan in advance, or only plan pointlessly.'

'So what have you actually done in the war?'

'What I was ordered to do, no more no less. I am afraid there's nothing very glorious in it, and none of the efforts I was compelled to make were in the least prejudicial to the enemy. I am rather afraid that I may have usurped the place I have here and the care you are bestowing on me.'

'Oh, you *do* get on my nerves! That's not an answer. I asked you what you *did*!'

'Yes?... Well, all right, what did I do? I marched day and night without knowing where I was going. I did exercises, I had inspections, I dug trenches, I carried barbed wire, I carried sandbags, I did look-out duty. I was hungry and had nothing to eat, thirsty and had nothing to drink, was tired without being able to sleep, was cold without being able to get warm, and had lice without always being able to scratch… Will that do?'

'That's all?'

'Yes, that's all… Or rather, no, that's nothing. Would you like to know the chief occupation in war, the only one that matters: I WAS AFRAID.'

I must have said something really disgusting, something obscene. They gave a little indignant shriek and ran off. I saw the revulsion on their faces. From the looks they exchanged I could guess their thoughts: 'What? A coward! How can this man be French!' Mademoiselle Bergniol (twenty-one, a colonel's daughter, with all the fervour of a Child of Mary,[19] but with wide hips that would predispose her to maternity) asked me insolently.

'So, you are *afraid*, Dartemont?'

A very unpleasant word to have thrown at you, in public, by a young woman, and quite an attractive one at that. Ever since the world began, thousands and thousands of men have got themselves killed because of that word on women's lips… But it isn't a matter of making these girls happy by trumpeting out a few appealing lies like a war correspondent narrating daring deeds. It's a matter of telling the truth, not just mine but ours, theirs, those who are still there, the poor bastards. I took a moment to let the word, with all its obsolete shame, sink in, and accepted it. I answered her slowly, looking her in the face:

'Indeed, mademoiselle, I am afraid. Still, I am in good company.'

'Are you claiming that others were also afraid?'

'Yes.'

'It is the first time I have ever heard such a thing and I must say I find it hard to accept. When you're afraid, you run away.'

Nègre, who wasn't asked, comes to my rescue spontaneously, with this sententious statement:

'The man who flees has one inestimable advantage over the

most heroic corpse: he can still run!'

His support is disastrous. I can feel that our situation is getting seriously out of hand and sense a collective rage rising up in these women, like the one that possessed the mobs in 1914. I quickly intervene:

'Calm down, no one runs away in war. You can't...'

'Ah-ha! You *can't*... but what if you could?'

They are looking at me. I scan their faces.

'If you could?... *Everyone would take to their heels!*'

Nègre can no longer restrain himself:

'Yes, everyone, no exceptions. French, German, Austrian, Belgian, Japanese, Turkish, African... the lot... If you could? I tell you it'd be like a great offensive in reverse, a bloody great Charleroi,[20] every direction, every country, every language... Faster, forward! The lot, I'm telling you, the whole lot!'

Mademoiselle Bergniol, standing between our beds like a gendarme at a crossroads, tries to put a stop to this rout.

'And the officers?' she snaps. 'Generals were seen charging at the head of their divisions!'

'Yes, so it's said... They marched with the troops once to show off, to play to the gallery – or simply because they didn't know what would happen, just as we didn't the first time. Once but not twice! When you've tasted machine-gun fire on open ground once, you're not going to go there again for the fun of it... You can bet that if generals had to go over the top, they wouldn't launch attacks so lightly. But then they discovered defence in depth, those aggressive old chaps! That was the finest discovery of the General Staff!'

'Oh, this is quite dreadful talk!' says Mademoiselle Bergniol, pale with fury.

It is painful to watch her and we get the feeling it might be wise to change the subject. Then Nègre turns the tables:

'Don't get all het up, mademoiselle, we're exaggerating. We have all *done our duty courageously*. It's not so bad now that we are starting to get *covered trenches* with all the modern conveniences.

There's still no gas for cooking but we already have gas for the throat. We have running water every day that it rains, eiderdowns sprinkled with stars at night, and when our rations don't arrive, we don't mind at all: we eat the Boche!'

He asks the whole ward:

'Be honest, lads, hasn't the war been fun?'

'It hasn't half been fun!'

'An absolute scream!'

'Hey, Nègre, what does Poculotte have to say?'

'The General told me: "I know why I see such sadness in your eyes, little soldier of France... Take courage, we will all soon be back to our pig-stickers. Ah, I know how you love your bayonet, little soldier!"'

'Yay, hoorah for the bayonet! Long live *Rosalie!*'[21]

'Long live Poculotte!'

'Thank you, my children, thank you. Soldiers, you will always know I am behind you at the hour of battle, and you will always see me in front of you, boots polished and brass shining, on the parade ground. We are together, in life, in death!'[22]

'Yes, yes!'

'Soldiers, I will send you against machine guns, and will you destroy them?'

'The machine guns don't exist!'

'Soldiers, I will send you against artillery and will you silence those guns?'

'We'll shut their mouths for good!'

'Soldiers, I will throw you against the Imperial Guards and will you crush the Imperial Guards?'

'We'll crush them into meatballs, into pasties!'

'Soldiers, will nothing stop you?'

'Nothing, General!'

'Soldiers, soldiers, I can feel your impatience, sense how your generous blood is boiling. Soldiers, soon I won't be able to hold you back. Soldiers, I can see it, you want an offensive!'

'Yes, yes, an offensive, now! Forward! Forward!

The whole room is now gripped by warlike delirium. People are imitating the rattle of machine guns, the whistle of shells, explosions. Roars and shouts of hatred and triumph evoke the frenzy of an attack. Projectiles are thrown, bedside tables shaken, and everyone joins in the furious fun. The nurses rush to calm it down and stop the noise disturbing patients in other wards.

Nègre has pulled the blankets off his thigh and stuck his leg in the air. He has put a képi on his foot and is waving it around to imitate a capering, conquering general at the head of his army.

Looking very serious, Mademoiselle Bergniol comes to my bedside:

'Dartemont, I have been thinking about what happened yesterday and I fear I may have offended you...'

'Please don't apologise, mademoiselle. I have been thinking about it, too, and I should not have spoken to you as I did. I've come to realise that in this war it is just not possible for people at the front and people at the rear to see eye to eye.'

'Still, you don't really believe what you said, do you?'

'I really do believe it, as do many others.'

'But there is still such a thing as duty, they must have taught you that.'

'I've been taught a great many things – like you – and I'm aware that one has to choose between them. War is nothing but a monstrous absurdity and nothing good or great will come from it.'

'Dartemont, think of your country!'

'My country? Another concept to which you attach from a distance a rather vague ideal. You want to know what "my country" really is? Nothing more or less than a gathering of shareholders, a form of property, bourgeois mentality, and vanity. Think about all the people in your country whom you wouldn't go near, and you'll see that the ties that are supposed to bind us all together don't go very deep... I can assure you that none of the men I saw fall around me died thinking of his country, with "the satisfaction of having done his duty". I don't believe that many people went off to fight in this war with the idea of sacrifice in their heads, as real patriots should have done.'

'This is demoralising talk!'

'What's really demoralising is the situation in which we soldiers are put. When I thought of dying, I saw death as a bitter mockery, since I was going to lose my life for a mistake, someone else's mistake.'

'That must have been terrible!'

'Oh, it's quite possible to die without being a mug. In the end I wasn't so afraid of dying. A bullet in the heart or the head... My worst fear was mutilation and the long drawn out agony that we witnessed.'

'But... what about liberty?'

'I carry my liberty with me. It is in my thoughts, in my head. Shakespeare is one of my countries, Goethe another. You can change the badge that I wear, but you can't change the way I think. It is through my intellect that I can escape the roles, intrusions and obligations with which every civilisation, every community would burden me. I make myself my own homeland through my affinities, my choices, my ideas, and no one can take it away from me – I may even be able to enlarge it. I don't spend my life in the company of crowds but of individuals. If I could pick fifty individuals from each nation, then perhaps I could put together a society I'd be happy with. My first possession is myself; better to send it into exile than to lose it, to change a few habits rather than terminate my role as a human being. We only have one homeland: the world.'

'But don't you think, Dartemont, that this feeling of fear you talked about yesterday has helped make you lose all your ideals?'

'That word fear shocked you, didn't it? It's not a word you'll find in histories of France, and that won't change. But I'm sure now that it will have its place in our history, as in all others. In my case I reckon convictions will overcome fear, rather than fear overcoming convictions. I think I'd die quite well for something I believed in passionately. But fear isn't something to be ashamed of: it is a natural revulsion of the body to something for which it wasn't made. Not many people avoid it. Soldiers know what they're talking about because they have often overcome this revulsion, because they've managed to hide it from those around them who were feeling it too. I knew men who believed I was brave by nature, because I had hidden what I was going through. For even when our bodies are wriggling in the mud like slugs and our mind is screaming in distress, we still sometimes want to put on a show of bravery, by some incomprehensible contradiction. What has made us so exhausted is precisely that struggle between mental discipline and flesh in revolt, the exposed, whimpering flesh that we have to beat into submission so we can get up again … Conscious courage, mademoiselle, starts with fear.'

Such are our most frequent topics of conversation. They lead us, inevitably, to define our notion of happiness, our ambitions, the goals of humanity, the summits of thought, even god and religion. We re-examine the old laws of humanity, laws created for interchangeable minds, for the whole flock of bleating minds. We discuss every article of her own morality, the morality which has guided the endless procession of little souls down through the ages, indistinct little souls which twinkled like glow-worms in the darkness of the world, and were extinguished after one night of life. Today we offer our own feeble light, which isn't even enough for us.

Through my questions, I lead the nurses into traps of logic, and ensnare them in syllogisms that completely undermine their principles. They struggle like flies in a spider's web, but refuse to surrender to the mathematical rigour of reason. They are led by the sentiments that a long passage of generations, ruled by dogma, has incorporated into the very substance of their being – sentiments that they have got from a line of women, housewives and mothers, who were alive in their early years and then crushed by domestic drudgery, worn out by the daily round, who crossed themselves with holy water to exorcise any thoughts they might have.

They are surprised to learn that duty, as they understand it, can be opposed to other duties, that there are seditious ideas vaster and more elevated than theirs, and which could be more beneficial to humanity.

Nonetheless, Mademoiselle Bergniol declared:

'No son of mine will be brought up to think like you.'

'I know that, mademoiselle. You could bear flaming torches as well as babies, but you'll only give your son the guttering candle that you were given; its wax is dripping and burning your fingers. It is candles like that which have set the world ablaze instead of illuminating it. Blind men's candles, and you can be sure that tomorrow they'll relight the braziers that will consume the sons of your loins. And their pain will be nothing but ash, and at the moment their sacrifice is consummated, they will know this and will curse you. With your principles, if the occasion presents itself, then you in turn will be inhuman mothers.'

'Do you deny that there are heroes, then, Dartemont?'

'The action of a hero is a paroxysm and we don't know what causes it. At the height of fear, you can see men becoming brave; it is a terrifying kind of bravery because you know that it's hopeless. Pure heroes are as rare as geniuses. And if in order to get one hero you have to blow ten thousand men to pieces, then we can do without heroes. You should remember that you would probably be unable to carry out the mission you give us. You can only be sure of how calmly you'll face death when you're facing it.'

When Mademoiselle Bergniol has gone, Nègre, who was following our conversation, shared his opinion:

'The delicate little dears! What they need is a hero in their beds, a real live hero with a bloody face, to make them squeal with pleasure!'

'They don't know...'

'They don't know anything, I agree. When all's said and done, women – and I've known plenty of them – are females, stupid and cruel. Behind all their airs and graces, they are just wombs. What will they have done during the war? They'll have egged on men to go and get their heads blown off. And the men who will have disembowelled lots of the enemy will receive their reward: the love of a charming, right-thinking young woman. What sweet little bitches!'

While he's talking I am watching the women going about their duties. Mademoiselle Bergniol is energetic in a methodical way, busying herself with studied cheerfulness: she seems transformed by the sense of duty that she upholds. Mademoiselle Heuzé is a big girl, homely and rather awkward, but the shape of her large mouth gives her a kindly appearance. Mademoiselle Reignier is full of goodwill, clumsy, a bit daft, and already too fat; in a few years she'll make 'a good, plump mother' without a trace of ill-nature. With Madame Bard, her nonchalance and the way she swings her strong hips, suggests desire; with the rather sultry gaze of a woman lacking a husband, her eyes linger on our bodies, a little covetously, perhaps. I avoid the attentions of grey-haired Madame Sabord, a fussy woman with dry fingers whose touch is unpleasant. Mademoiselles Barthe and Doré, one blonde the other brunette, both with bruised eyes, are almost inseparable, wrapping their arms round each other's waists, whispering confidences which make them burst into shrill laughter, like giggles, in a way men find irritating. There is something a bit too voluptuous in their sisterly embraces. Mademoiselle Odet offers everyone her sad smile, her veiled words and the ardour of her feverish eyes. She is too pale, too thin; her frail shoulders already bent beneath the weight of life at its start. You can see she will not have the strength to bear this life for long. We are grateful to her for sharing this short future with all of us, for caring for us when she needs someone to care for her, and the least we can do is to give a smile of encouragement in return for her smile, so full of self-denial.

I know nothing of them apart from these impressions and that's enough for me. I don't try to understand what brought them here. I am simply thankful that they are here, gliding gracefully around the ward, filling it with flowers and their various charms. I'm thankful, too, that they have lost that little edge of bourgeois arrogance they had at the start, when they spoke to us as if they were addressing their staff. I even allow myself the forbidden pleasure of catching them unawares with the ghost of a blush on their cheeks which they hide by turning away, or of suddenly looking deep into their eyes and finding the trace of some illicit emotional agitation which makes their hearts beat differently. But I stop myself on the threshold of this disquiet, like a gentleman at the door of a boudoir.

And above all I am delighted that we have become such good friends, that these young ladies (it's the young ones who display the most curiosity) spare me an hour of their time every day. The clamour of war is silenced by the murmur of their voices. Their words may not always be true, may be empty, but they are kind and gentle, and this pulls me back into life outside the battle zone – though it strikes me every now and then that my return here is unlikely to be permanent.

Every now and then the door of the ward silently opens, and a dark shadow appears beside one of the beds, mumbling unctuous words over the occupant. It's the hospital chaplain, the former head of the Saint-Gilbert school.

Now, I respect all faiths (and occasionally envy them) but I am always surprised at the furtive approach of some of these people, at their unconvincing smiles. If they are truly performing a holy and noble ministry then why do they behave like touts, and give the impression that they are soliciting your soul with a 'psst!'

from the end of some dark alleyway. This particular chaplain is of the type that seem to impose themselves on you by calculating your faults. Under their embarrassing gaze I suddenly feel like a monster of depravity, and I'm always waiting for them to say: 'Come, my son, and confide in me all your filthy little sins...'

Father Ravel took a particular interest in me in the beginning, and I suppose that the nurses, knowing my religious background, must have told him about me. In the period just after I arrived he would visit me every day and asked me to come and see him as soon as I could walk. I put this off as long as I could.

But he managed to drag a promise out of me, in a way that I find unfair. On the evening after my operation, seeing me weak and no more capable of resistance than a dying man, he persisted at great length and, still lost in the fog of chloroform, I said yes. Afterwards he kept reminding me of this promise and repeating: 'I am waiting for you', in a reproving tone that made it seem like I was the one acting in bad faith.

He did this so much that last week I eventually followed him out of the ward. He took me to his room and sat himself down in the chair beside the prie-dieu, where penitents kneel before Christ. But I've known that old trick with the furniture for a long time. So instead of kneeling on the prie-dieu, I sat on it. Once he had recovered from his astonishment, he questioned me, rather clumsily.

'So, my dear son, what do you have to tell me?'

'I don't have anything to tell you, sir.'

I realised that I should not expect any sophisticated conversation from him and that the only reason he'd brought me there was to catch me off guard and steal my sins. For him, every soul must be healed by absolution, rather in the way that some doctors use purges for every illness. I let him go on. He reminded me of my Christian childhood, and asked:

'Do you not want to come back to God? Do you not have sins to repent?'

'I don't have sins any more. The greatest sin, in the eyes of the

Church and the eyes of men, is to kill your brother. And today the Church is ordering me to kill my brothers.'

'They are the enemies of our nation.'

'They are nonetheless the children of the same God. And God, the father, presides over the fratricidal struggle of his own children, and the victories on both sides. He's just as happy whichever army sings the *Te Deum*. And you, one of the just, you pray to him to ruin and annihilate other just men. How do you expect me to make sense of that?'

'Evil comes from men, not from God.'

'So God is powerless?'

'His plans are beyond our comprehension.'

'We have that saying in the army, too: "Don't try to understand." It's the logic of a corporal.'

'I implore you, my child, for it is written: "Pride is the beginning of all sin: He that holdeth it, shall be filled with maledictions, and it shall ruin him in the end."'

'Yes, I know: "Beati pauperes spiritu". [23] It's a form of blasphemy, since He created us in his image and likeness!'

He got up and showed me the door. We did not exchange another word. Instead of the affliction at the sight of this lost sheep that should have been in his eyes, all I could see was a glint of hatred, the fury of a man who had been defeated and whose pride (yes, he too!) was wounded. I wondered how this fury could relate to the divine…

Still, I would have liked it if this priest had given me a few words of hope, indicated a possibility of belief, explained things to me. Alas, God's poor ministers are just as much in the dark as we are. You must believe like old women believe, the ones that look like witches, who mumble to themselves in churches under the nose of cheap, plaster saints. As soon as you start to use your reason, to look for a rainbow, you always run up against the great excuse, mystery. You will be advised to light some candles, put coins in the box, say a few rosaries, and make yourself stupid.

If the Son of God exists, it is at the moment when he bares his heart, while so many hearts are bleeding – that heart so full of love for man. Was it all to no purpose, had his Father sacrificed him pointlessly? The God of infinite mercy cannot be the God of the plains of Artois. The good God, the just God, could not have allowed such bloody carnage to be carried out in His name, could not have wanted such destruction of bodies and minds to further his glory.

God? Come off it, the heavens are empty, as empty as a corpse. There's nothing in the sky but shells and all the other murderous devices made by men . . .

This war has killed God, too.

The nurses leave the ward between noon and two o'clock, after our lunch. To avoid the embarrassment of relieving ourselves in their presence, we have regulated our bodily functions so that – unless it's unavoidable – they are only exercised in that period. The only job of the male army nurse who covers for them is to remove the bedpans. Those waiting for him to come look at the ceiling and smoke energetically to dispel the odour. Once the big rush is over and we no longer risk catching cold, we open the windows. Winter sunlight pours into the ward and we let it trickle between our hands, pale with idleness, so that they acquire a faint flush of pink.

Someone had given this male nurse the cruel surname of Caca. I know this name upsets him, know it because I knew André Charlet before the war, at university, where he was one of the star students, bursting with curiosity and ideas. In student reviews he published some brilliant sonnets, which represented life as a vast field of conquests, a heavenly forest full of surprises, into which ventured great explorers who brought back amazing fruit with unfamiliar tastes, women of savage beauty, and a thousand barbaric objects of refined savagery. When the mobilisation began he was one of the first to join up and he was severely wounded the following year.

Now I found him here, broken, drained, and dirty. A few months of war had brought about this metamorphosis, given him this agitated manner, emaciated body and yellow skin. It has left him with the mad terror that you can see behind his eyes. So that he could stay in the hospital he accepted this job and the disgusting duties that go with it. By being Caca, he gets to spend an extra three months in hospital, through some military decision or other allowing medical staff to take on temporary assistants. If he hadn't done this he would most likely have joined the auxiliaries unless he'd been declared unfit for service altogether. But he doesn't want to go before a panel except as a last resort for he isn't convinced that his health has been sufficiently ruined to exempt him from returning to front-line duty. He is alone in doubting it; we believe he is likely to die from tuberculosis, more infallible than shells.

I try to win him round, recalling our adolescent years together, our friends, our happiness, our former ambitions. But I cannot interest him. He smiles weakly and says: 'It's all over!'

'And what about poetry, old pal?' I reply.

He shrugs his shoulders: 'Poetry is like glory!', then leaves because someone is calling him. A moment later he returns with steaming bedpan, turns his head away in utter disgust, and sneers: 'There you are, poetry!'

Among his memories of the war, this one is truly appalling:

'It was in the eastern zone, end of August. Our battalion attacks with bayonets. You have no idea how idiotic those first assaults were, what a massacre. What distinguished that period without a doubt was the incompetence of our leaders – and they were sometimes victims themselves. They had been taught that battles were decided by the infantry, and cold steel. They didn't have the faintest idea about the effects of modern weaponry, of artillery and machine guns, and their big hobby horse was Napoleonic strategy – nothing new since Marengo! We were under attack and instead of establishing solid positions, we were scattered across the plains, unprotected, wearing uniforms straight out of a circus and then ordered to charge at forests, from 500 metres. The Boche picked us off like rabbits and then, once they'd done all the damage they could, they fled when we got close enough for hand-to-hand fighting. Finally on that particular day, having lost half our men, we managed to drive them out. But the bastards had a diabolical idea. There was a strong wind blowing against us and they set fire to the cornfields from which we were chasing them… What I saw there was a vision of hell! Four hundred wounded men, lying still on the ground, suddenly bitten and revived by the flames, four hundred turned into human torches, trying to run on broken limbs, waving their arms and screaming like the damned. Their hair went straight up in flames, like tongues of fire on the head of the Holy Ghost, and the cartridges they had in their belts exploded. We were struck dumb, unable to think of taking cover, as we watched four hundred of our comrades sizzling and twisting and rolling in this inferno, swept by machine-gun fire, unable to reach them. I saw one stand up as the wave of fire approached him and shoot his neighbours to spare them this horrible death. And then several of them, about to be engulfed by the flames, began screaming to us: "Shoot us, pals, shoot us!" and maybe some of us had that terrible courage… And Ypres! The night battles at Ypres. You didn't know who you were killing, who was killing you. Our colonel had told us: "Treat prisoners well, my children, but *don't take any*." The people we were facing had surely been given the same instructions.'

'But look, the worst is over, old pal. We'll soon be back in civilian life, and we'll return to what we were doing before.'

'No, it won't be like before. That's not possible. The war has diminished me. You knew me at university, you know my fellow students had me marked out as someone who would stand out in our generation, our teachers had faith in me, and men of distinction had

GABRIEL CHEVALLIER

already honoured me. I dreamed of a glittering career as a leader of men, at least an intellectual leader, but I also believed that my body was capable of serving my ideas. Now I've seen that my body is just an old rag, a straw in the wind; it's a deserter and it's taken me with it… A chap who shakes with fear cannot be a leader.'

'But we have all shaken with fear!'

'Not all. You remember Morlaix, that dolt who spent his life in bars with dubious women, who got ill at the very thought of opening a book, and whom we held in utter contempt? He's already a sub-lieutenant. He was completely in control at the front, incredibly plucky. To give you some idea – at the time when the trenches still weren't continuous, in a new sector, we were coming back with provisions through a foggy night. You couldn't see more than three metres ahead. So of course we get lost and we end up floundering around in some kind of swamp, going around in circles like we were blindfolded, hampered by the supplies we were carrying and unarmed. Morlaix decides what to do: "Go straight ahead, we'll see where we get!" So we march on and on, in silence… A shout makes us freeze: "Wer da?" We've walked straight into the German sentries. Now, listen to this, Morlaix has a pack full of hard-boiled eggs. Quick as a flash he chucks three of them ahead of him. Hearing them land, in the dark, the Boche thought they were grenades and fled. I could never keep my cool like that…'

'You have other qualities. The fact that a brute may be briefly useful on a battlefield doesn't prove anything against the life of the mind, quite the contrary. A man who creates is worth more than a man who kills.'

'I can't accept that a man can be incomplete, that he can show himself inferior in certain aspects of the game. In the war, I was a disaster. I cannot forget it.'

'You did no more and no less than everyone else. Stop punishing yourself.'

'I'm ashamed to think of it! I've writhed in humiliation at all the

120

times I've sobbed in fear, at the tears I've shed, a weakling's tears. Don't you see, I've betrayed all the beliefs of my youth, Nietzsche, strength… ah, sweet god… Now I am good for emptying chamber pots and I will never be more than a clerk.'

It was a strange case of depression and I think his physical illness played a large part in it.

I saw him do something shocking. It was at the time when Diuré was suffering so badly with his thigh. One day, on the pretext of relieving his pain, Charlet had insisted he change his dressing. Diuré finally agreed. The procedure completed, I saw Charlet take the bowl behind the wash-hand basins, take out a soiled piece of gauze and carefully put it inside a tin box that he slipped into his pocket. Intrigued, I called him over a moment later and asked:

'What's this then, you doing bacteriology now?'

'What do you mean?'

'What did you put in your box just then?'

He looked anxious.

'I don't know what you're talking about.'

Then, after a moment's thought:

'I can tell you and I know you won't talk about it. You remember Richerand, who was in the School of Chemistry?'

'A little chap, wasn't he, rather unprepossessing?'

'The same. I met up with him at the front. We were good friends and promised to help each other whatever happened. The promise helped sustain us a little. He didn't let me down. He stuck by me when I was wounded. It was he who bound up my wound and transported me to the first-aid post, through an artillery barrage, with the help of another soldier whom he had persuaded to come with him. There they were able to stop the bleeding, and so Richerand probably saved my life. I am all the more grateful to him for his devotion because I know he's very sensitive: a heap of nerves who has suffered a great deal in this war… He has just written to me (he's at Vieil Armand[24]): "All we do is attack. Save me!" Which I know is his way of saying, 'I've reached my limit, I've given up hope.'

'And so?'

'So... How do you think I can help him from here? I've been thinking about it since yesterday and it's urgent...'

He leaned over and whispered:

'I'm going to send it to him...'

'What "it"?'

'Phlegmonic pus. If he injects himself with it, he has a chance of being evacuated.'

We remained silent for a long time. I said:

'Do you realise what you are doing?'

He let his arms fall and murmured:

'I have no choice!'

I risked the supreme argument:

'One man leaves the front, another takes his place. By saving Richerand you are condemning someone else.'

He hadn't considered this. He looked at me reflectively.

'Too bad! Richerand is my friend. Do you want me to sit back and let him die? In a moment of depression he may do something foolish. I have no choice.'

He left me abruptly, one hand in his pocket, clutching the box.

The idea of denouncing him never crossed my mind, any more than it would with our comrades. Between us there is strict solidarity: we all have to do our jobs in the trenches but we consider that everyone is free to try and escape the front, and how this is done is none of our business; we congratulate those who succeed. Could I even judge Charlet? I thought of all those soldiers I had seen with the eyes of condemned men, suddenly overcome by a fatal presentiment. A man in the grip of such an obsession can no longer look after himself, fight to stay alive; he goes to his death like a sleepwalker... Could I judge Charlet? Where we had come from, you don't judge. You submit. To submit is to risk your life; not to submit is also to risk it. Charlet's gesture? Simply this: here is where our utter misery has taken us, this is what men are forced to resort to when their strength fails. We cannot blame: we know too well that weakness lies in wait for all of us.

It is hard to guess the age of Mademoiselle Nancey. Probably between thirty-five and forty. Sour face, thin lips, cold eyes and sharp voice; she lacks everything a man might seek in a woman, offers no physical feature that might stick in your memory. She is irritable, quick-witted, born to give orders, at no time could such a woman have possessed that hesitant grace, those little hints of consent that in most women can attract and keep a man. You can tell that she has never felt her heart heavy with longing and the sudden, irrational urge to offer it timidly. She is one of those women in whom love's safety valve doesn't work and so her energy must turn to other activity for release: cerebral tasks, the tasks of men. The hospital provides an excellent outlet for this energy. The indefatigable Mademoiselle Nancey does great service there, giving strong leadership to her little troop of nurses, never panicking at the sight of wounds, never moved by cries of pain.

In the mornings she leads the doctor on his rounds – a decent old civilian doctor, who signs the necessary papers, checks our condition, and asks his colleagues to assist in the most serious cases. He looks distractedly at the patients and asks:

'How's this one doing, mademoiselle?'

'He's coming along, doctor. It takes time.'

Without asking to verify this, he moves on to the next one:

'Number 12, doctor, that's the arm. We're carrying on with the irrigation. But number 23 is worrying us and is in pain. You should see him.'

And sometimes she says:

'Number 16 has healed up. We can discharge him.'

She prepares the paperwork, the doctor checks it, and the man has no choice but to go. The bonus period, those precious extra weeks that a patient who has recovered may still enjoy here, in complete safety, depends entirely on her. And bad luck for anyone who has crossed her! For having done just that, Boutroux (a thigh) left overnight, even though the scab on his extensive wound was only recent, still soft and swollen with pus. The idiot had come back drunk after an evening's outing, and caused a scandal. His vulgarity had been noted: he was a marked man. And so the very next morning, despite his incomplete recovery, out he went. His misbehaviour had cut his period of freedom by at least three weeks: time enough to get killed twenty times over.

The threat of this terrible punishment, premature departure, keeps the lid on everyone who might be tempted to give in to their instincts. We know from the press that the offensives in Artois and Champagne have failed utterly, that the bloody battles at Hartmannswillerkopf, which fill the news reports, will not be decisive. The war cannot enter a new phase before the spring. So it is important for us to gain time. Mademoiselle Nancey can choose to give or deny us this time, time which could save our lives. It adds to her prestige.

The basic rule is thus 'keep a low profile'. Among those closest to being fit for service, quite a few try to get in her good books by using whatever simple means they have. They offer themselves as drudges, sparing the nurses the most onerous tasks. Others go to Mass, while bragging that this assiduous churchgoing has nothing to do with their religious sentiments. (Others, it should be said, go to Mass out of conviction and no one mocks them for it.) I have the impression they are making a mistake. I don't believe for one minute that Mademoiselle Nancey will fall for their false piety and do them any favours.

As I've said, Mademoiselle Nancey and I are on very good terms. Better than that, we are flirting, a respectful kind of flirtation. She favours me with special attention, seeks my advice on various plans, asks my opinion on the news.

There is another little thing. Right in front of my bed there is a chest on legs, a sort of storage box. Whenever Mademoiselle Nancey comes by for a chat, she jumps up and sit herself down on this chest, obviously pleased to show how nimble she is. This sudden movement pushes her skirt up high, revealing a little glimpse of thigh above her dark stockings. (Her legs are muscular, but rather pretty: one of her best features, as she surely knows.) On one occasion my gaze alighted on this thigh and she caught my eye. I turned away in embarrassment. But I noticed after that she always sat down with the same revealing movement, and then stared at me without a blush. It seemed to me that she didn't need to uncover so much of her flesh... In short, I had been allowed to share the secret of this sturdy leg and its white skin. Henceforth it would be imprudent not to look at it – discreetly, but with feeling. To show that I was aware of it, that I appreciated it.

I am sure that, with the very best intentions, that is what it was. I recall the words of someone with experience: 'Women all have the same female pretentions and even the most virtuous among them like to convince themselves that they can tempt a man.' Yes, Mademoiselle Nancey sought to put a price on her virtue. Why refuse her this little pleasure which didn't threaten mine?

That leg is my guarantee of extra time in hospital. I can lie back and watch others sweep the floors.

It was bound to happen. I'm surprised that the changes in his behaviour which were definitely abnormal didn't alert me sooner. A young man, however much he's exhausted and demoralised, should quickly recover, but Charlet only got more depressed and gloomy.

His clenched fingers, facial tics and jerky movements, all indicated the state of his nerves when he entered the ward earlier on. Nonetheless, he began his duties as usual, though without greeting me.

At about one o'clock he suddenly loomed up in front of me. His face was terrifying, the colour of clay, plastered with brown, his eyes were red. He stuck his arm under my nose:

'Go on, smell it! Smell it!'

'Come on, what is this?'

He thrust his arm at me violently and I recoiled.

'Haha! You can smell it, can't you? You can smell the stink?'

He was staring at me with wild, burning eyes and I couldn't look away. Bringing his face right up to mine, he uttered these unbelievable words:

'*I am a piece of shit.*'

'Charlet, come on now, you're crazy!'

'Smell it!'

Even more than his fury, it was the spittle dribbling from his mouth that frightened me. Luckily, someone called out for him:

'Psst, Caca, over here!'

He leapt up and headed for Peignard, gesticulating wildly.

'My name is Shit, do you hear, and I will not tolerate your insolence!'

I realised then that he had gone completely off his head, and I feared for the safety of all these vulnerable, wounded men: Peignard with his foot, Diuré with his tubes, the unfortunate Breton. I called out to some of the more able-bodied patients to surround him while we got help. Now completely out of control, he tried to escape, shouting:

'I am your master, you degenerates! All men depend on me! I am the Truth, the ruler of the world!'

Finally three burly young men arrived from downstairs and took him away.

Charlet!

Here is the last vision I have of him in civilian life. One night in the early summer of 1914, under the chestnut trees in the square where we'd all meet every evening. White swans glided silently over the dark, silken surface of the pools by the fountains, the water dappled with light from a brightly illuminated café terrace. A distant orchestra lulled us with its gentle rhythms. And there was Charlet, bare-headed, slim and elegant, sure of himself, even a little spoiled by his precocious success, standing and reciting his own poems. I can still hear his intonation and remember one passage:

> *Tonight the air is heavy with the scent of the woodland grove*
> *Where she sleeps so calmly, beneath a ray of moonlight,*
> *Her body so white wrapped in the rich brown sash*
> *Of her hair, where I whisper my secrets*
> *The imperious Empress of my heart.*

And now, at twenty-two, he is insane. And his madness has taken the lowest form imaginable.

They change our dressings every morning. My turn usually comes around nine o'clock. A nurse approaches with her therapeutic kit and a brave smile (which costs her nothing). She takes hold of me, undoes the safety pins, unwinds the bandages, and takes off the sticky gauze, giving it little tugs that pull at the lips of my wounds. They in turn pass on the message to the rest of my body, which objects to such a sharp and sudden separation and makes me squeal with pain, something I find deeply embarrassing. The wounds are washed with permanganate and then treated with either tincture of iodine or a silver nitrate pencil. There's nothing to choose between them: both give me the same pleasant sensation of a red-hot iron being thrust into my flesh, and I am always surprised not to smell burning or see smoke rising. The large number of wounds prolongs my agony. While other wounds are still being cleaned, various points on my body, already soaked in iodine, feel like they've been placed on a grill, and I writhe about like a heretic struggling not to abjure his faith. My faith, in this case, being my wish to maintain my decorum despite the pain. The worst is kept for last: the wound in my thorax just below my shoulder blade. When I feel the iodine approaching, I tense up, holding my breath, as if a shell was falling. But it is only a pink hand which pauses and then with cruel suddenness pushes the wad of cotton into the gash in my back so that it impregnates me with its brown saliva, right to my lungs, or so it feels. I receive my final thrust to the heart.

I then spend a good hour cooking on a low flame.

Some days when I know I'm about to flinch, I resist. I camouflage my squeals with curses. And I have a very good mind to give this nurse a slap. How can a woman be so calm while making me suffer!

It's the bad moment of the day; it spoils my rest and blights my morning awakenings, which it follows closely. But once the pain has stopped, it feels like ages till the next treatment. The hours pass until I reach a peak of peace and calm, which then diminishes until the next morning.

Going to hospital, little more than a year ago, was a dreaded phrase. More than suffering, it suggested the ignominious idea of failure. The middle classes did not go to public hospitals; those places were reserved for workers, child-mothers, and those unfortunates who had wasted their inheritance, 'squandered the lot', and thus deserved the worst punishments, those, in short, who had gone to rack and ruin. Families would warn their wastrel offspring, their prodigal sons, that 'You'll end up in hospital!', that is, poor, alone and ashamed. Seeing the forbidding exteriors of these institutions, their gloomy corridors, the miserable huddles of mourners that sometimes emerged, used to make me think vaguely of leper colonies.

But now a hospital is the promised land, the greatest hope for millions of men. And for all the pain and suffering and harrowing sights it can contain, it is still the greatest happiness that a soldier can imagine. Once when someone was carried from an ambulance through the doors to this place his heart would sink, he'd feel afraid. Today, the man brought in on a stretcher knows that the admission note he gets from reception is a passport to life.

And if some senior doctor, blessed with divine powers, walked through the ward and told each patient he would heal his shattered limbs, saying 'Leave thy bed and walk!', the chances are that Peignard, Mouchetier and all the others who have been torn apart, after weighing up all the risks that a new, healthy body would entail, and remembering the icy sweat of terror that tortures strong, healthy men, would answer: 'No miracles, please!'

In my case, having been lucky enough to hit the battlefield jackpot with a 'lucky wound', my stay in hospital is rather like spending the winter in the Midi. After I've paid my debt of pain every morning (the cost of my board and lodging), I really do feel as if I'm on holiday, and the presence of young, graceful nurses, along with the attentions of Mademoiselle Nancey, complete the illusion. What do I need to do, apart from eat, smoke and read? When I tire of reading, I let myself slip into that state of extreme lassitude that comes from excessive rest, I rest from the rest... I plump up my weakness like cushions and lie back in comfort. I bask in the pleasure of not having to do anything, of my right – which I owe to a grenade – to be feeble. And I don't mind the shivers of the mild fever that comes with a long stay in bed.

And so, in my weak state, my eyes closed, I dream. But I don't dream of the future, which is very uncertain. Safe in the dark behind my lowered eyelids, I can listen to the great rumble of war, echoing in the depths of my ears, like the roar of the waves you can hear in a seashell. Despite myself, I think of the surprising chain of events that has brought me here, and it still amazes me.

7

CONVALESCENCE

MY WOUNDS HAVE HEALED and the moment has come when I must take my leave of the nurses in ward 11 at Saint-Gilbert where I have spent the best days of my life as a soldier. Mademoiselle Nancey entreated me to keep in touch: 'Don't forget to write to us. We like to know what happens to our patients after they leave us. And should misfortune strike you a second time, you know where we are.' With uncharacteristic gravity, Nègre said simply: 'Do your best to save your skin!'

We hear the familiar sound of the letterbox on the path opening and closing, and then a key turns in the door. Our father has come home for supper. Wiping his feet on the mat, as always, he asks my sister:

'Is your brother back?'

I come out into the corridor.

'There you are!' he says. 'We got your letter and we've been waiting for you every day.'

We embrace, somewhat ritually: a trial kiss, He must be wondering: has the war changed him? Our relationship has never been warm. My father expected better of me, and I expected better of him. I failed to pay sufficient heed to his advice, but then it seemed to me that the results he had achieved, with his much-vaunted experience, gave me the right to be wary. No doubt he loves me in his own way but unfortunately his manner of showing this when I was a child was never very convincing, and that impression stayed with me ever after. You could say we don't understand each other. A father has to put a lot into it if he and his son are going to understand each other, to find a way across the quarter century that separates them. This did not happen. In 1914 we were more or less at loggerheads. But when war came we extended the spirit of national unity to our family. Decency demanded it, given the dangers I was going to face. And now I am back, after thirteen months' absence and a battle wound, with the best intentions but still somewhat sceptical about the chances of finding a perfect accord.

We take our seats at the table, all in our former places, and I see that nothing here has changed. My father questions me:

'Fully recovered then?'

'I'm OK.'

'Yes, you look fine. That life has done you good.'

He's giving me a sly look and I realise, from the way he's squeezing the piece of bread in his hand, that something is making him unhappy. I quickly learn what.

'How did you manage not to get a single stripe?'

'I'm not interested,' I said, to cut it short.

'Another one of your strange ideas!'

Whenever my father alludes to what he calls my ideas, it's a bad sign. But he sticks to his guns and goes on:

'Charpentier's sons are pretty much the same age as you and one's a sergeant and the other an adjutant. Their father is proud of them.'

'It's nothing to be proud of!'

'Oh, of course, you're above that, aren't you!… Never been one to put yourself out to make anybody happy!'

My sister, fearing an argument where neither one of us gives way, butts in and changes the subject. They talk among themselves, leaving me out, about what's happening at home, their friends, invitations, visits, whatever... They have the same petty concerns as they had in 1914 and when I listen I feel I only left them yesterday. They do not appear to have the slightest idea of what's happening a few hundred kilometres away. And my father accuses me of egotism! Not that it matters. I am here for just one week – on convalescent leave, subject to immediate recall. But these people for whom I am fighting (for when all's said and done I'm not fighting for myself!) are like strangers to me.

They are not even interested in the war. My father won't condescend to ask me about it: that would mean admitting that a son can know more about something than his father. And that would be unimaginable for him; it is a very long time since anyone challenged his authority.

My father has arranged to meet me in the afternoon. I find him at the appointed time and I walk beside him along the crowded street where the window displays shimmering in electric light bring back scenes of pre-war life that I had forgotten. He has aged a bit since I last saw him and is now noticeably shorter than me. We are reaching that point where the father, diminished by age, shrinks, where the son gets taller and asserts himself. For a long time he seemed in my eyes to belong to the world of grown-ups, possessors of privilege, sources of all wisdom, and for a long time, too, I felt subservient to him. Today, I have a life of my own, beyond his grasp and out of his control. Faced with my growing independence, and my height, he shows a little more respect, while I more or less tolerate or ignore his unjust temper, now that I am free from him. There is a balance of forces, we treat each other cordially. But we are further apart than ever.

My father takes me to the brasserie where he meets his friends every evening. It's in the centre of town, and in the main room the owner keeps a corner reserved for them to spend part of their afternoons. They're in their sixties, businessmen and industrialists.

Some have that troubled look that comes with ill-fortune and declining years, others on the contrary have the satisfied air of successful entrepreneurs. They've all known each other for nearly half their lives. This is where they enjoy their leisure, well away from worries and domestic acrimony, and live off an old fund of memories and jokes that they have dug up from their youth. They are used to each other and respect each other's foibles, an essential condition for growing old comfortably in company.

They all look up when we arrive.

'Let me introduce my boy who has just come out of hospital after being wounded,' he says, shaking hands.

These important men interrupt their game of cards to greet me warmly:

'Excellent! Bravo, young man!'

'Congratulations on your bravery!'

'I say, Dartemont, what a fine chap!'

Then they go quiet, not knowing what further encouragement to offer me. The war is out of fashion, people are getting used to it. Military men on leave are everywhere, giving the impression that nothing bad ever happens to them. And I am just an ordinary soldier, and my father's business is hardly flourishing. These gentlemen have been generous to take such an interest in me.

They go back to their game: 'Whose turn is it to cut?' My father joins in. I stay alone at the end of a table, opposite an elderly gentleman methodically chewing gruyère and washing it down with beer. He looks at me for some time and I guess from his rather pained expression that he is trying to form a sentence. At last, with an engaging smile, he asks:

'You have some fun out there then, eh?

I stare in shock at this bloodless old fool. But I answer quickly and pleasantly:

'Oh, gosh, yes, I should say so, sir...'

He beams happily. I have the feeling he is about to exclaim:

'Oh-ho, those good old *poilus*!'

Then I add:

'...We really enjoy ourselves: *every evening we bury our pals!*'

His smile goes into reverse and the compliment freezes on his lips. He grabs at his glass and sticks his nose in it. In shock he swallows his beer too fast and it heads straight for his lungs. This is followed by a gurgling noise and then a little jet of spume that he spouts into the air and which descends on to his stomach, in a cascade of frothy bubbles.

'Something go down the wrong way?' I inquire, mercilessly.

His body is convulsed with catarrhal rumblings and spluttering. Above his handkerchief I can only see his yellow eyes, streaming with tears. Behind my hypocritically concerned expression, my mind is beginning a savage, vengeful scalp dance.

We leave soon after. I know what the gruyère man will say the minute we go out the door:

'I say, is Dartemont's lad some kind of troublemaker? No manners at all, that boy, you know!'

'I can't imagine he gives Dartemont much to be happy about!'

'Not a single stripe or medal after a whole year of war – makes you wonder, doesn't it?'

They will shake their heads as if to say 'everyone has his cross to bear' and order another cold beer to buck themselves up. And then one of them will make a suggestion: 'Are you all free this evening? I know a little place where we could have a bite of dinner and...' Between men, they are proposing a little debauch for themselves. And if a pretty girl should pass by then, ho-hoh!, they'll invite her to join them. They're so terribly lonely right now, those little lasses. Obviously, they understand a bit about the aftermath of this carousing: the gout, the pains in the liver... But what the hell! Mustn't mollycoddle yourself – everyone is suffering these days!

All's fair in love and war, eh?

* * * * *

I have a week left to treat myself to some pleasure, to gorge myself on it, store it up to last me for many months. It may be my final pleasure, and perhaps these seven days will provide the last memory of my life. No time to waste, let us start the pleasure hunt, track it down, grab it.

But then, what is pleasure? Make a list of possible pleasures. Meals? No, they can only be an accompaniment to pleasure, a seasoning. The theatre? No again. Plays are empty and false given the reality that's waiting for me. The joys of family life? A mother could perhaps understand me, make me feel I belonged, but I lost mine when I was very young. Friends? I would certainly like to see my friends again, exchange impressions as we go down our old paths. But my friends (I have three true ones) are scattered at the front; one was wounded in Champagne soon after me. The pleasures of vanity? It seems they exist. I don't know where you find such things. In various salons no doubt, but I have no access to such places, and no desire to go there.

Which leaves, then, the pleasures of the heart. The term is too romantic. Let's be accurate: a woman. I have known a few well, in various ways. But they were young and not very free. The first difficulty is to find them again, and then to revive their feelings for me, feelings that I have not exactly helped to sustain, for they spoke of eternal, absolute emotions and at the age of twenty, caught in the war, I could not sign an emotional pact binding for the whole future. I was thinking ahead, as often happens when you try too hard to act in good faith. So those possible lovers must have taken their hearts elsewhere. A woman's heart cannot remain unoccupied for long. The younger the hearts, the more demanding, and the more rights they claim. I didn't want to make any promises. Promising nothing, and being far away, I fear I've lost them all. Love is a transaction, at least of emotions in the rarest cases: you love to get something in return. Since I wasn't there, I couldn't give anything. And now I can only give seven days of an infantryman, whose life is at risk. Whose career has not begun and whose heart, it must be said, is unreliable. What woman would want me? To accept this gift, she would at least have to have known me before, kept a different image of me than the one I offer in the pathetic uniform that I was given at the hospital.

That leaves the pleasure that you buy, of inferior quality but pleasure nonetheless if you can afford the luxury version. Unfortunately I have very little money, enough to buy only cut-price pleasure, the pleasure of the poor, as loathsome as eating in a cheap café. What I need is a week of opulence and all I have ahead of me is a week of scrimping.

I take my chances; I go out.

I head straight for the places where, before the war, I was sure to find friends. I look in the cafés, go up and down the same streets over and over again. Everything that made this landscape familiar has gone, my city no longer knows me, and I feel alone. Once, in clothes of my own choice, I possessed a degree of confidence that my uniform has taken away. Women turn naturally to what is glamorous and elegant: all the officers, members of the General Staff, employees from military headquarters, in their fancy outfits, who can guarantee something lasting. I am afraid to approach a woman! Soldiers must go with soldiers' girls, and everyone knows it…

I wander around, at a loose end, and without much hope. I'm beginning to realise that life here has taken on a new rhythm, from which we're excluded and which leaves no place for one of those adventures I'm dreaming of. The women are beautiful, and have a more determined look than they used to; no trace on their faces of any secret sorrow. So where are all those lovers brought to despair by the separations of war?

I have the address of one of the young women I spent some time with in 1914. I decide to go and wait near the place where she lives in the hope of catching her coming in or going out. It's a slim chance but I have no better way of finding her.

I met Germaine D... yesterday evening, the fifth day of my leave. About time! I paced up and down the shop windows of a gloomy street which I knew was on her regular route home. And suddenly there she was, illuminated by a gas light. In spite of the new cut of her clothes, I recognised her walk or the way she held herself, something at least which told me it was definitely her. I watched her stranger's face coming closer, unaware of my presence, a pensive, inscrutable face which became distinct as she approached. I stepped out into the light. She stepped back indignantly – then blushed: it was her turn to recognise me. Without any reproaches, without showing any great surprise, she simply promised me an afternoon, this afternoon. Perhaps I could even see her tomorrow, too, but – 'Not for long, we've got people at home, and I can't do what I want.'

I took her to a pied-à-terre that someone had offered me. She was gracious enough not to look too closely at this makeshift flat, nor to criticise its dubious character and anonymity. She was gracious enough, despite my neglect, to give herself without hesitation, with that air of abandon and pleasure (at last!) of sensual women, grateful for what they are experiencing. By mixing our memories with the present, she had the skill immediately to re-establish an intimacy between us that cancelled out our year apart and naturally acquired the tone of our former rendezvous. And she had the generosity not to distract us from this precious time by complaining about my silence. She accepted me as she found me and saw me as she had before. It was that above all that I sought: someone for whom I was no longer a soldier. She left me with my little bouquet pinned to her coat. 'I am very proud of my medal!' she said.

I am in debt to charming, unaffected Germaine for the greatest joy I experienced during my leave: a few hours of forgetting spent in her company. In future, I will write to her.

Even the worst upheavals cannot change people's characters. This seven-day leave proved to me that my father's narrow-minded stubbornness would never alter, whatever I was doing. And what more could I do, today, than be a soldier? Being one, was I not completely satisfying public opinion and thus raising the standing of my family?

It is true to say that I'm a malcontent hero. If I am asked about the events of the war, I have the bad and unsociable habit of describing them as I found them. This liking for truth is incompatible with civilised behaviour. Those milieus where I was received and welcomed expected me to vindicate their smug passivity by my own optimism, expected me to display that scorn for the enemy, for hardship and danger, that good humour and spirit of enterprise that are legendary and so characteristic of French soldiers, the ones you see on the covers of almanacs, debonair and smiling in a hail of bullets. Civilians like to see the war as a fine adventure, an excellent distraction for young men, an adventure that of course has its dangers but compensates for them with the joys it offers: glory, romantic encounters, freedom from everyday cares. This convenient image tranquilised consciences, legitimised profits, and also allowed people to say, 'our hearts bleed' while living like pigs in clover. I have little faith in those hearts which feel the suffering of others so deeply. They must be made of some very rare material. You only truly suffer in your own flesh: in the 'flesh of your flesh' that suffering is already a lot less, except in the case of unusually sensitive souls.

I was well aware that it would have been polite, when offered a fine meal in a luxurious establishment, to put everyone at ease by declaring that we were on our way to victory and everything at the front was going along splendidly. In return for which they would have poured me a second glass of cognac, offered me a second cigar, while saying, in that indulgent tone that is reserved for soldiers: 'Come on now, a *poilu* like you, you won't get cigars like this in the trenches, so don't be shy!' In other words: you see, nothing is refused you!

But I did not tell of exploits where the Germans got a good hammering, I froze the most lively conversations. I was ill-mannered, I made myself unbearable, and people are glad to see the back of me.

My father has insisted on accompanying me to the station this evening. We don't have much to say to each other. We walk along the draughty platform, waiting for the train. My father is afraid of draughts, he's turned up his coat collar and I can tell he's impatient.

'Don't wait. Why catch cold for a few minutes that won't change anything?' I say.

'No, no, I'll wait!' he answers gruffly, like a man who has decided to set an example, to do his duty to the end, whatever the personal cost.

So we exchange a few unimportant words, and I notice that he keeps glancing furtively at the station clock. My departure is at an awkward time. I am aware that if my father leaves me soon and jumps on a tram, he can still meet up with his friends at the brasserie: Friday is their day. This is surely on his mind. Naturally I cannot mention the meeting without making him angry. We are standing side by side but our thoughts are far apart. A father and son? Yes, of course. But also, especially, a man going to the front and a civilian… The whole war separates us, a war that I know and he does not.

At long last the train arrives, one of those squalid, noisy army trains. Again I advise my father to go, on the pretext that it will take me some time to find a seat. He accepts a compromise:

'Yes, you're right, you'll be better off with your pals!'

We embrace. He stays standing in front of me for a moment, indecisively. From the way he's drumming his fingers in the air, I can tell he has something on his mind. He shares it with me:

'Do try to get yourself a stripe or two!'

'I'll try!' I say, being conciliatory.

'So, farewell, see you soon, I hope… And don't do anything reckless out there!' he says, without much warmth.

We embrace again. He turns and heads off quickly. Perhaps to hide his emotion… Before going down the steps into the underground passageway, he waves me goodbye a final time, waves in the air, a vigorous wave: the gesture of a free man…

I stand alone on the platform, by the train. I'm alone, with my haversack with food for two days, my water bottle, my blanket, my wallet with a bit of money close to my chest, my watch on my left wrist, my knife in the right pocket of my trousers, secured by a chain, my pocket scissors – all my worldly goods… I haven't forgotten anything.

I see the great, quiet city, sleeping – the city full of people who are not in danger, happy people and elegant, vivacious young women, who are not for soldiers. I can make out the streams of light of the main avenues of the city centre, where people are having fun as if nothing abnormal was happening.

The locomotive lets out steam and I can hear the guards' whistles. So I jump on the train quickly, into the nearest carriage. Its foul, warm breath hits me in the face, the breath of a drunkard. I step over bodies and people grumble as I try to find a place for myself. I'm back in the war…

DUG-IN

'The common soldier entertains no thoughts of becoming known, and dies unnoticed, among many others; he lived very much in the same way, but still he was alive; this is one of the chief causes of the want of courage in people of low and servile condition.'

La Bruyère (from The 'Characters' of Jean de la Bruyère, translated by Henri Van Laun, London, 188?)

1

QUIET SECTORS

'EIGHTEEN DEGREES,' shouts Baboin.

'Twenty-five paces,' I reply.

We note down the figures on a sheet of paper, then walk round a traverse. I count my strides until the next elbow in the trench, and push my stick into the ground. It has a red thread tied to it. Baboin looks through the viewfinder cut out of cardboard attached to his compass and tells me the degrees of deviation from true north; I tell him the distance. We are making a map of the sector. This entirely safe activity fills the afternoon, when we're free, and we intend to make it last as long as possible.

Baboin, a highway engineer in civilian life, is the batman for the lieutenant commanding our company. He's a small man with a beard and short legs, quiet and meticulous, who accepted this servant role to avoid the disadvantages of the front line. He's attached to the lieutenant's command post, where he more or less has the role of housekeeper: sweeping, emptying dirty water, warming up the meals, doing the dishes, washing underwear and cleaning clothes. He rarely leaves the shelter of the command post unless he's forced to. His only pride is his small, careful handwriting, which is a perfect copy of the models of calligraphy. His script reveals a natural submissiveness and a lack of imagination which goes with his character: he follows orders with the respect of a petty bureaucrat. He explained his position to me, which is a wise one, though I don't think I would be capable of such wisdom if it made me perform a role like his: 'Here it's a matter of not trying to be clever and getting home alive.' I have pretty much the same plan, but I know that in my case it can suddenly be compromised by an outburst of temper, that some instruction that I find offensive will make me quickly lose patience, even if it endangers my life. But I don't blame Baboin for the path he has chosen. He doesn't seem to find it degrading, or if he does he hides it carefully. I am grateful for his friendship, which is that of an equal, and which shows itself through gifts in kind, coffee and tobacco, of which he gets a copious supply from the kitchens. He holds me in esteem because I ask him for professional advice.

When I got back to the front I was lucky enough to find a job which I owe to my social status, something that had already gained me the attention of the nurses in the hospital. I also owe it to the skeletal state of the company to which I was attached. We are reinforcements, sent to fill the holes in a regiment that has returned from Verdun, where it suffered great losses. To restore the regiment's structure, they drew on the new arrivals, relying on the information contained in the regimental roll. The lieutenant summoned me to check that I matched my profession, and made me a runner.

Being is a runner is far better than being an ordinary squad soldier, which is 'the lowest of trades'. Every man's ambition is to get out of the squad. There are only two ways: get some stripes or get a job. In the middle of 1916 it's too late to try to move up through the ranks and the only chance of rapid promotion is in the attack units, where NCOs and officers are quickly decimated. But in units like these, being an NCO or junior officer does nothing to reduce the risks and offers few advantages. And anyway we're all civilians, only temporary soldiers, and whatever rank we may reach, our intention is to go home when the war is over – soon, we hope. The ambition that might have driven a sergeant in 1800 is denied us: field-marshals don't come from the ranks any more. This war brings no distinction, no advancement to those who risk their lives, it doesn't pay. For all these reasons, jobs are more sought-after than stripes. A cook is considered better off than the leader of a battalion in a great many cases and a company commandant can envy a colonel's secretary. A man who leaves for divisional headquarters is considered saved, without any doubt. He may still get killed, but it would be accidentally, by fate, like civilians can get run over or die in an earthquake. The problem for soldiers was how to get away from the front line, from the parapets and loopholes, how to avoid lookout duty, grenades, bullets, shells, to find a way back through the lines to the rear. You do this, and get a degree of safety, by becoming a telephonist, a signaller, a carrier pigeon handler, cyclist, observer, secretary, cook, interpreter, stretcher-bearer, sapper, etc. Those who got such jobs, 'cushy numbers', were called *dug-ins*[25] by the men of the forward pickets beyond the front lines. As soon as you leave the front line, you belong to the dug-ins, a category with many branches extending right up to the Ministry of War and General Army HQ. Once you've been 'dug in' your greatest dread is to be sent back to the squad.

So I am, to an extent, a dug-in. And therefore, unless something unexpected happens, my days as a bomber are over. I thank my lucky stars, because my unfortunate initiation the previous year has put me off fighting with hand grenades for good.

There are four runners (one per platoon), always at the beck and call of the company commandant, either to accompany him or to take his orders to the front line and bring back information. I am also secretary and topographer, when needed. These extra duties got me dispensation from fatigues.

Every evening at about six o'clock I go to battalion HQ to make a copy of the day's report for the company logbook. It's a twenty-minute walk through a deserted zone.

I return later along a pleasant path known as the *Reaper*

Trench. There's nothing grim about this reaper – the name comes from an old piece of farm machinery half-buried in the ground. The trench isn't deep and on one side you have a view across a broad meadow covered in wild flowers; in this month of June you can breathe in the sweet scent of the countryside. Mountain breezes make the grass ripple and wave like corn before harvest in peacetime. On the horizon the sun goes down over the dark pine forests like a hot-air balloon in flames on a holiday evening. On the other side of the trench the war is slumbering, but the sleeper can awake at any moment and treacherously dispatch the bucolic calm of the sunset, like a sentry caught unawares, crowning our positions with fire. This constant menace adds to the solemnity of the dusk.

We are occupying a rest sector in the Vosges where there was a lot of fighting a few months ago for possession of a few ridges that we now hold. This battle has lent a tragic aspect to the landscape, with piles of broken, twisted equipment and collapsed shelters, mysterious and silent like ancient burial grounds, dark and damp as catacombs. But still the men have got a bit of peace, and vegetation has reconquered the land, covering it with creepers and shoots and pistils and colours, spreading its blanket of perfumes that have driven out the smell of corpses, bringing its train of insects, butterflies, birds and lizards to dart and dance across this now benevolent battlefield.

Along the trenches overhanging plants brush our faces, and on the right of the sector, well back from the lines, I've found a place where no one goes, a place so green it dazzles you. The wind murmurs in the leaves of tall trees, still standing, and a pure stream cascades merrily over the rocks, before disappearing into the brush. It is there I live out the hours I steal from the war.

Down in the valley a road runs between the German trenches and ours, a distance of three hundred metres, a pretty, country road, bordered with spindly plane trees and covered with the fallen leaves from last autumn, a road forbidden on pain of death.

This empty highway has great charm and though men cannot venture on to it, their thoughts can wander there. As the mist of morning clears, the ploughmen in their look-out posts must be waiting for the crack of whips and clanking of harnesses as the horses are led to the fields. In the evening it can become a forsaken avenue leading to some mysterious castle, where ancient shades roam in the twilight beneath the trees. What makes this road so striking is that it leads nowhere, if not to the unreal, to peaceful places that now exist only in memory. Between the two armies, the phantom road offers a silent path for dreams.

At a desolate crossroads, I found an old metal Christ-figure, stained with rust like dried blood. On its stone plinth, scarred by bullets, a clumsy hand had scrawled: 'evacuate to rear'. I do not think there was anything blasphemous in it, no allusion to the divinity of the subject. The soldier wanted to say that the man on the cross had already paid his debt and had no further reason to remain at the front. Or perhaps he had wanted to show that, to have the right to be evacuated, you must have suffered agony, like the agony of Christ, in all your limbs, in your body and your heart.

Our front line runs along the foot of the mountain whose heights we control. Battalion and company HQs are spread out on the plateau, and a reserve company is stationed behind, in the forest. We overlook the German trenches that run round the ruins of the hamlet of Launois. Our over-extended sector is defended by sentries provided by the platoons to cover the flanks, posted at fifty to hundred-metre intervals. Very little artillery fire comes our way. Once a week, four German guns sprinkle us with about thirty shells. Once that's over, we can be sure we will be undisturbed for another week. Our own shelling is more random. From our second lines that snake round the cornice, I sometimes see shells from our 75s hitting the German earthworks or bursting in the countryside. But neither side is trying desperately hard; the gunners are simply carrying out exercises, because it is still a war and in war you fire guns. Nonetheless, one has to watch out for an unlucky shell: 'Those stupid bastards are quite capable of blowing you up for a laugh!' And recently we were almost victims of our own stupid carelessness for scorning these periodic bombardments: a 77 burst in the wall of the trench, three metres from where we were standing.

As for the infantry, it does its best to avoid disturbing such a peaceful and pleasantly rural sector. Any provocations won't come from us, unless orders from the rear force us to be aggressive. Activity is limited to rigorous sentry duty, fairly relaxed in the daytime, more attentive at night. We have got used to this sector and all we want is to stay here.

Every two days, a cyclist goes down to get supplies in the village of Saint-Dié. The following day he tours the shelters with his packs like a travelling salesman, distributing shoelaces, pipes, mirrors, combs, soap, toothpaste, notepaper, postcards, tobacco, and jotting down new orders like a proper tradesman.

Each group sends a man laden with water bottles to the canteen and he comes back after a three-hour walk, with thirty or forty kilos of wine hanging from his belt and shoulders. These devoted comrades are usually drunkards and one can be sure that generous sampling en route has lightened their load. 'Reckon we can hold out here all right!' say the men.

My duties allow me considerable freedom. In the mornings I sleep in, after staying up late, and by the time I've finished washing in a bowl, breakfast arrives. In the afternoons I set off with Baboin. And in the evenings, back at battalion HQ, I work alongside the lieutenant drawing up a map of the sector, using our notes and measurements. Around eleven I take my cane, a revolver and a gas mask, and make a tour of the trenches to find out what's happening and gather accounts of the day's events. If any grenades are going off ahead of us or if there is machine-gunning (they use enfilade fire against some communication trenches), I wake up a comrade. If it's a calm night – as it usually is – I walk alone. I go along the front lines, identifying myself to sentries who recognise my steps and my voice in the darkness, and exchange a few words with them. When I'm not in a hurry, I may stop and keep one of them company for a moment. Sitting on the fire-step, our heads above the parapet, we look out at the night, listen for sounds. I have discussions with the platoon leaders, who wait for me at agreed times. An hour later I wake up our company commandant, a primary school teacher who treats his men cordially and his staff with a hint of camaraderie: 'Nothing to report, sir!' 'All quiet around the 3rd platoon?' 'Completely quiet, sir!' When it rains, I heat up the last of the coffee on Baboin's spirit lamp. I bid goodnight to the lookout who has his post ten metres from there, and I return to our shelter where my three comrades are snoring.

One night I woke with a start; someone was shaking me roughly. I groaned, eyes still shut. A voice quivering with rage said: 'Jump to it, for christ's sake!'

It was the voice of Beaucierge, the runner for the 1st platoon, a good lad, rough and ready, who did not usually speak to me like that.

'What's got into you?' I demanded, crossly.

'The Boche are at the front line… We've got to go and see what's happening.'

What?… I understood: his voice wasn't quivering with rage but with panic. Still befuddled by sleep, I got my kit together mechanically, in silence. Outside, the night air was cool on my forehead and eyelids. There were no sounds of fighting. Had the enemy already occupied the forward trench?

'Where are these Boche?'

'No one knows. We got to go and look.'

'Who said we must go and look?'

'The lieutenant.'

Dirty business! I remember the embankment in Artois. I slip some grenades in my pockets, tighten my chinstrap, cock my pistol which I keep in my hand… who's going first?

'You know the trenches better,' claims Beaucierge.

Behind me I hear him sliding the bolt on his rifle, which he holds in one hand like they do in the colonial infantry.

'What are you doing?'

'Putting a round in the chamber.'

'Oh no, old pal, I don't want to get a bullet in my arse! In that case, you go in front…'

He prefers to remove the bullet. I move forward slowly, to give myself time to think: we have a choice of three routes to reach the front lines. I finally make up my mind:

'We'll take the covered trench.'

It's an old underground trench, constructed by the Germans, and comes out by the shelter of the leader of the 2nd platoon. If we are at all uncertain we can use our torches to see what's happening. We advance nervously, trying not to make a sound. The silence of the night is more terrifying than the sound of a grenade fight, which would at least tell us where the danger was. All of a sudden the underground trench opens up in front of us like a trapdoor. We go down a few steps, we lose sight of the sky which guided us, we descend into darkness. Holding one hand out in front of us, feeling the trench wall, we step forward one foot at a time, not putting any weight down until we are sure the ground is solid. It's fifty metres to the first elbow in the trench, after that it descends straight ahead. It takes us an infinitely long time to cover this distance. All we can hear is our breathing and our heartbeats. Beaucierge (clumsy as ever, the dolt!) bangs into something with his rifle. We freeze in terror, and stay stock still for a minute, dreading the flashes of fire that may be about to pierce the blackness.

But now here we are at the curve… Further down, some sixty

metres ahead, a faint light glimmers, and we can make out the murmur of voices. What voices? I stop my companion with my hand.

'We'll call out.'

'What if it's the Boche?'

'Then we'll know it. Better than walking straight into them.'

I call and the answer comes: 'Who goes there?'

'France!'

Soon the beam of my torch reveals a man who is one of ours. Phew!…We run up to him in relief. Down in the shelter, everyone is on the alert.

'So what happened to the Boche?'

'They've left again.'

We learn that three Germans jumped into our trench and attacked a lone sentry who, though taken by surprise, managed to shout the alarm. Luckily, not far to his right, Chassignole was still awake, and he is a man who doesn't easily lose his nerve. Chassignole is the one who claims that the damp gets into grenades and half of them don't work. After striking the exterior percussion cap he would hold the grenade up to his ear to make sure that the fuse was burning properly inside: a method of verification that could take your head off! If you pointed out his recklessness, he'd say: 'You've got five seconds, plenty of time!' So Chassignole started running at the Boches, throwing his famous grenades, his favourite weapon. The attackers took fright, jumped back over the parapet, and disappeared into the night.

The sentry is in a corner of the shelter, still dazed from a blow from a revolver butt that cut his head. We congratulate him for raising the alarm and not letting himself be taken prisoner. It's agreed that the raid was well planned and could have succeeded, that the Germans had found the weak point in our positions. It seems likely that their patrols had been observing the movements of our reliefs for several nights. And we are careless: sentries make a noise and light cigarettes without any precautions. Always hiding doesn't suit our temperament.

This was the first event to disturb the calm of the sector for a month. From now on, we will also patrol in front of our lines.

We have decided to celebrate the Fourteenth of July. The Republic has already given the troops one cigar and one orange each, and a bottle of sparkling wine for every four men, but we would hope for something a bit better in the way of festivities than this meagre generosity. The lieutenant had the idea of organising a fireworks display for that night, using flares; he had to abandon the idea of coloured flares in case it alerted the artillery. A conspicuous spot was chosen, in an abandoned trench, and the runners went to tell the platoons so that they could enjoy the show, and also keep on the alert in case the enemy reacted. In the end, it isn't so much a display of patriotism as a means to break the monotony of our lives for a few short moments.

A little before the event is due to start the lieutenant leaves his shelter accompanied by his runner, his batman, some quartermasters and observers. A dozen flares are arranged in a semicircle next to the parapet. At exactly ten o'clock we light the touch-papers. The flares whistle up into the night, and turn into twelve flickering light bulbs, spreading a pale, luminous dome beneath them. A few flares answer us from the opposite lines. We stare in wonder at this new lunar landscape, and, after counting three, we all shout 'Vive la France!' But our shouts are lost in the ring of mountains looming in the darkness and have no echo. The flares die, and our artificial joy goes out with them. No sound come from the German trenches, silence and darkness reclaim the land. We're disappointed. The party's over...

The only onslaught in this sector is of paperwork. The men at the rear bombard us with notes, and not a day goes by without the company having to provide the battalion, always as a matter of urgency, with reports and inventories, on stocks of food and munitions, on supplies of clothing, on specialists suitable for one task or another, on fathers of a certain number of children, etc. So much, indeed, that the runners are always dashing about to keep up with all the nonsense.

Thus I have got to know everyone, and everyone knows me, asking me questions about what's happening at the rear: a runner is also a vital source of information. Even the platoon leaders, who cannot leave the front line, hold me in respect and I sometimes help them prepare their reports. But the main benefit for me from this toing and froing, where the time we take isn't rigidly controlled, is that it allows me to stop at different shelters and talk to the men. Their numbers swollen by successive reinforcements, the units are made up of men from every part of the country and every part of the front, most of them having been wounded and having belonged to other regiments. They all have their own memories. Through their stories, I get to know every aspect of the war, for it is their favourite topic of conversation, being the thing that has brought them together and filled their lives for the last two years.

Naturally Verdun comes up a lot. There the use of artillery, the accumulation of means of destruction, reached a level of intensity hitherto unknown, and everyone agrees it was a hell in which you lost your mind. With the help of their accounts, confused as they often are, I reconstitute the epic story of the regiment in this terrible sector. It's a shameful epic, if, as historians will, you judge by the results. But a soldier judges from his experience under fire and knows that the conduct of a unit usually results from the situation in which it has been placed, and has little do with the courage of the combatants. This is what I learned.

Last April, the regiment was engaged in front of Malancourt, in a salient, a position 'out in the open', with no communication or support on the flanks, and it was kept in this position despite all the warnings from battalion leaders who had pointed out its vulnerability under concentrated fire. When the action started, two battalions stood to face the attack, but they were outflanked, overwhelmed by the masses of troops that swarmed out of the shell smoke, and taken prisoner, almost to a man. Only some support elements were able to fall back and these included one ambitious captain. This cunning officer, displaying considerable nerve in his presentation of the facts, estimated that no official enquiry would come and investigate what had happened on the ground. His report transformed our accidental defeat into a tale of defence to the last man, of the sacrifice made by a thousand soldiers, refusing to yield an inch of ground, and now buried in the ruins. This version, in perfect concordance with military doctrine, was immediately adopted by the colonel, who transmitted it to the division, adding a few amplifications of his own. For it is accepted, by some strange aberration, that a great loss of men proves the courage of those who command them – by virtue of that axiom of the military hierarchy which states that the valour of soldiers is created by the valour of their leaders, an axiom which does not have a converse form. So the colonel published a dispatch in which he exalted the nobility of the sacrifice and proclaimed his pride at commanding such valiant troops. The regiment would have therefore left Verdun crowned in glory, had a German aeroplane not had the poor taste to scatter leaflets on our lines in which the enemy command boasted of its success at Malancourt and added a list of the prisoners taken that day – several hundred men, officers as well as soldiers, all from that same regiment. There was no room for doubt: the sacrifice had not been consummated. Learning that these men, over whose loss tears were still being shed, were in fact alive enraged the colonel, who published a furious, scathing counter-dispatch.

The surrender of two battalions taken by surprise cast suspicion on a regiment that had been sent out into untenable positions. As someone had to be held responsible, the high command incriminated those who had disappeared, as they weren't there to defend themselves. It was recalled that the regiment came from the Midi and absurd old grievances that dated back to the beginning of the war were used against it. This military vilification put it into the category of unreliable units which had displayed weakness under fire. And that has earned us a long stay in the Vosges, exiled from honour. The colonel, who sees his chances of promotion jeopardised, complains bitterly. But the men don't hide their delight, and are in no hurry to regain 'esteem' which is so often deadly.

The survivors, men who have already endured dangers and torment beyond normal human comprehension, speak of Verdun with special horror. They say that when they got out they couldn't eat properly for several days because their stomachs had been so knotted with fear, because everything filled them with disgust. They have remembered nothing from Verdun except terror and madness. Except one thing, which always brings a smile to their lips. They tell of a crossroads behind the lines where they saw three gendarmes who had been strung up from a tree by colonial troops as they passed through. This is the only happy memory they have retained from Verdun! It never crosses their minds that gendarmes are men like them. The hatred of the gendarme, so traditional in France, has been intensified in the war by the scorn – or envy – that soldiers feel towards the non-combatant. And gendarmes not only do not fight, but they force others to do so. Behind the lines they form a network of jailers who force us back into the prison of the war. It is also said that during the retreat of 1914 they killed stragglers who no longer had the strength to march. So the execution of a few gendarmes lifts the spirits and avenges the forced labour they have inflicted on the men. Everyone feels like that and I have not seen a single soldier show the slightest pity for the three hanged men. There's no doubt that this 'special operation' has done more to boost the reputation of colonial troops that any brilliant military action would have done.

Who can say whether it hasn't indeed done a service to the High Command by getting the army of Verdun to laugh? Of course it's immoral. So this is the occasion to use the famous phrase which has already excused so many other immoralities: *It's war!*

A sergeant who has just arrived offers me another picture of Verdun. He describes a feat of arms:

'I was a grenadier sergeant. One evening we take up position on the flank of a devastated slope. No trace of barbed wire, or shell holes, position of Boche unknown. Once we'd sorted ourselves out, the commander, Moricault, an old bloke with a big mouth, summoned me. I found him in his little dugout, smoking his pipe. Handing me a quarter-litre of brandy he says: "Ah, good, th-there you are, Simon. I have need of you. Have y'self a nip of this!"

'He unrolls his map. "You're there, see? There, on the side, is, er, Permezel (another NCO). Good! You see? And there is a Boche machine gun that's bothering us. Now, you go and work it out with Permezel. You'll come from the front with your chaps, and he'll, er, come from the right with his. And at midnight, you blow the bloody machine gun to hell. Understood?" "Understood, sir!"

'You can't argue with the old buffer! So off I go and find Permezel, tell him the plan, sort out the details and synchronise watches. I pick three blokes to come with me: Rondin, a tall, beefy chap, Cartouchier, a miner from the north, and Zigg, an ace with the knife. Choice of weapons: bombs, shooters and shivs. We crawl forwards, hopping from one hole to the next, guided by flares. The racket from the bombardment helps a bit. The further we get from our side, the slower we go. It takes us a good hour. All of a sudden, Zigg tugs at my arm, makes a sign. I poke my head out of the hole, very carefully, and I see two helmets, maybe six metres away, Boche heads. I tell you, we were eye to eye, without making a peep. We all huddle down in our holes but don't take our eyes off each other. Don't stop to think! I give the nod to the others and, hop!, with one move we pile into them. There were three Boche, two get away and we nab the other one. But the pig rolls on the ground, trying to grab his rifle. Rondon catches him, gives him half a dozen good kicks in the ribs to calm him down and then we all get out quick, back to the commandant's dugout. Once inside we take a good look at our Fritz, a young bloke, brand new uniform, his mug a bit the worse for wear thanks to Rondin. Old man Moricault interrogates him in German but he's not saying anything. So our quartermaster captain gets up, and puts his revolver against his temple. My god, did he go white! And then he told us everything: they were all behind the ridge and were supposed to attack at four in the morning. That saved our bacon. The machine gunners put one belt through after another and at ten to four started firing even faster.'

'So the Germans didn't attack?'

'Not at four they didn't, but at nine. We were knackered, half-asleep. Only old father Moricault was up and about, with his pipe and cane and big mouth. He was the one who sounded the alarm, and then he grabbed hold of a machine gun. He had balls, that old bloke. The Boche were swarming around only sixty metres away and they were coming up fast.'

'They didn't get there?'

'No chance. We had six machine guns in action right off. Can't do anything against machine guns!… I never seen so many going down as I did then!'

'Not as many as I have', says the machine gunner sergeant who is listening to us. 'When we were fighting in open country, I was with the Zouaves. There was one time when there were three of us gunners dug in behind tree trunks on the edge of a forest, on a little rise. We opened fire on battalions that were coming out at four hundred metres, and we didn't stop firing. A surprise attack. It was frightful. The terrified Boche couldn't get out of the way of our bullets. Bodies piled up in heaps. Our gun crews were shaking with horror and wanted to run. *Killing made us afraid!*… I've never seen such a massacre. We had three Saint-Étiennes, they spit out six hundred a minute. Imagine it.'

'But when you saw the Boche six metres away in the shell-hole', I asked the grenadier sergeant, curious to know more, 'how did you decide to rush them?'

'It just needs a nod and a wave, like I say. We know the way it works. While the Boche were still making up their minds, we got going. It's the ones with balls that scare the others, and the ones who are scared most are buggered. You mustn't think in a situation like that. It's all bluff, war!'

Before moving to Verdun, for a long time the regiment had held the F— sector, which was so dangerous that units were replaced after three days on the front line. The men all tell me that during those three days they had practically no sleep at all, because of the great quantity of German trench mortars that were smashing up their positions. The 'aerial torpedoes' and heavy trench mortar shells are stealthy projectiles which cause terrible damage because of their considerable explosive charge. The explosion is not preceded by the whistle that alerts you to incoming shells. The only way to avoid falling victim to them is to spot them in the air after the small bang when they're launched, and try to work out where they will land, so as to get out the way. At night they provoke an obsessive fear that makes this method of attack the most demoralising of all. And on top of all this the mortar shells necessitate an exhausting amount of digging in order to repair collapsed trenches; cases of men being buried alive are common. Nerves are strained to breaking point. After a while, depression makes soldiers capable of just about anything. It's an open secret that at F— there were cases of soldiers deliberately injuring themselves. Many wounds were so suspicious that one brutal army doctor kept corpses on which to test the effects of projectiles fired at short range so that he could spot similar results on the injured men who were brought to him. This same doctor had some men court-martialled for having frostbitten feet. The soldiers who admit self-injury consider this is iniquitous: frostbite is an involuntary result of standing in frozen mud.

Initially, the easiest way of getting a good wound was to place your hand over a lookout slit that had been targeted by snipers. This had been used in several places. But bullets in the hand, particularly the left hand, quickly became inadmissible. Another method was to ignite the fuse on a grenade and put it and your own hand on one side of a splinter-proof shield: your forearm is blown off. It seems that some men had recourse to this. It could not be denied that to perform such an act of cowardice requires considerable courage and terrible despair. Despair, in the most punishing sectors, can provoke the most absurd decisions; men have assured me that at Verdun soldiers killed themselves for fear of suffering an agonising death. It is also whispered that at F— some veterans from the Bat d'Af wounded their own comrades. They polished shell shrapnel to make it look new, put it in a cartridge from which they had removed the bullet and then fired it into the person's leg at a spot agreed on in advance. They charged for it, and made a bit of money out of this dirty work. I have certainly heard soldiers expressing the wish to have a limb amputated to escape the front line. In general, the rougher, simpler men fear death but can bear pain and mutilation. Whereas the more sensitive ones are less afraid of death itself than the forms it takes here, of the agony and suffering that precedes it.

Soldiers talk plainly of these things, without approving or condemning, because war has accustomed them to seeing what is monstrous as natural. To them, the greatest injustice is that others dispose of their lives without asking them, and have lied to them in bringing them here. This legalised injustice cancels out all morality, and in their opinion all conventions decreed by those far away from the fighting concerning honour, courage, noble attitudes, and so on, cannot concern them, soldiers on the front line. The shellfire zone has its own laws, of which they are the only judges. They declare, without the slightest trace of shame: 'We're only there because we don't have any choice!' They are the navvies of war, and they know that the only person who profits from their labour is the boss. The dividends will go the generals, the politicians, the factory owners. The heroes will return to the plough and the work bench, as poor as before. They laugh bitterly when they hear that word, 'heroes'. They refer to themselves as *good lads*, that is, ordinary chaps, neither bellicose nor aggressive, the ones who march and kill without knowing why. The good lads, that is, the pitiful, mud-caked, moaning, bleeding brotherhood of the P.C.D.F.,[26] as they call themselves sarcastically. Cannon fodder, in short. 'Coffin candidates', as Chassignole puts it.

They approach the terrible conflict with a simple logic. The following exchange can give some idea of this. I had gone to get information from a sentry in a forward post. It was raining hard. The man was standing in the mud, dripping wet.

'There'll never be an end to this shit!' he grumbled.

'Yes there will, old pal, it can't go on forever.'

'Oh jesus!... If they stuck old Joffre here in my hole, and old Hindenburg opposite, with the lads on both sides cheering the bastards on, they'd soon sort out their bloody war!'

If you think about it, this reasoning isn't as simplistic as it seems. Indeed it's full of human truth, a truth that the *poilus* also express like this: *It's always the same ones that get themselves killed!*

The idea of duty varies according to one's place in the hierarchy, one's rank, and the dangers one faces. Among soldiers it comes down to a simple solidarity between men, in a shell-hole or a trench, a solidarity that doesn't consider the campaign as a whole or its aims, and isn't inspired by what we like to call ideals, but by the needs of the moment. As such, it can lead to self-sacrifice, and men risk their lives to help their comrades. The further one gets from the front, the more the idea of duty is separated from risk. In the highest ranks, it is entirely theoretical, a pure intellectual game. It merges with concern for one's responsibilities, reputation, and advancement, unites personal success with national success, which are in opposition for those doing the fighting. And it is used against subordinates just as much as the enemy. A particular conception of duty among men who possess unlimited power and not a trace of sensitivity to temper their doctrines can lead to vile abuses, both military and disciplinary. Such as this one, a decision made by a certain General N— worthy of Robespierre in its glacial ruthlessness, described to me by a corporal-telephonist sitting in front of his switchboard.

He had just been transmitting messages, his headphones over his ears, and I was asking him how the equipment worked.

'Can you hear what people are saying?'

'At a central exchange, yes. I just have to arrange the plugs on the board in a certain way.'

'Have you ever overheard any unusual conversations, ones that might reveal something useful about the war?'

'You learn more about people than events on the telephone. Important orders, unless they're very urgent, are sent in writing… But yes, sure, I remember one short, and tragic conversation. This was back in autumn '14, when I was telephonist for the division, before we were withdrawn. First you need to know that a soldier had been court-martialled. He had gone to the quartermaster to ask for new trousers to replace his, which were ripped. Clothing was in very short supply. The quartermaster gives him trousers that had belonged to a dead soldier, still bloodstained. Naturally enough, the chap is disgusted. "Take them, that's an order," says the quartermaster. He refuses. An officer turns up and tells the quartermaster to charge him with disobeying an order. Court martial straight away… Now, back to my telephone call. The colonel of the regiment asks to be connected to the general. I put him through, and listen in without thinking: "This is colonel X… Sir, the court martial has issued its judgement in the matter that you already know about, but I need to consult you because it seems to me that there are extenuating circumstances... The court martial has sentenced him to death. Don't you think, sir, that a death sentence is really too harsh, and that it should be reconsidered?..." Now listen to the general's answer: *"Yes, you're right, it's harsh, very harsh...* [There's a pause, long enough to count to fifteen.] *So, the execution will take place tomorrow morning, do the necessary."* Not another word.'

'They shot him?'

'They shot him!'

I know of course that general N— was only thinking of the national interest, the maintenance of discipline, the solidity of the army. I know that he acted in the name of the highest principles. But when the ordinary soldier here at the front considers the fact that in the name of the very same principles, with the same inhuman rigour, the same dogmatic certainty, this same general will take similar military decisions affecting thousands of individuals, then he can only shake with fear!

There is a man in the company who was at the Butte de Vauquois, the centre of the infamous 'mine war'. He tells of how in 1915 he witnessed an attack with flame-throwers aimed at capturing this disputed hill. The Paris fire brigade were brought to set it up. Tanks for the inflammable liquid were placed in a gully and pipes laid along trenches connecting them to the flame-throwers. The enterprise might have succeeded had it not been for the stubbornness of general S— who forced the fire-brigade captain to launch the attack on a day when the wind was uncertain. All went well to start with. The Germans fled in terror from the flames. But a sudden change in the wind direction blew the fire back at us, and our sector, in its turn, went up in flames. The installation of the equipment, which had cost us a great deal of effort, was completely destroyed, and we did not take the hill that day.

This same man, who is called Martin, also tells of how his company had been led by a young lieutenant, a graduate of Saint-

Cyr, who had been trepanned and had also lost the fingers of both hands, and yet had returned to the front as a volunteer. This officer came from a wealthy family and every week his mother would send a big parcel of food for her son's men. All this had made a great impression on Martin, who declared:

'You never know. There are sometimes even posh types who've got guts!'

'That's for sure,' agreed another. 'There are some who really believe in what they're doing.'

'Yeah, old pal,' says a third, 'and they're the most dangerous. Without them we wouldn't be here. They got 'em in Boche-land too, believe you me!'

'More than likely!'

'It ain't the same. Boche officers treat their lads a lot fucking worse than ours do.'

'That's what you hear but I reckon it's just the same as with us, they've got all kinds.'

'It ain't so much that our lot are all bastards. But when it comes to loonies, we take the fucking biscuit.'

'You remember that commandant we had in Besançon before the war, the old bloke who was completely barmy? What was he called, the wanker? Giffard, yeah, that's right, Giffard. He used to come and wash his underwear in the barracks with us. And when he was cross with his horse he'd make it sleep in the guardroom, I kid you not, the guardroom. You ask Rochat. Mad as a bloody hatter!'

'Biggest arsehole I ever knew was a captain who went around with a thing in his pocket that he used to measure the length of your hair. If it was too long, you'd catch it. In another pocket he had a pair of hair-clippers. He'd whack you across the nose with it, bang!, when you were presenting arms. So as soon as you had enough hair on your bonce for a parting, you had to get yourself to the barber.'

'Me, the worst was old Floconnet, the commandant we had

in Champagne. He spent his time hunting turds that had been dropped in the wrong place. The *poilus* used to go for a crap on a path on the edge of the village, and the old bloke never failed to come and have a good prowl round, every morning. He'd come up with this amazing scheme. He had a cane with a metal tip and he'd use it to pick up the paper on the ground and then he'd take it all to the adjutant and tell him: "Here, take this, see what it says, sort it out for me and give each of those dirty beasts four days in the glasshouse." Now, since the *poilus* all used envelopes to wipe their arses, by now it was brown paper! But it had belonged to someone, and their name was on it. In the end we used envelopes on which we'd put the address of the old bastard himself…'

'You ever hear about that adjutant they used to call Tapioca?'

Once they start a discussion like this it can go on forever. Everyone has his own store of tales to contribute and barracks life provides a large supply of them. It's strange to see how often these memories, that one would think were a bit out of date, keep coming up in conversations at the front. *Poilus* like to recall the days of their training (now seen as 'the good old days' in comparison to the present) and the reproach they always make to the new recruits among their comrades, young lads who are generally undisciplined, is the following: 'You can see that you've never done *active* service!' Another thing is that most of their memories are coarse ones. That's not because they choose those especially – it's because they do not have any others. Military life has always offered them far more vulgarity than nobility, and they would be hard put to find any ideal role models – whether corporals or adjutants, those above them are their oppressors, not necessarily evil but always as ridiculous as they are ignorant. And as for the senior ranks, apart from line officers who share their dangers to a certain extent, they are all upper-crust types whose follies are frequent, dangerous and protected by divine right.

* * * * *

Still in the Vosges, we are now in a new sector, tougher than the last one, on the summit of a mountain whose ridges we also hold. Throughout this region the two sides have fought to control the mountain tops, which provide commanding views, and bombardments have left many bald patches on the pine-covered slopes. The names of these peaks have all earned mentions in dispatches: Hartmann, Syudel, Linge, Metzeral, La Fontenelle, Teischaker, etc. We are above the valley of Sainte-Marie-aux-Mines.

The battalion HQ and the reserve company are stationed on the reverse slope of the mountain, in camps along the road running up from the valley on the French side of the border. The line companies hold two adjacent sectors, one on the high point of the mountain, the other which follows the descending contours of the terrain and runs off towards the German lines. This second sector, which is ours, is more dangerous because the position has no depth. An attack which advances 150 metres would push us back into the gulley right behind us. At the bottom of this gulley we would be at the mercy of enfilade fire from the German machine guns, and no fallback position has been created on the opposite slope. Fortunately, the sector is quiet. But if there was a surprise attack, our situation would be terribly precarious.

The ground has been pulverised hundreds of times by trench mortars. Nothing remains of the forest but a few tree trunks stripped of their bark that look like fence posts. We made ourselves as comfortable as we could. The platoons have a few covered saps in the front line. Further back, shelters are rare, rickety, and uncomfortable. In general, our shelters aren't as good as the German ones. This is probably because we thought we would be on the offensive. Our troops always believed they were holding their trenches temporarily and so it wasn't worth the effort of undertaking major work.

I have started my nightly rounds again. This time they are rather more exciting since the German lines are very close to ours – around twenty or thirty metres away. And at one point the gap is only eight metres. This proximity prevents the construction of any solid defences. So, given the way our sentries are spread out, I find myself alone in the darkness, closer to the Germans than the French. The watchers opposite can hear me walking and at any moment I could be seized by men positioned by their parapet, who would only have to reach out their arm to grab me. I hold my revolver at the ready and I've got a couple of grenades in my pockets. Any confidence these weapons give me is completely illusory; they would be of no help at all against several assailants, leaping out of the shadows, able to get back to their trenches in a few steps, taking me with them, before our lads had the time to intervene. In any case, our front line is guarded by eight double sentry posts, that is, sixteen men in all, spread out over five or six hundred metres. Before running to my aid they would first have to alert their comrades, always slow to get going after being woken up.

On very dark nights, when I have to feel my way along the trenches, there are occasionally heart-stopping moments when something makes a noise in the blackness. Night distorts things, makes them bigger, lends them shapes that can be disturbing or menacing; the least breath of air can bring them to life. Objects take on enemy silhouettes, and I imagine soldiers holding their breath all around me, eyes peering to seek me out, fingers on triggers; at any second I expect the blinding flash of a gunshot. They could kill me for the sheer pleasure of killing. I know this sector quite well but I keep stopping, wondering if I haven't got lost, and everything around me is strange, shifting, oneiric. A distance that I covered the day before without noticing now goes on forever, to the point where I begin to think our trenches are empty. But I am not here to be prey to childish fears: I try to laugh myself out of it... And at long last I find our sentries and go down into the warmth of an underground shelter where a candle is flickering and sleepers snore and splutter. I wake up the platoon leader, who signs my papers and gives me his. We exchange a few words and then here I am again facing the traps in the silent shadows. I stride off into the gloom, walking noisily, whistling a marching tune in the Germans' direction, hoping that my confidence will impress any enemies who are waiting to ambush me. I make my presence known before reaching the point where the lines almost touch: *I'm fooling them*... All this noise, I'm thinking, must surely make the enemies who are there, a few metres way, think that those who are advancing are unafraid, and it would not be a very good idea to attack them. I think the noise is multiplying me, making me seem like a crowd...

Back at HQ, the lieutenant greets me normally, seemingly unaware that I have just fought a terrible battle with the phantoms of the night and my imagination, and my heart is still pounding in my chest... And I smile cheerfully as if I've come back from a pleasant stroll in the country. But one day I may well not come back. I may not have had any trouble on my rounds so far, but nonetheless I only survive them thanks to the goodwill of the Germans. Still, I don't seriously think I am going to get killed. And when it's a fine night, and my path is illuminated only by the searchlight of the moon, that friendly and vigilant sentry, then this walk has a certain charm, along the side of these silent, disdainful mountains.

In the end we are only fighting a little war here, a war of convention, entirely regulated by tacit agreements. It's not to be taken too seriously, nothing to boast of. Very occasionally we face bursts of shellfire, coming from a ridge higher up where the Germans have their artillery. The noise of the explosions rolls around the valleys, making an avalanche of sound that crashes against the side of a distant mountain, which sends it on to another, until it is completely dispersed. Sometimes, too, we get attacked with hand- and rifle-grenades, to which we respond half-heartedly so as not to aggravate matters. In positions that are so close, so narrow, these things could quickly become very bloody. We never initiate any action ourselves. The regiment does its job decently enough but avoids any excess of enthusiasm like the plague. We leave feats of valour to others.

Every now and then one of our aeroplanes will fly over. They are Farman biplanes, old models, deplorably slow, known as 'chicken coops'. We feel sorry for their pilots and have the feeling the Germans must laugh at the sight of such ancient machines, which seem to date to the beginnings of aviation.

In short, this front is protected by a very thin line of troops. This light deployment allows divisions to be concentrated in active sectors. Here we rely on the towering bulwark of the mountains which would make any big offensive difficult. We are here to watch over these natural fortifications.

At about five in the evening a series of violent explosions shakes the entire sector, prolonged explosions accompanied by the sound of tearing metal that characterises trench torpedoes. Here we go! Immediately the bombardment takes on the rapid rhythm of a barrage, the explosions forming a background rumble broken at regular intervals by the impact of the heavy projectiles, enough to shake the mountain. Our own trench artillery responds rapidly. We quickly grab our weapons and run from the command post, on a narrow spur where we risk being surrounded. We must get through the first detonations before it's too late and the entrance to our trench is cut off. The reserve platoon, who have just climbed up a slope to join us, are pushing and stumbling behind, gasping for breath, shouting, rattling their weapons. We run under the whistling shells, through the yellow smoke, with huge pieces of shrapnel whizzing past like axes and smashing into the ground around us. For thirty metres the trench is as hot as an oven. Then we breathe cooler air, the menace of the flying cleavers is lifted from our necks, and we can see daylight. We're in the communication trench.

As this trench pushes on towards the rear, skirting the flank of a spur, the mountain itself rises up and protects us with a steep slope still densely covered with trees. There are now forty of us with a lieutenant, three hundred metres from our positions in a place that is almost completely sheltered. Shells seek us out but they burst above us or drop down into the gulley. They'd be very lucky to hit us in this dead angle. We just have to wait patiently.

The front-line platoons are ordered to fall back laterally at the first bombardment, closing up with the neighbouring companies. We aren't thinking about them, and it would be mad to try to link up with them right now. Each group is looking after itself, following set rules. Since shelling makes it impossible to hold this sector, the command has judged it preferable to abandon it altogether, then take it back afterwards with a counter-attack. But we know that this is simply a raid by an enemy group hoping to take prisoners. Caught by our own fire and finding the trenches empty, they'll clear out.

We listen to the bombardment. Violent explosions shake the ground even here. Shells that pass too low make us duck. A cloud of smoke hides our positions and despite our relative security, we're anxious.

After an hour, there are distinct gaps in the rumbling of explosions. The shelling gets less intense, falters, and quickly dies away. There are a few bursts of gunfire, then silence. Twilight descends. The reserve platoon forms up in battle order and advances cautiously. They don't encounter anyone. We get back to the command post, jumping over a few shell-holes.

Runners are sent off straight away to gather information from each platoon. The sector is unrecognisable. Trenches are blocked and I often have to walk along the parapets. Nearing the front line I call out to avoid walking into trouble. I reach the shelter on the far right of the company, its entrance facing the Germans, and climb down the rickety ladder. I find a few men with their sergeant.

'So, nothing serious?'

'Look!' says the sergeant.

I see a shape stretched out on the ground in a corner of the dugout, a broken body. One leg must be broken off at the hip because it's pointing in the wrong direction. The trousers are torn and reveal the pale thigh, almost cut off, which hasn't even bled. The other leg is also cut open.

'Who is it?'

'Sorlin.'

Sorlin, yes, I know him. A young man from class 16 who always gave me a friendly smile on my rounds... I bend down to look more closely. His eyes are shut but his mouth, that mouth that used to call out to me, is open and twisted. That young face that was always so cheerful bears an expression of terror. I hear the sergeant, a man of forty:

'A good kid, in this state! This war's a bloody disgrace!'

Stupidly, I ask:

'No other trouble?'

'Maybe you don't think this is enough!' he responds furiously.

I can feel how grief-stricken these men are, and their sadness is making them bitterly angry. I imagine what they've been through just now, the fear and panic under the bombardment, while I was back there in the trench, under cover...

'Look, sergeant, I think it's far too much, you know that. But I have to take back a report, they're waiting for me. I'll send stretcher-bearers.'

The other runners are also coming back to the command post. Two dead and four wounded in the platoon in the centre, none in the platoon on the left flank. In this now quiet sector, it's another evening of war, an evening of mourning. The lieutenant dictates a report which I write down to take to the battalion. Outside stretcher-bearers are asking where the wounded are. We guide them, in the darkness.

* * * * *

Later on I make my rounds. There's nothing but mounds of mud everywhere. Everyone is on the parapets, working. The trench, almost levelled, is being pegged out by a working party in a long line, their rifles lying on the ground beside them. Twenty metres away other shovels are clanging and you can clearly see shadows bending over the ground. The Germans are working on their side, and this whole part of the front is just one big building site.

Accompanied by a sergeant, we walk several metres out beyond our working party, driven by curiosity as much as bravado. A German shadow begins to cough loudly, to point out that we're breaking the rules, going beyond the limits of neutrality. We cough in our turn to reassure this vigilant watchman, and go back to our side. With no trenches separating them, these enemies, who could surprise their adversaries with a couple of leaps, respect the truce. Is this from a sense of fair play? Isn't it rather the wish, equal in both camps, to stop fighting?

About twice a month, our sectors get badly damaged by surprise attacks. Field guns and trench artillery, concentrating their fire on a narrow area, achieve a devastating density. Several thousand projectiles may be fired in just a couple of hours. Helped by the panic this creates and hidden by smoke, detachments penetrate the enemy lines with the aim of bringing back prisoners. In our first surprise attack we captured five Germans. Since then all our attempts have failed; it seems most probable that the enemy has adopted our method of evacuation, the only prudent one, and one which saves lives since units that remain in position will be annihilated. The Germans have never captured any of us.

A troop of about fifty men led by a sub-lieutenant, all volunteers, whom we call 'trench raiders', specialise in these little attacks. They live apart from the rest of us in the forest, and are exempt from other duties. They often go halfway down the valley where there's an inn run by three women, known to us by the name *The Six Buttocks*. The inn often echoes with the noise of their arguments, their quarrels with the artillerymen, which are often ended by pistols or knives when they are drunk. We shut our eyes to their exploits, because of their dangerous mission. It is understood that a good warrior must be a bit of an outlaw.

In between surprise attacks, the sector slumbers. The first mortar shells always indicate the start of a raid, and we expect them an hour or two before nightfall. With every raid there will be casualties among the lookouts responsible for warning of an enemy approach.

A general of rather martial bearing, escorted by a battalion runner, turns up unexpectedly at the command post, and declares: 'I have come to have a little look at your sector'. Giving me a wink, our lieutenant replies:

'Very good, sir, let us begin on the left.'

I hurry off and tell the first platoon; the warning will then be transmitted all along the line. That done, I wait for them to join me. As he walks along, the general questions our lieutenant on German activity, the state of their positions below us, the quantity of projectiles fired, etc. Suddenly, he halts by a sentry and asks him:

'If the Boche attack, my friend, what do you do?'

In a sector like this where we have the time to devote to the rule book, what to do in every situation is clearly prescribed and it's been drummed into us: in this case, fire two rifle shots, throw three grenades, set off the sirens, etc.

But our man gets confused, imagines that this imposing inspector is looking at him either sternly or with astonishment. He works out that it's a matter of making a quick decision since this is a surprise attack. And blurts out in panic:

'Yeah, right, well, I get my arse in gear…!'

The lieutenant is terribly upset. The general, who's got a sense of humour, leads him away and consoles him:

'Obviously those are not the terms that one would use at GCHQ... But it comes down to the same thing!... What's important is that he gets his... well, exactly that!'

I now find myself at the tail end of our little procession. We're going back up towards the platoon on the right. Two bangs in the distance, to the left: two mortar shells fired. For us? Wait three seconds. Two whistles. For us! Vroom! Vroom! Look out for the shrapnel... Reflex: they're using 77s.

'That was pretty close!'

'I've brought you bad luck,' said the general, with a smile that was a bit too calm to be convincing.

'No, sir, we're used to...'

Two more! Big ones... we dive for the ground. Vrrroom! Vrrroom! 105 time-shells. Shrapnel clatters down around us. Two black clouds above our heads.

'We should hurry, sir. This is a dangerous spot...'

'Lead on, lead on, lieutenant!'

Two more 77s. We go as fast as we can, and there is no question of any inspection.

We've just gone round a lookout post. There's a burst of gunfire. But I have time to hear a voice (good lord, it's Chassignole!) shouting out behind me, at the entrance to the shelter:

'Hey, lads! The shooting star has passed by!'

It's two in the afternoon. We're in the trench near the command post, not doing much. We hear a small explosion somewhere forward of us. We pay it scant attention: shells are always coming down somewhere or other.

Soon afterwards a man turns up, out of breath, asking for stretcher-bearers.

'A casualty?'

'Yes, rifle-grenade.'

'Bad?'

'Both feet more or less blown off. He was in the latrines – the grenade went off right there.'

That's the explosion we heard. The stretcher-bearers come back, put the stretcher down in the middle of the trench, and go into the shelter to get a form.

We recognise Petitjean, a nice boy, helpful and unassuming. He's very pale, but he's not making a sound. Blood is soaking through the crude bandages on his feet and running out at an alarming rate. I cannot stop myself comparing what he is losing from his body's total capacity with the time it will take to get him to the dressing station… There are three of us around him, fearing that it's cruel to come near him, to display our intact bodies, something he has just lost, probably forever, but also fearing that to move away would make it seem that we didn't care, that we were casting him into the isolation of the condemned, His silence makes us feel especially awkward: how do you show sympathy for someone who doesn't ask for your pity? He stares up at the sky which gives his eyes a light reflection of pale blue, like fine porcelain. Then he shuts them, closing himself off in the misfortune that separates him from us. Is he aware of the catastrophe that has struck him? Beneath his little moustache his lips are clenched and on his chest his hands are squeezed together so tightly that they are red and trembling. He is taken away before we pluck up the courage to say a word to him, and the lieutenant, who comes out of the shelter to shake his hand, remains standing beside us, sharing our silence.

It's a bright October day and we were enjoying the last warmth of the year before this unfortunate blow. You cannot lose yourself in any pleasure, the war is always there.

* * * * *

Early one morning a sentry at the bottom of the valley was woken from his reverie by the sound of footsteps in the trench. He turns and sees a German in front of him. His first reaction is to run. But the German raises his arm and cries: '*Kamerad!*' He's unarmed, has a little cap on his head and a package under his other arm. The sentry, still in shock and fearing a trap, calls the squad. They search the surroundings and find nothing suspicious: the man has definitely come alone. So they take him to the lieutenant. But no one speaks enough German to interrogate this odd prisoner who has dropped from the skies. He's a feeble-looking little man with a dull face and an over-fraternal smile. His eyelids flutter rapidly over furtive eyes, and he seems very pleased with himself. He still holds his package under his arm. Beaucierge and I are ordered to take him to battalion command. He trots along the trench between us. I ask him a few brief questions:

'*Krieg fertig?*'

'*Ja, ja!*'

'*Du bist zufrieden?*'

'*Ja, ja!*'

'You're a bit of a shirker, eh, brother?' says Beaucierge, giving him a friendly slap on the shoulder that makes him stagger.

'*Ja, ja!*'

'Not exactly belligerent, this little Christian, is he?' says my comrade.

'*Ja, ja!*'

'We're not talking to you, cabbage head!'

Our arrival is a big event. Word has got round that 9 company has taken a prisoner. Soldiers pour out of their huts and line the main street in the little village buried in the pine forest. At battalion HQ the excitement is similar. We all squeeze into the office, with *poilus* crowding the doorway. The commander appears and sends for a trench artillery officer who can serve as interpreter. Our German, estimating that his affairs are taking a turn for the better, stops standing rigidly to attention, and launches into a stream of protestations of goodwill while favouring us all with fraternal smiles. He tells his story to the officer who has just arrived, with rapid gestures, rather like a conjuror's patter.

He is a former auxiliary who was sent to the front last week. The day after he took up his post was the day of our surprise attack: one of our shells killed four of his comrades right next to him, at the entrance to a shelter, and he tells us how dreadful were the effects of our bombardment. He made up his mind then and there that the war did not suit him and took the decision to get out of it as quickly as he could. He prepared his flight while waiting for the right opportunity, as could be seen from his beloved package, which he undid to show us a pair of new boots, socks, a hairdresser's kit (that was his job), a shirt and a tin of fruit compote. That night, being on guard duty, he left his post, crawled to our lines and jumped down through a gap in our trench, at the risk of getting himself killed by both sides. He says that the war is a bad thing and seeks our approval. Which he gets, once the officers have left. Men run off to the kitchens and bring back coffee, bread, meat, cheese. We watch with sympathy while the deserter eats.

'He likes his grub, eh?'

'*Gut?*' I say.

'*Gut, gut!*' he replies with his mouth full.

'*In Deutschland nicht gut essen?*'

'*In Deutschland… Krrr!*'

He mimes tightening his belt.

'He's a laugh, this Boche!'

We have no other word than Boche for a German. To our mind this isn't a scornful term, it's just handy, short and amusing.

Beaucierge and I profit from our mission by getting ourselves something from the kitchens. The kitchens are the platoons' public forum; the citizen soldiers discuss public affairs there and get to hear news that arrives with the provisions. While a dirty, jovial cook grills up a bit of meat for us, we listen to what people are saying. Naturally the deserter is much discussed. The dominant opinion seems to be:

'He's not as fucking stupid as we are!'

The men nod their heads. But desertion remains the great unknown...

Relief troops are always sent to the front at night.

Our battalion is returning to the line after a fortnight's rest in the village of Laveline down in the valley. The climb up takes several hours of stiff marching, because it's a steep slope and the men carry full kits. The dark night, made even darker by the pine trees, obscures our path and our progress is erratic. We're sweating despite the cold.

A piercing whistle rends the night like taffeta, the rush of a shell makes us bend like blades of corn, the sudden peril overhead stops our hearts. There's a flash somewhere, like lightning. And then a clap of thunder, which reverberates down through the gorges to break on the valley floor. Then another, and another, explosion after explosion. Showers of fire light up the bare trunks of the pines. Furious, unstoppable blocks of metal, flying express trains, fall from the sky, surround us, drive us into panic. A storm of sound deafens us. We run up the slope, our legs breaking from the effort, our chests too narrow for bursting lungs that suck in air through the tight valve of our throats. Our hearts keep stopping, and we're dizzy and the blood rushes into our veins and then out, leaving them empty. Our eyelids are shut but the glare of flames imprints itself on our retinas... We're running for our lives.

Suddenly it stops. Men from different units, muddled together, sink to the ground to catch their breath. The night returns to protect us, the silence is comforting.

Then somewhere near me a risibly indignant voice is raised in complaint:

'They should be ashamed of themselves, endangering the life

of a man of forty, and a father of a family!'

'Hey. Listen to this old codger who reckons he's unsuitable corpse material!' jeers a Parisian with a rough accent.

'Shut your mouth you little whippersnapper!'

'You've fornicated enough already, grandpa! Let someone else have a go...'

'Watch what you're saying, lad! You're talking about our wives...'

'Leave your wife be! She's already had enough of your old mug and now she'll console herself with some young blokes. It's the old ones who have to croak first, everyone knows it!'

'They should protect the life of a family man. Not married, you little cub? You're useless!'

'And you want me to tell you what you are? You're an old pervert! You just want to stay nice and safe at home putting your wife up the spout while the lads are all here getting their heads smashed in. You're a bloody sadist!'

'Sadist!' repeated the other, stunned. 'Listen to this young hooligan!'

'That's what I said, a sadist! Luckily there's some justice in the world and you're a cuckold!'

'You little swine!' stammered the old man.

We could hear him get to his feet. But people held him back. The Parisian made his escape. He called back:

'Don't complain, old dear. It's supposed to bring you luck!'

This exchange banished the memory of the alarm. We set off again. We learn that there were victims at the rear of the column.

Back at camp, well-built shelters are in short supply and all occupied by battalion command and officers. The reserve company are accommodated in two *barraques Adrian,*[27] equipped with individual bunks. The men spend a good part of the day inside, for their stay here is seen as a rest period, and their only duties are cleaning or restocking munitions.

A short while ago we were together in our hut, the four runners and the cyclist. We were all lying on our mattresses, smoking, except for Beaucierge who was passing the time with jokes in bad taste and an attempt to provoke the cyclist into single combat. The latter got rid of him by threatening to cut off his personal food supply. Further off the *poilus* were drinking and playing cards, or sleeping.

A shot rang out a few metres away, followed by screams. A soldier was looking gormlessly at his smoking Browning. It's a common occurrence with automatics. Those who have them keep them loaded and when they want to take them apart for cleaning, forget to remove the bullet in the chamber. A number of accidents have resulted.

We went over to the injured man, who was still howling and pointing to his leg. While people went to get help, we started removing his trousers. The clumsy owner of the Browning was roundly cursed.

The young doctor arrived, looked at the injured man's thigh and laughed:

'Will you stop screaming! Can't you see that you've struck it lucky?'

The man immediately stopped making a noise and his face lit up. The doctor probed his leg:

'That doesn't hurt? Or that?'

'No!'

'People would give a fortune for a wound like that! And to get it when you were asleep! You've got yourself three months at the rear!'

The wounded man smiled. We all did. Once the wound had been dressed, we called over the owner of the automatic. His victim shook his hand, thanked him warmly, and left on a stretcher, congratulated by the whole camp.

Since then the chump has been glorying in his clumsiness. You can hear him say: 'It was me that got Pigeonneau out!' And even talking about: 'The day when I saved Pigeonneau's life...'

Winter has come and it looks like being a harsh one.

In the beginning, icy blasts swept down the sides of the mountains, followed by the first frosts. Then one morning we woke up in a strange, heavy silence, and the daylight coming into our huts had a special glitter. Snow had fallen in the night and covered everything. It hung on the pine branches in thick layers, like tracery on a cathedral window. From now on we live in a cold, Gothic forest, smoke rising from our little Eskimo huts.

I had been back at the front for more than six months when we received two important pieces of news, which would change my destiny. Our company was to be attached to another battalion, and our lieutenant was leaving us.

2

THIRTY BELOW

*'A soldier hates his own lieutenant more than the
lieutenant in the enemy army.'*

Maurice Barrès[28]

THE NEW ACTING COMPANY commandant is Captain Bovin,
a man already well known throughout the regiment.

This captain had for some time held the role of adjutant
to the colonel and in this capacity he was feared, especially by
other officers and staff. The men at the front, on the other hand,
feared no one, on the basis that: 'they can't move us any further
forward!' Those I had spoken to depicted Captain Bovin as a kind
of eminence grise, distributing favours and blame as he liked;
here, blame can often get you killed... Crossing him meant jeop-
ardising your career, if not your life, and it was easy to do, either
with outbursts of temperament or youthful behaviour, or, fatally,
by displaying your independence. He was also condemned by
many for abusing his power by giving himself several laudatory
mentions in dispatches, notably at Verdun, where he had stayed
safely at the rear with the quartermaster. As an administrator
whose paperwork kept him out of danger, he was accused of using
this same paperwork against those who were risking their lives.

But his favoured position had just come to an end. The regiment
had a new colonel at its head and this colonel considered that a

captain with his eye on a commandant's shoulder stripes needed to have served at the front.

Captain Bovin lives up to his reputation in his appearance and behaviour. He's about fifty, very tall, with a jaundiced complexion. He has yellow teeth, the cruel smile of a Moor, the eyes of a Chinaman; he is bearded, greying, with a slow, solemn walk, and a hypocritical air of austerity. I find him mediocre, fussy, mean-spirited: he has the mind of an office manager combined with that of a barracks adjutant, with full power over a hundred and fifty men. The type of man you loathe at first sight, a man who likes to intimidate people, and who also likes – more seriously and always a bad sign – servility in his subordinates. In short, we all knew it was a bad day for the company when he turned up. We also got the strong impression that his batman was spying on us.

My own relations with such a man could only be difficult and were unlikely to end well. He ordered me to draw up a map of the entire sector, a task which cost me ten days' torture. In a temperature of twenty below, I had to measure abandoned trenches, with the snow up to my knees, and stand still on the ground checking deviations and noting down figures. My shoes froze to my feet. Once I'd completed the map, the captain sent me straight back to the front line. I was back in the squad.

This sector lies at an altitude of about 1,000 metres. Our company is attached to the other battalion, on the top of the mountain, a part of whose slopes we hold. Our positions consist of a single line of trenches, well protected by barbed wire. Along the whole length of this line, every 150 metres, short trenches lead out to bunkers at a salient, which function as 'holding points'. Each of these little forts has a steel-barred door, so that the garrison can close itself off in the case of any attack from the rear by enemy units who have infiltrated our main trenches. It's a weak defence system, suitable for a quiet sector. We're on the edge of the forest.

The road comes almost to the trench and along this road, behind our posts, there are shelters for company command, for the quartermasters and so on, hidden by the trees. In fact the rear of the position, inadequately prepared, would become untenable under bombardment. But our only serious enemy is the cold.

We hold the last position on the left of the company. It's a narrow shelter, dug out to the same depth as the trench and covered over with rows of logs. Furniture consists of a sleeping platform, a metal stove, and a little bench. Five of us live there: four privates and a corporal. Lookouts stand in front of the shelter on a kind of platform protected by shoulder-high gabions.[29] In the daytime the sentry stands in the trench. Keeping guard is our chief duty, and it's a very tough one. From dusk to dawn we have to cover fourteen hours of sentry duty between us, two men at a time, making seven hours per team. Our sleep is thus interrupted every two hours.

The temperature has dropped even lower. At night it varies between minus 25 and minus 30 degrees. The sentries keep the fire burning in the shelter but the stove only works if it stays red hot. Thus we go straight from the inside temperature, about 25 degrees, to the temperature outside, where we stand still in the trench looking out for enemies who cannot possibly come and who, just like us, are only thinking about how to keep warm. And since on the front line we have to sleep fully clothed and kitted, we endure the jump of fifty degrees with no other protection than the blanket we keep tightly wrapped around us.

No one can endure this torture for two hours, and our cramped position does not even allow us the space to walk up and down to stop freezing again. So we have a private arrangement to take it in turns as lookout every half hour. One watches while the other warms up. If you need help you pull a wire which rings a bell in the shelter.

We fight against the cold as best we can. The icy north wind pierces and slashes us with blades of steel. Our woollen caps protect our heads and ears, we wrap mufflers round our faces leaving only our eyes uncovered and our corneas freeze so that all we see is blurred as if we were looking through water. Above this construction of scarves we balance our helmets and sometimes add a blanket over them which hangs down on to our shoulders like a big hood. We've been given rubber mountain boots which we wear over felt slippers. But the boots are uncomfortable and dangerous, the insides get soaked with sweat and they cause us to fall over on the slippery snow. I have found another way of protecting myself from the cold, less effective but sufficient as long as I jump up and down on the spot every now and then. I keep my shoes on and put my legs inside two empty sandbags which I tie on at the knees. Then I take other sacks from which I've cut out the bottoms and make myself thigh covers. This outfit has the advantage of giving a surer grip on ice; it allows you to run and I am well aware that running is the first necessity for a fighter, who must always be prepared for a rapid retreat. On my hands I wear three pairs of gloves on top of each other.

The nights seem to last forever. Cracking ice mimics the sound of wire cutters but we have stopped worrying about it. We concentrate on guarding ourselves, on the sectors of our bodies which stiffen up as if our arteries were carrying ice floes. Standing still gives us a treacherous sense of warmth, wraps us in a dangerous fleece of inertia, and it takes an effort of will to start moving again, which stirs up the cold before rekindling the fires of our blood. The first glimmers of dawn seem like deliverance.

Around seven we get coffee, frozen wine which tinkles in the cans, and loaves of bread that's so hard you'd need an axe to cut it. We put the loaves on the stove where they soften and give out water, then gorge ourselves on the tepid, spongy bread. And we take little sips of the boiling hot coffee heated up in our tin mugs. After a winter night, a polar night, it's life itself that we're gulping down.

* * * * *

It didn't take Captain Bovin long to show his measure. The Germans leave us in peace on our mountain, but he has burdened us with more and more duties that can only add to our suffering without having any military benefit whatsoever. Profiting from the passivity that the low temperatures have imposed on all soldiers, he has transformed our sector into a barracks. He swamps us with tasks that aren't urgent, takes no account of our exhaustion, and robs us of the scant free time that would be left to us by duties that are already quite onerous enough.

Several times a week, he summons the company to alert in the middle of the night. All the men have to line up in the trenches and await his inspection. He thus makes us endure two extra hours of cold. These alerts have no value. Most of the men are old hands by now and know far better than the captain how to defend a forward post like ours. In any case, we have the feeling that a few shells would quickly take the wind out of his sails, and we wait for the time when we're in an active sector so that we can show what we think of him. The men respect a leader who is strict in critical moments and risks his own skin, but they have the deepest contempt for one who persecutes them without having proved himself.

During the day the captain puts us to work on the grounds that we should not be idle: maintaining the trenches, digging latrines, cleaning anything that can be cleaned – the results of which are soon covered by the snow. He has also come up with the idea of sending detachments to the rear for training exercises, something unheard of until now.

Getting fuel is enough to keep us busy in the afternoons. We get through a great deal of wood. Every day we have to cut down a pine in the forest and carry it piece by piece to the shelter where we saw it into smaller sections and then chop these into logs before stacking them up inside. Always busy, we are also always tired since we can only sleep for short periods between our turns at guard duty.

Our worst enemy now is our captain. We fear him more than German patrols and during the night we're more alert to noise from behind than in front. Through his tyranny he has managed to produce the ridiculous result that we turn our attention from the enemy facing us to focus it in our own camp. Two guards who warmed themselves up, with the approval of their comrades, were court-martialled for abandoning their post in the face of the enemy, and NCOs have been reduced to the ranks for pointless reasons. It has reached a point where we've set up a system of alarms to protect ourselves from our leader. As soon as he pops up somewhere, his presence is announced through a network of strings, hidden in the barbed wire, linking the positions, which rattle empty bully beef tins. The garrisons on the slope also pour water down the trench every evening so as to add to the layer of ice that makes the approach to the bunkers hazardous. We're the first to suffer from this, but it obtained the desired result. During one of his rounds, the captain slipped and fell heavily, injuring his back. His runners had to hold him up so he could get back to his command post. This news was greeted with whooping and firing in the air, rather like an Arab equestrian fantasia. After that, the tyrant doesn't show himself in our patch. But he takes his revenge by leaving us no respite.

Our silent hatred for the captain continues to grow. Here is a man who should be helping us to bear our suffering and instead is causing us more misery than the enemy. The soldiers would kill him more readily than a German – and with more reason, they believe.

I'm living like an animal, an animal who has to eat and then sleep. I have never felt so stupefied, so blank, and I realise that wearing people out, leaving them no time to think, reducing them to a state where they feel nothing but the most basic needs, is the surest way of controlling them. I understand now how slaves submit so easily, because they have no strength left for revolt, nor imagination to conceive it, nor energy to organise it. I understand the wisdom of oppressors who prevent those they exploit from using their brains by crushing them with exhausting labour. I sometimes feel I've almost reached that state of utter subjection that comes from weariness and monotony, that animal passivity that accepts anything. I feel close to submission, which destroys the individual. My critical faculties are dulled; I hesitate, waver, and capitulate. Military routine, with all its petty rules and regulations, doesn't need my consent and drafts me into the herd. I am becoming a true infantryman, one whose intellect stands permanently to attention; I do what I'm told, one little cog in the machine. Everyone, from a general down to a corporal, gives me orders by right, absolute and unquestionable, and can strike me off the list of the living. In the field of human activities, mine consist of digging a latrine or carrying a tree trunk. Could I tell an NCO that these things are harder for me than for others? It would be useless for he'd probably misunderstand me; it would be unwise because he'd take advantage of it. Captain Bovin had certainly guessed it, and he put me here. (And consequently he's the only person in front of whom I'll slave away with a cheerful smile on my face.)

And first and foremost I have to mix in with, identify with, those with whom I share my life, to whom I am bound by a pact of self-preservation. I must go back to being a caveman and make my contribution to sating the appetites of my horde. I must dig and saw and carry and clean and make fire, think only of my body. How can I explain to my comrades that in the conflict between body and mind, in my case the latter is usually the winner? But my mind, here, is a privilege and it has been withdrawn; it is out of line, it causes a nuisance to the squad. The riches of the mind are monopolised by the General Staff, who redistribute them as shells showered down on the rabble.

And yet sometimes at night, looking out at the snow shining into infinity beneath dazzling moonlight like an aurora borealis, I come to think that there, alone before my icy ramparts, I am watching over the sleeping country, that it depends on me for some part of its security, that my chest is its frontier, and I feel a little bit of pride in keeping with the traditions of GCHQ. To while away the hours I experiment with noble motives, try out the joys of simple patriotism. But I'm already quite aware that a well-aimed burst of gunfire will restore my disgust for such fine sentiments.

If a German should come to attack me, I know for sure that I will do all I can to kill him. So that he doesn't kill me, above all; and then because I am responsible for the safety of four men in our bunker, and if I don't shoot I could expose them to danger. I am bound to these farmers who are always bullying me for being lazy. The solidarity of a chain gang.

But in the daytime if I looked down the sight of my rifle and saw an exposed German at 150 metres, who didn't know that I could see him, it's very unlikely I'd shoot. I don't see how I could kill someone like that, in cold blood, my rifle resting comfortably on my elbows while I slowly take aim, how I could kill with premeditation and not as a reflex.

Fortunately there is so little question of killing that we don't even bother to hide the lights of our cigarettes. Perhaps we risk a bullet. But there's something in the little act of defiance of smoking openly that avenges the terrible biting cold.

Now that I'm a soldier of the trenches once more, I can understand the kind of fatalism to which my comrades succumb, in this war where nothing ever happens, nothing changes, everything looks the same; a war where all we do is keep watch and dig ditches, suffer silently in the muck and mud; a war without limit or respite, where we don't do anything, don't even defend ourselves, just wait for the chance shell that has our name on it. I can understand what these two long years, the hundreds of nights on sentry duty, the thousands of endless hours looking out into the dark, what they represent for those who've endured them. I can understand that they have stopped asking themselves questions. And yet it still amazes me that this herd of cattle, of which I have become a part, still struggles so much against death.

As I'm ferrying back supplies, I go past the highest point of the position, bent down from the weight of a dixie in each hand and a large haversack on my back. In a trench I bump into an NCO. We're in each other's way, I raise my head. Oh…

'Nègre!'

'Hey, my old son!'

Once we've stopped telling each other how happy we are to meet again, my old neighbour from hospital explains that he's been in the same regiment as me for the last two months, as a sergeant-observer working with the colonel. But he was detached to the 1st battalion, which explains why I hadn't bumped into him before.

'Incidentally, how's our dear friend Poculotte doing?'

'Very well, thank you.'

'And what's he saying?'

'Sssh! The general has become very circumspect. But between you and me, I think he's got something big planned.'

'So, still going on the offensive?'

'More than ever! We are preparing Austerlitz.'

'What are we waiting for?'

'Sunshine. We have to wait till spring.'

'And in the meantime?'

'In the meantime, the general is busy raising the pay of NCOs. He sets great store by this measure for the maintenance of morale, based on the principle that a factory's output is always highest when the foremen are well paid.'

'And the workers?'

'They are far less important. The baron is truly becoming a great politician and a profound thinker!'

'And what about you, what are you doing?'

'I'm observing. First of all I observe the places where shells fall, so that I don't go near them. Wisdom teaches us: God saves those who save themselves. For save yourself read keep a low profile. You understand that I'm too interested in the war not to want to see it through to the end… And then, during quiet periods, I observe what the Barbarians are up to with my little lorgnette.'

'Nègre, I'd like to ask you a question that still bothers me. What do you think of courage?'

'You're still stuck on that one! That question has now been definitively answered. Specialists were closeted away working on it. So here's what you need to know: a Frenchman is naturally courageous; no one else is. Technicians have proved that the only way to get a German into combat is to give him ether. This artificial courage is not the real thing. And what are you up to?'

'Me? Between you and me, I'm working like a dog.'

I ask Nègre to recommend me as an observer. He promises to do his best, and to come back and see me.

After two months in the bunker, we are relieved, just as it's getting warmer. We are almost sorry to leave the mountain peaks. Life was very tough but we were not in any real danger. Down in the valley we learn that Captain Bovin is on sick leave. The men sneer at the news:

'He's scared of going to a sector where things are hot! Rule number one: you can always be sure that a bastard who does his service at the rear will be yellow when it comes to fighting.'

A young reserve lieutenant by the name of Larcher, a cheerful, cordial man, comes to take command of the 9th. We return to our old sector and find the battalion resting in a village at the foot of the mountain.

The company adjutant, whom I knew when I was a runner, attaches me to command HQ as a secretary-topographer. Once again I've been saved from the squad, once again I've got myself a cushy job.

We soon go back up to the front lines. This time I'm staying in an encampment in the forest, with comfortable log cabins for shelter. The windows look out on to a clearing at the top of which are the trenches leading to the front line. I've got a basic office job: I transcribe orders in several copies, prepare summaries for the colonel, keep the campaign plans up to date.

Weeks go by quietly, disturbed only by the usual surprise attacks. For a couple of hours, the mountain is shaken, the ridge breaks up under an avalanche of mortar shells, our batteries roar in response, explosions resound in the mountain gorges, and heavy artillery shells burst in our vicinity. In the evening we draw up lists of our losses in men and matériel. Thus we learn of the fatalities, rather inattentively, like town-hall clerks registering deaths.

It's not so cold now. The sun is getting its strength back. The snow melts, the forest turns a darker green; we splash about in the mud. Contingents of birds set up camp in the pine branches, green shoots pierce the soil. The coming of spring cheers us up and also secretly worries us. Springtime brings the start of fresh battles; it is the harbinger of new hecatombs. We hardly believe in decisive victories any more and we know that offensives are usually more costly for the attackers than the defenders. The chances of getting killed remain our overwhelming concern.

Nonetheless, on the front line where I sometimes go to note down some organisational detail, the lookouts are happier because they're not suffering so much. They stand around outside their little huts, chatting and joking, living in the present for fear of imagining the future. They play games for pennies with cards or counters. They smoke a lot and always keep their friend, their wine flask, close at hand.

3

THE CHEMIN DES DAMES

'Man in battle... is a being in whom the instinct of
self-preservation dominates, at certain moments, all other
sentiments. Discipline has for its aim the domination of that
instinct by a greater terror.
Man taxes his ingenuity to be able to kill without running the risk
of being killed. His bravery is born of his strength and it is not
absolute. Before a stronger, he flees without shame.'

Lieutenant-Colonel Ardant du Picq, *Etudes sur le combat* (1880),
trans. Col. John N. Greely and Major Robert C. Cotton (1921)

WE ARE IN THE TOWN OF Fismes, an accursed place, with the
sad, forbidding aspect of any large industrial centre. This one is a
centre of the war industry, surrounded by railway tracks, bays and
platforms for loading and unloading, encampments of Moroccan
soldiers, and aerodromes; a centre which is a convergence point
for endless columns of lorries, artillery, ambulances, etc. Long
processions of men remind you of shifts leaving factories, and
through them weave the motorcars of the generals, the ironmas-
ters. Their foundries glow before us, up on the ridges, and the
noise of their huge anvils fills the sky as their heavy hammers
pulverise human flesh.

Our billets are disgustingly dirty but they are only there to
provide a day or two's shelter for men passing through, human

sacrifices whom there's no need to bother about. Mere cattle pens. We are in Fismes, gateway to death.

We are also in Fismes, the town of total debauchery. All along the streets there is nothing but grocery shops spilling out on to the pavement. We've never seen such great pyramids of mouth-watering charcuterie, of tins with gold labels, such a choice of wines, spirits, fruit. Not many objects, though, for this is not the place to buy things which last. Just food and drink, every-where. The sharks who run these shops treat us like scum and announce their prices defiantly. We've never paid such prices and the soldiers complain. The salesmen reply with a cold, impla-cable look that says: what use is your money if you're not coming back? A good point! A particularly large explosion in the distance decides matters for even the most economical; they fill their arms and offer their money.

Let's eat and drink ourselves to death...

Since die we must!

In the street I stop an artillery NCO whom I knew in civilian life. He's a tall, calm lad, a little older than me, with the direct gaze of a child. In the past, I'd never seen him angry, or even irritated. He doesn't seem to have changed. We find a table in a café and I question him. He tells me he's acting as a detached observer, alongside the infantry, living in the trenches with the men. I ask him:

'Do you know the sector?'

'Only too well! I took part in the attacks of 16 April.'[30]

'Where was that?'

'Outside Troyon. I set off with the African troops, Mangin's famous army.'

'Is it true that they were massacred?'

'You know how it is. No one sees any more than their own patch. But in mine it was slaughter. I can tell you about it, I was part of the waves of assault under Colonel J—. In the battalion we marched with, only about twenty men came back.'[31]

'Why did it fail?'

'Simple enough: the Boche were waiting for us. Our attack had been planned for months, and everyone knew about it.'

'Yes, I'd heard that. In the Vosges they announced that we were planning something very big in the Aisne, that Nivelle had decided to blast through German lines with his artillery. In short, all-out attack, without any attempt at hiding.'

'Imagine it! The Boche also had artillery, and several divisions of troops. They brought them up. While we were making roads and paths and setting up munitions depots, they were installing armoured turrets for their machine gunners, they were constructing entrenchments, tunnels, and concrete bunkers, they were putting up new lines of barbed wire. They had all the time in the world to prepare their trap. The day of our assault, they just fired at will. In two hours our offensive had stopped dead. In two hours fifty to a hundred thousand of our men were out of action. We'll never know the exact number.'

'And what happened to you in all this?'

'By the day of the attack I'd been waiting in the line for more than a week. The caves and countryside all round, the "Creutes marocaines,"[32] Paissy, Pargnan, etc., were all bursting with troops. Shiny new heavy artillery had been put in position in the ravine, three hundred metres from the trenches. Men and wagons and artillery everywhere: it was a fairground. The Boches did nothing, but their aeroplanes flew over very low and calmly noted all this movement, all our guns, our stores, our assembly points... At seven in the morning on 16 April we went over the top. At first we were unopposed, and their forward trenches were empty. We moved across the rest of the plateau and went down into the German ravine. The Boches had evacuated and then dug in at their undamaged second lines on the ridges on the other side. They let us rush down the slope and get to the bottom. And then they unleashed their barrages of artillery and machine-gun fire. Nivelle's great offensive was broken there, less than a kilometre from its start, without having engaged the enemy at all.'

'How did you get out of there?'

'In the night.'

'You were stuck in there all day long?'

'There was no way of doing anything else. Those who hadn't been cut down had dug themselves into shell holes to escape the bullets. We couldn't move. We had literally buried ourselves right in the middle of a shooting range.'

'What was Colonel J. saying?'

'He was in a tight spot! He'd sent black soldiers to the rear to ask for reinforcements several times but never saw any of them again. Then we heard the sound of grenades which meant the Germans must be counter-attacking nearby. "Do you know this sector?" the colonel asked me. "Not well, sir." "Too bad! You're going to take this note to the general." He gave me a big black soldier to accompany me. But we had to get through this wall of fire. We crawled from hole to hole, clambering over the corpses...'

'A lot of corpses?'

'Lines of them, piles of them! There is only one way to describe it: we were walking through meat... At last I managed to reach the plateau with no other damage than having my kit bag smashed by a bullet; I lost my revolver, my gas mask, my field glasses... Once on the plateau we hurried along the trenches to the divisional command post, in a cave in the Troyon ravine. The cave was full of officers, all shouting at each other because they were so afraid. Quite a comedy! I show them my note and they start to shout at me, too: "First of all, where have you come from?" "Where were you?" "With Colonel J., sir." "That's a lie, Colonel J. was taken prisoner at nine this morning..." These chaps were completely crazy! "No, sir, I have just left the colonel, who is afraid of being surrounded and sent me to ask you for reinforcements." "What reinforcements? I have no men left..." "There are still a few territorials," said another. "We'll have to see…" I wait for maybe an hour… Finally a captain comes up to me, looking suspicious: "Are you sure you can find Colonel J. again?" "I think so, sir." "In that case, you will take the detachment that is waiting outside." Outside, I find about forty territorials, led by an adjutant, their faces drawn in terror, carrying boxes of grenades. And all these poor buggers start to curse me: "Shitty little artilleryman, fucking bastard! Why couldn't you keep your mouth shut? What do you think we're going to do down there? That's not where we should be, at our age…" What a bloody mess! I tell them: "Look, if you don't want to come, stay here. But I've got to go back." Their adjutant decided: "Go in front. I'll follow at the back to make them march." I set off once more through the bombardment, at the head of forty old codgers, more dead than alive, moaning and wailing and stopping every twenty metres to make up their minds. We arrived in the night, just in time to join the retreat.'

'You left your dead on the field?'

'Of course we did. There were a few hundred of us survivors and there were thousands of dead and wounded.'

'And then?'

'Nothing, all over! The Boche took back their old positions with no opposition from us. If in turn they'd attacked seriously they would have driven us right off the Chemin des Dames, no doubt about it. But they were happy enough just to shell us heavily.'

'A real disaster?'

'You could say so. A shameful business, enough to ruin the French army.'

'Did this disaster provoke the mutinies, do you think?'[33]

'For sure. You know how passive the men are. They've all been sick of the war for a very long time, but they still follow orders. For the troops to actually revolt, they had to have been pushed to the absolute limit.'

'Wasn't there talk of traitors?'

'I can't comment on that, I can only tell you what I saw. As always a host of contradictory rumours were going round. It seems to me it can all be explained quite simply. When they wanted to make them attack again, the *poilus* felt they were lost, thrown into the slaughterhouse by pig-headed incompetents. The cannon fodder rebelled, because they had waded through too many pools of blood and they couldn't see any other way of saving themselves. It was their leaders, some of their leaders, who provoked them. Just think how they sent poor chaps to the firing squad, men who had already endured years of suffering, but not one single general was condemned. The revolt was a consequence of the massacre and you have to seek those responsible for it among the General Staff.'

'I've heard vague claims that it was the politicians who hindered the military action and without this we'd have been successful.'

'No, absolutely not! People can argue the toss as much as they like but one fact remains: the sixteenth of April cost the lives of 80,000 men in the French army. After such a bloodbath, there could be no question of going any further. I've seen what happens when you are led by raving lunatics only too closely!'

'None of this is exactly cheering news!'

'You don't still believe that intelligence plays any great part in war, do you? You would be the only one...'

'Sure. It's just that we are heading for the Chemin des Dames...'

'Don't panic. Look at me, I came back OK. Have another drink!'

Back at camp, I am discussing how long we'll be on the front line with a couple of runners. A cyclist turns up bearing new information, gathered here and there. He says:

'It isn't a question of time, nor of whether an attack succeeds. To be relieved, units must have suffered at least fifty per cent losses.'

This news hits us hard. Losses of half our men! I think about this: there are four of us here, none older than twenty-five. Two must die. Which two? Despite myself, I look at the others for fatal signs, something which might mark out people chosen for a tragic destiny. I'm picturing their waxy, lifeless faces, I'm choosing two comrades in our group to become corpses...

Of course this logic can be wrong, and it could be that all four of us come back. But if you stick to the figures, it's accurate.

Since this conversation I'm unable to be with a man from our unit without asking the question: him or me? If I want to live I have to condemn him resolutely, mentally kill my brother in arms...

This is what they call the *war of attrition*.

We're on our way.

The regiment goes through Fismes one last time, at a quick march with a band in front. A macabre parade before civilians who've seen plenty of them already and are only staying here to make money.

And suddenly: 'Present... arms! Eyes right!' On a little mound stands a general with shiny boots on his legs, a fearless expression on his face, and his hand on his képi. Something strikes me about that hand: his thumb is turned down, like the sign made by the emperor in ancient arenas...

'*Ave*, old man! *Morituri te salutant.*'

We're approaching the explosions. At the entrance to the village of Euilly we have to go over a canal on a wooden bridge surrounded by debris from shelling. Crossing the Styx.

Leaving the village, the road is full of craters, the newest distinguished by the colour of the earth. At any second a shell could come down on us. There's nothing to do but advance as fast as we can. Model T Ford ambulances driven by Americans pass us by, creaking and clattering and looking as if they're about to topple over. We can hear the groans from inside. As they jolt across the bumps their canvas covers flap up, affording us a glimpse of the ashen-faced wounded, and their bloodstained bandages.

A lull allows us to reach unharmed the foot of a steep escarpment below a spur of the Chemin des Dames ridge. Our commandant halts the battalion to get his bearings. But others passing shout to us that we should not stay there. So we rush up the slope, bent over with our heavy loads, using our hands to get a grip where the ground is slippery.

Twenty metres from the top we find the entrance to a vast cave system, big enough to shelter several battalions. As the last men get inside, a furious bombardment comes down above and below us. We were just in time.

In this bandits' lair we await our turn to move up to the front. Shells whistle down outside the cave entrances, all day and all night.

Two a.m.

Leaning on my elbows on a little table with a candle, I'm keeping watch in the depths of the shelter. We relieved our comrades a few minutes ago. Battalion command has been set up in a very long sap, a kind of narrow gallery with a couple of sharp corners, ten metres underground. The reserve sections are also sheltering in the same sap. Everyone is asleep, except the lookouts at the cave mouths, and me, separated from them by the steps down and the turnings in the tunnel, and by groups of soldiers lying on the ground, curled up in jumbled heaps in the shadows, dead to the world. There must be a hundred men in the sap and you have to walk over them to get through. I feel their heavy presence, and their trust in me; it's a lonely feeling. Some of them toss and turn violently in their sleep, start and shudder, or suddenly cry out in anguish, which makes me jump.

While watching over these sleeping minds, my own mind, working feebly, considers our situation. We are at the Chemin des Dames. I read the names we all know: Cerny, Ailles, Craonne, terrible names... I study our position. Our front lines are at most a hundred metres in front of us, and behind us there is less than fifty metres before the ravine into which the Germans are trying to push us. At the foot of the ravine, the plain stretches off into the distance, a plain so pulverized and desolate that it looks like a sea of sand (I looked at it when we were coming to find the battalion command). Recently the enemy has been attacking strongly in an attempt to take possession of the whole line of plateaus, and these attacks have advanced. At the point we are defending we've just a hundred and thirty metres left in which to hang on to the heights. We're at the mercy of a well-organised major attack. And here, deep in the shelter, if the front line breaks we are powerless – with fifty steps to climb to reach the surface – and would be captured or suffocated by grenades. Not a happy situation...

Three a.m. Absolute silence...

A lead-tipped cane whacks me on the head, makes my ears ring, sets off the visceral panic that I know only too well. A violent gust of air slaps me in the face, blows out the candle and plunges me into the darkness of the grave. A furious bombardment is crashing down on us, ploughing into us, making the timbers of the sap creak. I hunt for matches, relight the candle, shaking like an alcoholic. Up above me it must be total destruction. The bombardment reaches an extraordinary intensity, then takes on the rhythm of machine-gun fire, like a kind of backbeat broken by the deep explosions of big time-shells, seeking us out in our caves.

My comrades, shielded by the thick walls of the sap that muffle the sound, are still sleeping, exhausted, like sleeping soldiers everywhere. I leave them in their unconsciousness for a while, face the fear alone. The violent bombardment surely means an attack is coming. Will the sections at the front hold out?... We'll have to fight. Fight? I click off the safety catch on my automatic pistol.

A powerful explosion makes the flame tremble once more. I hear cries of panic from the depths of the darkness: 'Gas! Gas!' Then I shake those around me: gas! We put our masks on, pigs' muzzles that make us monstrous and grotesque. We look especially pathetic with our heads bowed down on our chests. Now a hundred of us in this pit are listening to the destruction above us, and inside us, listening to the prompts of fear eating away our nerves. Will it be this time, any moment now, that we will die, like you die at the front, torn to pieces?

We hear other voices:

'One entrance has collapsed – pass it on!'

The mortar shell has buried the two lookouts. The horror commences...

'Who was on lookout?'

We wait to hear their names, like the numbers in a funeral lottery. Their bodies must be disinterred, right away.

The battalion commander occupies a niche at the side of the trench, a little underground cabin that he shares with his adjutant. We hear him asking:

'What's happening?'

'We don't know, sir.'

'Send out runners.'

Men draw back rapidly, try to hide themselves, trembling with fear.

The adjutant gets angry:

'Runners, now, jump to it!'

The men reappear, with ghastly faces.

'Find out what's going on with the other companies, go in twos.'

'We'll be blown to pieces for sure!'

'Wait by the entrance till things calm down a bit,' he adds.

They go off to their position.

Machine guns!... The rattle of machine guns. The sound of these terrible weapons cuts through all the other noise, stands out from the bombardment... We go quiet, our hearts constricted: now it starts...

'Are the runners back?'

'Not yet, sir.'

'Send more.'

'He's mad!'

Two ashen-faced men move off slowly, hunched over. The adjutant holds up his finger, cocks his ear:

'It's getting quieter, isn't it?'

Yes... so it would seem. The bombardment is slowing down. The rumbling is replaced by bursts of firing. But nothing is sure in this unknown sector.

There's a clatter on the stairs. Two runners have returned, streaming with sweat, eyes vacant. They give their news to the commander:

'The Boche advanced on the 9th. They were stopped.'

'Were the companies badly hit?'

'Badly enough, sir. Several shells in the trench. They're calling for stretcher-bearers.'

'Is Larcher OK?'

'Yes, sir. He says there's no danger for the time being and if the Boche come back, they'll be ready for them.'

Saved, this time! We get the list of casualties: eleven men out of action in the 9th and seven in the 10th.

Around nine o'clock, the adjutant takes advantage of a lull to inspect the sector. While he's away the bombardment starts again. He is brought back wounded, gravely, it seems. The battalion doctor comes to attend to him and he is carried away. The run of misfortune continues... We stay with the commandant. Our fate depends on his decisions. In the quiet sectors his attitude was more than cautious, it made us smile. This may be good: he won't lead us into any reckless actions.

The bombardment rumbles on, but it has slowed down.

On the second night I have to go and fetch provisions from the edge of the Troyon ravine, and I return loaded with loaves of bread wrapped in a tent canvas. A cluster of trench mortars nearly catches us just outside the entrance to the shelter. By the light of a flare we can make out Frondet, on guard duty, who is crossing himself whenever there's an explosion, like an old woman in a thunderstorm. My comrades laugh as they tumble on to the stairs. And I am thinking: 'Prayers, intercessions, get whatever consolation you can, you poor old man!' Frondet is a well-bred chap of thirty-two, who had a good job in industry abroad, and he has kept his good manners here. He endures without complaint the promiscuity that war inflicts and the coarseness of his companions. But his well-known piety does not save him from being afraid. On some days he looks like an old man. He has one of those lined faces with sad eyes and a desperate smile that mark out a man consumed by an obsession. When fear becomes chronic it turns an individual into a kind of monomaniac. Soldiers call this being down in the dumps. But in reality it is a type of neurasthenia that follows excessive nervous strain. Many of the men are sick, without being aware of it, and their febrile state can make them disobey orders or abandon their posts just as much as it can drive them to fatally rash deeds. It is often the only reason for certain acts of bravery.

Frondet himself clutches at his faith and his prayers but I have often realised, through the poignant humility of his gaze, that these things do not give him enough consolation. I secretly pity him.

* * * * *

We have spent two days crushed together in this pit, where the air is tainted by our breath and stale sweat, and the bitter stench of urine.

We're targeted with furious bombardments several times a day, for no obvious reason. The constant danger denies us any respite. We are always afraid of an attack, of being forced out into a desperate struggle, of hearing shouts in German at the entrances or grenades exploding on the steps. We cannot see anything at all, and depend entirely on the companies who are fighting in front of us.

The Germans haven't shown themselves again. But on a front like this where soldiers are nervous and on constant alert, artillery will be called in at the slightest sign of danger; the guns splutter into action at the first enemy flare, and then set the whole zone ablaze. The alert spreads like a trail of gunpowder. Within a few minutes, the eruption spreads across the plateaus. There is never total silence, the trench mortars continue their stealthy work, so terrible for our nerves, and their shells land all over the place. The number of victims continues to rise.

Our commandant hasn't even reconnoitred the sector and never sets foot outside his little cabin. Apart from the adjutant who takes his orders, no one has set eyes on him. He relieves himself in a dixie which his batman goes and empties over the parapet outside. His meals are prepared for him on a spirit stove and he seems to spend the greater part of his day lying on his bunk. He has lost all dignity and no longer even attempts to keep up appearances. We know too much about what is becoming of all of us to judge him too harshly, but we deeply resent the way he unnecessarily exposes his runners to danger. He despatches them two by two under shellfire and sends out teams one after another without giving the first ones the chance to accomplish their mission. There is no useful information these men can bring back and the squad leaders would be the first to ask for help if they needed it. We feel that our commandant, no longer fit for his duties, will get us all killed stupidly, that fear is driving him mad without removing the rights that come with his officer's shoulder stripes. We have stopped believing that anyone is leading our battalion, and this makes us very confused. Fortunately, we are well aware of the quality, the courage, of the three company commandants, who know how to judge a situation and always stand firm alongside their men in the trenches. Lieutenants Larcher of the 9th, and Marennes of the 10th, both about twenty-six, are rivals in audacity. The former can always be found at the most exposed spot in his sector. The latter, according to runners, sits on the parapet to observe the German positions. Then there is Captain Antonelli of the 11th, who gets possessed by a raging fury whenever he goes into action, one which would certainly carry him to the front rank in a counter-attack; older than the other two, he wants to show he is their equal. All three would give their lives rather than surrender their trenches, and are an inspiration to their men. They compensate for the inadequacy of the battalion leader, receive his orders with contempt, and decide what needs doing between themselves. We count on them.

In a sap at the front line we discovered the bodies of some men from the battalion that we had relieved. We assume they died of asphyxia after a gas attack.

I have in my hand a little pocket Kodak that I found on one of them. I would like to keep it because the camera belonged to sub-lieutenant F.V— (of whose death I thus learned) whom I had known slightly at university where he was studying for a degree in literature. But I realise that doing so might be misinterpreted. So I put it back on to the little pile of personal effects, though I doubt it will ever reach his family. Others will perhaps have fewer scruples, without the excuse of remembrance.

Later on I slip the camera beneath the other objects. Not because I still want to take it. But it reminds me of its owner. F. V— showed great promise, and this death is heart-wrenching because just a hundred metres from here it struck someone who links me to the days before the war. The death of those whom we only knew in the war, however sad it is, does not have the same significance, the same resonance.

Our heavy artillery has begun methodical shelling at a rate of one round every five minutes. They fall short: 155s and 220s almost invariably come down on our own lines. One sergeant was thrown into the air, several men have been wounded. There is every reason to believe that during most bombardments we are getting hit by shells from our own side. Men keep running back, cursing, demanding they extend the range of fire. We send more and more messages and signals. To no effect. An angry sub-lieutenant comes to us:

'It's a disgrace! Where are the heavy artillery officers? We've never seen a single one and there's nothing else we can do.'

'What a bunch of swine! They're afraid of getting their boots dirty! They save their skin and don't give a damn about ours!'

He sets off again, tears of rage on his face. The firing goes on: regular, idiotic, unbearable. This is surely one torment that the men in the trenches could have been spared.

I am woken by a peculiar pain.

I am curled up in a narrow recess underneath a shelf full of papers, cards and bits of equipment. I am sleeping in the dark, forgotten, on a pile of sandbags that I found there.

The first thing I'm aware of is the thunderous roar of the bombardment outside. The second is the pain, which is now localised and makes me panic. But it's nothing, surely... no need to get excited... it will pass. Except that I have to face the facts: *I have a bad stomach upset*. I have to go outside. Go outside? All hell is breaking loose up there. The shelter is shaking and shuddering under the crashing waves of heavy shells. The roar of drumfire comes in, blast upon blast... I cannot go out!

A ridiculous, obscure little drama, and one in which my life may be at stake... My guts are fermenting, distending, pushing at my muscles which cannot hold back for long. My body is letting me down... OK, I've got to go!... Up there? I think of the latrines, near the entrance where the mortar shells are landing. I imagine the shrill, blinding night, the flashes of fire, the screech of the shells that you hear a tenth of a second before the blast. I cannot go, I cannot go out there! No, look, you don't get yourself killed for an upset stomach, you overcome it. It would be too stupid!

Alone, knees pulled up, hands clenched on my stomach, eyes shut, I am struggling with all my might, making a superhuman effort. I am writhing, sweating, holding back my cries. I've never endured anything like this. And it's not stopping... Can I hold out? I must, I must hang on...

'But just go and do what you've got to do!' I see myself coming back normally, the deed done, freed of my burden, intact and proud, as if I'd just accomplished some heroic act (and would it not be one?). I see myself, my face calm, my body purged, thinking: he who dares... 'But you know very well that you won't go.' No, I will not go...

This bombardment will never end...

I am weakening. The band of muscles is stretching, the safety valves will not hold. My joints are all knotted up by the effort, like an attack of rheumatism. I have to get out of here!

I extricate myself slowly, stand up, make my way across this mournful crypt, bent almost double, holding my leaden stomach which is making my legs give way, feeling for the walls, looking for space to put my feet in between the sleeping men. I keep stopping to hold back violent contractions, hopping about on the spot.

Once you leave the central area of the cave and turn right there is a long sloping passage leading to the surface. I am breathing cooler air now but it is acrid, and the explosions are becoming sharper. I can distinguish the slow glug-glug of the 210s, which have a very long range, and the way some speed up when they fall into the ravine. Short bursts of machine-gun fire. A faint crackling sound that must come from grenades. Trench mortars battering away, exploding slowly like mines in a quarry...

A sudden shaft of light, which seems to come from an air vent, illuminates the shelter and shows the entrance, the end of the tunnel, fifteen metres away. Then there is a strange kind of moonlight, a flare going off. This sight makes me freeze in the shadows and I begin to question myself like a patient hesitating at the door to the dentist's surgery. I think I feel a bit better. Yes, I definitely feel better, it was a good idea to walk... But the spasms start up again. I go a bit further on and in the darkness I bump into the two lookouts, who have come inside to shelter.

'Where are you going?'

'To the latrines.'

'You ain't exactly picked the best of moments to drop your trousers! Just listen to it out there. It's still hammering down.'

'Yes... you could be right.'

I squat down on a box. Being so close to all the flares and flashes is giving me more strength to resist. The lookouts continue:

'You can be sure the Boche have picked out the spot from aerial photos. They're chucking it down at us, the bastards! But anyway it's daft to let lads go outside, since you can't see a bloody thing. Everything's going up, you don't even know where the front lines are any more.'

The incoming shells are more distinct now, longer gaps between them. I'm going to try my luck.

'Get yourself ready,' they say. 'Better be quick!'

I'm out, trousers undone, bent over. I find the plank and let myself go, eyes shut. All my faculties are concentrated in my ears on which I depend to warn of any danger, decipher the sounds.

Vouououou... I rush back to the entrance, holding my trousers up with my hand. The mortar shell bursts very close by, its storm whistles over me, shrapnel slams into the ground.

'Not hit?' shout the anxious lookouts.

'No,' I say, coming inside.

'You can bet that would have stopped you in mid-flow! Pity you can't even take a shit in peace round here!'

I have to go again… I wait for a bit. Silence and darkness are returning to the night. The din of gunfire is no longer constant, the pauses are longer. Now's the time. My second visit lasts longer, and no shell disturbs me.

I make it back to the shelter and rest for a while with the lookouts, worn out and preparing myself for another attack of this treacherous colic. My body is empty and weak and the morning chill makes me shiver. My suffering has been pointless and ridiculous. My companions are complaining:

'How much longer are they going to leave us here?'

For long enough, I fear. That is, for a few more days. But the days last forever in this sector of condemned men, whom only luck can pardon.

The artillery's fury continues to intensify. Day and night we have no peace of mind. Day and night the shells, like a host of madmen with pickaxes, are smashing their way through to us, digging ever deeper. Day and night the projectiles doggedly rain down on this scrap of land that we have to defend. We know that an attack is in preparation, that there must be a denouement to these days of wrath. We know that the general staffs of two nations have begun a struggle over these plateaus in which their vanity and military reputations are at stake, that the result of this will raise one up and bring disgrace to the other, that this bitter, relentless battle which brings only despair to the soldiers who are fighting it is an ambitious calculation on the part of a few German generals who measure on the map every day how many centimetres still lie between them and the objective they brag of attaining, that they are vexed at the obstacles and delays we put in their way and blame these on the lack of courage of their own troops. We know that it will take deaths and more deaths on both sides for the one who launched the battle to be frightened by their losses and stop their campaign. But we also know that it takes an awful lot of victims to frighten a general, and the one stubbornly opposing us is nowhere near giving up yet.

The great offensives on the Western Front, which have all come to a standstill, make available a vast quantity of weaponry which is making local actions extremely bloody. Since Verdun, artillery barrages have become standard. The most minor assault is preceded by a bombardment aimed at flattening the enemy defences, and decimating and terrifying the garrisons. When firing is well aimed, those men who escape only do so because it is impossible to hit every single bit of land with shells. Those who are spared start to lose their reason.

Nothing I know has such a devastating effect on the morale of men in the depths of a shelter. The price they pay for their safety is nerves shaken and shattered to a terrible extent. I know of nothing more demoralising than this stealthy pounding, which hunts you down underground, which buries you in a stinking tunnel which may become your tomb. Going back to the surface requires an effort so great that you cannot force yourself to do it unless you overcome your terror at the start. You have to struggle with fear as soon as you have the first symptoms otherwise it will possess you and then you are lost, dragged into a breakdown that your imagination precipitates with its own, terrifying inventions. Your nerve centres, once they've been shattered, send out the wrong messages; even your instinctual self-preservation can be undermined by their absurd decisions. The greatest horror, aggravating the breakdown, is that fear still leaves men with the capacity to judge themselves. So you see yourself in the depths of ignominy and cannot regain your self-esteem, cannot justify yourself in your own eyes.

That is where I am…

I have fallen to the bottom of the abyss of my self, to the bottom of those dungeons where the soul's greatest secrets lie hidden, and it is a vile cesspit, a place of viscous darkness. Here is what I have been without knowing it, what I am: a fellow who is afraid, with an insurmountable fear, a cringing fear, that is crushing him… It would take brute force to drive me out of there. But I think I would rather die here than climb up those steps… I am so afraid that I have lost my attachment to life. And I disgust myself. I depended on my self-esteem to keep me going and I've lost it. How could I still display any confidence, knowing what I know about myself, how could I ever put myself forward, ever shine, after what I've discovered? I could fool others perhaps, but I would know I was lying, and this sham sickens me. I think of how I pitied Charlet in the hospital. I have fallen just as low as him.

I have stopped eating, my stomach is knotted and everything disgusts me. I drink nothing but coffee, and I smoke. In this perpetual night I no longer know one day from the next. I just sit in front of my little table, leaning over papers; I write, I draw, and take my turn as lookout for part of each night. Men I would rather not see pass by and sometimes bump into me; the wounded cry out in the corner where they have been left temporarily. I concentrate on pointless tasks. But I only hear the shells. The whole of the Chemin des Dames is shaking, and inside I am shaking with it.

I believe that if I had sufficient willpower to go out and go through a bombardment, it would free me from my obsession, like a highly dangerous vaccine can temporarily immunise those who can tolerate it. But I do not have that willpower and if I did I would not be so prostrate. And even then I'd have to revive it day after day.

I have even suspended my bodily functions: I no longer need to go to the latrines. I spend my free time out of sight in my little cubbyhole, listening to the noise outside. Every explosion of the bombardment hits me in the chest. I am ashamed of the sick animal wallowing in filth that I have become, but all my strings have snapped. My fear is abject. It makes me want to spit on myself.

In my cowardice, I rejoice at the fact that I have found an empty litre bottle complete with cork under the sandbags of my bedding. Periodically I turn on my side and piss in it, in short bursts, so that no one will catch me at my shameful little ruse. I am careful to empty the urine slowly throughout the day, so that it soaks into the ground. What a swine I have become!

Death would be preferable to this degrading torment... Yes, if this must continue much longer, I would rather die.

My mind is torturing me:

'You're just as much of a coward as the commandant!'

'But I'm not the commandant...'

'And if you were?'

'Then my self-respect would triumph.'

'And how about your self-respect as a soldier, what happened to that?'

'It wasn't a role I chose freely. And I'm not an example that anyone is supposed to follow.'

'And your dignity, dog?'

'Why, oh why are you asking all these questions?'

'Because the war is in these questions, in this internal conflict. The more you can think, the more you must suffer!'

And so mental suffering, which saps a man's morale and diminishes him, is added to physical suffering: 'It's your choice: degradation or shells.'

We must endure both...

'*Secret.*

Attachments: Operations order and map.

From Colonel Bail, commandant of the 903rd Infantry

Regiment, to battalion leader Tranquard, commandant of the 3rd
battalion of the 903rd.

Battalion leader Tranquard to make immediate preparations
for attack. Two companies to join the attack. Reserve company to
assemble in "Franconia" trench and be ready to reinforce assault
troops.

Objective: "Helmets" trench, from point A to point B as
indicated on map.

Zero hour: 5.15 a.m.

Units to be in place at 4.30 a.m. Artillery fire to begin at 5 a.m.

Battalion leader Tranquard to follow instructions detailed in
operations order regarding lateral liaison, signalling, ammunition
supply, evacuation of wounded, etc. But he is to take all measures
necessitated by the nature of the terrain or special circumstances
which he judges will contribute to success of operation.

Battalion leader Tranquard to keep Colonel Bail informed on
his preparations and to confirm to him at 4.30 a.m. by agreed
signals that his unit is ready for action.

Colonel commandant of the 903rd Infantry Regiment.

Signed: Bail.'

And, in the colonel's hand: 'The objective must be taken, the
regimental division expects nothing less. I am counting on the 3rd
battalion.'

It's ten o'clock at night. We are bending over the adjutant's
shoulder to read the terrible document he has just received from
the commandant.

The death sentence, the death sentence for many of us… We
look at each other and our looks reveal our distress. We have
not the courage to say a word. The runners set off, bearers of the
tragic news.

The news soon travels through the cave, wakes the sleepers,
fills the shadows with whispers, makes those lying down jump to
their feet with a start, like men who know they are doomed.

'We're going to attack!'

And then there is a heavy silence. The men fall still again, take refuge in the darkness to hide the agony on their faces.

Everyone is stunned, knocked senseless, throats squeezed by a noose of anguish: we're going to attack! Everyone retreats into his own forebodings and despair, tries to reassure, to control his unwilling, indignant, rebellious body, battles against hideous visions, images of corpses... The grim vigil begins.

'Quickly, take down the orders!'

I write. I write what the adjutant dictates, the words that prepare the massacre of my comrades, perhaps of me.

I feel like an accomplice. I also carefully copy several maps for the company commandants, drawing a line in red pencil to mark the objective. Like some staff officer at HQ... But I am part of this...

The orders are sent off. Now there is nothing to distract me. I imagine zero hour. For us, too, the day will be hard. There is no doubt we'll also be moving to the front.

Soldiers are going to attack; soldiers are going to perish. Would I give my life for the 'Helmets' trench? No! And the others? No! And yet dozens of men will give their lives, of necessity. Hundreds of men, who are so unwilling to fight, are going to attack.

We have no more illusions about combat... One single hope holds me up: perhaps I will not be compelled to fight. A shameful hope, a human hope!

I manage to get a little sleep.

The battalion adjutant calls us together and we can tell from his troubled manner that this is something very grave.

'The runners will march too!' he blurts out.

'Are you mad?' replies one of his compatriots.

'It's the commandant's decision.'

'Bastard! What good will it do?'

'We're all marching?'

'No. Half of you will march with the companies. The other half will stay here to carry orders. How many are you?'

'Not including signallers, cyclists and batmen, there are eight of us available.'

'Who wants to march with the companies?'

No one answers. The adjutant divides us into two groups. But when he is about to indicate which ones will go, which ones are condemned, he feels the weight of eight pairs of eyes fixed on him. He lowers his head, he cannot make the decision.

'Would you like to draw lots?'

There is nothing to say to that. We accept. He tears up two bits of paper into strips of different lengths and hides them behind his back.

'How do we do it? The short strip means you go to the front, the long one you stay here. OK?'

'Yes.'

He offers Frondet the two thin folds of paper sticking out of his fist. We stare at the fist which holds our fates, four lives. Frondet reaches out his hand, hesitates...

The explosion of a trench mortar which has landed outside blows out the candle flame. We shudder. Frondet jumps back:

'You, take one!' he tells me.

I pull out a strip which the men in my group stare at dumbly: it's the short one. Opening his fist, the adjutant confirms it. There is an agonising moment for everyone.

'All right, the question is solved!' I say with as much indifference as I can manage and a little smile that is supposed to mean: I couldn't care less!

The winners move away, shamefacedly. So as not to have to witness our pathetic attempts to keep a stiff upper lip. So as to spare us the cruel spectacle of their relief.

My three comrades are Frondet, Ricci and Pasquino. I guess that they resent me because I drew the wrong number. I put on a nonchalant air one more time, as much for them as for the adjutant who is observing how we are taking it:

'You'll see, it'll all turn out OK. We've made it back before, haven't we?'

No one is fooled by these assurances and I go off and huddle down in my corner where I do not have to hide my trepidation.

It is three in the morning. We will soon leave the shelter. I concentrate on my gear, to give myself the best chance. I know that freedom of movement is of capital importance. Since it's summer, I decide to leave behind my coat and second pack. I will march with my food pack, my canteen full of coffee, my gas mask and my pistol. The pistol is the best weapon for close combat. Mine holds seven rounds and I have a spare magazine in my left pocket. I am not so afraid of facing a German: it is a duel in which skill and cunning play their parts. But the shells, the barrage of fire, the machine guns…

If needs must, I could get some grenades in the trench. I do not like grenades. Still…

But I can't believe this is happening!… Ah, my pack of field dressings…

All around me men are now also getting themselves ready, cursing loudly, in a clatter of weapons and kit.

Then suddenly, from god knows where, the order comes which turns the terrible thoughts that preoccupy us into an immediate reality, and puts an end to our last respite:

'Outside!'

Frondet, very pale, is at my side: we must march together. We are swept into the ranks and drawn along with the irresistible force of the crowd. As I'm going up the steps I bang my leg against a box of grenades. The pain makes me pause for a moment.

'What's your problem? Shitting yourself?' growls a voice behind me, and I'm shoved forward with the brutality that comes from furious resentment and makes soldiers seem brave.

I'm stung by this vulgarity, and reply:

'Shut your mouth, you moron!'

The altercation does me good, spurs me on a bit.

Outside.

The fading darkness is still lit up by flares, cold shafts of light which dazzle us then leave us blundering in murky confusion. All our attention is focused on moving, marching. Force of habit is so strong, slavery so well organised that we go forward in good order, docilely, towards the one place on earth where we do not want to go, with mechanical haste.

We quickly reach the front line. Frondet and I go to meet Lieutenant Larcher, commander of the 9th. He calls to us from inside his shelter:

'Stay there, in the trench, with my runners.'

The first light of dawn sadly reveals the silent, dreary, ravaged battlefields where there is nothing but destruction and putrescence, reveals the ashen, dismal faces of men in muddy, bloodstained rags, shivering in the cold of morning, the cold in their souls, terrified attackers, praying for time to stop.

We drink eau-de-vie that has the sickly taste of blood and burns the stomach like acid. A foul chloroform to numb our brains, as we endure the torture of apprehension while waiting for the torture of our bodies, the living autopsy, the jagged scalpels of steel.

4.40 am. These minutes before the bombardment starts are the last of life for many among us. Looking at each other we dread already guessing who the victims will be. In a few moments some men will be ripped apart, flattened on the ground, will be corpses, objects of horror or indifference, scattered in shell holes, trampled underfoot, their pockets emptied, buried in haste. And yet, we want to live…

One of my neighbours offers us cigarettes, insists that we empty the packet. We try to refuse:

'What about you? Keep some for yourself.'

'I'm going to cop it!' he answers stubbornly, gasping like a dying man.

'Don't be so bloody daft.'

We take the cigarettes and smoke feverishly, before the inevitable. All possibility of retreat is gone.

A few trench mortar shells burst behind us. Machine guns rattle, bullets ping against the parapet that we must cross.

Our future is in front of us, on the ploughed-up, lifeless soil over which we must run, offering our chests, our stomachs…

We wait for zero hour, for our crucifixion, abandoned by God, condemned by man.

Desert! But it's too late…

'I've been hit!'

The shell just exploded there, on my right. I got a blow on the head that left me dizzy. I put my hand to my face, and took it away, covered in blood, and I do not dare assess how bad it is. I must have a hole in my cheek…

I am surrounded by whistling shells, explosions, smoke. Screaming soldiers barge into me, madness in their eyes, and I see trails of blood. But I am only thinking of myself, of my own calamity, my head down, hands on the embankment, like a man who is vomiting. I don't feel any pain.

Something detaches itself from me and falls at my feet: a flabby, red piece of flesh. Mine? My hand goes back to my face in horror, hesitates, starts with the neck, the jaw bone… I clench my teeth and feel the muscles working… Nothing. And then I understand: the shell has blown a man to pieces and slapped a human poultice on my cheek. I shudder with disgust. I spit on my hand and wipe it on my jacket. I spit on my handkerchief and rub at my sticky face.

The artillery thunders, obliterates, disembowels, terrifies. Everything is roaring, flashing, shuddering. The sky has disappeared. We are in the middle of a monstrous maelstrom, pieces of sky come crashing down and cover us with rubble, comets collide and crumble, sparking like a short circuit. We are caught in the end of a world. The earth is a burning building and all the exits have been bricked up. We are going to roast in this inferno...

Bodies whimper, dribble, soil themselves in shame. Thought prostrates itself, begs the cruel powers, the demonic forces. Tormented minds throb weakly. We are worms, writhing to escape the spade.

This is the consummation of ignominy. There is no disgrace we will not accept. To be a man is the depth of horror.

Just let me get away. Let me live in shame and infamy, but let me get away... Am I still me? Is this piece of jelly, this stagnant human puddle, really me? Am I alive?

'Get ready, we're going over!'

Ashen-faced, stupefied, the men draw themselves up a little, check their bayonets. The NCOs bark out commands, like sobs.

'Frondet!'

My comrade's teeth are chattering, shameful: my own image! Lieutenant Larcher stands in our midst, tense, holding himself up by his rank, his pride. He climbs up on the fire-step, looks at his watch, turns:

'Ready, lads, here we go...'

The final seconds, before the leap into the unknown, before the holocaust.

'Forward!'

The line shudders, the men clamber up. We repeat the shout, 'Forward', with all our might, like a cry for help. We throw ourselves behind that cry, into the stampede of the charge...

Standing upright on the plain.

The feeling of being suddenly naked, the feeling that there is nothing to protect you.

A rumbling vastness, a dark ocean with waves of earth and fire, chemical clouds that suffocate. Through it can be seen ordinary, everyday objects, a rifle, a mess tin, ammunition belts, a fence post, inexplicable presences in this zone of unreality.

Heads or tails for our lives! A kind of unconsciousness. The brain stops working, stops understanding. The soul separates from the body to accompany it, like an impotent, weeping guardian angel. The body seems suspended from a thread, like a puppet. Shrunken up, it rushes forward and totters on its soft little legs. The eyes distinguish only the immediate details of the surroundings and the act of running absorbs every faculty.

Men are falling, opening up, splitting, shattering. Shrapnel misses us, blasts of hot air envelop us. We hear the impact of bullets hitting *others*, their strangled cries. Every man for himself. We are running, each of us marked out. Now fear acts as a spring, multiplies our animal powers, makes us insensible.

The maddening chatter of a machine gun on the left. Where to go? Forward! There lies safety. We are charging to capture a shelter. The human machine is set in action and will only stop when pulverised.

Moments of madness. At ground level we can see flames, rifles, men. The sight of men enrages us. In that instant our fear is transformed into hatred, into the desire to kill.

'Boche! Boche!'

We are there. The Germans wave their arms about. They flee their trench and escape down a communication sap. A few desperate ones are still firing. I see one, threatening.

'You bastard! I'll get you!'

I spring like a tiger, with admirable agility and coordination. I jump down in the trench next to the German, who turns to face me. He raises one arm, or two, I don't know how many, or with what intention. My flying body dives, with unstoppable force, helmet first, into the stomach of the man in grey who falls on his back. And now I jump on this stomach, heels together, with all my weight. It buckles, gives way under me, like crushing an insect. Only then do I remember my pistol...

Now there is a second German in front of me, gaping with fear, open hands raised to his shoulders. OK, good, he's surrendering, leave him be. Perhaps I should not have hurt the other one but he was taking aim at me when I was already only twenty metres away, the fool! And it all happened so fast!

I stare at the prisoner, my fury suddenly calmed, not knowing what to do. At that moment, a bayonet, forcefully thrust from above on the plain, goes through his throat, and sticks into the side of the trench, so that the rifle's sights bang against the parapet. One of our men follows the weapon. The German remains suspended there, knees bent, mouth open, tongue hanging out, blocking the trench. It is ghastly. The one I stamped on is groaning. I step over him without looking down and get away as fast and far as I can.

Our assault wave has swarmed into the trench screaming. The *poilus* are like wild beasts in a cage. Chassignole shouts:

'There's one, over there! Let's give him a lesson!'

Another soldier grabs at my arm, pulls me along and, pointing at a corpse, tells me proudly:

'Look, that one was *mine*!'

It is an instinctive reaction, joyful savagery born of extreme stress. Fear has made us cruel. We need to kill to comfort ourselves and take revenge. Yet those Germans who escaped the first blows will come out of this unscathed. We cannot set upon unarmed enemies. We concentrate on rounding them up. From one sap where they had thought they'd die, twenty of them emerge, jabbering '*Kamerad*!' We notice their skin, green from terror and grey from malnutrition, their shifty, nervous glances like those of animals accustomed to ill-treatment, their excessive submissiveness. Our men push them about a bit, not with malice any more but with the astonished pride of conquerors. Naturally, we go through their pockets. We feel a degree of contempt for these pathetic enemies, a contempt that protects them:

'So that's all there is to the Boche!'

'We really got the drop on them!'

The *poilus* all crowd round, eagerly searching for a bit of booty to calm their overexcitement. We expected more resistance and our fury suddenly has no object.

Lieutenant Larcher comes into the trench and gives orders to the sergeants:

'Set up lookout positions straight away and post sentries. We must prepare to meet the counter-attack.'

'Let them try, the bastards!'

Success has given us enormous strength and confidence. We feel extraordinarily resilient, which comes from our desire to live and our fierce will to defend ourselves. Our blood is up and right now, in broad daylight, we fear no man.

Our artillery is striking hard in front of us, to wipe out any reaction from the enemy. The German batteries haven't shortened their range and continue to pound away at the positions we left. We are in a quiet zone. We take advantage of this to organise ourselves. Our fervour diminishes bit by bit, our courage vanishes like a drunkard's stupor, anxiety about the future returns. The men demand to be relieved, since they have done what was expected of them. We are hoping we will be withdrawn from here tonight. But a lot of things can happen before nightfall.

The exhausted artillery has more or less ceased fire and there is no sign of the enemy. We take advantage of the calm to escort the prisoners to the rear. There are four of us to take fifty of them. They offer no resistance at all and on the contrary seem very happy with the way things have turned out, and keen to get safely under cover at last. No sap leads from the captured trench back to our positions. We have to cross the plain, in full view of the Germans, but we are shielded by their own men on whom they will not fire. This protection allows us to take a look around.

On ground that is still smoking, our men, who regained consciousness of reality along with pain, are lying, howling like beasts. They are pleading not to be left to die alone on this plateau that is now bathed by the warm rays of the sun, shining joyfully for men who are whole and happy. But we cannot help them before nightfall. Those who are less severely wounded drag themselves along on their broken limbs with desperate energy, driven by the horror of the battlefield and the lack of aid. In a shell-hole one of them manages to use his knife to cut off the last strips of flesh holding his foot, which is hampering his progress by getting caught in the rough terrain. We take him with us. The gravely wounded have their hands clenched over the gashes in their bodies from which their lives are pouring in fountains of blood, lives whose memories they are replaying behind closed eyes, talking to themselves in the gathering fog of death. Others lie stretched out and still, calmed, of no importance: dead, just identity tags that we remove from their wrists to add to the lists. We also find scattered limbs, an arm, a leg, inert objects. A grimacing head has rolled off on its own. Mechanically, we look around for a body with which to join it in our thoughts.

When we are about twenty metres from our trench, we signal to the prisoners to pick up and carry some of the wounded. Those at least will be saved if there is still enough life in them. Shells start to fall again in our vicinity.

Confusion reigns at the command post, the chaos that comes with critical moments. There is a constant coming and going of runners, stretcher-bearers and officers, everyone swopping contradictory news, good or awful, based on whatever remarks distracted men have made on the hoof and which the general anxiety has quickly twisted and exaggerated. The sap has been swamped by a unit of reinforcements, detached from another battalion, making a lot of racket because they are afraid they'll have to join the battle. We push our way through this mob and get asked the same question as anyone who comes from outside:

'Much damage?'

We reach the adjutant and give him Lieutenant Larcher's report and the list of losses: a quarter of the men. We recognise the voice of the commandant, who has not left his little dugout;

he is phoning through to tell of our success, his success. We find our comrades again. They tell us that Ricci is dead, and in a corner we see Pasquino, completely dazed, struck dumb by shell shock, sobbing hysterically, making sounds rather like a muffled kazoo from his throat, and waving his arms around to signify the unbearable, like an idiot.

We ask to take the Germans to the colonel ourselves. Permission is granted. Together with Frondet we set off quickly, bringing Pasquino along so we can leave him at the first-aid post. After passing over the wounded to stretcher-bearers, we take the main trench on the opposite slope. Mortar shells are landing on the plateau and shrapnel whistles over our heads. The prisoners flatten themselves on the ground, jostling each other and emitting guttural cries. We force them to get up and march calmly. We have no wish to show fear in front of them, especially as we envy their luck: the war is over for them and they will be better nourished with us than they were before. We also know we are in a dead angle and not in much danger.

The shellfire increases. 210s are methodically hammering the ravine and the access routes; the enemy is trying to cut off our communications.

At last we reach the colonel's command post. We herd the prisoners into the cave where they are immediately surrounded by curious onlookers, and we go to tell an NCO of their arrival. Then we make ourselves scarce as fast as we can so no one can give us a mission that would oblige us to go out again during the intensifying bombardment. We are trying to gain time, as much time as possible.

We find the corner where all the cyclists, batmen and cooks from HQ are waiting. They ask us questions, give us food and drink, offer us cigarettes; they cover us in kindness, atoning for the safety that they are lucky enough to have. Their company has a soporific affect on us. We listen to the distant noise of shells above the thick vault that protects us: the thought of going back out there frightens us terribly. We shuffle about indecisively for a couple of hours, waiting for a lull, and sometimes approach the exit then go back in again. The cave is packed with men like us who have found shelter here and are putting off the moment when they must expose themselves once more. You can tell them by their worried air.

But eventually we know we will have no excuse for further delay. Abruptly we throw ourselves out of the exit, and run towards the front.

'We're getting a real hammering!'

Rolling fire has started hitting the ground around us, chasing us down into the bottom of the sap, making the beams of the shelter creak and filling it with gusts of warm air that smells of gunpowder. Candles flicker out, voices tremble. Then the bombardment silences us, overwhelms everything, devastates... The Germans are probably going to counter-attack...

Along with Frondet, we have tucked ourselves way in some dark corner, far from the adjutant, mixed in with men from the company. We are keeping our heads down, we do not want to be found and, if we hear someone calling, we will not answer. Enough is enough! We have done enough today. We don't want to go out, to cross the plateau under a barrage of shellfire, bank on another miracle to save our lives. We hide our faces, pretend to be asleep. But we listen intently, in terror and despair, to what is happening above us – sick with fear. A herd of elephants is up there, trampling and pulverising. The shells are masters of the earth. We are afraid, so afraid...

'It goes on for ever and ever... we won't escape!'

An explosion at one of the exits. The wounded scream, and scream...

* * * * *

The adjutant waited too long to pass on the orders. The companies were relieved long ago by the time we leave the battalion command post, and now it is the time for the artillery to start up again.

Fortunately, the clear night helps our progress, There are fifteen of us, all the runners, going as fast as we can. We can hear the explosions on the plain; our artillery is starting its work, and the Germans will not take long to respond.

The trench ends up at the foot of the ravine, from where a road leads to a crossroads named *The Crooked Farmhouse*, a bad spot. The explosions are ever more frequent and the night is furrowed by very low whistles, carrying off into the distance.

'The 75s are giving their best!'

We walk in silence. The mist hanging in the narrow valley muffles sounds. But still I listen hard to the trajectories tracing above us. I can soon make out whistles that sound suspicious: incoming, ending with the 'plop' typical of gas shells. No one suspects it yet, and if I give a warning I'll be laughed at. But I stay on my guard.

'Get down!'

We throw ourselves into the ditch. It is as if a line of overhead hoppers were coming off their rails and tipping out their cargo of explosives. The ravine resounds with detonations, shrapnel cuts through the night. More convoys of 150s come into their station in the sky, and tip over. The crossroads we need to pass is a volcano. We must wait. The screech of gas shells slips into gaps in the uproar.

Silence. A few seconds of silence, then one, two minutes' silence. We rush into this silence as if we were running across a collapsing footbridge. Our breathing has trouble keeping up with us, and starts to lag behind, groaning hoarsely.

The crossroads, the farm, the stench of gunpowder, fresh, smoking shell-holes...

'Right in the middle of the road!'

'Let's get out of here!'

If the German battery chief had ordered the gunners to open fire at that moment we would have been killed. We take off down the road which skirts the rear of our positions and leads to the canal. But the shells are cunning, and now they're exploding on our right.

'Into the field!'

We jump down. The 150s hit the ground at the same time as we do, near the farmhouse. Screams follow the explosions.

'Everyone still here?'

'Yes, yes, yes… one, two, three, four, five… fourteen!'

Good! The men who have been hit aren't ours – the others can look after themselves.

'We got out just in time!'

'Look out!'

Two seconds' anguish, every muscle clenched as death approaches. The thunderbolts miss us, scatter. Flick the switch: restart heart and lungs.

'Look out!'

The breath of these monsters flattens us on the ground, the explosions suck out our brains, empty our heads.

'Ah, shit!'

'Bad luck to get ourselves smashed up because of some idiot. We should have…'

'Look out!'

The blast of red fire spays up, very close.

'Aaaaaaaah… I'm hit…'

'Who's that?'

'Gérard,' a voice answers.

Vououou… Vrrroom… Vrrroom-vrrroom…

'Another one!'

Vrrroom-vrrroom-vrrroom… Vrrroom…

'Christ, we're all going to cop it! Let's get out of here!'

'Yeah, let's go!'

'Can Gérard walk?'

'Yes.'

A desperate dash, running for our lives, falling to the ground whenever shells come down. We are totally exposed on the road, surrounded by explosions. Zing! A piece of shrapnel hits a helmet... No more thoughts: run. All our will is concentrated in our lungs.

Ss-vrrraouf...The terrifying flash... that's it, this time... Me, me!...No, I'm not hit... But there must have been some damage... Three seconds' self-examination. Then an unrecognisable voice. Mine?

'Stop, stop!'

'Casualties?'

'Yes, right in front of me!'

'Who?'

'I don't know.'

'Then look, for christ's sake!'

'Who's got a torch?'

'Me!'

I take the torch, go forward, flood the ground with light. Horror! A corpse stretched out, a shattered head, half empty, brains like thick pink cream.

'One dead!'

'No wounded?'

'No.'

'Forward, forward!'

We can't go any faster, don't even hit the ground when we hear a shell. The explosions drive us on like whiplashes. We run and we run, veins pounding, vision clouded by red mist from the strain, the last effort.

'Halt!'

We have outrun the bombardment. We fall to the ground, try to gather our strength.

Zzziou-flac... Zzziou-flac... Zzziou-zzzziou-flac-flac... Gas shells are coming closer and the 150s seem to be coming back too. We get going. The road slopes gently down. Further on there's a sinister fog, which smells bad.

'Gas masks!'

They make walking very difficult. The eyepieces get steamed up, we breathe in hot, thin air with difficulty, and our pace slows.

Vouououou... The percussion shells are coming in again, targeting us. We pull off our masks and run for it, breathing in the poisonous air. But only for a short while. The road climbs again and the fog disperses. Finally the shells become much more intermittent.

The men with the heaviest loads slow down. The danger is moving away. We all flop down behind a bank which protects us from any last shrapnel.

'Christ, some bloody relief that was!'

We answer with nervous laughter, the laughter of the insane. Oh, and by the way, the dead man?

'Parmentier!'

Parmentier, yes Parmentier! Poor chap!

We laugh again, despite ourselves...

At first light we reach a village. Gérard, whose shoulder wound does not seem too bad, leaves us to go to a first-aid post. Then the adjutant goes off, looking for the commandant and some stretcher-bearers. We stay in the village square, beside a fountain.

'We're done in!' says Mourier, the runner for the machine-gunners, 'I'm going to try to find us a field kitchen.'

'You'll find bugger all!'

'They're bloody scarce!'

Off he goes. He has only walked a little way, hands in his pockets, when he encounters a police officer on horseback. He doesn't bother to give him a glance.

'Hey, you, have you stopped saluting? shouts the officer, rearing his horse.

We hear Mourier's angry answer, just before he disappears into a row of ruined houses:

'Where we've been, you only salute the dead!'

4

IN THE AISNE

'The unexamined life is not worth living'

Socrates

WE HAVE BEEN MOVING AROUND for a month or more.

At battalion HQ we enjoy the privilege of being able to leave our packs with the support unit transport. And some, myself included, have replaced their rifles with pistols, and thus also freed themselves of bayonets and bandoliers. This contravenes regulations but is tolerated, and we would in any case be hard pressed to find our own rifles again, now that they have mysteriously disappeared. It is quite possible that we bear some responsibility for these disappearances, but no one is ever going to get to the bottom of it. After years of war, we are firmly convinced – a rifle is of no use at all to soldiers like us, whose role is to rush around in the trenches and whose constant concern is to avoid any unexpected encounters with the enemy. On the contrary, it has major drawbacks: the care that has to be taken of the breech and barrel, its heavy weight, the way it slides about on the shoulder. Some prefer to get themselves short-barrelled carbines, easier weapons to handle, which you can attach with a strap. The ways we have managed to acquire arms to suit our taste remains obscure. But in short we have adapted our weaponry 'to the demands of modern warfare', which consist of avoiding anything that is fired at us, and our choices come with experience. It is in decisions like these that we can recognise the much celebrated initiative of the French soldier, with which he makes up for the deficiencies of the rule book concerning armies in the field.

Thus equipped according to our tastes, haversacks at our side, blankets across our chests instead of bandoliers, and canes in hand, our marches are turning into tourism. Those who are interested in the countryside can enjoy discovering panoramic views, picturesque bends in the road, a deep, crystal-clear lake at the foot of a valley, pastures as green as freshly painted railings, bright borders of birches round a park, an old house with rusty wrought iron and broken shutters which retains nobility in its decrepitude like a grand old lady fallen on hard times. Mornings are sweet delight, pale blue mist clearing to unveil wide vistas blushed with luminous pink. All of a sudden, the chime of church bells breaks the silence, while the farmyard cock warms himself in the sun, lord of all he surveys. We share the adventure of new billets in the evening, a village to explore with all it has to offer in the way of grocery shops, bars, wood and straw – and women, if we stay awhile. But women are rare and the countless men who lust after them get in each other's way. The excess of desires protects their virtue, and the beneficiaries of this are usually men stationed at the rear who have permanent quarters in the village.

We make up a little detachment at the head of the battalion, behind the commandant on horseback who is himself preceded by all the cyclists. The road opens before us, clear and empty. As we pass through towns and villages, we are the first to spot a pretty girl standing on her doorstep. My comrades, almost all from the south, greet her with an exclamation which needs to be heard with the right accent: *Vé, dé viannde!* Which makes it clear that their aspirations are not focused on the soul of this child.[34]

Behind us, men from the companies struggle with their loads of packs, light machine guns, and full bandoliers. They need marching songs to forget their fatigue. Drawing its recruits from Nice, Toulon, Marseille, etc., the regiment has kept its local traditions in spite of the incorporation of new elements from all over the country. One song is particularly popular. It celebrates the charms of a certain Thérèsina, a young woman who always extends a warm welcome to working men. Every couplet praises a different part of her superb body. The best bit, kept till last, is more or less the same as that which gourmets appreciate in chickens. More men join in, voices swell, and the song ends on this apotheosis:

> *Bella c...nassa,*
> *Quà Thérèsina,*
> *Bella c...nassa,*
> *Bella c...nassa,*
> *Per fare l'amoré.*
> *Thérèsina, mia bella,*
> *Per fare l'amoré.*
> *Thérèsina, mia bella,*
> *Per fa-ré l'a-mo-ré!* [35]

This evocation of the charming Thérèsina, half-Niçoise, half-Italian, has helped us up many a steep hill and over many a difficult stretch, as if possession of this military Venus must be the reward for our efforts.

Soldiers from the south are very demonstrative. During breaks, while we are all sitting around outside our billets, they shout out from group to group, and amiably insult each other in their colourful patois.

> *'Oh! Barrachini, commen ti va, lou miô amiqué?'*
> *'Ta mare la pétan! Qué fas aqui?'*
> *'Lou capitani ma couyonna fan dé pute!'*
> *'Vaï, vaï, brave, bayou-mi ouna cigaréta!'*
> *'Qué bâo pitchine qué fas!'* [36]

At the front, where there is the risk of the Germans listening in to our telephone communications, this patois is used as a code. I remember once hearing our adjutant announce a bombardment of our sector thus:

'*Lou Proussiane nous mondata bi bomba!*'

I do not understand everything. But I love this sonorous tongue, which evokes sunny lands with all their optimism and nonchalance, and lends a particular pungency to their tales. Sometimes when we're sharing a hut I have the impression of finding myself mixed in with an exotic tribe. These people experience the north as an exile. They say: 'We've come to fight for others. It isn't our country that's being attacked.' To them, their country is the shores of the Mediterranean, and they have no worries about their frontiers. They are astonished that people can fight tooth and nail over cold regions, blanketed in snow and fog for six months of the year.

Yet they perform their enforced role as soldiers just like everyone else – only with a bit more noise and cursing. They are easy people to get on with.

The battered division has gone to recuperate on quiet roads and in peaceful villages. Survivors of the Chemin des Dames have brought back a series of anecdotes which they embellish and gradually transform into feats of arms. Now that they are no longer in immediate danger, the simplest men forget how they shook with fear, forget their despair, and display a naïve pride. Poor men who paled in terror under the shells, and will do so again at the next engagement, make themselves into a legend worthy of Homer, without seeing that their vanity, which has nothing to feed on apart from the war, will become part of the same traditions of heroism and chivalrous combat that they usually scorn. If you were to ask them 'Were you afraid?' many would deny it. At the rear they start talking again of courage, dupes of this tawdry illusion. They like to impress civilians with tales of the horrors they have witnessed, exaggerating their own sangfroid. They bask in the joy of having survived the massacres, blot out the others that are being prepared, and the fact that their lives that they managed to save last time round will soon be threatened again. They live in the present, they eat and they drink. 'No need to worry!' they say, and in that they are mistaken.

Rewards and medals have been distributed, with the usual injustice. Men like lieutenants Larcher and Marennes, for example, who held the battalion together, have received hardly any recognition. When a battalion performs well, its leader is the first to get medals, and if he does not indicate those among his subordinates who showed merit, the higher ranks ignore them. In fact Commandant Tranquard abandoned us at our first break, without so much as a by your leave, and without bothering to put the affairs of his unit in order – 'like a yellow-belly' as people said. The men at the front fight amidst chaos; there are no witnesses, no umpires to record their successes. They alone can judge where honour is due. This makes most proud proclamations ridiculous and most honours a disgrace. We know of all the usurped reputations which nevertheless carry weight at the rear. Medals are a mockery when some share out the honours and everyone else shares the risks. And as for stripes, they quickly became absurd distinctions; we tore them off long ago. Their only value is for those passing their time in the military zone at the rear who want to impress people when they're on leave. For us, the front means the trenches.

We have been walking in the Vosges, revisiting the solemn, majestic forests and the silent mountain passes. We have got as far the Col de la Schlucht, opposite Munster. At the foot of the high peak of the Hohneck, its summit still covered with snow that had survived the summer, we were billeted in isolated encampments. In this valley of boredom we were only troubled by our own anti-aircraft batteries, whose shells fell back on us. Some victors of the last battles were thus stupidly wounded.

After Pétain's offensive, we returned to the Chemin des Dames, captured at last, to the area around Vauxaillon, to the left of the Moulin de Laffaux. Because of our advance, this sector was still disorganised. Paths led to the battalion command post, set up in a little house on a hillside and the runners had their shelter in some ruins.

Along with Frondet, I slept in a narrow passage which we shared with an unexploded shell from a 150 which had come through the wall. A main road led on to the front lines. Down on the plain we found a village hidden by trees, and German positions were scattered around the rich, unspoilt countryside.

We only got shelled at mealtimes in the field kitchens, and spent our leisure exploring the old enemy positions, which had been knocked to pieces by a bombardment lasting several days. On the Mont des Singes we found a number of German corpses, purple and swollen, in an advanced state of decomposition. Grimacing and terrifying, these hideous cadavers had been left to the worms which were coming out of their noses and mouths like some gruel that they vomited as they were dying. They awaited burial, eye sockets already picked clean, hands blackened and shrunken, clenched on the ground. In spite of the smell, the most hardened and greedy soldiers searched them again, but in vain. These unfortunates had already been robbed once by their conquerors, as revealed by their open jackets and turned-out pockets; all the trophies were long gone. Hatred played no part in this pillaging of their remains, merely the desire for booty, traditional in war, to the point of being its true motive, which could only find satisfaction on dead bodies, on quite rare occasions.

At least the corpses proved that the enemy was also taking serious losses, something we did not often have the means to verify. Then we alerted the sanitary brigade to their presence, and stopped going to see these rotting conquerors with empty pockets.

* * * * *

Now we are in another sector, and it looks like this time we will be here for a while.

On our right is the little village of Coucy, crowned by a medieval castle with round towers. On our right is the English army which is holding the Barisis sector. The reserve battalion occupies a huge limestone cave network, a '*creute*' – with entrances on the opposite slope beneath a plateau. Below us lie a valley, fields, a forest, and in the background, a canal. We take it in turns at the front line, between two sectors that have not been devastated and are covered with wild flowers.

The soldiers have returned to their monotonous duties: keeping watch and digging trenches. Men are increasingly dispersed, are expected to work to their limits. The hours of guard duty are extended. While some regiments only go up to the trenches to attack and do not stay there, ours hardly ever leaves them, except when it is moved. Our losses are generally less, but the work is exhausting. After two weeks at the front line, the battalions are moved back to the reserve positions, as close as they get to rest. At night, detachments are sent off in fatigue parties but in the daytime men remain in the cave with little to do and pass their time playing cards, engraving shell cases, sleeping, sewing or writing.

The days pass, indistinguishable in their tedium. Shells always find a few victims. There is nothing interesting in the communiqués and it is clear the war has no reason to stop.

In the morning the ground is hard, a thin film of ice covers the puddles and long-fallen leaves crackle underfoot. Winter has come and we have to prepare to spend it as well as possible. 'One more winter!' cry the men in despair. They draw up a balance sheet of four years of war. They have seen many of their comrades perish and have narrowly escaped death themselves several times, and yet the Allies have still not managed to carry out a major offensive which has shaken the enemy line or liberated a significant portion of territory. The battles of 1915 have won nothing but local advantages, paid for too dearly and without strategic importance. At Verdun we were on the defensive, the Somme was inconclusive, and last April's offensive was a crime that the whole army has condemned. We followed our brothers' rebellion at a distance and our hearts were with them: the mutinies were a human protest. Too much has been asked of us, our sacrifices have been wasted and abused. We know very well that it is the docility of the masses that permits so many horrors, our own docility… We are kept ignorant of battle plans, but we see the battles themselves, and we can judge.

No end seems in sight. Every day men fall. Every day we have less trust in our own luck. There are still some old hands in the platoons who have been there from the start, hardly leaving the front. Some of them believe themselves immune, invulnerable, but they are rare. The majority, on the contrary, estimate that the luck which has saved them will eventually turn. The more times a man has a lucky escape, the more he has the feeling his turn is coming. When he thinks back at the dangers he has undergone, he is caught by a retrospective terror, like someone who pales after having narrowly avoided a serious accident. We all have a fund of luck (we like to believe), and if you draw on it for too long there will be nothing left. Of course there is no law to this and everything comes down to probabilities. But faced with the injustice of fatality, we hang on to our lucky star, take refuge in absurd optimism, and we must forget that it is absurd or we will suffer. We have seen plenty of evidence of the fact that there is no predestination, but it's the only notion we have to keep us going.

Here everything is planned for killing. The ground is ready to receive us, the bullets are ready to hit us, the spots where the shells will explode are fixed in time and space, just like the paths of our destiny which will inevitably lead us to them. And yet we want to stay alive and we use all our mental strength to silence the voice of reason. We are well aware that death does not immortalise a human being in the memories of the living, it simply cancels him out.

The rose-pink morning light, the silence of dusk, the warmth of midday, all these are traps. Happiness is a ruse, preparing us for an ambush. A man feels a sudden sense of physical well-being and raises his head above the parapet: a bullet kills him. A bombardment goes on for hours but there are only a few victims, while a single shell fired for want of anything better to do lands in the middle of a platoon and wipes it out. A soldier comes back from the long nightmare of Verdun and on an exercise a grenade detonates in his hand, tearing off his arm, ripping open his chest.

The horror of war resides in this gnawing anxiety. It resides in the continuation, the incessant repetition of danger. War is permanent threat. 'We know not the place or the hour.' But we know the place exists and the hour will come. It is insane to hope that we will always escape.

That is why thinking is so terrible. That is why the most simple-minded, illogical men are the strongest. I do not mean our leaders: they are playing out a role, doing what they are employed to do. They have the satisfactions of vanity and they have more comfort (and some of them weaken nonetheless). But the soldiers!

I have noticed that the bravest are the ones most lacking in imagination and sensitivity. This is understandable. If life had not already accustomed the men in the front lines to resignation and the passive obedience of the humble, they would run away. And if those defending the front were highly strung intellectuals, the war would soon become impossible.

The men at the front are dupes. They suspect this may be the case. But their inability to think very far, their habit of following the crowd, keeps them here. The soldier on the parapet is caught between two powerful forces. Ahead of him, the enemy army. Behind him the barrier of gendarmes, the chains of hierarchies and ambitions, held together by the moral pressure of the country, which lives with a concept of war that goes back a hundred years, and cries: 'Fight to the finish!' On the other side the people at the rear respond: '*Nach Paris!*' Stuck between these two forces, the soldier, be he French or German, cannot go forward and cannot go back. So it is that the shout sometimes heard from the German trenches, '*Kamerad Franzose!*', is quite probably sincere. Fritz is closer to the *poilu* than to his own field marshal. And the *poilu* is closer to Fritz, because of the suffering they share, than to the men in Compiègne.[37] Our uniforms are different but we are all proletarians of duty and honour, miners who labour in competitive pits, but above all miners, with the same pay and risking the same explosions of firedamp.

One quiet and sunny day, two enemy combatants, at the same time and place, put their heads above the parapet and see each other, thirty metres apart. The blue soldier and the grey one, having prudently reassured themselves they can trust each other, venture a smile and gaze across in mutual astonishment, as if to ask: 'What the fuck are we doing here?' That is the question both armies are asking themselves.

In a corner of the Vosges sector there was a platoon that was on good terms with the enemy. Each clan got on with its tasks openly and cordially greeted the opposing clan. Everyone freely enjoyed the fresh air and incoming projectiles consisted of loaves of bread and packets of tobacco. Once or twice a day a German would shout '*Offizier!*' to signal that their bosses were making their rounds. This meant 'Look out! We may be forced to lob a few grenades over.' They even warned of an attack and the information was accurate. Then the story got out. An inquiry was ordered. There was talk of treason and court martials and some NCOs lost their stripes. The fear seemed to be that the troops would come together to end the war, overruling the generals. Apparently this outcome would have been something terrible.

Hatred must never diminish. That is the order. But in spite of everything we are losing our appetite for hatred…

* * * * *

'16 February 1918.

...The Boche have been very aggressive in the past twenty-four hours. They had had the foolhardy notion of carrying off some of our men, and to prepare for this unpleasant attack had subjected us to an intense bombardment. This began last night, which was clumsy of them since it put us in a bad mood by compelling us to get up. They carried on this morning and just now attempted an assault which failed. We didn't even see the tips of their noses. In front of our lines we have grown a thick crop of barbed wire, and it seems most probable this artificial vegetation stopped the marauders. That, and the fact that our own artillery returned their politeness with typically French good grace and generosity.

'This evening it seems that the people opposite have abandoned their dark designs on us. They must be starting to realise that the road to Paris is a bumpy one and that in order to get there it might be better to borrow a Cook's Guide than to adopt the manners of Roman conquerors.

'There was a spot of damage. The destroyers of cathedrals smashed one of our shelters which, fortunately enough, was empty at the time. We will add this to our bill.

'Yesterday we knocked down one of their aeroplanes. We followed the progress of the combat from its beginning way up high to the last shots exchanged one hundred and fifty metres above our heads. Our fighter, circling round the German two-seater, forced it to land behind our lines: the observer was killed and the pilot wounded. Our men ran over and brought us the wicked archangel on a stretcher. The commander interrogated him but couldn't find out much. His boots were removed to allow his wounds to be dressed and one of his feet was bare. We were very struck by how clean this foot was, toenails perfectly manicured. It made us respect this defeated enemy with broken wings: we thought of our own, black, infantry feet... Imagine a dishwasher comparing her chapped hands to the delicate hands of a duchess!

'It has to be said that the Germans also knocked down one of ours last week. But the cowards were five against one. The pilot of our single-seater, blinded by the sun, was caught high up by a whole squadron. At first he fought to break through the ring of enemy planes surrounding him. And then he dived below the clouds to escape. The squadron dived down after him, all six aeroplanes levelling out just above the ground at 200 kph. Behind our Spad, which was losing speed, five two-seaters were taking turns to use their machine guns. They flew over us at three hundred metres. The birds of prey killed the dragonfly. The light-coloured aeroplane dropped vertically, like some crazy diver leaping off a springboard with outstretched arms. It crashed behind a little wood, a kilometre away. Our hearts stopped for a few seconds and we felt we were falling into the void with him. There is something supernatural about these aerial battles for us, earthlings with heavy legs, caked in mud.

'What else can I tell you? I did a bit of carpentry recently. I wanted to make myself a little bunk bed. A difficult task, since we don't have any tools. I had to run halfway round the whole sector to find one bad hammer, a broken saw, a few pieces of plank and some nails. Still, I am quite pleased with my construction even if it is a little fragile. My labours brought me rest. Bear in mind that I can sleep perfectly well on the ground or a table. But I had not found any surface that was right for my size, and the little pallet is definitely more comfortable for a long break.

'It's been cold but sunny, perfect walking weather. When you climb up on the ridge that protects us, you can see hills, woods, roads down in the valley – off in the distance a lake glistens, and there are crenelated ruins, so many things. It is lovely. It would be so nice to go down there along the grassy path. But the path is out of bounds and the valley is deadly. The Boches would be quite capable of killing a peaceful stroller. No doubt about it. We are crafty old warriors and they won't get us so easily.

'We have no idea what actions are being planned. We eat jam and smoke English tobacco that our cyclists buy from our neighbours. Ensuring we get plenty of provisions is our chief preoccupation. Currently, my immediate goal is a new pair of trousers – and maybe a couple of shirts and some socks. I am preparing my attack. I will probably avoid the quartermaster and attempt an enveloping movement on the storekeeper. I hope to open the engagement with some serious preparation, such as the contents of a two-litre "water" bottle...'

I am writing to my sister. There is no truth in what I write, no deep truth. I am describing the outer surface, the picturesque side of war, a war fought by enthusiasts that does not involve me. Why do I put on this dilettante tone, this false assurance which is the opposite of what we are really thinking? Because they cannot understand. For those at the rear we write letters filled with suitable lies, lies 'to keep them happy'. We tell them about *their* war, the one that they will enjoy hearing about, and we keep ours secret. We know our letters are destined for fathers to read aloud to each other in cafés, so they can say: 'Those young devils don't have a care in the world! Huh! I tell you, they've got the best of it. If only we were still their age...' To all the concessions we have made to the war, we add our sincerity. Since they cannot estimate the true cost of our sacrifice, we tell more tall stories, with a sneer. Me just like everyone else, everyone else just like me...

One evening in early March, already quite warm.

We are holding the regiment's right sector. The battalion command post is on the side of a rugged ravine, and smoke is rising from our camp kitchens at the bottom. A little higher up is the start of the plateau where we have established our front lines, about a thousand metres ahead. In this bleak, bare place, our view is limited by three arid slopes. But on the left we have a vista of a smaller, gentler valley. In the mornings the trees tremble in a fresh breeze blowing across the plain and the sun piercing the mist drapes it with rosy pink, like tulle on a woman's skin. Rolling hills form the background, harmoniously arranged with that unaffected charm you find in landscape paintings of the French countryside.

All is quiet, as usual. We are waiting for the end of a day like the rest, in the great idleness of war that is only broken by various little tasks. We have a good shelter, quite spacious and bright, solidly constructed, partly underground. We enjoy the calm, safely outside our cave.

All of a sudden, the peace is shattered by a massive artillery barrage. Despite the distance, we can feel the shock waves of exploding mortar shells. From the first shots, we recognise the frenzied rhythm of a major attack. Shells soon start whistling low overhead. They have missed the ridge and explode on the other side of the ravine, which fills with black clouds of smoke. Powerful time-shells burst in the air, blotting out the sky. There can be no doubt about it: this is preparation for an assault or an all-out attack, made all the more dangerous by the fact that at the end of the long access trenches we only have a single front line, and the troops manning it are spread out widely.

This looks very bad. We were not thinking about the war and now must face it with all its dangers. Men are going to die, perhaps some are dead already, and we are all threatened. We get our kit together nervously, so as to be ready for whatever comes. Our hearts are less submissive than our bodies and you can read our anxiety on our faces.

Our little group is not at full strength. In peaceful sectors like this one, people wander off on whatever pretexts they can find. We have no idea where the others are.

The battalion leader sends off two runners to alert the reserves in the rear. They set off through the upper end of the ravine. Two more go to find the colonel. Must we go forward? That is the only question that matters.

Our own artillery goes into action. Now we can hear the howls of our 75s. The air is full of the roar and rush of shell after shell. The din gets louder.

The commandant summons the adjutant who returns quickly.

'Runners to the companies.'

Two men take the trench that leads to the company on the right. But it is on the left that the bombardment seems to be doing most damage... There is only one runner left and a runner is never sent out alone under shellfire. The adjutant hesitates... At that moment we see a man running across the ravine and clambering up the slope, and soon he appears, breathless and soaked in sweat. It's Aillod from the 11th. He lets out the sigh that means: 'Saved!' But the adjutant calls out his name:

'You're to go to the 9th with Julien.'

'Yeah, sure, the same ones get sent every bloody time!' he responds feebly, standing in front of me.

I see how terror has replaced joy on his face, and I meet his gaze, the gaze of a dog who is used to being beaten, a man picked out to die. That gaze makes me ashamed. Without thinking, and just because it is unfair, I shout:

'I'll go!'

I see his gaze come back to life, its gratitude. And I see the astonishment of the adjutant:

'OK, good, off you go!'

I know this sector because I have been through it to check our maps. I set off and Julien follows me... It is a twenty-minute walk, with detours, to reach the command post of the company on the left, at the end of our front line.

We soon emerge on to the plateau where the ground is shaken by shock waves from explosions that are now even more intense, violent and resonant. Waves of steel are crashing down in front of us, in a great wall of smoke as if an oil well had caught fire. We dive on into it, driven by the force of the order we have been given, prisoners of discipline just as surely as if we'd been handcuffed.

I become aware of what I am doing. I am a volunteer, I asked to go through this avalanche… This is madness! No one has volunteered for ages, no one wants to take upon themselves the responsibility for what will happen, to usurp the role of chance, to expose themselves to regretting having been struck down.

Something strange is happening to me. My character is such that I always take logic to its limits, accept my acts in all their consequences, envisage the worst. Now I've embarked on this mad adventure by a simple reflex, without taking the time to consider it. But it is too late to go back. I will go where I have promised to go.

Now we are entering the zone of heat and chaos. Shells are exploding nearby, throwing up showers of metal; fierce gusts of air make us stagger. Behind me I catch the sound of Julien panting like a dog trotting after his master's carriage. It's not our pace that's making him breathless, it's suffocating terror. I know that these surprise bombardments are short but extremely violent. For an hour, this is Verdun, this is the Chemin des Dames, this is as relentless as it gets. And we are under it. Either I must take some sort of moral decision or collapse in shame. I can feel fear rising up, hear its moans, and I know its livid mask will cover my face, making me gasp like a fox fleeing the pack…

Logic dictates to me: to be a volunteer is to accept all the risks of war, *to accept to die*… I need this consent to continue, need this agreement between my will and my action…

'So, you accept?'

'Yes! I do.'

'The final sacrifice?'

'Yes, yes, just get it over with!'

This slim, blond boy, with his pale skin and well-proportioned body (the legs a little too heavy, for my taste), this boy of twenty-two who looks sixteen, this soldier with a schoolboy's face, his forehead still smooth, and his mocking smile, they say (how could it not be mocking?), and his eyes that stare into the depths of beings (I know how my mechanism works, I have taken it apart often enough), this Jean Dartemont, is going to die, on this March evening in 1918, because a man said: 'It's always the same ones who have to take the risks', because in the gaze of this man with whom he could not have had an hour's enjoyable conversation he found some unbearable glimmer of reproachful light, which was immediately extinguished by the habit of submission...

Striding forward vigorously like a true infantryman, Jean Dartemont is going to get himself killed on this plateau of the Aisne and he is not calling for help from either the notion of duty or God. As for God, he cannot love him without loving the shells that he sends, which seems absurd to him. If he calls upon him, it is only confusedly: 'I am giving the most that I can give and you know what it is costing me. If you are just, then judge. If you are not, then I have nothing to expect from you!'

He is going to get himself killed, this boy, because he thinks it is inevitable. Just for self-esteem. Ever since he began to think, he only envisaged life in terms of a success. Precisely what success he did not know, except that this success would be inseparable from an inner success, sanctioned by himself. Such a conception does not allow him to face death resolutely without having the *intention* of dying.

At that moment, he has it. The mind has mastered the body, and the body will no longer shirk at marching on to the final agony.

I can read myself clearly because I have been turning over these questions for years. The answers had been prepared for the day when I was in the final extremity. That is the moment when I must hold to the principles that I have made for myself.

I will witness my death. Only one thing shocks me: the feeling of pity that death evokes in the living. They look on a corpse as the remains of someone defeated. I will get myself killed in a little local action, one that will not even get mentioned in dispatches, stupidly, in some corner of a trench. They will say: 'Now Dartemont, there was a chap who might have made something of himself but he never got the chance'. The earth will cover my corpse and time my memory. They will not know what happened inside me at the final moment, will not know that I volunteered for death, defeated myself – the only kind of victory that is precious to me. But I am well used to ignoring the opinions of others. Who cares what stories they will tell!

I still need to face pain, which I dread. I consider the worst pains I have endured: neuralgia, a bout of typhoid, a broken arm. But I cannot recall the feelings. Pain has no place in time, its duration is short. It will be numbed by shock at the start. Then the flesh will give out its dramatic cries. An hour, two hours... If it is unbearable then I will end it with the loaded pistol I have ready in my hand. But at least the mind will keep this lucidity: 'I thought as much.' I will not be left with that appalling terror-stricken gaze that you see on those taken by surprise, who had not already given their consent.

My mind is imagining what will happen to me so intensely that I am already wounded as I am marching; my stomach is open, my chest smashed in, each shot that spares me nonetheless penetrates my flesh, cuts it and tears it and burns it. The sacrifice is consummated. The blow I am awaiting, from one second to the next, cannot be worse. It will only be the last blow, the *coup de grâce*...

'Let's stay here!' shouts Julien behind me.

I had forgotten him. I turn round and see his haggard face. He points out a sap to me, one running across our trench which is caught in enfilade shellfire.

'Let's stay in there for a moment.'

'Stay if you want, I'm going on,' I say rather cruelly.

Since my decision is made I have no reason to take cover. But the briefest pause, the least hesitation would weaken my resolve.

Now I cannot throw everything into question again. And besides, what Julien is suggesting is stupid, based on fear of going further. We would hardly be protected in a little deserted sap in which I do not know of a single shelter.

I set off and he follows me again without saying anything. I am truly not afraid. The trench is blocked: I clamber over the pile of earth without any rush, hardly even ducking, and find myself on a level with the plain. Mechanically, I glance across the devastated landscape. A shell explodes on my right, the red gleam in the middle of the black ball of combustion imprints itself on my retina.

We are approaching the company sector. I am still unscathed, but I hang on to my idea: to die. I push away the hope that tries to insinuate itself. With the hope of escaping reappears the wish to flee. My mind continues to offer me up to the shrapnel, still waits for the blow that will finish me off. I repeat to myself: get my face smashed in! This familiar phrase suits me very well, it diminishes the thing's importance.

We come out into the front line, and turn left. The explosions merge into one, the whistles from the two artilleries, the noise of shrapnel and shells, are all mixed together. Under a heavy bombardment it is almost impossible to distinguish the incoming shells. I am amazed that all this violent rage is spread above us without any consequences. The trench is deserted for a long stretch.

At last we find a small group of men squeezed up against the parapet. A look out peers furtively out over the plain. He shouts to us:

'We've seen the Boche down there!'

Down there is precisely where we are going. Too bad! Our mission is to reach the lieutenant, to pass on news. Onwards!

We go round a few traverses. Suddenly I find myself facing a revolver: a French one. The lieutenant has come with an escort to find out what's happened. We tell him that his men are still at their posts. He turns round and takes us with him. For two hundred metres, the position had been badly damaged by box barrage fire, aimed at cutting off the place where the enemy wanted to attack. After this point we were moving away from danger. Soon we reached the command post and went down into the shelter.

'Wait here,' says the lieutenant, 'until it's over.'

Life was given back to me.

'What got into you?' they asked, when I returned to the battalion.

'We were saying, Dartemont's trying to get himself a commendation.'

But I've already got my commendation. I awarded it to myself, and I don't give a damn for those of the army, which sanction the circumstances and ignore the motives.

In my comrades' attitude, there is amazement and something like blame, as if they're saying to themselves: 'he knows all the dodges, that one!' They cannot accept that I went off simply because I wanted to. My gesture seems inexplicable to them and they search for an ulterior motive. If I confided to Aillod that I just risked my life because of him, even though my role protected me, it would surely astonish him. In war, one does not do things for sentimental reasons! And, if I told the men about the decision I had taken just now as the shells came down, if I told them what I had been thinking, they would not believe me. How many have anticipated their deaths resolutely? I have gained nothing by following the impulse that drew me along. But I acted for myself. I am happy enough with this spontaneous act and with the way I accepted my responsibilities.

We get the casualty lists. The wounded arrive on stretchers and their cries bring misery to the twilight. A German corpse is also brought in, a soldier who fell just in front of the company and who was found in the grass. So the Germans really did get right up to our lines and this corpse is the proof of our victory. He has no papers on him, no army number. Enemies always conceal the identity of soldiers on patrol so as not to reveal the positions of their divisions.

At an early hour I go and stretch out on my bunk in the dark, and reflect on this evening's events. So, in order to be courageous, I now have a fairly simple means at my disposal: to accept death. I recall that once before, in Artois, when it was a matter of going out and facing machine guns, I had adopted this idea for some hours. Then the orders had changed.

Those who go forward – and it is most of them – saying to themselves: 'Nothing will happen to me' are ridiculous. I cannot sustain myself with a notion like this, for I'm well aware that the cemeteries are full of people who had hoped they would come back, who had convinced themselves that bullets and shells made a choice. All the dead had put themselves under the protection of some personal providence, distracted from all the others to watch over them. Without that, how many would have come to get themselves killed?

I know I am incapable of courage unless I have decided to give my life. Without that choice, there is nothing but flight. But you take such a decision on the spur of the moment and you cannot make it last for weeks and months. The mental effort is too great. Hence the rarity of true courage. We generally accept a kind of lame compromise between the destiny and the man, which reason rejects.

Until now I have shown absolute courage twice. This will be the greatest thing I will have done in the war.

Then I think of the words of Baboin: 'Don't try to be too clever...' Today I tried to be clever, and, if I want 'to come back' it would be a good idea not to give in to such impulses too often...

* * * * *

There is a growing rumour that a major German offensive is soon coming, but no one knows where. The offensive is a direct conse-quence of the Russians' withdrawal which has freed up a lot of enemy troops. It is said that our command is ready for it and has taken the necessary steps.

The army has placed its confidence in General Pétain, who has shown some concern for the troops' welfare. He has a reputation for not wanting to squander the lives of his men. After the carnage organised by Nivelle and Mangin, generally considered here as bloodthirsty monsters, the army needed reassurance. We know that the two victorious operations led by the new commander-in-chief, at the Chemin des Dames and Verdun, were wisely conducted, with adequate matériel. Pétain has understood that this is a war of weaponry and that reserves are not inexhaustible. Unfortunately, he came too late.

The prospect of great battles ahead is enough to trouble us. But being attacked does not frighten us any more than an offensive led by us. On the contrary we estimate that it is prudent to wait. Selfishly enough, we hope that this business will not start where we are.

The days are bright. Now every night we hear droning in the sky. German aeroplanes are flying over the lines above us, on their way to bomb Paris. We lack the means to block their passage. But we wave to the invisible aviators:

'The patriots are going to catch it!'

'It might do them some good. What civilians need is a few hours of bombs falling smack on their bloody heads!'

'Yeah, then see if they still shout "never surrender"!'

'What's really stupid is destroying ancient monuments.'

'Oh, right, that's a good one! Isn't your hide worth a monument? You think anyone gives a damn if you're blown to buggery?'

'Let the old Parisians have a taste of it for once!'

'It'd be a good laugh if they dropped a big one right on the Ministry of War!'

'Shut your mouth, you defeatist!'

'Listen to this bloody turncoat! You little twerp, you yellow-belly tin soldier!'

'The first thing to do in war,' says Patard, the artillery telephonist, 'is destroy. That way it's over quicker.'

That is his guiding principle and he acts on it. Whatever is intact, he smashes up; whatever is smashed up he finishes off; and whatever isn't guarded, he steals. His pockets are full of strange objects. He is the biggest filch anyone has ever seen, the terror of kitchens, canteens, and shops. His most famous exploit is to have 'pinched' the breeches and boots of his divisional general. It happened at the Chemin des Dames. At the back of a dugout, Patard was busy making imitation police headgear that he had the notion of selling to the men of his regiment. But he needed some braid to decorate the caps. In order to obtain it, he offered to go to the division during a bombardment to exchange a piece of broken equipment. It was while he was poking about down there that he came across the fine linen breeches hanging from a nail, red ones, exactly the colour he needed. Since a pair of boots was standing alongside, he took them as well, and made his way back to the trenches. The general made an almighty fuss, but never suspected that his breeches, cut into fine strips, had ended up on the heads of the gunners and that he was saluting them every time he encountered his men. Having cut off the shoes and changed the colour of the 'aviator' boots, Patard fashioned himself a pair of gaiters, with which he shamelessly declared himself quite enchanted: 'The general certainly didn't rob me with these, old chap!'

His time at Verdun, accompanied by his pal Oripot, was the occasion for another remarkable achievement. This is how he tells it:

'So, we turn up at the front with the sarge and all our clobber, somewhere near Vaux. The sarge was a decent bloke but the sector was a dump: craters all over the place, shells raining down, and all the brass hiding underground. "OK," I says to the sarge, "it ain't worth the trouble of unwinding the phone line just so it'll get cut, is it?" "Do what you like," he says. "All right then," I says, "I'll go for a wander with Oripot and find us a bit of nourishment." "What you going to find?" he says. "There's always something to find," I tells him. After sniffing around this desert for a bit we come across a sort of vault at the back of the Vaux fortress, which was a food store, absolutely stuffed with nosh of every kind, all you could wish for. But there was no way of sneaking in. The door was guarded by a pair of territorials, real sticklers. "What do you want?" they asks me. "A bit of grub, eh!" "You got a docket?" "No," I says. "You gotta have a docket!" "What docket?" They explains to me how it works. "Right," says I, "I'll go and get one of these dockets!" Back we go to the sarge and tell him the set-up. "But I can't sign one of those!" he says. (You always get a few dopes even among the educated.) "You just have to sign it as Chuzac!" That was the name of a former group officer who had got on the wrong end of a mortar shell. We go back to the territorials with a docket for food for twenty-five lads. Oh, fellers, you wouldn't believe it! Five big cans full of *gniole* and kilos of chocolate, and jams, and meths for the camp stove, and you name it! We found ourselves a nice deep shell-hole where we melted the chocolate in the brandy. In twenty-four hours we'd drained all five cans. Then back we go to the two codgers with another docket, and another, and another, till it was all over. "You haven't suffered any losses, then?" asks the territorials. "We're in a safe spot!" I tells them. Stupid old buggers!'

'But wasn't there fighting going on around you?'

'That I couldn't tell you. I suppose so, but I didn't see anything. We weren't sober for the whole three weeks in our crater. We ate and drank our way through eight hundred francs.'

'How's that?'

'The regiment got the bill a month later. The territorials had sent the dockets on up to the commissariat. It seems the nosh had to be paid for.'

'Was there any trouble?'

'You bet there was. They had themselves an inquiry. But what you gonna do with an inquiry at Verdun! They couldn't suppose that two blokes had treated themselves to eight hundred francs' worth of brandy and chocolate in three weeks. You can say only two, because the sarge didn't have much.'

'Life was cushy at Verdun, believe you me!' declares Oripot.

'The funniest thing,' Pacard goes on, 'is Oripot's brother, who's a priest...'

'He's a decent lad!' exclaims Oripot.

'Decent he may be, but he's still a twat! He was writing to this sod here, telling him you mustn't drink too much, think of your family. I was reading his letters cos it's easier to see when he's asleep... Mustn't drink, says his brother. Damn it! If you don't get pissed, what's the point of having a war?'

One morning at reveille, the front starts to growl fiercely on our left, beside Chauny. We recognise the thunder, the hammering that the earth transmits like a conductor and which passes through the air in mournful waves. Something very bad is going on and it isn't far away.

We are not getting any information. The rumbling goes on all day and starts again the next morning. We don't get any letters or newspapers, always a bad sign.

On the third day we learn that the German offensive has broken through the British front. We learn that artillery is firing on Paris. The battle is turning to a disaster. But optimistic informants claim that the retreat is a trap laid for the Germans in order to 'thrash' them in open country. For what it is worth, we make do with this rumour and wait to hear more.

A new military doctrine is being spread around: 'territory is not what matters.' How true! And yet we are rather close to Paris to start innovating. And why if this is true have so many men been massacred to take a salient or occupy a ridge?

On the fourth day, enemy observation balloons are openly flying behind us. We are going to be outflanked... It seems unlikely that we will emerge unscathed from this situation.

Leave is suspended. Orders come, instructing us to transport weaponry and munitions to the rear. We are on fatigues for two nights.

Then the orders are countermanded. We restock with cartridges and boxes of grenades. After that no one knows. We have battle orders, some dealing with resistance where we are, others with evacuation. Our command is hesitating between the two. Our own preference is for the latter, and it seems to us impossible to resist a heavy attack with the small numbers we have holding our lines.

More days of uncertainty go by. The sector livens up. We are getting some heavy incoming shells, which are obviously range-finding. Our fate is clear!

'They'll have another go to get it right!' mutter the men in the trenches.

'Will it stand up to a 210?' we ask ourselves as we look at our shelter.

'With a long-range 210 they can't miss!'

This realisation does not do much for our morale, and we would dearly like to avoid fighting. We are now in the first days of April and the Germans are near Amiens.

Without any warning, our front lines are evacuated at night. The companies have been brought back to our second lines on the ridges, and we have just set up our battalion command post in the rear, in a huge cave, full of men, its approaches crowded with vehicles laden with matériel and with ragged territorials.

The following morning the bombardment resounds opposite

us and we get the last ricochets. The Germans are smashing up our abandoned positions. Then we are informed that they have broken through and are making slow progress. Our troops are falling back but doing them some damage on the way. All day long the artillery roars and machine guns crackle. Coucy is heavily bombarded. We do not leave the command post, we cannot see what is happening ahead of us, and we do not know where our units are.

The companies take advantage of the night to take up new positions. The battle starts again at daybreak and there is much confusion. Shells fall at random. We abandon the cave, retreat across the countryside, following the ravines. We spend part of the day on the slopes of a wooded hill. Every quarter of an hour the sky is filled with a tremendous whistling noise. 380s crash down into the soft earth of the valley but none of them explodes. Later on we skirt the ridges and come back down on to the plain following the slopes of a spur.

There we learn that the battalion has mustered ahead of us, on the far side of the canal, and runners get the order to rejoin it. In groups of two or three we set off along a quiet stretch of road. On our way we pass some of our men leading a tall German prisoner, wearing a leather helmet, looking extremely cross and agitated. He is an airman who was flying a spotter plane very low over our platoons and was shot down with rifle fire.

The battalion is drawn up along a bank going up from the road. We are pointed to a sloping field that blocks the horizon and told that 'the Boches are up there, in the grass behind the ridge'. They must be able to see us and are hesitating: the battle would degenerate into hand-to-hand combat. No one fires and our little detachments continue to move around freely in the open. The proximity of our enemies does not bother us, far less than a bombardment would. We fix bayonets. We hold our fire until they stand up: we will see clearly. They are only men like us. But the Germans do not try anything.

At sunset we get the order to fall back. We cross back over the canal, which must mark the furthest point of the enemy advance. We do all this in silence, without casualties. We return to the high ground. Ammunition wagons gallop by. Around us the 75s open fire. Fresh troops arrive whose duty will be to defend our new positions. The retreat has been carried out in good order, without too much damage, without our leaving the enemy with prisoners. It must be said that the attack was somewhat half-hearted, the Germans counting on their strategic advantage to compel us to withdraw.

We vanish into the night, heading for the rear. We are marching towards fresh dangers but there will be time enough to think of them when we have to face them. For now, our role here is over. This happy retreat feels like a victory. Soon sounds can be heard from our column, the men are singing and swearing. We've got out of it alive, one more time.

5

IN CHAMPAGNE

A MARCH LASTING SEVERAL HOURS in torrential rain has brought us to the heart of 'dry' Champagne.[38] The downpours pen us like cattle in a slough of despond, where all we can see is running water, dampening and depressing our spirits. Miserable huts, soiled with the mud that cakes our boots, remind us of prison camps. Our clothes are soaked, our food cold, and we have no way of making a fire. Fatigue stretches us out on the damp straw of our pallets but steam rises from our bodies and we cannot get warm. We had not seen a single tree or house in our surroundings. This is an inhospitable, hostile land, where nature itself denies us the smallest bit of joy.

We stay for a week in the tarpaulin shacks, surrounded by deep puddles, lacking anything which could make our lives more agreeable.

One morning the captain who is temporarily in command takes us off to reconnoitre the support positions that we must soon occupy. Our sector is located between Tahure and the Main des Massiges, names made famous by our offensive in 1915. It is well equipped and the trench system is very deep, as it was in Artois. Everywhere we find old battery emplacements and empty shelters, in the walls of the trenches. The reserve battalion occupies the reverse slope of a ridge, behind another ridge that hides the summits where the trenches are. On our right you can see in the distance a great expanse of green, which contrasts with the bare, grey landscape, like a desert, that we have under our noses. They say it is the Argonne.

The battalion command post is a dugout in a trench, roofed with a good thickness of logs, and with openings at ground level to let in the light. It is relatively comfortable. We are not going any further forward today.

On our way back we make a halt in a ruined village some four kilometres from the front lines, where the colonel has set up his headquarters in some very fine shelters built against the wall of a quarry. They look as stylish as mountain chalets and are fronted by an arcade protected by sandbags in zigzag rows. The neat and tidy surroundings are impressive.

Through the windows we can see secretaries in their indoor clothes, writing and drawing at large tables, cigarettes in hand. Typewriters imitate the sound of machine guns in a way that is silly and unseemly. Batmen hurry about, bringing bowls and bottles of eau de cologne, and cooks carry folded napkins over their arms, like maîtres d'hôtel. We hardly go near these privileged ones, these courtiers, who keep us at a distance as if we were of no account. They are afraid lest among our number are Gascon cadets[39] who might rise too swiftly in their careers under the benevolent eyes of the great and powerful. Everyone here is defending his position and scents a rival a mile off. A fall from favour may mean a return to the front line, the threat of death. This world of employees knows all the servants' gossip and office secrets. The desire to flatter, to make oneself indispensable, leads to an excess of zeal. There are corporals here who would strike fear in the heart of a battalion leader.

The officers of the colonel's entourage (his deputy officer, an information officer, an officer for the 37mm cannon, flag bearer, etc.) are carefully shaved, powdered and scented; these are men who have time to devote to their toilet. In particular they must be good company, clubbable, able to tell a funny story over dinner. They do not concern themselves with the actual war except in extremis, and, if at all possible, at a good distance.

Finally the colonel shows up. He's tall and slim, with a long Gallic moustache, dressed in khaki, cap pulled down over one ear, chest pushed out – very much the musketeer. (In civilian life, with light trousers and white gaiters, he would make a classic ageing philanderer.) He pulls himself to his full height when he sees a soldier, fixes his magnetic gaze upon him, and salutes him with a fulsome gesture which might signify 'All honour to you, bravest of the brave!' or 'Always follow my plume!'[40] Unfortunately, at the moment of a skirmish, that plume will stay put rather far in the rear... I am only going by appearances, and I do not know the true worth of the colonel, apart from his theatrical salute. But I never trust people who give themselves airs.

His audience over, the captain rejoins us. We leave Versailles...

Just before we set off for the front, a new battalion leader has come to take command of our unit. This is our third commandant since I became a runner, not counting the temporary captains. Changes like this always worry us. Our fate can depend on the cool-headedness of our leader, and our well-being depends on his moods.

The newcomer has a distrustful manner. He handed me all the operations maps he found in the shelter and told me: 'Check all these and bring them up to date.'

So twice a day I take my gas mask, my helmet, my revolver, my cane, my pencil and papers and set off alone on topographic reconnaissance. It is a hard job to identify the terrain because bombardments have levelled it all, destroyed all the landmarks. I have to establish a point using some detail from the trenches and determine other points on the basis of this one. The sector is absolutely vast, the front line for three companies stretching over about twelve hundred metres, on the flank of the first

GABRIEL CHEVALLIER

summits of the Champagne mountains, whose peaks are held by the Germans. Their dominant position compelled us to fill in parts of the trenches dating from their occupation and to dig new communication trenches which they could not see or hit with direct fire from machine guns. The result was a tangle of trenches that I have to explore to get my bearings, indications on the map being somewhat fanciful. I often climb over barriers of sandbags, making myself visible at ground level for a few seconds, and I wander through abandoned trenches which are crumbling away and getting covered by grass. The slope facing the Germans is deserted. I find myself in total solitude for hundreds of metres, and, if I were to get seriously wounded, no one would have the idea of looking for me in places where I am the only one to venture. In the beginning I had a few bullets fired at me, luckily from five hundred metres; they served to warn me of the danger presented by these old ditches. I go back there, though, taking all due precautions, as much for pleasure as necessity. I love the isolation, the silence, I love discovering old dugouts with mushrooms growing on their damp walls, which have all the poignant mystery of ruins. These particular ruins have their own pathos, and I imagine the destinies of the men who spent time here, many of them now dead. Along with pleasure comes pride in knowing secret places, which become my own domain, on this land that one army observes and another defends.

My first concern is to mark those shelters and dugouts that are in good condition. It inevitably happens that the zone I am exploring as I make my rounds gets hit by some shells. I then run for the nearest shelter. I am more afraid of shells than bullets. Because of their stupid noise and the way they rip apart the body. Bullets are more discreet and operate more cleanly.

I spend a lot of time at the front lines, to the point where look outs start to wonder what form of madness compels me to roam around places that they would dearly like to leave. The colonel wants the fullest details and demands that the thickness of each barbed-wire entanglement be indicated on the map. Since it is out of the question to go and take measurements in front of our lines, I estimate as best I can by looking over the parapet. It is a tricky task which could, with a moment's distraction, earn me a bullet in the head.

My conscientiousness does not spare me from reproaches. Recently, and with his customary asperity, the commandant held out a map to me and said:

'You don't really know what you're doing. That squad isn't there.'

After a fortnight we have been able to judge that our commandant is not an ill-natured man. But he does have bad manners and the burden of responsibilities weighs heavily on his mind. I replied with good humour:

'It is you who are making a mistake, sir. The squad is indeed there and I will show you on the ground whenever you like.'

'You are sure of this?'

'Quite sure, sir.'

'OK.'

He must have checked for himself later. He did not mention it again and ever since then he exercises his authority more politely.

We have just heard the news about the offensive at the Chemin des Dames: a new breach has been opened in our front lines and is getting wider by the minute. They say that the Germans turned up in Fismes a few hours after they launched the attack, catching by surprise a paymaster general, some airmen, etc. To those who know the region, the speed of their advance is overwhelming. It is also overwhelming to know that the enemy is marching on Fère-en-Tardenois, where we have seen fields full of munitions stretching off into the distance, vast depots of matériel that they are going to capture.

Two strong surprise attacks on neighbouring sectors to our right and left caused us some losses. The Germans are harassing us with shells without any warning. I have been caught several times by unexpected shelling, and the other day nearly got killed on some low ground. Everything is going badly. The end seems further away than ever... I am at the end of my tether. I think to myself:

'I've had enough of this! I'm twenty-three years old, I'm already twenty-three! Back in 1914 I embarked on a future that I wanted to be full and rich and in fact I've got nothing at all. I am spending my best years here, wasting my youth on mindless tasks, in stupid subservience; the life I'm living goes against everything that is dear to me, it doesn't offer me any goal but burdens me with privations and constraints, and may well finish with my death... I've had enough! I am the centre of the world, as each of us is for himself the centre of the world. I am not responsible for others' mistakes, I have nothing to do with their ambitions and their appetites, and I have better things to do than pay for their glory and their profits with my blood. Let those who love war make it, I want nothing more to do with it. It's the business of professionals, let them sort it out between themselves, let them do their job. It isn't mine! By what right can these strategists do with me as they please, when I can see through all their ruinous, murderous elucubrations? I reject their hierarchy which is no measure of true worth, I reject the policies that have led to this. I have no faith in those who organise massacres, I despise even their victories for I have seen what they are made of. I have no hatred, I only detest mediocrities and fools, and often enough they get promoted, they become all-powerful. My patrimony is my life. I have nothing more precious to defend. My homeland is whatever I manage to earn or to create. Once I am dead, I don't give a damn how the living divide up the world, about the frontiers they draw on their maps, about their alliances and their enmities. I demand to live in peace, far away from barracks, battlefields and military minds and machinery in any shape or form. I do not care where I live, but I demand to live in peace and to slowly become what I must become... Killing has no place in my ideals. And if I must die, I intend to die freely, for an idea that I cherish, in a conflict where I will have my share of responsibility...'

'Dartemont!'

'Sir?'

'Go and check where the 11th have positioned their machine guns. On the double.'

'Very good, sir!'

We are back at camp, having a rest without any pleasures or distractions. Inside the barracks the sun bakes us alive, but we cannot stay outside either, on this dry, chalk plateau, flayed by the heat, that could have come straight out of the kiln.

Our armies are still in retreat. In the newspapers that reach us irregularly, we are following the German advance. Its successes worry us, not because they foretell defeat, for we do not believe final defeat is possible now that the Americans have joined in, but because they are postponing the end for months or years. The words victory and rout have no meaning for us any more. A corpse is just a corpse, whether it is at Charleroi or in the Marne. We have all had years of this war, been wounded, and our wish to stay alive is stronger than ever.

We were struck by a flu epidemic and a lot of men were evacuated. I had an attack myself. On the evening when we were being relieved, fever took hold of me, and as I was leaving the trench, my legs gave way. Luckily I found a cart that brought me here. I've just spent four days flat on a straw mattress, not eating.

Today, at the beginning of the afternoon, I'm in the office with the adjutant. He is sitting on a bench and smoking, and I am rolled up in a blanket. We are both thinking about the latest events. He claps his hands to his temples, raises his eyes to heaven, and, in his southern accent, cries:

'What a bloody mess!'

'This would all have been finished long ago if we hadn't made so many mistakes…'

'When you think that they actually rejected peace!… Imagine, rejecting peace!… Sweet God!… It could hardly be any worse!'

The latch on the door snaps open and a head peers in. We see it is Frondet, dirty, unshaven, with his tortured face and feverish eyes. Seeing we are alone he comes in. He looks strange and is smiling oddly. He looks at us searchingly. And then this well-bred, high-principled believer opens his mouth in a sneer and very quietly utters these terrible words:

'*They* are at Château-Thierry[41]… Maybe it's going to end!'

His words embarrass us… There is a long silence in which we both ask ourselves, on the brink of treason, whether to accept or reject his implied outcome to the war.

Then the adjutant pulls up his sleeves, and rubs his hands together. The gesture of Pontius Pilate…

'What we all want is to get back home!'

On the night of 6 July we make a halt in the village where the colonel is based. Our commandant goes to collect his orders, and tells us on his return:

'In three days' time the Boche will attack right across the Champagne front. We have this from unimpeachable sources.'

We camp among the ruins which are becoming the base for reserves. I work through until morning with the adjutant, preparing various urgent communications.

It is most likely that the Germans will unleash their preparatory artillery barrages during the night and their troops will advance at dawn. This is the standard tactic in a big push. It has the advantage of surprise and leaves a whole day for troops to advance through unknown country. To counter it, every day at nightfall we withdraw our troops from the front line trenches over a depth of two or three kilometres, leaving behind a few sacrificial victims charged with signalling the enemy approach by launching flares. The troops take up defensive positions on the ridge, protecting a line that the enemy must not be allowed to cross. Just before daybreak our battalions go back to their usual front line positions and make it clear by their activity that they are still there. It is vital that the enemy does not know about this manoeuvre. Basically, we are doing to him what he successfully did to us in April '17 at different points on the Chemin des Dames. He will squander his bombardment on empty trenches and then throw himself against well-manned positions equipped with machine guns. The battle will take place on ground of our choosing.

While we were resting, the sector had been arming itself at a prodigious rate. We wake the next morning to find guns all over the place. The biggest, the 120s and long-barrelled 155 GPFs, and the 270s which fire enormous shells, are hidden behind walls and banks. On the right, shells have simply been piled up in cornfields which provide them with natural camouflage. The countryside is suddenly packed with all kinds of artillery, its dark, gaping mouths menacing the other army. They say there are tanks at the rear and General Gouraud is ready for anything. All these preparations give us some confidence.

The sector's gun batteries are doing their own preparatory work, their aim being to make life difficult for enemy troop concentrations. Between sunset and three in the morning each battery fires several hundred shells filled with mustard gas. The new batteries remain silent, for the Germans must not suspect their presence until the fighting starts.

All the activity is on our side and at night. In the daytime we've never known the sector so quiet. Not a single explosion or rifle shot, not a German aeroplane to be seen; the enemy isn't even sending up observation balloons any more. Deep silence reigns, off into infinity, beneath the clear, blue sky. You can make out all the little sounds of a summer's day in the country, made by unseen creatures; the buzz and hum of insects, the beating of countless wings, and the faint rustle and crackle of the corn in the heat. Yet this peace is one more portent of what is to come. We read in the reports that a similar torpor preceded the offensives at Amiens and Château-Thierry.

My name is on the list of those due for leave at the next departure. I am waiting for the attack, or my leave. Which will come first?

A few days go by. It's leave… I hurriedly bid farewell to my envious comrades.

It's 15 July and I am off to visit friends in the suburbs. On the tram I open the newspaper. Banner headlines announce the defeat of the German offensive in Champagne. My first instinctive thought is: 'I got out of it!' My second is about the men in my regiment, who are fighting at this very moment, being shelled and counter-attacking. I am too closely bound to them to forget. What state will they be in when I return?

My friends, who are industrialists, have a son who is about to be called up, and his mother is worried. So she has decided to help her son's career by finding him the connections that could get him into a sector where he would not be in too much danger; their choice was motor transport. This provident mother had used her wiles to establish good relations with a general attached to the regional command and to persuade him to accept an invitation to visit their home. She had been warned that this general had a mania for writing little plays in verse, somewhere between tragedies and revues. To cement their relationship she came up with the idea of putting on one his dramas at a charity fête in aid of a small hospital that she manages. It is to this fête that we have been invited.

I am presented to the general. The embarrassment is mutual.

Neither of us knows how to properly reconcile hierarchy with normal social relations. Cap in hand, I salute, but without standing to attention, and make a slight bow. But I prevent myself from saying 'Delighted to meet you!' (a soldier in uniform cannot be delighted to meet a general, even at a social occasion). He looks at me.

'Aha! Excellent! Good day, young man!'

He does not ask about the war. It's not his department.

This is the first time I've met a general in private life; I observe this one closely. He's a stout little man with a red face, who walks with his legs apart like a cavalier. He is wearing the old-fashioned uniform of black tunic and red trousers over elasticated boots. He has a poet's long, flowing locks, a nasty glint in his eye, the air of a cunning satyr. The table is set for twenty and he has been placed on the immediate right of the lady of the house. He speaks in a clipped military manner, picks and chooses among the different dishes, and puts his nose to women's arms as if to check how fresh they smell. His sense of humour bears an unpleasant trace of the barracks; he tells funny stories that are somewhat coarser than one is used to accept in polite society. Moreover he eats heartily and gulps down the burgundy with impressive intrepidity. He does not look up from his plate except to sniff his female neighbours and leer at their décolletage. Since he is the man who must protect young Frédéric, the son of the house, one finds these manners absolutely charming. One responds favourably to his jokes.

After coffee, the cars take us to the nearby aerodrome. A Bessonneau hangar has been transformed into a theatre. A stage has been built, benches set out, and acting roles given to young aviators, of whom the bourgeoisie of this place have provided rather a lot. Soldiers from the camp, wounded from the hospital, and local people are all there. The general, surrounded by various dignitaries, sits in the front row in an armchair. The curtain rises. As was to be expected, the revue celebrates the virtues of the race and the valour of our fighters. One after another, an infantryman, artilleryman, horseman, machine-gunner, grenadier, etc., come on to the stage and recite Cornelian couplets with very warlike vehemence. At the end of each tableau, a luminous France, draped in tricolour sheets, clasps them all to her bosom. The general's sublime alexandrines, in which 'trench' rhymes with 'French' and 'savagery' with 'Germany' are greatly relished by the civilians, who stamp their feet with restrained enthusiasm. It is a real shame to let such energy go to waste; they should be given weapons immediately and taken to Champagne...

The general receives many congratulations, which he accepts with the modesty of genius. My obscurity luckily prohibits me from offering my own: a common soldier cannot have an opinion on something that emanates from a great leader. At last he is accompanied to his staff car. He carefully settles himself down on his cushions and makes his departure, distributing little limp waves as he goes, like a bishop giving blessings.

The lady of the house then discovers that the envelope he has given her for her hospital contains a derisory sum, the kind of tip one might give a maid. Some observe that his behaviour at dinner was not of the best, and I foresee the moment when he will be denounced as a miserable skinflint . . . But the appearance of Frédéric tempers any criticism: the child has not yet been placed! Until further notice it is advisable to find the general charming, refined, spiritual...

I realise how useful it is for a young man in troubled times to have a rich father and energetic mother... I tell myself, too, that generals are less fearsome when they put their names to verse rather than battle orders. At least the one who has just left only murders language.

When I return to my sector, all is in order again. People tell me what had happened.

On the evening of 13 July, a surprise attack near the village of

Tahure gained us some German prisoners in assault kit. From them we learned that the German attack, postponed by our poison-gas shells, was fixed for the following morning. Orders were immediately given, runners set off in all directions. At eleven in the evening, Gouraud's forces were put on full alert, the infantry took up combat positions and the artillerymen stood by their guns. On all sides hundreds of thousands of men were anxiously awaiting the moment when the silence would be shattered.

At midnight, a great blaze of light filled the horizon. The German artillery was starting its bombardment. But even before its first salvo had hit the ground, the sky turned crimson on the French side. Our own artillery was beginning its job, with greater fire-power. And we were striking our blows on massed troops, while the enemy's shells were hammering down on empty positions. We were the ones causing destruction, not only of troop units and dugouts, but of the morale of men who would very soon have to go through this storm.

They attacked at dawn, as predicted. Our artillery reduced its range from our abandoned trenches to a point ahead of our line of defence. Batteries of 75s specially adapted for barrage fire went into action. Successive waves of German forces, sticking to their timetables, piled up at the same place and were flattened without being able to cross the fire zone. From its new positions, our infantry machine-gunned them at good range. The attackers' situation became untenable, they had to fall back and more were killed by the mustard gas we had put in the trenches when we left them. During the day of 14 July the great German push (the push 'for peace') was broken, having failed to make any serious breaches in our positions. Over the next days our troops reoccupied their former emplacements without encountering much resistance. As the men sum it up:

'The Boche came a cropper!'

Few traces can be seen of the hard battle that has just taken place. The trenches have already been repaired and the fresh shell-holes merge with old ones on this lifeless ground which has been pulverised so many times. Once again, the defenders have won.

In our own group there was only one victim: Frondet, who died of shock. During the bombardment, a 210 shell had pierced through the logs covering the shelter where the battalion runners were based and rolled on to the middle of the floor, without hitting anyone or exploding. But there were three terrifying seconds, in the sudden presence of this monstrosity that might go off and pulverize the petrified men. Frondet's heart gave up.

'He just stayed there like that...'

'His mouth gaping, his eyes wide open, like the face of some bloke in a film calling for help.'

'We thought he was kidding at first...'

Poor Frondet! Yes, I can well imagine the expression on his face – the expression they have all had, without ever knowing it...

'You know, when you have a great shock...'

'After that blow, we just stood there for a good quarter of an hour unable to say a word.'

'We had the feeling that if we spoke we'd set the thing off.'

'Did the battalion catch it badly?'

'The 11th got it worst. Three platoon leaders and forty men cut down.'

'And the 9th?'

'Not much. They were lucky.'

We are not being relieved. Reserves must be getting rarer. We go back to our usual tasks.

One morning I am making my rounds of the sector. Down in the ravine I bump into my company commandant, Lieutenant Larcher. Proud of his own courage, of his influence over the men whose dangers he shares, he is rather scornful of the battalion's 'dug-ins' – like me – and he shows it. Although I am often there and he knows it, he pretends to be surprised:

'What are you doing here?'.

'Checking the maps, and inspecting a bit of the sector.'

'I'll show you round.'

He takes me with him. Fifty metres on, we find a machine-gun emplacement. The lieutenant climbs up on the fire-step and I climb up beside him. Our chests are fully exposed above the trench. We are surrounded and overlooked by enemy lines. I know this spot and I have climbed up here on my own already, but very briefly. Today it is up to the lieutenant to decide how long we will stand here. He points out a bank of yellow clay some three of four hundred metres away.

'The Boche are there, and there, and there...'

He smugly goes through all the enemy positions, in detail... I see: this is a game of pride! Here we both are, with no witnesses, very calm, risking our lives. I ask a few questions coldly and he gives me the answers. Neither the questions nor the answers are of any interest. He is thinking: 'So, you dabble in inspecting the lines, like an amateur. I'll soon put you off that!' And I am thinking: 'I am just as capable of taking risks as some little lieutenant, however brave he's supposed to be...' But the Boche have a lot of patience this morning!

Rat-tat-tat-tat, ss-ss-ss-ss. Bullets whistle around us. The lieutenant has jumped down into the trench and he pulls at my sleeve.

'You'll get yourself killed!'

I calmly descend. I am surprised, not by the bullets – which were to be expected – but because he gave way so fast. He stares at me. We are both thinking the same thing: 'Well, well...' I am sure I have not gone pale. Abruptly, he shakes my hand.

'So, there we are! Enjoy your stroll, old chap!'

'Thank you, sir,' I say in the normal tone of a subordinate.

These are the childish amusements we still get up to in August 1918! Good lord, I am sure that if I had commanded a company my men too would have said: 'That Lieutenant Dartemont, he's got guts!' It is true that perhaps I would then have been killed a long time ago...

Two surprise attacks have shaken the sector.

One evening at sunset, outside the battalion's deep shelter, we were happily assembling our bags ready to be relieved later that night. Some men had already put their gear on the road below where the trucks would arrive.

Machine-gun fire overhead makes us look up. Above the German lines two aeroplanes are ducking and diving round each other and exchanging fire. Everyone's attention is fixed on the sky. Before choosing our preferred victor, we are all peering to see which one has our colours...

Rrrran, rrrran, rrrran, rrrran, vraouf, vraouf, vraouf-vraouf... Bombardment, earth shaking... Vououou... 150s coming straight at us. We throw ourselves down the steps of the sap, tumble down into the depths of the shelter... We are overcome with the stunned stupor that always accompanies the start of an attack, gripped by terror. The dark question rises up from the depths where it slumbered: 'Is this the hour?' We look at each other, mutely: 'Who's it going to be? Who'll be hit in the next second?' And then the silent prayers, the refusal: 'no, no, not me!' We are extremely shaken. Heavy shells are exploding right outside the entrances to the shelter, the trench has been targeted exactly, the acrid smoke comes down in waves and makes us cough. Now, we are eight hundred metres behind the front lines. Such deep shelling makes us fear some major attack.

The telephone rings. The commandant answers:

'Yes, sir, we're getting it... don't know yet... on the right especially... Yes, sir... I'll keep you informed.'

Will men be sent out?... The dull rumbling tears at our chests, the accurate shelling makes it hard to stop shuddering.

'Runners!'

The adjutant peers through the darkness. In a corner there is a short argument: the runners are defending their lives. 'It's not my turn to go... Not mine either.' And then the judgement is passed: 'You and you.' Four men set off for the companies, breathless even before they have started running. We look away as they pass to hide our shameful joy: any of us might have been chosen... They wait on the top steps. After a burst of firing, they take a deep breath, throw themselves outside, heads down, like divers.

We wait for them to come back. It will take a good half-hour.

Two runners arrive from the 9th and one of them, white-faced, is wounded. Lieutenant Larcher sends the news that everyone is at his post and that there is no sign of the enemy.

The telephone rings again. In the rear, the colonel is getting impatient, under pressure himself from divisional command. The runners shake with fear and try to hide. But the commandant has the good sense just to grumble, 'Let them come and look for themselves if they're in such a hurry!' and not to risk the lives of more men.

We spend another twenty minutes wondering whether the Germans are not about to arrive...

Then we notice that the bombardment is slowing down.

'All over!' says the adjutant.

Chests heave deep sighs of relief, the tension falls. A little later, other runners bring the first reports. The enemy penetrated the front-line trenches of the 10th and took some prisoners, we don't yet know how many. The lieutenant will send details as soon as he's clarified the situation.

In the meantime we go to look at the damage. It is night outside. The trench has caved in and we get stuck in the churned-up soil. The front is silent, the evening chilly. We worry again about when we will be relieved.

Finally the company report arrives. We can reconstruct the progress of the attack. The aerial combat had been a fake so as to distract the attention of our look outs. Assault troops had been massed in abandoned trenches between the lines. At the first explosions, they surged out, rushed to our lines, surrounded a detachment of machine-gunners and threw grenades into a dugout. Our casualties were eight missing, three dead and seven wounded. One of the dead had just been given leave and was to have set off the next day to get married.

No problem as far as the dead and wounded are concerned: their names are added to the profit and loss sheet. But command cannot accept that men disappear, cannot accept the surprises or hazards of war. Someone must be responsible. The machine-gun officer and the company commandant are both incriminated and they turn against each other. The former claims that 'the infantry gave no support to my machine-gunners.' The latter replies that 'the machine-gunners should have given covering fire to my men.' The actual truth was simple: the Germans had come up with a plan that they executed with precision, leaving our squads no time to organise any defence. At the start of any engagement there is always a degree of wavering and they profited from it. Their success was regrettable but deserved, and the combatants, who are impartial, agree on this. One would not be able to give such an explanation to the men at the rear. Blamed by divisional command, the colonel lets the battalion leader know of his displeasure and he then takes his revenge on the company commandants. Blame cascades down through the ranks and ends up, as always, on the back of the soldier. But the soldiers take this philosophically. 'One thing's for sure, and that is that those lads who went off with the Boches have had their lives saved!' Whereas the three dead are indeed dead. In a hut at camp I heard Chassignol discussing the events in measured terms, a water bottle of wine in his hand:

'If the old colonel reckons he's smarter than me at the look out, he can have my gun any time he likes. Then he can thrash it out with Fritz!'

'If they ain't pleased with our work then all they got to do is pension us off!' said another.

'Ha, they'll pension you off with a dozen bullets in your guts, you stunted foetus! Rest homes and pensions are nice little fiddles for invalids!'

'And why wouldn't I be an invalid?'

'Because you ain't anything. You're nothing. Nothing! You're part of the *quota*, just a tool, about as much as a shovel handle. If you're still alive, it's because the shells couldn't be bothered with you!'

We had a score to settle with the enemy. It had to be done. The battalion prepared a surprise attack which took place a fortnight later. The affair cost us several wounded and thousands of projectiles. But the Germans had known only too well that a riposte was coming and had evacuated their trenches as soon as we fired the first shells.

Latterly the division has been made up of two French regiments and one regiment of American blacks. We encounter them in rest periods because their camp is next to ours. The *poilus* fraternise with their new brothers in arms. Blacks and whites sit together drinking the heavy wine they serve out in the canteens, and swop bits of equipment. The Americans are more generous, being better off. They are holding a sector on our left but I have stopped going there because it is so dangerous. They keep all their weapons ready to shoot, safety catches off, whether it is revolvers in their pockets or rifles propped up against the wall of a shelter. If one gets dropped, it goes off. If someone gets killed, it is an inevitable accident of war, something of which they only have a vague notion. They came to France like they would set off to the lands of Alaska or Canada, to become gold prospectors or fur trappers. They go out on crazy, boisterous patrols in front of their lines, making a lot of racket, something which does not always turn to their advantage. They throw grenades like fireworks at a festival.

They have hung up tin cans on their barbed wire and fences at which they shoot from every direction. Behind the line there are bullet holes everywhere, from American bullets.

Our men tell of an event which happened in their camp. One of their sergeants is distributing the coffee ration in the kitchens. Each soldier goes up and holds out his mug (theirs are double the size of ours, half a litre). One man drains his mug. He goes back to the sergeant and demands a second helping. 'No!' says the sergeant. 'No?' 'No!' The man then pulls out his revolver and shoots the sergeant dead on the spot. NCOs run over, grab the murderer, tie a rope to a tree and hang him without further ado. The onlookers all roar with laughter, enjoying the comedy... The *poilus* love this story. They reckon that people who hold the lives of others so cheaply will be excellent soldiers. We are counting on them to finish the war.

The days go by and our victories continue, one after another. There is no doubt that the end is in sight. Clemenceau and Foch are popular, but we cannot admire them: they threaten our lives and their status goes up as our numbers go down.

Our lives now become ever more precious as we see the chance of saving them. We are less and less prepared to risk them. Thus we stop complaining about having to hold our positions for so long, since everywhere else our troops are attacking.

The night is disturbed by a dull sound, the murmur of an ocean, masses on the march. It starts far off in the rear, comes out of the distance, spreads across the plain, rises up towards us like a flood. Something is happening out there in the darkness, something vast and spectacular...

In the morning we see heavy artillery down in the ravine where the reserves are encamped. Tribes of artillerymen drive us out of our shelters. We are informed that henceforth we are not allowed to use the roads, which are reserved for convoys; the infantry must stick to the paths.

This deployment of forces and the new regulations confirm the news that is starting to spread: Gouraud's forces are attacking. Preparations continue through the following nights. We lie awake listening to the great hum of human activity. Once daylight comes, everything stops, everything slumbers. The number of big guns keeps rising. In the battalion's dugouts and shelters, the men exchange views:

'We're going to be relieved.'

'Yeah, probably. They can't expect us to do the attacking after leaving us here in the shit for five bloody months!'

'It's the colonials who are coming. They've been seen at the rear.'

For two days we wait optimistically for the assault troops to arrive. On the third day we learn that the assault troops are us... This news is not greeted with enthusiasm.

We receive quantities of paperwork, including maps on which I have to work flat out marking objectives and routes. We have to move several times to make way for the rising tide of artillerymen. On the fourth night we crowd into damp saps, packed in too tightly to stretch out. We don't sleep any more, we are too tired and worried. The power suggested by all the rumbling in the nights reassures us slightly. Men coming up from the rear say that there is artillery everywhere. Those who come from the front report that our 75s, covered with a simple camouflage of painted canvas, are lined up on the plain between our first and second lines.

We feel sure that 'it will work'. But we also know that it cannot work without losses and that we have to *go over the top*, that chilling phrase.

Our battalion will form the regiment's second wave.

* * * * *

The evening of 24 September. We are entering the fifth and final night. Three years ago, to the day, I was waiting on the eve of the attack in Artois.

We go up to take our assault positions where we have to be before the bombardment which will begin very soon. We are marching with an infantry company. The men are fully equipped, without heavy packs, but with food rations for several days. A captain adjutant-major has been working alongside the commandant for the past few days.

We crowd into a big sap on the left sector, on the side of the ravine which separates the front lines. We are too many to fit in the shelter and I predict another sleepless night. But I have made up my mind to get some sleep. Partly as a precaution, to build up a store of sleep on which I can live for the next day or two. Partly because it is bad to spend the eve of a battle lying awake and thinking about all that might happen when nothing can be done to change it. I manage to get to the front of the line and find some bunks in a small dugout. I share one with a comrade. I wrap myself up and sleep.

I wake later. The darkness is full of people's backs, of bodies jumbled together. I see one man leaning on his elbows staring pensively into the flame of a candle.

'What time is it?' I ask.

'Two o'clock.'

'Has it started?'

'Yes, it's been going on since eleven.'

And indeed I can hear rumbling in the distance. No shells are coming down above us at the moment.

'What time do we go?'

'Five twenty-five.'

Three hours of safety and oblivion left... I go back to sleep.

Someone is shaking me violently.

'Up, now, come on, we're attacking...' I hear.

We are attacking?... Oh, yes, right, now is the time... There is agitation all round me. Candlelight reveals tense, hardened faces, reflecting the anger that is a reaction to weakness. Everyone is asking questions:

'Is it going OK up there?'

'Are the Boche hitting back much?'

I have got to rush! I leap off my bunk, roll up my blanket and tent canvas, still thick-headed. I must concentrate on my gear: my two haversacks, water bottle, gas mask, maps, pistol... Have I forgotten anything?... Oh, yes, my cane, my chinstrap... I have scarcely got everything when the order is shouted:

'Forward!'

We are near an exit. I take my place in the line, follow the others. We are already at the foot of the steps, we are going up, we are going to go out... the terrible moment when you surrender yourself...

Outside... Whistles and screams of the bombardment we have unleashed... Into the colourless chill of dawn, like splashing your face in a tub of icy water. We are all shivering, our faces green, mouths thick with that foul smell that bad awakenings belch up. We wait in the communication trench to give the column time to get organised.

Whipcracks lash the air, so low it seems they might take our heads off; it is the mad onslaught of our 75s whose barrage precedes our assault. Above that the heavy artillery forms a vault of gasps and growls across the sky. A vast net of trajectories is spread over the earth and we are caught in its mesh. Waves of sound collide, break, swirl and eddy overhead. Impossible still to make out what contribution the enemy is making to this over-whelming storm of steel.

Still, some distinct explosions indicate incoming shells, though none of them land near us. We stand motionless on the threshold of the battle, all retreat cut off. Our voices are as pale as our faces. To get a grip on myself, I turn to my neighbour and, speaking slowly and precisely with feigned indifference, as if I am using a foreign language, tell him:

'The strap on your water bottle is unfastened, mind you don't lose it.'

'Forward!'

We set off down the communication trenches. Here we go. Soon we are descending the slopes of the ravine, covered with a sinister mist that smells like gas. We put on our masks then remove them again because we can't breathe. We go up the reverse slope and come out on to the plateau.

We are now at the enemy positions. There is such chaos that we have to leave the trenches and move forward on the plain. We are entering a repulsive landscape, where nature has been stripped bare, closed off by a horizon of swirling, booming, thick yellow smoke. Five hundred metres ahead, thin columns of men are taking possession of this erupting expanse, conquering the flanks of a deserted, ravaged and sulphurous planet. From time to time, black balls with red hearts burst among the columns: enemy shells.

I tell myself that there is a certain grandeur to this spectacle. It is quite moving to watch these pathetically small, fragile groups of men, little blue caterpillars, so far apart, marching to meet the thunder, disappearing into the gullies and ditches and re-emerging on the slopes of this valley of hell. It is moving to watch these pygmies controlling the advance of the cataclysm, commanding the elements, wrapping themselves in a sky of fire that clears and ploughs all that is ahead of them.

All grandeur and beauty suddenly vanishes. We are passing scattered, broken corpses, men in blue lying flat in the nothingness on a litter of blood and entrails. One of the wounded is writhing, grimacing and screaming, his arm torn off, torso ripped open. We all know him. He was the batman for the intelligence officer, a giant of a man who was even more 'dug-in' than us...

We turn our eyes away so as not to see the reproach in his, we hurry on so as not to hear his imploring cries.

This is where we really enter the battle – our flesh on full alert...

It's nine o'clock. The sun is shining.

After many pauses, we have reached the rim of a valley whose floor is still hidden by a light mist. Above this mist on the other side emerge the slopes held by the enemy, with their menacing trenches. We have advanced for two or three kilometres over abandoned positions. The enemy had pulled back, covering its retreat with just a few sacrificed troops who surrendered without putting up any fight. We passed a detachment of prisoners dazed by the night's hammering.

Soon the black American regiment appeared; they were following us. They formed a line along the ridge, their mass silhouetted against the sky. Thousands of bayonets glistened at the ends of their rifles. They were laughing. Many of them had already swopped their weapons and gas masks for German equipment.

'It's stupid to stay up there in full view!' some observe wisely.

But no one is listening to them. We are a bit intoxicated by our victory. Our losses were very low. We fraternise with the Americans.

We waste a good hour like this. Flights of enemy aeroplanes appear overhead. Fighters circle gracefully, gathering information on our positions, which does not bother us.

At last the Americans march off along a communication trench which leads down into the valley. We wave to them cheerfully as they disappear, full of confidence.

We have another long wait. The mist has cleared, our bombardment ceased. For the first time today we hear machine guns...

Now it is our turn. The battalion goes off along the wide communication trench, which is open to enfilade fire from the ridges opposite along its entire length. One man in front of me separates me from the commandant, himself preceded by the captain adjutant-major.

The enemy can see us. 77s and 88s start to strike the parapets with terrible precision and regularity. Machine guns support them. A swarm of bullets is buzzing round our ears, tormenting us... Then there is some kind of bottleneck ahead. The front of the column stops moving. We stay there, crouched down and panting, offering ourselves as targets all the way down this slope. The shells are getting ever closer. Our situation is hopeless if we continue to go down the trench. We will leave hundreds of dead men behind us.

There is a terrible explosion right next to us. People are shouting:

'Get in the shelter, quick!'

Our commandant, his face ashen, turns back, pushes past us and throws himself down the steps of a German deep shelter a few metres way. I can understand his panic. The shell went straight into the captain adjutant-major, blew up in his chest and scattered him in pieces, but, miraculously, did not claim any other victims. By terrifying the commandant, this death saved all of us.

We crowd through the shelter's two entrances. Just as I am going in I recognise Sergeant Brelan, a teacher, with whom I have had some friendly chats in the past. I draw back:

'After you, sergeant!'

This gesture takes two seconds, time enough for a few shells or ten bullets to find me... Refinement, a wish to impress? I do not think so. It was more a matter of concern for my morale, a way of warding off panic. More than anything I am afraid of fear itself overwhelming me. One must use any bit of folly to control it.

For the next two hours, heavy shells hunt us in our underground shelter, where we spend the rest of the day.

* * * * *

We take advantage of the clear night to continue our journey down the valley, whose floor is covered with a bog about two hundred metres long. We cross this by a narrow footbridge which the Germans had left intact to give themselves a way of escape. A few big time-shells go off just above us.

Our successive waves of troops from this morning now form a single line at the foot of a four-metre bank, the limit of our advance. Above the bank there is another stretch of flat ground, swept by German machine-gun fire since nightfall. The Americans were stopped here with heavy losses. Corpses rolled down the slope where in the darkness they got mixed in with the sleeping bodies of the living. We attack at first light.

Our preparation starts a little before dawn. Our shells are coming down just in front of us. But they fail to demolish the bunkers from which the machine guns are firing with fury.

Then a battery of 75s fires short. We can clearly hear the four bangs when the shells depart and they are above us with terrifying speed, exploding only a few metres ahead. The bog prevents any retreat. It feels as if death will strike us from behind, and we have a quarter-hour of total panic under these fratricidal blows. We fire off all our red warning rockets to tell them to increase the range. The fire then stops but by then we are too demoralised to attack. And in any case the machine guns are still sweeping the open ground.

Day has dawned. Heavy shells are seeking out the footbridge to cut off our communications. They throw up showers of mud.

In the afternoon the machine guns go silent. We move forward without any opposition. At the entrance to a sap lies a German corpse, a hole in his temple: one of those who held us up.

We advance very slowly for some days, with lengthy delays caused by invisible machine guns. The land we conquer is covered with our corpses. The Americans, who do not understand how to use cover or shelters, have been badly hit. We have seen them changing positions following the whistle, as artillery fire is striking the middle of their sections, throwing men into the air. They launched a bayonet attack on the village of Sochaux across open ground. And left behind hundreds of dead.

Overall, the artillery fire is not doing us a lot of damage and the Germans only have a few guns to use against us. But it is true that they use them well, holding their fire till they have spotted troops massing. Mostly, though, they are covering their retreat with machine-gunners who must have orders to hold us down for a certain time. Over broken, bare ground, well concealed machine guns have an extraordinary effectiveness that tests us cruelly. Some resolute platoons stop whole battalions. We do not see any of the enemy. Some surrender at the last minute, others escape into the night, their mission accomplished. All this confirms once again that the attacker, obliged to use dense troop formations, has the more dangerous role. If we had chosen a defensive strategy in 1914, we would have avoided Charleroi and done considerable damage to the German forces.

After several trying days in the rain and cold, we have now assembled on the highest summit of the Champagne mountains, looking down over the vast plain where the Ardennes begin.

It is afternoon, and the sun is shining. Two or three German batteries are harassing us, but fortunately their shells are landing behind a little trench that shields us from the shrapnel.

We hear a faint humming, which rapidly increases in volume, becoming so loud that it even drowns out the explosions. It comes from the sky... Soon afterwards a whole wing of bombers, bearing our colours, flies overhead. We count more than two hundred machines in triangular formation, covered by fighters, at about two thousand metres. Their mass, flanked by hundreds of machine guns on the fighters, gives the impression of an irresist- ible force, unaffected by enemy gunfire which causes no visible damage. The armada disappears from sight into the clear sky.

Later on we hear the echoes of a string of explosions that shake the earth: the aeroplanes are flattening a village, destroying an assembly point.

At twilight, the artillery has gone quiet. We descend the slopes in small groups. Fog comes down, spreading its veil over the distant landscape. All we can still see are a few shining patches: rivers and lakes that reflect the last light of the day. Then they too disappear.

I have taken command of a stray group of a dozen men, including two American runners who have been attached to us since the start of the offensive. One carries a shovel and the other a pick, and both have large packs of blankets. They have chucked away all their weapons, considering them useless, keeping only items of protection and comfort. Such a precise grasp of the needs of the present fills us with admiration.

We spend the night in a crater caused by one of our 270s, big enough to hold a platoon.

The following morning, we see two American officers approaching. One of them asks us questions and I manage to pick out a few words:

'I am... Colonel... Have you seen?...'

I realise that we are in the presence of an American colonel who, baton in hand, is looking for his regiment. Using sign language I explain that I don't know any more than he does. Or rather I cannot express to him what I do know. Which is that through complete inexperience his regiment has lost three quarters of its strength in six days. (Did he not notice the bunches of men in khaki strewn across the plateaus, slowly turning from their natural brown to the green of decomposition?) The other quarter, with some disgust at this war whose results they have seen, must have gone and pitched their tent well away from the fighting, somewhere near the canteens and supplies. Deeply upset, the colonel headed off in the direction of rifle shots. The notion of this colonel who had lost his regiment kept us amused for the rest of the day, which we passed very peacefully eating tinned food and smoking. Shells were falling a long way behind us, and there was little danger from bullets.

Unfortunately the battalion was reassembled in the evening, so we can't go it alone any more. During the night we march forward again, a very hesitant march, broken by interminable pauses. Morning finds us on a fine open road, where our column is all too visible. The battalion digs in on the ditch on the right and we camouflage ourselves as best we can with foliage and tent canvas.

At about one o'clock a German aeroplane circles over us, banking round several times to have a good look at what is happening below. He must find the area much changed... Someone is shooting somewhere but the bullets don't come near us.

The day ends badly. Around five o'clock we are directly targeted by shellfire. A battery of 150s and another of 88s catch us in an enfilade. The firing is precisely aimed at the length and breadth of the battalion. At the very moment when it was furthest from our minds, terror seizes us by the throat, and the guts. We are pinned down under a systematic bombardment. Once again our lives are at stake and we are powerless to protect ourselves. We are lying in the ditch, flat as corpses, squeezed together to make ourselves smaller, welded into a single strange reptile of three hundred shuddering bodies and pounding chests. The experience of shelling is always the same: a crushing, relentless savagery, hunting us down. You feel individually targeted, singled out from those around you. You are alone, eyes shut, struggling in your own darkness in a coma of fear. You feel exposed, feel that the shells are looking for you, and you hide among the jumble of legs and stomachs, try to cover yourself and also to protect yourself from the other bodies that are writhing like tortured animals. All we can see are hallucinations of the horrible images that we have come to know through years of war.

The projectiles bracket our position. Almost all of them are hitting the road and the field to our right, behind a hedge. There are wounded men ten metres ahead of us, and more further off. Our victorious battalion is now begging for mercy, humiliated by some brute beast. I am thinking that today is the second of October 1918, and that this war is near its end… and I must not, I must not get killed!

This one has my name on it!… Ssss… First the crash so loud that it shakes your head almost off your shoulders, leaves you dizzy… and then the enveloping smoke that burns your eyes and nose and fills your chest with its unbreathable stench. We're coughing and spitting, our eyes are streaming. The shell came down on the road two metres away. If you stretch out your arm you can touch the edge of the crater…

Behind us an explosion of a 150 is followed by screams. Someone says Lieutenant Larcher has been wounded: Larcher the invulnerable, who had been in the thick of every fight for the last two years. And now he is stupidly wounded in a roadside ditch by a retreating enemy which has at most ten field guns! It is ridiculous and unfair! And if Larcher can be hit then surely none of us can avoid the same stroke of fate!

Every new burst of fire leaves us gasping for breath. And where is our own artillery, for christ's sake? We lie prostrate for an hour suspended between luck and death until the two German batteries run out of shells.

Night falls. The stretcher-bearers set off into twilight heavy with the smell of gunpowder, leaving in their wake the cries of agony from their charges. More tragically still, the stretchers carried by the last teams to leave are silent ones. On one of them lies Chassignole, the bomber.

Petrus Chassignole, class of 1913, in service at the front since the start of the war, was killed this evening, 2 October 1918, after fifty months of suffering.

* * * * *

We move around this plain for several more days. The runners are based at a crossroads in a battered forest, which is sometimes even hit by our own 75 shells.

A little further forward what remains of our units are attacking the village of Challerange where the enemy has dug in deeply and seems to want to put up a fight. The Germans launch a surprise counter-attack and take some prisoners.

Support from our own artillery is inadequate.

It has been raining and the nights are cold. For ten days now the men have slept on the bare ground and have had to fight with hardly any sleep and nothing hot to eat. They are tired, and sick; quite a number are evacuated. We are all asking to be relieved.

At last we are, after an offensive of eleven days in which we have advanced about fifteen kilometres. This victory has cost us half our troops. A company in the battalion now consists of no more than twenty fighters.

We are taken away on trucks, utterly exhausted. But alive. Maybe we will be among those who come back from the final relief...

6

CEASEFIRE!

WE WERE MOVED BY train and truck, and a few days after leaving Champagne we found ourselves back in the mountains of Alsace.

They sent us straight to the front lines. Soldiers who had just attacked were already on alert on the fire-steps, having repulsed a surprise assault by the Germans that had greeted our arrival. For the *poilus* the war drags on relentlessly with its long hours of guard duty and sudden dangers. We know that there will be no let-up from now on, no end to the efforts we must make. The word is that high command is planning an offensive on this front, attacking the flank of the German armies. This time we cannot count on assault troops coming up from our rear at the last moment. This one will be for us, and we know how much victory will cost...

Above Saint-Amarin we are holding the ridges of the Sudel and the Hartmann overlooking the Rhine valley. But I haven't yet explored our positions. When we took over the sector, our battalion was kept in reserve. And for the last couple of weeks I have been attached to the intelligence service in the colonel's office, where Nègre – taking advantage of someone going on leave – had got me a post. He even imagines getting me promoted to corporal. I tell him this is a ridiculous idea after five years of army life. But he is serious:

'If you don't have a job to go to, you could take up a career as an NCO. Your war service counts double. You only need another five years to have the right to retire with a pension. Think about it! They're going to need good people to rebuild a career army. With a bit of luck you could soon find yourself with an adjutant's baton!'

'You're very kind! But what about you, old chap, why aren't you signing up again?'

'I've got better things to do. It's time I pretended to be an honest man so I can end my days in prosperity.'

'And how will you set about doing that?'

'I am going to become the most jingoistic patriot you can imagine, the scourge of the Boche, the whole bloody shebang!'

'That's rather out of fashion these days.'

'Foolish boy! How else are you going to recoup your losses and get a nice return on your outlay?'

'Oh, come on, Nègre! We're going to tell them a bit of the truth once we get home!'

'You're still young, my boy! Who'll want to hear the truth? The people who've profited from the war, who've been lining their pockets from it all the way through? What do you want anyone to do with your truth? You're a victim, you're a victim, who's going to care? Where have you seen anyone showing pity for idiots? Get it into your head once and for all: in a few years' time, that's what we'll look like: idiots. It's time to change sides!'

'Perhaps you're right as regards people in their fifties. But the new generation will listen to us.'

'And to think I had hopes for you!... Listen, you soppy idealist, the new generation will say: "They're either trying to shock us or just drivelling." You're about as perceptive as mothers who really think their words of warning will keep their lovesick young daughters out of trouble.'

'So you'll support a new war?'

'I'll support whatever they like!'

'And you'll participate?'

'Next time round, rest assured your old pal Nègre will be crippled by rheumatism, unfit for service, will have found himself a nice, safe position. I'll have got myself a little trade, maybe some kind of factory, whatever, and I will be shouting: "Go on lads, on to victory, fight to the finish!"'

'And you think that's decent?'

'You really have wasted these last five years! Unfortunate young man, you make me tremble with fear for you! How will you survive life?'

'Don't you believe that a man can have opinions and stick to them?'

'Men's opinions are based on the size of their bank balance. *To have or not to have*, as Shakespeare would say.'

'Before the war, sure, I agree. But things will have changed. Such exceptional events must surely result in something worthy, something noble.'

'There's no nobility except in the face of death. Only a man who has been tested to the very depths of his soul, who has faced being blown apart by the next shell can talk of nobility.'

'You're being unfair to some of our leaders...'

'Oh, that's great! Be gentle with them, say thank you, slave! You know as well as I do that the leaders are just pursuing their careers, playing poker. Their reputation is at stake. So what? If they win, their name liveth for evermore. If they lose, they retire on a fat pension and spend the rest of their lives justifying themselves in their memoirs. It's all too easy to be sincere when you make sure you're well out of harm's way.'

'But even so there have been some great figures, like Guynemer and Driant.'[42]

'Obviously there have been men of conviction and others who've done an honest job. Guynemer, sure! But remember that he performed way up in the heavens, before a bloody great public: the whole earth. That makes you a man to remember! How do you compare him with the poor idiot who's come out of the depths of

Pomerania singing *Deutschland über alles* for the greater glory of old Kaiser William, and who has understood what's going on far too late? And what's he got in common with the *poilu* who's looking forward to getting his face ignominiously smashed in the mud with no one to see it and no one to shout about it? He's risking everything: he's risking his skin. What does he get out of it? Drill and parades. Once he's back on the streets, he's going to have to find a job. The boss will find him smelly and uncouth... Let me give you the balance sheet of this war: fifty great men to go down in the annals of history; millions of dead who won't be mentioned any more; and one thousand millionaires who lay down the law. A soldier's life is worth about fifty francs in the wallet of some fat industrialist in London, Paris, Berlin, New York, Vienna or anywhere else. Are you getting the picture?'

'So what's left?'

'Nothing! That's the whole point, absolutely nothing! Can you believe in anything after what you've seen? Human stupidity is incurable. All the more reason to laugh at it. Why should we care? We don't give a damn! So let's get back in the game, accept the old lies that keep men going. Laugh at it, for god's sake, just laugh!'

'But if we tell...'

'Tell what?... You want to starve to death later on?'

'But can't we tell the truth about the war without taking on all the institutions of power?'

'My boy, all the institutions lead to war. It's the crown of the whole social order, we've learnt that. And since it's the powerful who decide to go to war, and the minorities who do the fighting...'

'We'll tell them...'

'Oh, you're too much... Enough. I'm off to see if the Prussians are ready to go home yet.'

I share a bright and comfortable little shelter with Nègre, with a good stove. We are in a camp tucked away among the pines on a mountain slope. While my friend is off on his rounds, I'm sweeping up and chopping wood. In the evenings we prepare reports on the day on a drawing table and compare our maps of the sector with aerial photos sent by the division.

We spend our free time in animated debates, which usually leave me confused given Nègre's passion for argument and his tendency to push logic to the limit. But our debates make no difference to our friendship. That's the main thing.

We can feel that the end of the war is near.

Our telegraphists have been intercepting radio messages. We now know that an armistice is under discussion and that the Germans have asked for peace terms from GCHQ. It is nearly over.

At around six o'clock one morning, an artillery spotter wakes us up.

'That's it. The armistice takes effect at eleven o'clock.'

'What did you say?'

'Armistice at eleven o'clock. Official.'

Nègre sits up and looks at his watch.

'Another five hours of war!'

He puts on his helmet and takes his cane.

'Where are you off to?' I ask.

'I'm going down to Saint-Amarin. I'm deserting. I'm going to get myself under cover and I advise you to spend the next five hours at the bottom of the deepest trench you can find and not go out. Return to the womb of our mother earth and wait for delivery. We are as yet but embryos on the threshold of the greatest birth ever seen. In five hours we will be born.'

'But what are we risking?'

'Everything! We've never risked so much, we risk catching the last shell. We're still at the mercy of an artilleryman in a bad mood, a barbarian fanatic, a mad nationalist. You don't by chance believe that the war has killed all the halfwits? They belong to a race that will never die out. I'm sure there was a halfwit in Noah's

Ark and he was the most prolific male on God's blessed raft! Keep your head down, I tell you... Cheerio! We'll see each other again in peacetime.'

He hurries off, vanishing into the morning mist.

'At the end of the day, he's right,' said the spotter.

'Then stay here with me. There's not much danger here.'

He lay down on Nègre's bunk. No sounds of war disturbed the morning. We lit cigarettes, and we waited.

Eleven o'clock.

Total silence. Total astonishment.

And then a murmur rose up from the valley, answered by another from the front. A great outburst of shouting, echoing through the naves of the forest. It seemed that the whole earth was exhaling one long sigh. And that an enormous weight was falling from our shoulders. We cast off the hair shirts of anguish that mortify our chests: we are finally saved.

It is a moment that brings us back to 1914. Life rises up again like the dawn. The future opens before us like a magnificent avenue. But it is an avenue bordered by tombs and cypresses. A bitter taste mars our joy, and our youth has greatly aged.

The only goal offered to us through all these years of war was the horizon, crowned with explosions. But we knew we could never reach that goal. Gorged on the living and the dead, the soft earth seemed accursed. Young men, from the land of Balzac and the land of Goethe, whether they were taken from universities, workshops or the fields, were provided with daggers, revolvers and bayonets, and were pitched against each other, to butcher and maim in the name of an ideal which we were promised would be used wisely and well by those at the rear.

At twenty we were on the bleak battlefields of modern warfare, a factory for the mass production of corpses, where all that is asked of the combatant is that he is a unit of the immense and obscure number who do their duty and take the shells and the bullets, a single unit in the multitude that they destroyed, patiently and pointlessly, at a rate of one ton of steel per pound of young flesh.

Through all these years, when they had broken our spirits, and though we no longer had any conviction to drive us on, they sought to make us into heroes. But we saw only too well that hero meant victim. Through all these years, they demanded from us, hour after hour, the total acquiescence that no moral strength could allow us to repeat continually. Certainly many had consented to die, once or ten times over, resolutely, to have done with it all. But every time that we kept our lives, having made a gift of them, we were pursued even harder than before.

Through all these years, they forced us to gaze on the rotting, dismembered corpses of those who had been our brothers, and we could not stop ourselves thinking that these were the images of what we would be the next day. Through all these years, while we were young, healthy, and full of hopes that tortured us by their tenacity, they kept us in a kind of final agony, like a death watch for our youth. Because for us, the ones still alive today, the survivors, the moment that precedes pain and death, more terrible than pain and death, has already lasted for years...

And peace comes suddenly – like a burst of gunfire. Like a stroke of good fortune for a poor, exhausted man. Peace: a bed, meals, quiet nights, plans that we have still not had the time to form... Peace: this silence that has fallen over the lines, and fills the sky, and spreads across the whole earth, the great silence of a funeral...I think of the others, those in Artois, and the Vosges, and the Aisne, and Champagne, of our age, whose names we have already forgotten...

'It feels really funny, doesn't it?' says a soldier passing by.

Our new colonel has just been told that the Germans are abandoning their lines and coming to meet us. He answers: 'Give the order that they must not be allowed to approach. Open fire if necessary!' He seems furious. A secretary explains: 'He was waiting to get his general's stars.' He must find our joy deeply offensive.

Then we decide that we too should go down to Saint-Amarin to celebrate the armistice. We will return this evening. We doubt that the intelligence section has any more intelligence to receive or to give. Since eleven o'clock we are no longer soldiers but civilians held against our will.

We stroll down the paths joking merrily.

Vououou... We throw ourselves to the ground, up against the tree trunks. But instead of an explosion, we hear a roar of laughter.

'Bloody fool!'

The man who had imitated the whistle of a shell answers:

'You're not used to peace yet!'

It is true. We are not used to not being afraid.

Down in Saint-Amarin, everyone is drinking, shouting and singing. Women are smiling, and getting cheers and kisses.

I know the café where we will find Nègre, and we head straight for it. He is indeed there, and it's evident that he's already slightly drunk. He climbs up on the table, knocking over glasses and bottles, and, to welcome us, points to the crowd of soldiers with a grand gesture:

'And on the 1,561st day of the fight-to-the-end era, they rose from the dead, covered in lice and glory!'

'Bravo, Nègre!'

'Soldiers, I congratulate you, you have attained your objective: Escape.'

'Long live Escape!'

Nègre comes down from the table, warmly embraces us, finds us seats at his table and calls the landlord:

'Hey there, good Alsatian, wine for these thirsty victors!'

I shout above all the noise:

'Nègre, what does Poculotte think of the events?'

'A good question! You know I saw him? At eleven o'clock on the dot I announced myself at his residence. I've waited five years for that moment. "Is there something you want, sergeant?" he says, arrogant as ever. But I soon sorted him out: "My dear general, I have come to inform you that as of now we are dispensing with your services and leaving it to Providence to take care of filling the cemeteries. We further inform you that during the rest of our lives we would never like to hear any more of you or your estimable colleagues. We wish to be left in fucking peace. Peace! General, you are dismissed!"'

Six months later our regiment is marching through the suburbs of Saarbrücken, where the *poilus* have been wreaking romantic havoc. They have naturally been exploiting their success with the last of their energy.

On the low balcony of a little house, a pregnant woman, whose appearance and complexion reveal her nationality, gives us a rather daft smile, points to her belly, and, with amicable shamelessness, calls out:

'*Bedit Franzose!*'

'Don't you think,' says a soldier, 'that they've been feeding us a lot of nonsense with all that stuff about "race hatred"?'

NOTES

1 Author's note: I have discussed this in another book: *Le Petit Général*.

2 Author's note: 'The courage, the recklessness, call it what you will, is the flash, the instant of sublimation; then flick! The old darkness again…' William Faulkner, 'All the Dead Pilots', 1931.

3 The 'raging little Borgia' was Joseph Caillaux, former prime minister and more recently minister of finance, a Radical and pacifist. During his brief spell as prime minister he had averted war with Germany during the Agadir Crisis of 1911. His wife, Henriette, had shot dead the editor of *Le Figaro*, Gaston Calmette, after he had accused Joseph Caillaux of partiality in office, and had threatened to publish some potentially scandalous correspondence between Caillaux and his wife (who had at the time been his mistress). The trial of Madame Caillaux was the most sensational in France for many years, and ended with her acquittal thanks to the oratory of her lawyer, Labori. 'Caillot' – pronounced the same as Caillaux – 'de sang' is French for blood clot.

4 The buildings of Les Invalides in Paris include a retirement home for war veterans.

5 François Achille Bazaine was commander-in-chief of the French army during the Franco-Prussian War. He surrendered the city of Metz and a force of 180,000 men to the Prussians in October 1870.

6 Pseudonym of Emmanuel Poiré, a popular political cartoonist.

7 Charles Martel, 'Charles the Hammer' (688–741 AD), Charlemagne's grandfather, most famous for leading the victory of Christian Frankish and Burgundian armies against the Muslim forces of the Umayyad Caliphate at the battle of Poitiers (or Tours) in 732.

8 Louis IX.

9 In fact he is supposed to have said 'Paris is well worth a Mass'.

10 Differences between French and British army ranks can be confusing. Here, it is worth noting that an adjutant (*adjudant*) is a sub-officer, immediately above a sergeant, and has some of the same duties as a *lieutenant* (same spelling and similar role to the British one). A *commandant* is an officer one rank above captain, thus almost but not quite the equivalent of a British major. A French *major*, however, is a staff warrant officer, above an adjutant and below a lieutenant. And to make matters more complicated still, at least for luckless translators, a *major* was also the term used for an army doctor, at least until the late 1920s.

11 In fact Cicero wrote 'Quousque tandem abutere, Catilina, patientia nostra?', 'How long will you abuse our patience, Catiline?'

12 He is referring to an infamous quote from General Joffre, who, when asked in October 1918 by leading politicians what his strategy was, replied 'I'll just keep nibbling at them for the time being.'

13 The German offensive that began the war had initially been very successful and by September Paris was in danger. During the Battle of the Marne between 5 and 12 September, a French counter-offensive drove the Germans back to lines where the armies remained for much of the rest of the war. On 7 September the French 6th Army was helped by the dispatch to the front of 10,000 reserves from Paris, of whom some 6,000 came in Paris taxi cabs sent by General Gallieri, the city's military governor. The taxis – whose drivers apparently received 27% of the actual fare for the journey – became a symbol of national unity, though in fact their military role was relatively insignificant.

14 Bat d'Af was the usual name for the Bataillons d'infanterie légère d'Afrique, also known as 'Joyeux', who mainly served in the French colonies of north Africa. Many of the men in the Bat d'Af had previously served relatively short prison terms, usually for crimes of violence or immorality. Discipline in the Bat d'Af was especially tough.

15 Author's note: This is the effect of foreshortening. A pilot flying over the battlefield would obviously not have seen a blue plain but a plain dotted with blue. In the same way, the earlier expression 'kingdom of the dead' may seem excessive to those who judge coldly at a distance. What must be understood is the state of mind

of a young man who, after a night of danger and exhaustion, suddenly finds himself facing hundreds of corpses – thousands, even, if you take account of those too far away for him to see. This young man is there as a participant… A man who watches a bombardment from a distance might find the sight curious, even amusing. But take him a kilometre closer, where he can look down on what is happening, and his judgement will be strangely different. One should thus not be surprised if emotions bring a few distortions, but remind oneself that no exaggeration, no invention, could ever surpass the horror of the reality.

16 This is a precise description (author's note).

17 These were used as revetments to retain the soil at the sides of trenches.

18 The 75mm field gun was the main artillery piece used by the French, effective in open country but not much good against trenches.

19 A devout Catholic organisation for young women.

20 The battle of Charleroi in August 1914 ended with the first major German victory of the war and the flight of thousands of civilians. The French Fifth Army, commanded by General Lanrezac, was eventually forced to retreat. Though Lanrezac took much blame for this (Joffre claimed he lacked 'offensive spirit'), the retreat probably saved the French Army from complete destruction.

21 Rosalie was French army slang for the bayonet. The name comes from a popular (at least among patriotic civilians) song by the Breton poet and singer Théodore Botrel. 'Rosalie is so pretty that she had two or three million admirers… Rosalie loves to dance to the sound of the cannon… she is white when the dance begins but crimson when it ends…' etc. Having been turned down for military service because of his age, this Catholic and Royalist became the official 'Bard of the Armies' and toured the front entertaining the troops.

22 Poculotte is using part of a well-known declaration by General (and Comte de) Rochambeau, which he made in 1781 when he brought French troops to aid Washington in the American War of Independence.

23 Blessed are the poor in spirit.

24 A spur in the Vosges mountains, also known as Hartmannswillerkopf, the scene of very fierce and bloody fighting at several times in 1915.

25 The French term is *embusqué*, literally 'under cover'. An ambush is *une embusquade*, a sniper *un tireur embusqué*. Although the WWI French word is sometimes translated perfectly well as 'shirker' or 'skiver', there are British equivalents from the same period. Thus a 'dugout', as well as being a shelter in a trench, often referred to men, mainly officers, recalled to active service from leave or retirement or a comfortable job. And a 'dug-in' was the name given to anyone with a relatively safe job at or near the front, a term usually used with a mixture of scorn and envy.

26 Pauvres Cons du Front. Poor sods of the front line.

27 Huts made from wood and metal, similar to Nissen huts.

28 Author's note: This quote is from *Leurs figures*. So this is of course Barrès at a late stage of his development, a Lorrainer and nationalist. [*Leurs figures* (1902) was the third novel of Barrès's trilogy, *Roman de l'énergie nationale*.]

29 Gabions were large wicker tubes, open at both ends, rather like a roll of carpet, used mainly in breastwork defences around gun emplacements and, as here, around look-out positions.

30 The artillery NCO is describing the beginning of the Second Battle of the Aisne, a catastrophic attack on well-entrenched and defended German positions on the Chemin des Dames, a road running along a high ridge for some 30 kilometres between the valleys of the Aisne and Ailette rivers. It began on 16 April 1917. There were approximately 40,000 French casualties on the first day alone. The 'Mangin' to whom he refers was General Charles Mangin, known as 'the butcher'. It was Mangin who bought thousands of troops from French colonies in West Africa, especially Senegal and Niger, to join the slaughter. On 21 February 1917 Mangin wrote to the Ministry of War asking for 'as many black units as possible, so as to save French blood'.

31 A battalion usually consisted of about 1,000 men.

32 One of a number of cave networks in this area, given its name because of the role played by Moroccan troops in the fight to capture it from the Germans.

33 After the disaster of the Second Battle of the Aisne, a wave of

mutinies spread through the regiments who had suffered most. Sixty-eight divisions were affected, about 40,000 men involved. Actions ranged from simply refusing to move to attacking officers, waving the red flag and singing the Internationale.

34 'Look, a nice bit of meat!'

35 'c…nassa', of course, is 'cunt', and I do not think any reader needs to know Occitan, or this variant of it, to understand the rest.

36 'Hey! Barrachini, how are you, my friend?'
'Son of a whore! What you doing there?'
'The captain took me for a ride, the son of a bitch!'
'Come on, my beauty, give us a cigarette!'
'Ah, you're a lovely lad!'

37 Compiègne in Picardy was French General Staff HQ for much of the war. It was in a forest outside the town that the armistice was signed in 1918.

38 'La Champagne pouilleuse' (meaning lousy, verminous, miserable…) is the name given to an area of the Champagne region east of Reims with chalky soil, formerly very barren and impoverished. It is contrasted with 'La Champagne humide' and sometimes, rather awkwardly, called Dry Champagne in English.

39 The Gascon cadets were the youngest sons of nobles from Gascony in southern France, sent into the service of Louis XIII (r. 1610–1643). Supposedly romantic and swashbuckling, they were the source for Alexandre Dumas's *The Three Musketeers* and Edmond Rostand's *Cyrano de Bergerac*.

40 The reference is to something the future Henri IV is supposed to have shouted to his troops before the Battle of Ivry in 1590: 'Follow my white plume: you will find it on the path to honour and glory!'

41 'They are at Chateau-Thierry', that is, only about 90 kilometres from Paris, putting the capital within range of the biggest German guns.

42 Two national heroes. Georges Guynemer, a popular fighter pilot, lionised by the press, missing in action in 1917 at the age of twenty-two. Emile Driant (1855–1916), career soldier, journalist, politician, and prolific writer of war fiction coloured by nationalism and Catholicism. One of the first high-ranking officers to be killed at Verdun.

TRANSLATOR'S ACKNOWLEDGMENTS

FOR THEIR VALUABLE ADVICE on some difficulties in this translation, many thanks to Pete Ayrton, Martina Dervis, Donald Nicholson-Smith, Ifor Stoddart and Chris Turner. I am also very grateful to Deborah Lake and Mick Forsyth, two extremely knowledgeable historians of the First World War in general and the French army in particular, for their help with military terminology. My thanks, too, to Andrew Kinross for the kind loan of some useful background reading.